Panic Spring

# Panic Spring

*A Romance*

Charles Norden

[*Lawrence Durrell*]

EDITIONS

Copyright © Lawrence Durrell 1937.

Introduction copyright © 2008
Richard Pine.

Preface and annotations copyright
© 2008 James Gifford.

The right of Lawrence Durrell to
be identified as the author of this
work has been asserted by him in
accordance with the Copyright,
Designs & Patents Act 1988.

ELS Editions
Department of English
University of Victoria
Victoria, BC, Canada
V8W 3W1
www.elseditions.com

Founding Editor:
Samuel L. Macey
General Editor:
Luke Carson

Book design by Jason Dewinetz.
Printed in Canada.

LIBRARY AND ARCHIVES OF CANADA
CATALOGUING IN PUBLICATION:

Durrell, Lawrence
   Panic spring : a romance / Lawrence
Durrell ; edited and annotated by James
Gifford ; introduction by Richard Pine ;
afterword by James A. Brigham.

(ELS monograph series,
ISSN 0829-7681 ; 99)
Originally published: London: Faber
& Faber, 1937, under the pseudonym
Charles Norden.

Includes bibliographical references.
ISBN 978-1-55058-381-6

   1   Gifford, James, 1974–
   I   Title.
   II  Series.

PR6007.U76P3 2008        823'.912
C2008-903273-X

# Contents

vii    *Editor's Preface* — James Gifford
xv    *Introduction* — Richard Pine

PANIC SPRING

1    Marlowe
19    Blackdaphne
33    Rumanades
43    Phaon
49    Moving In
55    The Portentous Pattern
63    Walsh
79    The Mummy
97    Francis
147    The Music
165    World Without End
181    Atque Vale
205    The Curtain

225    *Afterword*:
*An Unacknowledged Trilogy*
— James A. Brigham

233    *Works Cited & Selected Bibliography*

# Editor's Preface

JAMES GIFFORD

1937 was a momentous year for the young Lawrence Durrell. *Panic Spring*, his second novel, reflects the rapidly developing milieu in which he was conceptualizing his craft and organizing his influences. Durrell had lived in Greece for twenty-five months when *Panic Spring* first appeared in print, and on the advice of Faber & Faber, the novel was released under a pseudonym after revisions and expurgations – although Durrell's name appeared with the copyright, making the authorship an open secret. The surname Norden derives from Henry Miller's virile Van Norden in *Tropic of Cancer*, a work that preoccupied Durrell at this time and that had prompted him to begin a correspondence with Miller in 1935. This was also a turning point when Durrell began to influence others as well – his correspondence from the Greek island Corfu, where he then resided, was spreading widely.[1] While his first novel *Pied Piper of Lovers* highlights the personal preoccupations that would linger across his career, *Panic Spring* shows the synthesis of influences he would later reconstruct into a late Modernist enterprise, as it appears in *The Alexandria Quartet* and his subsequent novel sequences.

Both of his first novels, from twenty years before his rise to fame, come at a critical juncture, both in Durrell's career and in modernist writing in general. His modernist readings are clear, as is their influence and his struggle with it, and his own late modernist experiments were beginning to be noticed by his contemporaries. These early works provide a readily apparent genealogy of the development from traditional narrative through modernist experimentation in Durrell's *oeuvre*. This is the stylistic point at which Durrell moves from a realist mode similar to that seen in Orwell's novels to an experimental frame that ties him to late modernism. *Panic Spring* is the key point in this transition, offering the missing aesthetic development that is not clearly traceable in Durrell's peers: the integration of the mannerisms of literature from the 1890s to the 1920s in tandem with a late modernist discomfort with these often still-living predecessors. D.H. Lawrence, Ezra Pound, T.S. Eliot, Aldous Huxley, Norman Douglas, W.B. Yeats, Stéphane Mallarmé, Remy de Gourmont, and Richard Aldington all figure prominently, very frequently modulating further allusions to much earlier authors in the English canon while transforming contemporary movements of the 1930s. Yet, their influence is discomfited, as if they are tied to the social obligations and milieu that were reaching a breaking point prior to World War II.

Durrell's works from this period overlap significantly, and he tended to deride his first two novels, preferring to begin considerations of his career – and even then only when necessary – with *The Black Book* in 1938.[2] This appears to have been largely a matter of convenience and posture: *Pied Piper of Lovers* was too autobiographical for a private personality like Durrell, and *Panic Spring* reveals the formative influences he was synthesizing that appear less overtly in his subsequent works. Apart from being compelling works of the late inter-bellum period, contemporary to and often anticipating George Orwell's pre-war fiction, these first two novels inform Durrell's later works in important ways, primarily because they show his influences and preoccupations more clearly. *The Black Book* appears Milleresque at times, until the reader attends to the broader range of allusions and source materials in *Panic Spring*, which recast *The Black Book*'s origins and influences significantly, as can be seen in the word repetitions that echo D.H. Lawrence's characteristic style.

The affinities with Orwell's novels are also uncanny. Orwell later used the same character names and a windfall of 50 pounds (dollars for Orwell) that sends the budding artist-protagonist off on a foolish spree in his 1936 *Keep the Aspidistra Flying*, an exact parallel to Durrell's 1935 *Pied Piper of Lovers*. Durrell repays the favour here by using the same class-based pun on mispronunciations of "*Ro*-mance" (opposed to "Ro*mance*") that Orwell strongly emphasizes and by setting the chapter "Francis" in a firm in which the titular character makes good by producing expert advertisements. In Orwell's novel, a poet who works for an advertising firm has a sexual relationship with his girlfriend in a dilapidated boarding house while working in a series of bookshops, in which he notices and derides lower class pronunciations while extolling a classless society. The scenarios are, otherwise, quite different, and Orwell invests little energy in describing the perspective or feelings of his female character, Rosemary. Durrell reverses Orwell's gender dynamic, and on the whole, Durrell's Frances receives a far greater proportion of narrative consideration than does Orwell's Rosemary. This echo rings truer when Durrell's Gordon (a repeated character that predates the protagonist in *Keep the Aspidistra Flying*) is granted the same occupation and experiences as Orwell's Gordon Comstock. The two young authors would subsequently joust publicly in *The New English Weekly* in 1937, with Orwell condemning the politics of *The Booster* and Durrell quipping that such critiques "could be turned on George Orwell's own flying aspidistras with more profit" ("Booster" 78). Orwell would, nevertheless, write a famous review of Miller's *Tropic of Cancer* that became his "Inside the Whale," and he notably went to Spain wearing Miller's overcoat, given to him en route by Miller in Paris.

With Orwell as a comparative focus, Durrell immediately proves to be more genuine in showing his Decadent in addition to his Modernist influences. Moreover, in contrast to his later "entertainments," as he called them, such as his espionage-thriller *White Eagles Over Serbia* or the comedy series *Antrobus*, these early novels engage in stylistic experimentation that struggles within the traditional narrative structure. Although *Panic Spring* has been largely ignored by critics of Durrell's works and by broader studies of this period – perhaps in large part due to the difficulty of obtaining a copy of the text – it is very much a part of the critical transition in Anglo-American late modernism and English Surrealism that occurred in the late 1930s. Its immediate successor, *The Black Book*, stands in stylistic kinship with Beckett's *Murphy* (1938), Miller's *Tropic of Cancer* (1934), and Djuna Barnes' *Nightwood* (1936) at the turning point to a late modernist aesthetic (Miller, *Late* 7–9, 12–13) – these kin are also all alike in having protracted delays in publication, which makes *Panic Spring* unique in that it bridges that moment of delay in Durrell's career. In contrast with Gascoyne's surrealist first novel, *Opening Day* (1933), Durrell also successfully negotiates the formal complexities of the novel form, allowing for experimentation within a tautly managed structure. His is perhaps the first surrealist novel to do so successfully, but this transition is very clearly anticipated in *Panic Spring*.

Durrell began work on his more critically well-known *The Black Book* in May or June of the same year, which makes the two novels overlap in composition by seven to eight months. During this same period in late 1935, Durrell completed his highly surrealist short story "The Cherries." While significantly revising the Faber & Faber proofs for *Panic Spring* in 1936, he completed "Asylum in the Snow" and finished what was possibly the third draft of *The Black Book*, sending copies of both to Miller in less than two months from Christmas 1936 to February 1937. This nexus of creativity broadens, and in addition to publishing *Panic Spring* under a pseudonym from Miller's work, Durrell began to publish overtly Surrealist works in a joint venture with Miller, Alfred Perlès, and Anaïs Nin: *The Booster*. This journal eventually became *Delta* under Durrell's direct editorship. It focused increasingly on English surrealist poetry and attracted contributions from several rising writers of the late 1930s, many of whose careers were disrupted and overshadowed by the war: Dylan Thomas, Antonia White, Elizabeth Smart, Tambimuttu, Kostas Palamas, Kay Boyle, Audrey Beecham, and Anne Ridler. This same period saw the rise of Durrell's influence on David Gascoyne, whom he published in *Delta* and invited to co-edit the poetry issue. The young poet had already taken a leading role in translating Surrealist works, rapidly displacing Samuel Beckett after the young Irish author's first work translating contemporary French Surrealist materials. Gascoyne took the lead when both, with other English authors, translated Paul Eluard's *Thorns of Thunder* in 1936, coinciding with the London Exhibition (Gifford 36–64). This network widened rapidly during the period of *Panic Spring*'s composition and publication, including Durrell's sharing the manuscript of *The Black Book* with Gascoyne.

When Durrell's correspondence with him started in 1935, Miller had concurrently begun a parallel correspondence with the British poet and art critic Herbert Read. At some point prior to October 1936, he began openly sharing Read's materials with Durrell, in particular to develop a conversation about the London International Surrealist Exhibition. This led rapidly to his and Durrell's quasi-anarchist resistance to Surrealism's communist political affiliations, which Read himself then shared. However, Durrell and Miller maintained the surrealist methods of "pure psychic automatism." Durrell began to respond to these materials in detail, especially Read's political lecture from the Exhibition, and this is reflected in the formal experimentation of *Panic Spring* – he rejects the political for the personal. It is then no surprise that the island, Mavrodaphne, markedly resists the governmental upheavals in Greece, to which the novel alludes, and instead nurtures individual creativity. A non-hierarchical form of mutualist individualism also guides the actions of the characters while the only authority figure, Rumanades, who is also overtly tied to capitalist excesses, weakens until he is prematurely aged and diseased. Fonvisin fled from the Bolsheviks in Russia, and Walsh is eager to know if poetry in London is "still communism." Francis escapes sexual exploitation as a female labourer, and the luxury of independent means is poignantly desired by Marlowe as he regards his circle of friends at the novel's conclusion. Yet, neither Rumanades' excessive wealth nor the contemporary revolutionary zeal displace the individual's hour in the sun or the mutualist life of the village – this trend continues in Durrell's works, and these "politics of the unpolitical," akin to Herbert Read's, are frequently misread as apathy or elitism. This situation is anticipated in Durrell's extensive responses to and creative engagement with Surrealism via Read and Miller, which antedates his meeting with André Breton by a year, marking this novel with the signature of an artist caught in the midst of a struggle between conflicting aesthetic allegiances, which are themselves caught between deeply conflicting political aims.[3]

Finally, in addition to demonstrating a stylistic development into the late modernist mode that Durrell adopted after *Panic Spring*, the novel also ties his later works to his earliest. As James A. Brigham points out in his article in this volume, characters recur across Durrell's first three volumes, as do specific locales and descriptive tropes. In contrast with Beckett and Barnes, this makes Durrell's ongoing reconstruction of his narrative materials clearer than is typically possible with a writer developing his or her craft. Affinities are easily found between Durrell's first novels in the 1930s and his last in the 1980s. The publication of Miller's first two novels is akin, but Durrell is the only author in this nexus whose early novels were actually brought to a final form and published under his own eye.

The anticipations here of Durrell's later works are clear: the mummi-fication chapter prefigures the social satire via embalming in *The Revolt of Aphrodite*; the leap from the high cliff is repeated in his novel *The Dark Labyrinth* (originally published through Tambimuttu's Poetry London as *Cefalu*); the dark tension between satire and prejudice in an English protagonist's view of the Levant in general and Greece specifically; and so forth. Perhaps more importantly, the novel treads ever-closer to the stylistic break being nurtured among Anglo-American writers at this moment, a break from High Modernism to which his subsequent *The Black Book* contributed: the refusal to move time forward; the employ-ment of multiple, conflicting narrative perspectives; a neo-colonial landscape that depicts decadence without a viable nostalgia for empire; and the bitterness of a dark humour that treads narrowly between the ridiculous and the allegorically damning. These features mark the in-creasing shift in 1930s writing but without the overt political aims of the Auden Group: a feature likely due to the neo-anarchist individualism Durrell then espoused in tandem with Henry Miller, and with which both infected the New Apocalypse poets. Although Durrell does not appear in the New Apocalypse anthologies, he and Miller published and mentored most of the Apocalyptic poets in the 1930s and prompted the anarchist shift in the thinking of Herbert Read, who was a direct influ-ence on the New Apocalypse (Gifford 53–60). Durrell is also referred to repeatedly in Apocalyptic anthologies, where his stylistic influence is clear, though he is cast as too individualist for the military nature of the movement, making G. S. Fraser comment "even such a brilliant vision-ary of defeatism as Lawrence Durrell...cuts apart from the movement" ("Apocalypse" 6).[4] This individualist "defeatism" is abundantly evident in the retreat from politics and the world in *Panic Spring*, a retreat that informs the "Private Country" of Durrell's subsequent works.

CRITICISM

Included with this edition are an Introduction by Richard Pine and a reprint of an early article by James A. Brigham that contextualizes the novel. Durrell's works have attracted an eclectic range of scholarly criti-cism since his rise to prominence in the 1950s, although his ties to his Modernist predecessors and late Modernist contemporaries are often neglected in favour of his works from the same period of the Angry Young Men. In part, this text and the critical works included with it seek to correct this oversight. The scholarly work on Durrell has developed into an impressive body on its own, but it is only now becoming more fully integrated into twentieth century literary studies.

Also, while many critical investigations discuss Durrell's early works, due to their rarity for the past seven decades, very few scholarly essays have focused exclusively on the novels on their own, preferring instead a comparative approach to Durrell's later fiction. The Bibliography in-cludes these comparative works, which analyze *Panic Spring* in relation to Durrell's *oeuvre* and his development as a writer, as well as entries for Durrell's contemporary writings.

THIS EDITION

This edition draws on the Faber and Faber first edition in 1937 in com-parison with the subsequent American edition by Covici Friede later in the same year, nearly contemporaneous with the firm's bankruptcy. A few obvious typographical errors have been silently corrected, and spellings with ligatures have been modernized throughout. In contrast to Durrell's later works, there are no authorial revisions between the two editions, which has simplified my task.

ACKNOWLEDGEMENTS

Any effort to return lost works to our attention involves a network of academic support and personal encouragement. My appreciation is profound, and I recognize that this work would not have been possible without the assistance of several people. Candace Fertile first made Durrell's early novels available to me, the University of Alberta afforded me the opportunity to teach such works, and the Social Sciences and Humanities Research Council of Canada supported my research while preparing this text. I am also indebted to Edward Bishop, who encouraged my interests in editing, the Special Collections staff of the University of Victoria for extensive assistance with their astonishing holdings, and the International Lawrence Durrell Society for its long-standing academic support. I am particularly thankful for the Durrell School of Corfu's ongoing encouragement of these activities, for providing a location for intensive research, and for developing networks to support this project in particular. Were it not for the DSC, I would not have been able to complete this project.

I must also make a special note for James A. Brigham, who first called for the publication of these materials in 1979. Jay's papers were donated by his widow to the University of Victoria while I was there as a post-doctoral fellow conducting research in the McPherson Library. I had the opportunity to organize these papers early in 2007. During several late nights sorting his correspondences and manuscripts, I realized the staggering extent of his humble and private labours to aid others in their scholarly work. I discussed this editing project in its earliest stages with Jay in 2003, to which he responded with much enthusiasm. I can only hope that bringing these works back to the public, nearly thirty years after his first call to do so, is a suitable tribute to his contributions to literary studies.

### Notes

1 Another notable feature is the degree to which *Panic Spring* reflects Durrell's life on Corfu. Although many parallels to Corfu are generalized in the book, in a signed copy of the novel dedicated in 1937 to a "Mrs Holdsworth," he pasted in a map of Corfu and re-titled it "Map of Black Daphne," the name of the fictional Ionian island. Moreover, this was the first of several "island books," as Alan Warren Friedman describes them, and its submerged theme of revolution anticipates Durrell most famous island book: *Bitter Lemons* and its recollections of Enosis on Cyprus. Durrell wrote the first draft for *Panic Spring* largely between his arrival on Corfu in March 1935 and its completion in the following December. The opening scene also parallels his own delays in Brindisi during the attempted coup in Athens by Venizelos.

2 Exceptions to this tendency exist, such as the Ace Books pulp edition of Durrell's *The Dark Labyrinth*, which places *Panic Spring* first in Durrell's list of published novels, despite the pseudonym. *The Dark Labyrinth* is very much a return to the issues that concern Durrell in *Panic Spring*, including another fictional Greek island, and it was his next novel after *The Black Book*, so its temporary return to his acknowledged publications is not particularly surprising.

3 For more detail on the political tensions involved in Durrell's ties to the Surrealists and his intrusions into the Miller-Read correspondence, see James Gifford, "Surrealism's Anglo-American Afterlife" (36–64). Significantly, Durrell first voiced his notion of the "Heraldic Universe," an artist's individual creative world, in a direct point by point response to Read's most political speech on communism during the 1936 London International Surrealist Exhibition.

4 Notably, Fraser later went on to write a book-length study of Durrell and was with

him in Egypt during World War II while writing for the New Apocalypse. Fraser was also involved in the *Personal Landscape* movement led by Durrell and Robin Fedden, the title of which demonstrates their personal and individualist stance.

# Introduction

RICHARD PINE

## 1. Durrell, Greece, and the "Heraldic Universe"

It is almost a commonplace for commentators on Lawrence Durrell's time in Greece to remark that on the opening page of *Prospero's Cell* – the memoir of his years of residence in Corfu – he wrote "Greece offers you...the discovery of yourself" (1). *Panic Spring* and *Prospero's Cell* (both of which almost run parallel to each other) are records of the means by which Lawrence Durrell found himself as a writer on Corfu. In his first novel, *Pied Piper of Lovers*, Durrell fictionalized his early childhood in India, which he regarded as paradise, and painted a sorry picture of his hero, Walsh Clifton, after he had been sent "home" to a London which, to him, was thoroughly alien. After this expulsion from the childhood paradise, and his self-imposed exile from England, Durrell moved towards a discovery of himself as a poet, a novelist, a husband and a "foreign residence writer" in his years in Corfu (1935–39). Having spent ten miserable years in England – to which he scathingly referred as "Pudding Island" – Durrell substituted for his lost paradise this Greek interlude of less than five years, during which he allowed – and welcomed – the infusion of Greekness into his soul to replace the lack that his removal from India had caused.

Like Marlowe, one of the characters in *Panic Spring* (1–3), Durrell himself had waited in Brindisi for conveyance to Corfu, the principal of the Ionian islands.[1] Brindisi is (despite – or perhaps because of – its significance as the death-place of Virgil), famously a place of departure, the *terminus* of the iconic Appian Way from Rome. Today, many ferry ports offer an exit from Italy to the eastern Mediterranean, but in the

1930s Brindisi was the principal jumping-off point for Greece – that part of Europe which remains, essentially, the nub of the Balkans, neighbour to Albania and Bulgaria and to its old enemy, Turkey, under whose Ottoman Empire most of modern Greece (excepting the Ionian islands) suffered severe cultural, political, social and economic oppression until the war of independence in the 1820s.[2]

The delay experienced in Brindisi by Marlowe exactly coincides with that of the newlyweds Lawrence Durrell and Nancy Myers from 11th to 14th March 1935, as they waited for a safe passage during a turbulent period in Greek political and social life. In that month, an attempted coup by the republican Eleftherios Venizelos failed (as had a previous attempt in 1933), resulting in his flight from Greece on 13 March and his subsequent exile to Paris, where he died in 1936. Venizelos' coup was not, as Durrell calls it in an apparent aside in *Panic Spring*, a "revolution" (11); Durrell was aware that such a successful businessman as Rumanades – the owner of Mavrodaphne, the island where the novel is set, who was "soaked in the politics of his day" (33) – would have been thoroughly at home, if not involved, in the tensions within Greek society that gave rise to such eruptions as the attempted coup. Nonetheless, it was followed by a period of unease, culminating in a military dictatorship under royalist General Ioannis Metaxas from August 1936 which was maintained until the opening of the second world war, and the invasion of Greece by the Axis forces in 1941.[3]

Although there are only marginal comments in *Panic Spring* on the political situation, Greece permeates the novel, as India had permeated *Pied Piper of Lovers*. The political events of 1935, when Durrell was writing *Panic Spring*, and in 1936 when he had immediately begun its successor, *The Black Book*, reflect the climate within which modern Greece was evolving. Not only was there a conflict within Greek society between monarchists and republicans, but this division was also symptomatic of much deeper questionings by Greek people of what Greekness meant to them. This quest for meaningfulness, on the part of Greek politicians and writers from the 1880s onwards, was enshrined in the concept of the *Megali Idea* or Great Idea, and was intimately involved with the wished-for expansion of Greece to embrace the ancient boundaries of Hellenism, including Constantinople.[4] It culminated in an ill-conceived military disaster known as the Anatolian Catastrophe of 1920–22, which resulted in the expulsion of the very numerous Greek population from Anatolia (the western part of Turkey) where they had been settled for centuries, centered on the port-city of Smyrna (present-day Izmir). Durrell was perfectly aware of this tragedy in the Greek soul. As he wrote in a preface to Ilias Venezis' *Aeolia* (in 1949),

The tragedy of his expulsion from Anatolia still weighs heavily
upon the heart of the modern Greek, whether he is a metropoli-
tan or an exile from the bountiful plains and wooded mountains
of Asia Minor. He cannot forget it. If he is an exile he returns
again and again to Anatolia in his dreams: he broods upon it
as Adam and Eve must have brooded upon the Garden of Eden
after the Fall. The blazing fires of Smyrna lit up the skies of the
whole Levant.... But it is more than the injustice, the cruelty, the
madness of the whole episode which sticks in the mind of the
modern Greek. It is also a sense of a lost richness, a lost peace of
mind.... It has become a memory which he touches from time
to time, like a man fingering a cicatrice. The author of this novel
is such a man, and in order to understand the appeal which his
work has for the modern Greek, one must first turn one's face
away from Europe to gaze out across the blue straits to where,
once, in the rich fastnesses of Anatolia, life was ample and rich,
and a man owned his own peace-of-mind. The golden ambience
of *Aeolia* springs out of an imaginative reconstruction of a way of
life which has vanished, the re-evaluation of an inheritance which
has been forfeited. (v-vi)

The tennis match between royalists and republicans in Greek politics was
exacerbated by this disaster, which (if a disaster can be a cornerstone)
became the cornerstone of modern Greek politics until the present day,
and certainly during the time that Durrell lived in Corfu and Athens,
and subsequently in Rhodes.[5] It was not only concerned with social and
political issues but also with the structure of Greek society,[6] and, while
it was submerged during the German occupation in the second world
war, it emerged immediately after (in fact, before the German war had
ended) in the bitter civil war that still divides Greece, especially in rural
areas. This was not only because of its typically internecine character but
also because it brought to the fore the deep divisions as to how the Greek
polity should be organized, on mainly economic and social grounds, and
led to a further period of military dictatorship in 1967–74.

Such divisiveness cannot but have made itself obvious in Corfu in
1935–36 and, despite its absence from the pages of *Prospero's Cell*, it was
at the back of Durrell's mind as he proceeded in his philhellenism after
his departure from Corfu, his stay in Athens (1939–40), when he is
said to have volunteered for the Greek navy, and his work as a British
information officer in Egypt, during which he associated with his friend
George Seferis, like himself a poet-diplomat, who was attached to the
Greek government-in-exile based in Alexandria from 1941. Yet it is not
political and social division, but the promise it offered of spiritual unity,

that made Greece significant to Durrell. In *Panic Spring*, the politics are first noted and then abandoned for the personal world. Greece – and particularly Corfu – remained the imaginative source of Durrell's sense of man-in-the-world, of man's relation to nature and man's philosophical place in the world.

Durrell frequently commented, both in print and in private notes, on the unsatisfactory nature of childhood (one fragment in a notebook remarks on "childhood with its gross psychological damage")[7] and most explicitly in *Tunc*: "People deprived of a properly constituted childhood will always find something hollow in their responses to the world, something unfruitful" (26). It stems from a "central lack. The weakness of the marrow. A racing heart…. The central determinant…is that buried hunger which is only aggravated by the sense of emotional impotence" (26). He might well have been describing the lack felt by his characters Walsh, Marlowe and Francis, as well, of course, as himself, to satisfy which they undertake a quest which can, however, never be satisfied; as Durrell also said, in interview, "je suis un refugié de moi-même."[8]

Walsh, who has emerged from *Pied Piper of Lovers* with his Indian childhood as an increasingly distant and increasingly cherished memory, with his mourning for the dead girlfriend, Ruth – a memory or flashback as far as *Panic Spring* is concerned – and with his disgust at the decadence and squalor of London at his back, carries much of Durrell's own preoccupations at that time (Ruth excepted). So too does Marlowe. Had his father lived, Durrell might well have written (as does Marlowe) "I shall go mad…if I don't get out of England" (8). And Francis' London has poignant echoes of the Bloomsbury experienced by Walsh in *Pied Piper of Lovers*, and directly recounted by Kipling in his autobiography and, in fiction, by Patrick Hamilton (in *Twenty Thousand Streets Under the Sky*): "outside, in that mournful hinterland of lamp-splashed blackness, the trams soughed and crooned, moving up and down the shiny roads like pillars of fire, thick with crowding humanity. A heavy wind flicked the rain up off the pavements to the ankles of the passers-by, and lugged at the passing umbrellas" (123–4). It was to escape "the shouting and braying of life" (153) that each character seeks the island (and finds his or her quiet in the music of Beethoven). Discomfort is both physical and spiritual, and the compensation of a Greek island, even when unexperienced or imperfectly imagined, is more than alluring. Walsh's composition, "Never Come Back" (66), could easily stand for his – and Durrell's – attitude to London and England at that time.

Where Walsh is a refugee from London and from the death of his girlfriend, Marlowe is in flight from an injury in World War I – "the legacy of a wrecked nervous system" (6) and in "an hysterical panic" (9) – one of the first indications of the significance of the book's title. The state of mind and body is reminiscent of Septimus Smith in Virginia Woolf's *Mrs Dalloway* (1925) whose shell-shock is graphically portrayed as a condition only just beginning to be understood by doctors as anything other than cowardice (cf. Shephard). It's an unusual detail in a Durrell novel, and his later wartime victims are treated differently. But Marlowe, who is also a refugee from schoolmastering (highly suggestive of Evelyn Waugh's *Decline and Fall* [1928]),[9] seeks quiet and calm, and Durrell's choice of a Greek island for the experiment with quietism (which I discuss below) seems natural in view of his own quest.

Thus Greekness defined Durrell – and many of his creations – viscerally from here onwards, as no other country could. India was his imagined homeland, but it was now inaccessible (and he would never return there); England, despite his unhappiness during his years there, had an affective hold not so much on his imagination, as on his nervous system. But, despite the peregrinations in his life after 1939–40, Greece continued to exercise an emotional, intellectual and psychic pull on his imagination. Egypt – the site of his most acclaimed and most controversial work, *The Alexandria Quartet* – could not exert such an influence, and Provence, where *The Avignon Quintet* is largely set, despite giving him his final home over a period of more than thirty years, was a home *alternative* to the Greek "spirit of place" which had endowed him with his initial sense of selfness and belonging. In *The Greek Islands* he wrote with emotional intensity that "among the most venerable words still extant you will come across words like 'man' – *anthropos* means 'he who looks upwards.' In common use also are earth (*gee*), sky (*ouranos*) and sea (*thalassa*)" (26). Corfu was also, sentimentally, the place where he had discovered the work of Henry Miller, had had intimate discussions with the Armenian writer Gostan Zarian,[10] and had encountered his (and his younger brother Gerald's) mentor, Theodore Stephanides. Therefore his association with Corfu was both intimately local – grounded – and cosmopolitan.

The complementarity of *Panic Spring* and *Prospero's Cell* in respect of the fusion of intellectual debate and observation of nature is striking. The natural world not only infuses one's daily life but displays its *super*natural capacities, as the characters who live within it are affected by phenomena owing nothing to reason. In exploring these phenomena, Durrell was close to the perceptions which fuelled the life work of his brother Gerald, who, following the example and guidance of Stephanides, became one of the world's leading naturalists and zoologists. Attention to nature, both ecologically and psychically, binds humans to their environment and makes them aware of the forces of nature that are greater than they, and – barring an ecological man-made disaster on a world scale – continue to influence *us* rather than *vice-versa*. In a BBC television documentary, Durrell gestures towards the wind in the trees, speaking of its *susurrus*, and says "that's Greece speaking to you" (*Spirit of Place* n.pag). Such attentiveness is not merely that of an observer, but of one who is inevitably suffused by what the land, sea and sky are saying to him. In this sense too, therefore, Greece *made* Lawrence Durrell, and this is evident in every aspect of *Panic Spring*.

Whether or not Durrell had read J.M. Barrie or E.M. Forster, two titles suggest the thematic import of "Pan." Barrie's *Peter Pan* (1904 as a play, 1911 as a novel) concerns a boy who refuses to grow up, plays his pipes, and who escorts children from middle-class London (the "lost boys") to his make-believe island of Neverland to live an unreal life elsewhere: "I ran away the day I was born," because "I heard father and mother talking about what I was to be when I became a man.... I don't ever want to be a man" (Barrie 28). Perhaps Rumanades' boatman Christos (Christ), blatantly labeled as a "diligent fisher of men" (39), is a similar fisher for lost children, for whom, to adopt the title of one of Barrie's chapters, "The Island Come[s] True."

Forster's short story "The Story of a Panic" (1902–4) relates an experience of a group of English tourists in Italy when manic forces of nature manifest themselves, inducing a sense of overpowering fear:

> It was a cloudless afternoon in May.... We were all sitting at the
> edge of the small clearing for the sake of the view, and...all sounds
> died away – at least that is my account: Miss Robinson says that
> the clamour of the birds was the first sign of uneasiness that
> she discerned.... As I looked over the green fingers of the valley,
> everything was absolutely motionless and still; and that feeling of
> suspense which one so often experiences when Nature is in repose,
> began to steal over me.... A fanciful feeling of foreboding came
> over me; so I turned away, to find to my amazement, that all the
> others were also on their feet, watching it too. It is not possible
> to describe coherently what happened next: but I, for one, am
> not ashamed to confess that, though the fair blue sky was above
> me, and the green spring woods beneath me, and the kindest
> of friends around me, yet I became terribly frightened, more
> frightened than I ever wish to become again, frightened in a way
> I have never known either before or after. And in the eyes of the
> others, too, I saw blank, expressionless fear, while their mouths
> strove in vain to speak and their hands to gesticulate.... Who
> moved first has never been settled. It is enough to say that in one
> second we were tearing along the hill-side.... I saw nothing and
> heard nothing and felt nothing, since all the channels of sense
> and reason were blocked. It was not the spiritual fear that one has
> known at other times, but brutal overmastering physical fear....

> And it was no ordinary humiliation that survived; for I had been
> afraid, not as a man, but as a beast. (14–16)

The possession of humans by panic fear, leveling them with the natural and bestial worlds, in which Pan as a goatsherd (and player of the *syrinx* or Pan-pipes) is the presiding deity, is reproduced in each of the panic leaps or jumps or springs to which the characters in *Panic Spring* are tempted – from the manic urge to get out of an oppressive London (Marlowe's "panic was tinged with excitement…. He had…struck out wildly on impulse in a new direction" [9]) to the need to identify with nature and let it take its course. One of these occurs when Walsh almost performs a death-defying leap into the sea from a high rock known as "the Jump" (156) and another two pages later during a walk taken by Marlowe: in the latter, he hears a flute (the archetypal instrument of the god Pan), and in both, he thinks "Perhaps one of the shepherds" – the discovery is left undone, and the uncertainty dominant.

"Pan" and "panic" were constants in Durrell's mind, perhaps because he himself had made that leap into Greece and the Ionian, with all the mystery of his own destiny and that of the Corfiot landscape: at the time of writing *Panic Spring* he was also contemplating a story entitled "The Aquarians" as part of his putative "English Book of the Dead," and while doing so he also conceived a society devoted to "Pan-worship," perhaps to complement the water-based Aquarians with the earth-based hoof and horn of the goat.[11]

The two ideas – Pan as the eternal child and Pan as the god of nature – meet each other in Durrell's novel, where the need to preserve the self and the imperative to submit to nature and its music create a laboratory for his characters to identify and protect themselves while acknowledging forces greater than themselves. In all Durrell's work, the grandest panic gesture is in the titles and the closure of *Tunc* and *Nunquam*, when a gigantic, heraldic leap is taken (after Petronius) – *aut tunc aut nunquam* ("it was then or never"; Petronius 74–5),[12] and the cruelest is the retreat into autism of Sebastian's child in *The Avignon Quintet*.

During his years in Corfu, Durrell was formulating and reforming his idea of a "Heraldic Universe," which became the subject of several letters to Henry Miller.[13] The Heraldic Universe, and quietism (which was an element in *Panic Spring* because it was a contributing idea to the Heraldic Universe), are thus central to Durrell's thought and writing in 1935–36. According to one of Durrell's notebooks, "Einstein altered views of universe by new notion 'matter' and question mark over Western notion of causality. Meanwhile in interior world investigation of the 'Soul' led us into the galleries of mirrors – unconscious – with its key concepts like ambivalence and the bisexual psyche of Plato – his 'Eros.'"[14]

Durrell's singular achievement in his notion of the Heraldic Universe was to draw the aesthetic scheme proposed by Wilde ("a truth in art is that whose contradictory is also true" [1078]) into the scientific scheme demonstrated by Einstein. As he writes in the *Key to Modern Poetry* (the text of lectures given at the University of Cordoba, Argentina), "to think according to the terms of relativity one has to train the mind to do something rather extraordinary: to accept two contradictory ideas as simultaneously true" (31).

Despite the apparent complexity of the subject it is, in fact, easily assimilated: it concentrated on the exclusivity of the self, and in the best sense of the word it was utterly self-ish. Much complicated theory has been applied to the Heraldic Universe, perhaps because Durrell himself spoke of it in different ways at different times, but in essence it was a "kingdom of the imagination" populated entirely by the writer and within which he was able to subject himself to a process of self-definition: "It is the nature of thought to strike a locus around itself.... Pure thought, in thinking of itself, can remain thought."[15] Coupled with Durrell's acceptance of the notion that "our consciousness determines the space in which we live,"[16] this becomes the site and strategy of the Heraldic Universe: a membrane between the thinking mind and the external world.

As he wrote to Miller, "Each man is entitled to his own reality, interpret it as he wants. THE HERALDIC REALITY.... What I propose to do, with all deadly solemnity, is to create my HERALDIC UNIVERSE quite alone... I AM SLOWLY BUT VERY CAREFULLY AND WITHOUT ANY CONSCIOUS THOUGHT DESTROYING TIME" (*Durrell-Miller* 43, 18). The Heraldic Universe both emphasized, and was intended to defeat, the sense of absence and otherness that eluded and impugned the artist. To inhabit it was equivalent to achieving "reality prime." In theory it was like Fernando Pessoa's "heaven where I secretly constellate myself and where I possess my infinity" (Pessoa 18). "Transcending logic," Durrell wrote of poetry, "it invades a realm where unreason reigns, and where the relation between ideas are sympathetic and mysterious – affective – rather than causal, objective, substitutional. I call this the Heraldic Universe, because in Heraldry the object is used in an emotive and affective sense.... The Heraldic Universe is that territory of experience in which the symbol exists" ("Heraldic" 72).

Jonathan Bolton, who traces Durrell's evolution of the concept during his Egyptian years, quite simply calls it "a symbolic realm forever shifting in relation to one's position in time and space, connecting dream and reality, transcending causality" (86) and correctly points to its origin in the Corfu of *Prospero's Cell* "in which observations on the culture and people of Corfu combine with his notion of the Heraldic aspect of reality to create an intimately personal and imaginative evocation of place"

(89). His mention of the "signature of place" directs us immediately to Durrell's idea of "landscape and character,"[17] and suggests that the contemporaneous *Panic Spring* is another re-working by Durrell of the Corfiot experience. It also helps us to "find" Mavrodaphne, although it need not be an actual or real island, and its cartographics are impossible to establish by reference to the co-ordinates Durrell gives us in relation to the other Ionian islands. Nevertheless, a private clue in an author's presentation copy of *Panic Spring* makes it very clear that Durrell regarded Corfu itself as the blueprint for Mavrodaphne.[18]

In a positive, rather than a negative, sense, the idea of being suspended in limbo (first experienced by Marlowe during the *hiatus* at Brindisi) is equivalent to a spiritual or psychic test-tube in which life is arrested while the character, or sensibility, or soul, is formed. In an exchange between Gordon (skeptical), Marlowe (convinced) and Francis (undecided) the status of a limbo-life is discussed: for one, it is "a gap in the continuity of things"; for another "it doesn't exist for any of us really" (a suspicion that will pervade many of his later characters in contemplating life – existence – itself) (172).

Critics have remarked that *Panic Spring* is concerned with the life-force, that its characters are seeking affirmation of their destinies, and that for this reason they value their release from Mavrodaphne back into the "real" world following the death of Rumanades. It has equally been said that they experience a sense of death in Mavrodaphne. Certainly, there is, in the novel, plentiful evidence of both. The presence of life, or the presence of death, does not necessarily imply acceptance of life or of death. I think, however, that they seek nothing more or less than the in-between, the *limbo* between different kinds of reality (the past, which is unhappily known, and the future, which is unhappily not) in which to explore who, in this non-moment of being, they might actually be, before the past overwhelms them once again or the future imposes itself upon them. This was very definitely what Durrell himself sought in Corfu as he left "Pudding Island" behind him ("Never Come Back"...?) and anticipated World War II and all the uncertainties that that would bring in its unfolding. In saying that his books were "a sort of spiritual autobiography,"[19] Durrell was underlining the need for the writer to wear his heart on his sleeve, and at the same time admitting that life was a perpetual quest.

Miguel de Molinos (c. 1628–1697), author of *The Spiritual Guide* (1675; English translation 1688),[20] was the apostle of quietism. Since his semi-protestant text advocated the individual's direct approach to God without the mediation of the Church, he was prosecuted and sentenced to life imprisonment. Quietism in itself may have attracted Durrell if he had known of its possible connection with Catharism, with which

*The Avignon Quintet* would be significantly concerned, due mainly to Durrell's interest in heresy and deviance. Molinos was defended by Mme. Guyon (1648–1717), author of *A Short and Easy Method of Prayer* (1685), who was confined in the Bastille at the behest of Louis XIV after her ideas had been condemned by Jacques-Bénigne Bossuet (1627–1704), bishop of Meaux (hence their presence in Marlowe's traveling library).[21] Marlowe wants to "adapt" Molinos "to a personal need: to build upon it a personal philosophy of passivity and contemplation" (55). Marlowe calls it a "Portentous Pattern," presumably because it signifies – or at least promises – a major re-adjustment in his life of fundamental significance. Marlowe is not seeking Molinos, he seeks quietism *through* Molinos and, as Ray Morrison correctly observes, "his ideas on quietism become a unifying strand of spirituality that runs throughout *Panic Spring*" (201).[22] Durrell himself was not following Molinos in his discussion of quietism, but using him as part of what we might call a perennial culture (similar to Aldous Huxley's "perennial philosophy"), an eclectic collection of philosophies and strategies until such time as he could hammer them into a sufficient and adequate unity.

In a letter to Miller, Durrell refers to his reading at that time of W.H.R. Rivers' *Conflict and Dream* (1923) and Ernst Kretschmer's *The Psychology of Men of Genius* (1931): "it's all dove-tailing into my heraldry" (*Durrell-Miller* 35). In Greece, he wrote, "I discovered the Ancient Greek philosophers like Heraclitus and discovered their Indian parentage" ("From the Elephant's" 59). This is one clue to his imaginative method in proclaiming the Heraldic Universe. The trick, as he would call it, consisted in being able to seize the grain of heraldry in a proposition and to abandon the chaff. The choice of propositions, from Heraclitus to Bergson, from Mayan culture to Buddhism, from Wordsworth to Whitehead, led him to what we shall see was a Yeatsian idea, that "there is a faint hope of a great synthesis which will conjoin all fields of thought, however apparently dissimilar, to make them interpenetrate, interfertilise. This is the sense in which it is worth being a poet" (59). The elements in the Heraldic Universe, and thus resonating in Durrell's literary imagination, were assembled by a magpie mind which accepted or rejected as he saw fit.[23]

It was this self-definition, or self-discovery, that Durrell believed he had achieved in Corfu and which, on the mythical island of Mavrodaphne, he portrayed in Marlowe's exploration of quietism and his experience of the Beethoven concerto in the chapter "The Music," the central section (thematically speaking) of *Panic Spring*, in which Rumanades gives a record recital of Beethoven's fourth piano concerto, which amounts to a character in the novel in its own right, rather than a sound effect. This is of profound importance for our understanding of how Durrell envisaged the Heraldic Universe or the state of achieved quietism. Writing from

Corfu to Alan Thomas during the writing of *Panic Spring*, he said of the concerto, "I know it now – every stitch of it – more intimately than I know Nancy. I've got it in my bowels. Sort of empathy. I've *been* it. I act it, sleep it, shit it, sleep with it – everything" (Durrell, *Spirit* 34–5). The novel was originally conceived as "Music in Limbo."

The concerto – by a great composer whose music straddled the cusp of Classical and Romantic styles – was significant at the time of its composition because it was the first occasion on which the soloist began *solo*, uttering a personal statement before the traditional opening with an orchestral *tutto*: "I am here-in-the-world." Like the Elizabethans, who are at the core of the allusive structure of *Panic Spring*,[24] Beethoven was a revolutionary, challenging forms and pursuing an individual vision.[25]

The effect of the music on Marlowe amounts to such an achieved state: he recognizes the solo opening heraldically, "as a signal of a form which was yet to be" (151). He

> followed the traceries of its sound, with the feeling of doom
> which Hamlet must have known, following his father's ghost
> along the vertiginous battlements of the castle. The music
> was a ghost beckoning them on across precipices of feeling,
> with sureness of foot that only a spirit could know which had
> crossed every division of sense and perception and sloughed its
> substantial body. (152)

The central movement of the concerto – a mere seventy-two bars of extraordinarily affective music – questions the authority of the orchestra both passionately and mercilessly through the speech of the solo piano. It is a question of identity: the perception of identity and the *agón* that must ensure its survival. Gordon wonders "If there is any magic in the world, where is there a more terrible statement of it than here" which makes him "tense with fear," while the piano playing *versus* the strings "dissolv[es] the harshness of its enemy with simplicity" (153). It was a moment "as an equivalent of infinity, timeless, indestructible" (153). Marlowe "had reached a stage of empathy, in which he himself had become the mystic piano-communion with quietness" (153). For the brief moment of the resolution of the music, those who could give themselves to it (and Marlowe, the seeker of quietism, certainly could) experience the Heraldic Universe.

### 2. Structure, Format and Character

One reason for critics' difficulty in labelling Durrell is that, as G.S. Fraser observed, Durrell "durrellized" experience rather than allowing it to shape *him* (*Lawrence* 18); and Alfred Kazin saw him as "fundamentally a writer concerned with pleasing his own imagination, not with making deeper contact with the world through his imagination" (191). Durrell is a one-man show, and although he would occasionally admit to an influence – particularly if he was passionate about the source, such as the work of Rank and Groddeck or, from literature, Kipling's *Kim* ("je reste un vrai enfant de *Kim*") (Montalbetti 78) – he was, for most of the time, guarded about his reading matter and deliberately vague, especially when grudgingly giving an interview to visitors who seemed not to be on the same artistic wavelength.

He therefore appears to be volatile, hard to pin down, and his willful, if sometimes obscure, allusiveness (especially to Keats and Shakespeare in *Panic Spring*) should not be taken too seriously. Durrell always admired Rimbaud's "semantic disturbance" (Pine, *Mindscape* 127–8),[26] and of symbolism as the root of heraldry and closely related to metaphor as the communication of meaning between subjective sensibilities. His personal volatility (Rimbaud's "*je est un autre*") allowed him to change perspectives as frequently as his imagination required, leading to critical accusations of inconsistency where consistency was never intended.

The structure of *Panic Spring* is, accordingly, described by Ray Morrison as "a discontinuous narrative of a highly subjective order," due to "arbitrary handling" of elements which had begun as a simple story (158). Morrison further remarks that Durrell went "to considerable lengths to disrupt surfaces so that the reader is forced to look for a coherence at a deeper level" (160). This novel, like so much else of Durrell's poetry and fiction, is thus a hybrid of both surrealism and cubism, as it displays these different, disrupted, surfaces according to the novelist's fancy, rather than to what the characters themselves – or indeed the reader – might prefer.

Various stylistic devices penetrate the narratives of these characters, of which the purple passages relating to embalming and other arcane matters are the most outstanding. Throughout his work, Durrell espoused purple passages or set pieces, which punctuate the narrative flow. Later examples include Capodistria's account of breeding homunculi in *The Alexandria Quartet*, but the most common and frequently recurrent was his interest in dolls, effigies and *simulacra*, of which the re-creation of the dead Iolanthe in *Tunc/Nunquam* is the most vivid.

Simulacrum is an apt term for the making of likenesses, since it is in origin an Elizabethan word, meaning "to simulate," and its extra double-meaning in Durrell-speak, of being either a likeness *or* an exact replica, leads us to consider the issue of ontology – of the actual being of the being – and the gnostic refusal to believe that what one sees is actually what it purports to be. The creature in Mary Shelley's *Frankenstein*, the portrait in Wilde's *The Picture of Dorian Gray* and the inside-outside world depicted in the film *The Matrix* are examples of the baroque and bizarre way in which *simulacra* can invade the mind and lead it astray in the matter of belief. In *Panic Spring* the embalming of Manuela would be simply one of Durrell's typical purple passages if it were not for the fact that, after she has been installed in her tomb, her husband encounters her alive. Pastiche, caricature, plagiarism, faithful or deviant reproduction, are all occasions on which the question "is it real?" becomes a minefield.

In *Prospero's Cell* the *personae dramatis* – whether the visitors or the islanders – are rounded so far as they represent the aspects of island life that Durrell is anxious to record and celebrate and, to some extent, to transcribe into characters larger than the lives they actually live: his landlord Anastasius, Father Nicholas, and of course the island's mummified patron saint, Spiridon. In *Panic Spring* they are much more two-dimensional (again, I refer to both the islanders and the visitors who are collected for the island's owner by Christos). They are depicted only insofar as Durrell requires them to illustrate a philosophical or even a literary point. It would not be until he came to consider the *personae* of the *Alexandria Quartet* that they were permitted to take on independent existences and inner lives that resonate beyond their individual iconic relevance. Walsh is the only character in *Panic Spring* with a literary and psychological pedigree, and, one feels, the "proto-agonist" representing Durrell's own psychological hinterland and preoccupations. As a "waif" (40), who is later referred to as "the boy" (161) he is still the unformed entity who is described in the very first words of *Pied Piper of Lovers*: "the child was born…" – he carries his uncertainty into the island of "Mavrodaphne," and presages the naïf Darley, the central figure of the *Alexandria Quartet*, in relation to his more sophisticated *alter ego* and literary superior, Pursewarden, and may even transmute into Felix Charlock, the hapless inventor in *Tunc/Nunquam*.

I have already suggested that at this stage in his career Durrell was more interested in ideas than in characterisation, and to an extent this persisted throughout his work, even though his growing experience later permitted him to create three-dimensional people. Marlowe even refers to the island peasants as "playing-card kings and queens" (170), but the same applies almost as easily to him and his fellow visitors: one of them says of Francis that she was "a cardboard silhouette of a stock emotion" (212). In a notebook belonging to the Corfu years, Durrell jotted in his preparations for his life's work (conceived overall as "The English Book of the Dead") that

> It must be made clear that these are not "characters": a character
> is an integer in a temporal series: whereas these are personalities

embodied by reminiscence: the biological structure of a continuum. Space is my concern, not matter: so these men and women are not substance but the figment of substance seen in a mirror: I judge them not as man but as part of the scenery.[27]

The people walking or stumbling about in the first four novels are isolated (my use of "isola," from which we get "island," is deliberate).[28] They hardly interact, except as one might lay a king on a queen or try to marry a knave with an ace. Each has his own inherent difficulty to work out, and is trying to establish an agenda for doing so. Durrell is the puppet-master who manipulates their actions and, more importantly, their emotions and ideas. Durrell himself can identify with his characters to a remarkable extent because their difficulties were his own at that time (he was twenty-three years old) and their projection onto Walsh, Marlowe and Francis was his way of inscribing his own agenda as a writer and as a man. By the time he came to write the *Alexandria Quartet*, deeper emotional and intellectual experience permitted him to create deeper characters – characters more capable of interaction – and to set them against the background of war that would be the hinterland of almost all his subsequent writing, so different from the apparent idyll of Corfu in which *Panic Spring* was written and *Prospero's Cell* conceived.[29]

Leaving his poetry aside, Durrell wrote deeply felt, intellectually and emotionally ambitious novels, and he also wrote potboilers, intending, until Henry Miller told him otherwise, to write them under his new pseudonym, Charles Norden. In each case, Durrell as a writer and as a person is immanent, whether teasing out an esoteric argument between two characters, or spinning a yarn – as in the none-too-successful *Sicilian Carousel* which, he told me, he wrote "as a makeweight while I am waiting for the cistern to fill up with the successor to *Monsieur*" (*Mindscape* 54). *Panic Spring* is somewhere between the two, even though Durrell was embarrassed by its preciosity, calling it "a damn bad book," but he did think that it was much better than *Pied Piper of Lovers* (Mitchell 262), and writing to Miller that it was "a cheap romance, wishy-washy stuff. Sheer lochia" (*Durrell-Miller* 54).[30] The ambition to explain the Heraldic Universe is there, and hardly surprising since he was hard at work in his notebooks of the time to "hammer his thoughts" on this subject "into a unity" – a strategy by which he would live his personal, spiritual and writerly life. The didacticism of the novel – to be re-enacted in *The Dark Labyrinth* – makes its situation somewhat difficult for the reader, even though the ideas and emotional anxieties of the individual characters are palpable and almost convincing.[31]

*Panic Spring* was dedicated to Durrell's lifelong friend, Alan Thomas, as "a final valediction to sentiment" – a pleonasm, perhaps, but one which emphasizes the self-examination required to make it – which presages his next novel, *The Black Book*, which he described as "a savage charcoal sketch of spiritual and sexual etiolation" (*Black* 10), and in which he followed Henry Miller's destructive pursuit of their effete heritage. In this, there was no place for sentiment. At the close of *Panic Spring* Durrell's Walsh declares "We're all dead…. We're the last of the romantics" (211). It is almost without doubt that Durrell was alluding to Yeats' poem "Coole and Ballylee 1931," which includes the lines

> We were the last romantics – chose for theme
> Traditional sanctity and loveliness. (293)

If *Panic Spring* is a farewell to "traditional sanctity and loveliness" it suggests that the wished-for *quietus* of the Heraldic Universe has been denied to the writer, as indeed Durrell saw it dashed away from him repeatedly in his career, until he settled in Provence in 1958.[32] At best, achieving the Heraldic Universe would be a fleeting experience. But on a wider level, "the last of the romantics" evokes a line from the diary of one of his closest but most enigmatic friends, Anaïs Nin, whom he met in Paris through Henry Miller in 1937: she wrote in September 1939 "We all knew we were parting from a pattern of life we would never see again, from friends we might never see again. I knew it was the end of our romantic life" (364). For Durrell, there would be no more Corfu, or "Mavrodaphne" as he called it, but a great deal more in his life of the "panic spring," of the need to act in defence of his imagination.

Thus, while the Heraldic Universe is the location and focus of our hopes and dreams, it can only be an occasional landfall. No artist, in whatever medium, can hope to establish such an equilibrium for more than a brief moment. Every mere word, colour or sound tone qualifies the absolute nature of the Heraldic Universe so that, in the very act of poetry, the desired state is created and destroyed. Conceived at the outset of his career as a nirvana, the Heraldic Universe, like the island itself, is a landfall Durrell rarely touched during the "long strip" of his career (as he called it),[33] an imagined place that he could inhabit only when he could hold the balance between the keenly competing forces. In its brevity it is the ultimate metaphor.

Durrell School of Corfu
Greek Independence Day
25 March 2008

## Notes

1 The major Ionian islands are: Corfu (Kerkyra), Paxos, Lefkada (known under Venetian rule as Santa Maura), Ithaca, Zante (Zakynthos), Cephallonia and Cythera. Spellings vary according to methods of transcription.

2 In 1937, the central year of Durrell's time in Corfu, and the year of publication of *Panic Spring*, the Swedish-Finnish writer Håkan Mörne (1900–61) published *The Melting Pot*, his account of the imminent disruption of the Balkan countries; he, too, started from Brindisi and, to use a typically Durrellian expression of arrival, made Corfu his first landfall.

3 It was, as Richard Clogg remarks, "part of the general trend towards royal dictatorships that occurred throughout the Balkans during the late 1930s" (118).

4 The fall of Byzantium/Constantinople in 1453 "was a national disaster. After a thousand years and more, Hellenism was without the background of a state, and without political leadership" (Politis 38). It would continue in such a condition for over 350 years, until the first attempt in the 1820s to wrest independence from Turkey and to form a modern Greek state.

5 He was appointed to a British information position in Rhodes and other Dodecanese islands in the eastern Aegean 1945–47 to oversee the transfer of power in the islands from Italy to Greece.

6 Cf my "War, *Agón* and the Greek Literary Imagination."

7 A notebook now in the Durrell Archive at the Université Paris X at Nanterre.

8 Loosely, "I am a refugee from myself." Typescript of an interview with Jean-Luc Moreau and Jean-Didier Wagneur in the Durrell Archive at Université Paris X, Nanterre.

9 Corfu, which Waugh had visited in 1927, appears peripherally in *Decline and Fall*; Waugh wrote "It seemed to me then one of the most beautiful places I had ever seen. So much was I impressed, that when, later, I found myself writing a novel about someone very rich [Mrs Beste-Chetwynde] I gave her a villa in Corfu as I thought that, when I was rich, that was one of the first things I would buy" (Hastings 148).

10 Gostan Zarian (1885–1969), novelist and autobiographer, lived in Corfu 1935–38; Durrell's essay "Constant Zarian: Triple Exile" is in *From the Elephant's Back*, ed. Peter Baldwin (Birmingham: Delos Press, 2008). A portion of their correspondence has also been published (Matiossian 75–101).

11 Pan recurs in several of Durrell's works, including his short story "Oil for the Saint; Return to Corfu," in which he recounts creating a statue to Pan inside a cave beneath the Shrine of Saint Arsenius on Corfu (286–303).

12 Book XV, par 44.

13 Cf. *Durrell-Miller Letters* pp. 18, 25, 35, 42–3, 45, 82, 346.

14 Durrell Archive, Southern Illinois University, Carbondale [SIUC] box 42/15/6 (a notebook for *Clea*).

15 Southern Illinois University, Carbondale, 42/8/1.

16 Ibid.

17 Cf. Durrell's essay "Landscape and Character."

18 This particular copy contains a map of the "Ile de Corfu" on the front pastedown, signed in blue ink by Durrell as "Durrell" on the endpaper. According to the private owner, "On the map, in red ink, the author has made a presentation 'To Mrs Holdsworth with all good wishes this tardy copy of Panic Spring / Thanks / Charles Norden..1937 / Map of Black Daphne'"

19 Moreau-Wagneur interview, loc. cit.

20 An accessible reprint is available: *The Spiritual Guide*. Jacksonville, FL: SeedSowers, n.d.

21 Jeanne-Marie de la Motte Guyon, *Moyen court et très facile de faire oraison* (1685); an accessible English translation: *A Short and Easy Method of Prayer*. Destiny Image Publishers, Shippensburg, PA: 2007.

22 Ray Morrison misunderstands me on this point when he observes that in my exploration of quietism and Molinos, I overlook "Durrell's mocking treatment of the often spiteful Marlowe which occurs throughout the novel" (151).

23 The danger of imputing influences to an author which cannot be substantiated is that it encourages an unsustainable set of associations. In his study of Durrell's early novels (which contains the most substantial exegesis of *Panic Spring* to date), Ray Morrison identifies parallels between Durrell's thinking and that of Schopenhauer in his *The World as Will and Representation*, for example when he suggests that the origins of Durrell's Heraldic Universe "at first seem to arise out of…Schopenhauer's philosophy of the will and its music" (5). But it is an exaggeration to say, as does Morrison, that "by the time Durrell writes *Panic Spring* (1937) and *The Black Book* (1938) he relies heavily on *The World as Will and Representation*" (52), and that "Schopenhauer's view of reason influences not only this novel but much of Durrell's later work" (248). (*Panic Spring* was in fact written between March and December 1935, and *The Black Book* between January and December 1936.) Morrison himself admits that Durrell mentions Schopenhauer only obliquely. There is no evidence that Durrell possessed a copy of – or had read – Schopenhauer's *The World as Will and Representation*, although it may have been among the books abandoned by Durrell in Corfu in 1939 when he fled. In a 1984 interview, Durrell referred to Schopenhauer as "probably" one of the founders "of our philosophy," and he did possess a copy of Schopenhauer's *Parerga and Paralipomena* in a 1970s reprint which may have contributed to his writing of *The Avignon Quintet* (Pine, *Mindscape* 412–3). At this earlier stage in his development we can only be certain that Durrell was engrossed in the work of Einstein on relativity and of Henri Bergson concerning the meaning of time and free will, that of Georg Groddeck, Freud and Jung on the *ego* and the *id* and, slightly later, Otto Rank on the trauma of birth and the artist's relation to society. As far as literary influences were concerned, Durrell admitted (in 1975) to *Panic Spring* being "a pretty good anthology of the styles of the writers I then admired, Huxley, Graves, Aldington, Lawrence" (Mallinson 35).

24 "Marlowe," of course, is one of the most iconic names among the Elizabethan writers, and Marlowe himself refers to Dekker in *Panic Spring*. In later works, characters will bear the surnames of other Elizabethan writers, including Nash(e) and Campion. Durrell himself was a lifelong devotee of the Elizabethan writers, possessing copies of many playwrights including some of the more *recherché* such as Sir John Harrington, Thomas Lodge and Samuel Rowlands. He planned, but never executed, a study of "The Elizabethan Writer," in preparation for which he compiled biographical notes on fifty-five writers.

Durrell's fascination with the "Elizas," as he called their writings, originated in the vigour with which they carried the energy, mystique and violence of the middle ages over the cusp of the sixteenth-seventeenth centuries into the age of modern English letters and literature – their language was newly minted, exploratory, spunky, fearless, redolent of the schisms and controversies of the age. Durrell sensed that his own age might also engender a re-awakening, a rebirth of verbal, grammatical and intellectual energies, and, having encountered Henry Miller's influential *Tropic of Cancer* in the middle of writing *Panic Spring*, he attempted his own *transitus* in *The Black Book*.

In *Panic Spring* he says "we get nearly all our ideas from the Elizabethans" (107), and engaged in a protracted correspondence with Henry Miller on the subject of *Hamlet*, which, he said, "epitomised" the "English death" (42). Those ideas inevitably involved the issues of conscience, violence and destiny, and, in company with Miller, he embarked on a period of destructive writing in *The Black Book* in which he killed the England that had been strangling him, and re-invented it on his own terms. Miller had said of himself that he was "a necessary monster. A divine monster. A hero. A conqueror. A holy destroyer. A destroyer of dying rhythms. A maker of living rhythms" (Nin 139). In *Tropic of Cancer* he wrote "everything which the fathers and mothers created, I disown" (256); he greeted *The Black Book* as "brutal, obsessive, cruel, devastating, appalling" (*Durrell-Miller* 55). In *Panic Spring*, however, there is less evidence of the desire to attack the world, and much more of a need to come to terms with it: but each character seems to encounter defeat at the hands of either nature or the supernatural, with the curious exception of Fonvisin, a doctor and one-time embalmer, who "could honestly look forward, without fear, and greet the new age; could rejoice as he saw the bare cold spars of the new thought on the horizons. The rejection of all that was finished was sincere and complete. He had said, more than once: 'I am glad when I think of the new age coming with its collective sanities. I am glad to kick all the old totems and bugaboos into the muck-heap. I am glad to destroy all the traditional attitudes and create the new values of scientific thought'" (84–5).

25  The first performance of the fourth piano concerto took place at the same concert when the fifth and sixth symphonies were also heard for the first time.

26  See Durrell's poem "*Je est un autre*" (106–7).

27  The notebook, labelled "Corfu/Egypt," is in the Durrell Archive at Université Paris X, Nanterre.

28  In this sense Durrell's fourth novel, *The Dark Labyrinth*, belongs to the group which I have called 'a quartet of loneliness,' (the third was *The Black Book*), since its didacticism and explicit treatment of the search theme is carried by highly lit mannequins (*Mindscape* 179–197).

29  Morrison is incorrect in inferring that *Prospero's Cell* was actually written in Corfu: Durrell himself said in the preface to the first edition that "this book was composed in Alexandria" (*Prospero's* xi).

30  Lochia [λοχια] is the Greek term for the discharge from uterus and vagina after childbirth.

31  A prime example of how the potboiler might graduate to the level of high literature is the unpublished *The Placebo*, a simple, basic story which Durrell then rewrote several times until it became *Tunc/Nunquam*.

32  He would not acquire his final home, in the town of Sommières, until 1966.

33  In conversation with Richard Pine, October 1988.

# Panic Spring

For
ALAN GRADON THOMAS
*as a final valediction
to sentiment*

*Chapter I*

# Marlowe

PERHAPS the greatest damage done by the Greek Revolution, reflected
Marlowe, on the fifth day of his incarceration in the Hotel Superbo,
Brindisi,[1] was to the tempers of those travellers who had been held up
by it. To himself, travelling southward without wanting to waste much
time or money in Italy, the whole business was a catastrophe, if a slightly
droll one; and, if his own state of mind was indicative of general feeling,
then certainly tempers had begun to take a sinister turn. Waiters were
being snarled at by middle-aged ladies whose lives had been hitherto
without blemish; the pages had been on the run since daybreak; and the
hall porter (most kindly and servile of creatures) had been bombarded
with questions and orders until his head began to swim and his weak
legs to tremble under him.

The two large lounges (known as *palm lounges* on account of their
cluttering forest of tubbed plants) were crowded to capacity – brimful
of people of every nationality who sat, sipping vermouth or coffee, and
rattling staccato papers which were three days old. Revolution, naturally
enough, was the topic of the hour – revolution in general and the Greek
Revolution in particular.[2]

Revolution! Marlowe reflected with humour on the word in relation
to the case. Stirring his pungent coffee he pondered the theft of the entire
Greek Navy; the peregrinations of a great politician, and the declara-
tion of Crete's independence; the widely advertised land manoeuvers,
the aerial bombardments; the uncertainty of the Government as to
whether foreign shipping should be allowed to enter Greek ports – an

1

uncertainty which was countered by a simple, if capricious expedient: that of granting the permission each morning, and of countermanding it as suddenly each night. Revolution forsooth!

But after five days the sense of drollery had worn very thin, especially as each morning saw the arrival of a new train or seaplane, bearing more passengers who, being bound southward like himself, were as certainly chained to the raucous Italian town, and the vast but already over-crowded hotel.

The number of English missionaries had increased in two days from five to eight; sober, perspiring, unfailingly genteel, they trotted to and fro among the lounges, absorbed in a plan for the doing of relief work among the revolutionary forces when the war ended. Strange, bread-like faces! Marlowe was diverted at tea-time by the sight of them as they swept into the lounge, their faces stolidly trying to express spiritual hope and ecclesiastical geniality; he watched them scatter and deploy, like a covey of vultures, and finally settle in a half-circle about the fireplace. How grimly they drank their sweet tea, how happily they purred!

The hotel was full of English men and women of all shapes and sizes and religious denominations: and they were beginning to sort themselves out, and build a dozen little Englands here on alien ground. Tea was almost exclusively served, and muffins were at a premium. Marlowe, with the impartial boredom of an umpire, watched and prayed.

A group of planters, brought together by a common taste for Anglo-Indian station[3] gossip and lascivious anecdotes; three young men flaunting the habit and habits of Franciscans; a writer with an aptitude for witticism and a reputation for satire;[4] a don; a journalist; two incurable foxhunting men – the list was continually growing. Finally that hulking, worried, husky colonial, interned in a cracked pith helmet from which he showed a decided reluctance to be parted, even at meal-times, and who was too shy to join any of the groups. He had taken to nodding at Marlowe whenever he passed, and Marlowe, who nourished a secret dread of colonials and their company, fearing that an encounter was imminent, had taken to answering the nod by a ferociously intimidating *moue*.

Somewhere in the south an offensive on the rebel front was about to commence. The hall porter spoke with great conviction and fervour about the Government atrocities. It appeared that among all the other conflicting rumours, guesses and reports, official and unofficial, was an excitable wire from Athens[5] which stated the number of casualties to be several thousands. As no decisive action had yet been fought (the report was afterwards amended to three killed and one fainted in street rioting), as, indeed, the opposing forces had not yet been persuaded to get within whistling distance of each other, such a statement had been quite unnerving.

Mrs. Sardanapalus, who had handed all her jewellery over to the Banco Italiano directly she heard of the trouble, became positively skittish about danger; the rebels, she said, would be sure to capture the steamer on which she was to travel. With her large hands she gave a brief but impressive sketch of the scene, flirting with danger. "On all sides," she said, rolling her dark eyes, "on all sides at once. . . like they do in China. . . and drive us on a sandbank. What do you think, Mr. Marlowe?"

"Madam," said Marlowe gently, with the faintest expiring trace of Dr. Johnson,[6] "there are so few sandbanks in the Ionian."

"Ah! you English are so cold in the faces of danger."

Marlowe tried to hide a wry face in his inadequate coffee cup.

"More," he said. "White this time."

"Yessir."

Mrs. Sardanapalus, leaning back in her chair, began to breathe heavily; the don had engaged the writer on the subject of rheumatism; the journalist was debating knotty theological points with one of the foxhunting men, to the silent scandal of the missionaries.

"In the beginning was the Word. You can't get away from that, m'boy." The journalist became mildly explosive, and the men of God pringled with horror. The denial of God!

"Phew! But it makes hot," said the tiny Polish Jew banker.[7]

"It does."

Marlowe, regarding the dregs of his cup, speculated vaguely on the state of his inside. Hollow and hot his belly felt with cigarette smoke and coffee: layers of smoke and hot coffee layered up inside of him.

The porter came back and announced (incurable gossip that he was) that he had received a further titbit of official news over the telephone. He was an artist in creating suspense. He would not give up the news until a concert of voices, demanding it, told him that he had the whole lounge for audience. Mrs. Sardanapalus bristled in her chair, and lapsed into her native Italian, voluble and emphatic as a motor-bike. The words seemed to explode between her teeth, sparkling and rattling in that combustion chamber of artificial pink gum.

Having achieved his effect, the porter told them in three languages. A heavy fall of rain had considerably intimidated both sides; there was some talk of waiting until midsummer; at any rate, nothing could be done until the respective generals had been dug out. Both sides, however, were going to issue bulletins to announce that the situation was under control.

"That means," said Mrs. Sardanapalus, "we shall be able to make our departure on the boat to-night."

Marlowe, a more astute student of temperament if not of politics, corrected her.

"It might go on for a long time yet," he said, with exasperation. "There's no knowing. Neither side's won."

"Yes," said the porter. "Perhaps a month – perhaps two."

"Ach!" erupted the banker. "It is a nation of fools. A nation of fools, Sir. To make war. *War!*"

In the half-second's silence that followed, a tiny bomb of conversation, beautifully audible, exploded among them.

"Have you heard," said a gnarled voice, forcing its way through the stuff and clutter of an Australian argot, "have you heard the one about Mae West?"

Christian Marlowe went upstairs to his cavernous uncarpeted fourth-floor bedroom, and lay face downward upon the bed, confronting his own special daemon.

The racing shoals of dock-water, reflected and metamorphosed, crossed and crossed the ceiling at his back, assuming and rejecting patterns in gold and grey. The familiar crepitations of the harbour water leaked through the rotten floors of the building, mingled with the noise of shutting doors, and languid voices.

Siesta! The sounds, the scents, the heat and the inaction, took possession of him like an anaesthetic: the bed-clothes heavy with the dust which permeated them like a fine snuff: the sagging of the floor boards: the paint blistering on the shutters: and above all that facile change and interplay of the lemon tides upon the ceiling. He knew, too, that the long mirror at the end of the room waited in humid silence to mock him with his own reflection.

Lying there, in a drowse, it was natural for him to imagine himself back at Shelling again, slowly frying on the gridiron of apathy and routine. The faint scrape of footsteps next door corroborated his memory, suggesting the movement of a stampeding class of urchins, crowding the doorways to the playground. Somewhere a steamer's bell rang with sharp emphatic strokes. For so long now had he been living by the sound of bells that, from pure reaction, he felt that he must do something to answer the sound. Distracted from the intention of sleep he put an arm over his eyes and wondered vaguely what there was left for him to do until tea-time. True, he could count his money: but he already knew, to a lira, how much he had. There was nothing to be gained by such an expenditure of energy, nothing to be gained by assuring himself that he carried his total fortune in a pocket-book over his heart.

Last evening, he remembered, he had been asked what he did for a living. He wished now that he had taken some advantage of his adventure: had answered that he was a man of means, instead of admitting weakly that he was a pedagogue. Yet, he supposed, it would not have been easy to convey the idea of his bravado to Mrs. Sardanapalus: a man who throws up his profession, draws every penny of his savings, and strikes a trail for a Thule[8] however ultima is not, by average standards, so much brave as foolhardy.

Indeed, had he but known it, the question which had caused him a moment's anxiety had been, on her part, purely rhetorical. She had seen, with those wise if vulgar brown eyes, that Marlowe had, in his person, his manner, all the stigmata which characterise the sedentary slave. The fountain pen, for instance, clipped awry in the vest pocket of his threadbare blue suit. For what reason would a man carry a fountain pen in such a place of convenience unless he were in perpetual need of annotating exercise books? Why the dints and creases at the elbows and knees of his newly pressed suit? Mrs. Sardanapalus had seen what she had seen. Yet, if she had missed seeing in him the stuff out of which an adventurer is made, she was hardly to be blamed. No one felt less like one than Marlowe himself. Walking, the whole of his small body expressed the lifelong possession of a gown floating behind; sitting, he doubled himself unconsciously over a book, or a cup of coffee, with the uneasiness of one who has long been accustomed to the frightening stares of a class of barbarian Britons, and whose response to their staring has been the shading of the eyes with the palm of one hand. He gave the impression of having cultivated his mannerisms through a sheer lack of privacy; and at Shelling there had been no privacy, except perhaps at night, in the musty little room which had been nominally his own. He had not yet learnt how to use freedom and his present "genteel sufficiency."

The history of Marlowe would, I suppose, be unremarkable against the histories of many of the men of his generation. As the history of achievement it is wholly disappointing. To say of a man that he was born and that he died, is to suggest that his life is lacking in distinction. Of Marlowe it might have been said that he was born, and he taught; teaching and death being compatible as forms of not being. The rest was incidental except for that major interlude in the life of his genera-tion, the war.[9]

The Great War did not make him what he was; his propensity for the life of books and routine had been marked long before that. School life, as a form of monasticism, had always appealed to him, and war, with its infinities of emotional havoc, consolidated in him the demand for something settled and fixed; something that moved within boundaries of routine, and gave the illusion of being, as it were, finite. In a sense he had never really left school, and the return to it was the comfortable return to something he knew. For the first year or so he could not fully grasp the richness of being able to sit in quiet while the class worked, staring away across the lush Kentish fields, dreaming his own particular dreams; or walking peacefully in the cool cloisters, smoking, and chatting to his common-room cronies. If he ever remembered the gibe, "Those who can, do; those who can't, teach", it was with annoyance and pity for the poor fool who could scorn something which held out so many opportunities for tranquillity. After all, he might have argued with perfect justice, he had his drinks and his smokes, his leisure hours in which to sit in one of the broken wicker chairs of the common room and argue knotty points of Greek syntax with Fender, the Junior School classics man; he had his holidays in which to walk in England, Wales and Ireland with Latimer, his bachelor Head. And above all, he had the privileges of routine to keep his mind pinned down to the work in hand. No, there was nothing much to sneer at in the work.

His own mild literary yearnings, not strong enough to justify a whole-time indulgence in writing, were gratified from time to time by the production of stories and essays, neither of which showed any inclination to reach publication state. For the rest, he managed to live: he was tolerably content.

He was not religious: but he had in him a streak of that emotional urge toward devotion of some kind, an urge which naturally seeks about for antiquity and archaism. He was of none of the religions, yet he used their magic freely for his own ends, sometimes, it is true, without quite knowing how or why.

In the years that followed the war, he played safe, confident in the powers of tranquillity, and the friendship of his fiery headmaster, Latimer, who spent whole holidays with him, tramping the moors, sleeping in pubs, or hiring small cars for long trips. Latimer was like a charm with his inexhaustible vitality, his thick hair, his genuine and pugnacious pleasure in arguing, on any subject from tariff reform to the ubiety of God, whenever and wherever he could. With all the fanfaronading confidence of the Irishman, he led, and Marlowe followed him.

But if the war had not altered him, it had marked him.

Where its other victims had been made a present of medals or amputations, or a mangle of limbs, to Marlowe, as to many others, it had left the legacy of a wrecked nervous system. The mere slit of shrapnel across his ribs had been, as it were, complimentary.

Naturally there were no very distinctive characteristics of this disease. Even Latimer, who was his constant companion out of school hours, remarked nothing but a slight accentuated twitch of his hands about a pipe. To Marlowe the secret horror was not of loss of reason, but of physical paralysis; the former would at least have been some sort of refuge from conscious life, the latter too much of a prison.

But the classes had begun to tell on him after a few years. For some reason, not quite patent to himself, he had begun to distrust the boys, and, what was more, dislike them; whereas before they had affected him deeply neither one way nor the other, he now began to resent having to spend his days, perched before them on a dais, subject to the publicity of all eyes. And in the wake of this distrust had followed a series of small mannerisms, unconscious to him, and a change of manner marked enough to alter his reputation in the school. Normally the most mild of men, he became subject, under provocation, to fits of deadly cold rage, when even a public beating could not satisfy his merciless sense of justice. Even Latimer, who was hot-tempered enough himself, was staggered by these waves of anger. Once or twice, to his secret wonder, he had to act as mediator between a boy who had misbehaved and the master who resented such a breach of rules to the point, it seemed, almost of blind fury.

"They're swine," said Marlowe on one occasion, with vehemence that Latimer found extraordinary for a man who was normally so reserved. "Damn little vandals and swine. I'd like to beat the trousers off every one of them." There is no doubt that he was right. They were swine, with that peculiar swinishness characteristic of the sons of gentlemen, and which, I suppose, is really a projection on their natures of the cast iron system that makes and/or breaks them.

It was curious, this growing obsession of fear and disgust for twenty anonymous, inky sixteen-year-olds, and the bleached and musty class-room in which he dictated their servitude. At times it used to worry him that he should feel the doom of to-morrow's work ahead, and fear it. Explicable it would have been, if his loathing had centred on a definite personality among those twenty boys; this collective hate was not so much inexplicable as worrying. For, though each year shifted boys out of his form and substituted others in their places, his obsession was not lessened; rather was its effect cumulative, growing, until he reached a point where rage had to be consciously controlled, and weariness simulated in its place. At this time the holidays were a blessing.

But it would be a mistake to suppose that he was occupied solely with these problems of helotry. His obsession had not gained quite such a large hold on him. Of late the discovery of philosophy had opened new and pleasing avenues of thought, and supplied occupations as interesting as his former work. He published a short enthusiastic monograph on the effects of Quietism in English Literature, which was well reviewed, and on which Latimer would offer no comment but the bitter quotation:

> "Cannibal Christians out on a spree,
> Eating their God to eternitee
> Fee Fi Fo Fum."

He discovered, among other people, Molinos,[10] and was very much impressed by the doctrine of spiritual passivity; he even planned a book to write when he had time, which would take the central idea of the Guida Spirituale, and relate it to a scheme of his own for contemplation; though why, as Latimer said, it should interest him when he himself hovered between chilly agnosticism and fits of exalted pantheism, God alone knew. But Latimer himself was something of an enigma, with his hypocritical school-lectures on God and Man and, occasionally, Woman; and the bland way he patronised the Lord God in the chapel twice every day.

So life continued for some time, Marlowe dividing his interest between philosophy and the problems thrown up by his hated class. Shell Form, he observed at the end of that year, was going to be the home of more dunces and morons than, probably, any other form in England. This too was satisfying in a curious way.

When the holiday arrived Marlowe said good-bye to Latimer and went north to Cumberland. Parting with his Head made him at once conscious of how much Latimer's vivid friendship had meant to him. Some little part of this he managed to express as they were standing on the platform, waiting for the express to come in; but the major meaning of the thing, like all friendships, was inexpressible without a descent to low and uncomfortable sentiment. Marlowe slowly began to fill his pipe as the bell rang for the train. A minute later, leaning from the window to shake hands, he smiled and said:

"Well, for the present, Latimer, luck."

And Latimer's answer was characteristic of him as he stood, brushing his thick hair off his forehead with his hand and grinning with his white teeth.

"To the devil with the Hail and Farewell, Marlowe. Well, here you go."

He walked along beside the maundering train, saying:

"And don't go eating God in my absence, will you? It's indecent."

"Fee Fi Fo Fum," nodded Marlowe gravely.

As the long line of clattering carriages struggled out westward, Latimer put up a long arm and shouted:

"Don't forget to drop me a line."

Now, lying in this musty hotel bed, while the pictures of his recent life flitted across his mind, he was again a little amazed and panicky. The line he had dropped Latimer contained no fuller explanation of his action than that which he had sent his father. "I shall go mad," he had written in both, "if I don't get out of England."[11]

Latimer had replied: "Go to, creature. Sublimate your desires, but get back in good time for next term, coz I don't want to lose you, and if you're late the board will sack you." His father, more gravely practical, and less interested, pointed out the stupidity of a man spending most of his savings on one holiday. "You never mentioned your journey to me when you left here," he added plaintively, "or I would have used moral suasion with you. Dear me! It seems rather a waste, and now your brother Frederick has returned to settle near your school in Kent, and start a brewery. He wants a partner and is prepared to offer you the option on the position. At any rate drop him a line at the address in the margin and think carefully, dear boy, think carefully."

Lying there with his eyes shut, Marlowe could only conjure one picture of the situation, which explained and excused it. Himself as an adventurer of some sort, battered and sea-cured, setting off for nowhere in particular, with no particular idea in view. It was really confoundedly silly of him. Yet the panic was tinged with excitement. After all, he had burnt his boats, whatever that means. He had decided and struck out wildly on impulse in a new direction.

From the cottage on Cumberland he had watched the approach of the new term with a curious apprehension which he had not known before: an hysterical panic. Even now, recalling the fear which had made him pack his trunks secretly, sneak out of his father's home, he was a trifle afraid of its theatrical flavour. Really, could this strange dread of a form of inky schoolboys have driven him out of England – thrown up in him an impulse to escape to which he had responded so easily? And why, above all, the schoolgirl hysteria of his letter to Latimer?

I feel I'll never be fit to teach again. Don't ask me why. I must go my own way from now. If I have got nothing new in sight when my money gives out you must ask your cousin in Wales to take me on. Back to Shelling I will not come. My dear Latimer, bear with me, and put in my resignation, will you? For yourself I feel I should have some logical explanation, but haven't. Sitting here, in this Italian lounge writing, while a Greek revolution blows over, I feel a little apologetic and silly. A little giggly and old-maidish. For some time past I felt the atmosphere tightening. It was harder to breathe. There was a weight pressing on my brain. Then snap, and I exploded. I'm still a little numb from the shock. Where am I going? I don't know. Why? I can't clearly say. For how long? At the moment I feel, forever. Perhaps I'll fetch up at Mt. Athos.[12] Southward ever southward. As I say, I may never have to teach again. My brother is opening a brewery in Kent and offers me a partnership. I may take it. Who knows? At any rate I'll be near you if I do. In thy orisons be my sins remembered.[13]

And so on. Latimer's air-mail reply showed that he refused to take Marlowe seriously. What was there queer in a pedagogue taking a holiday? "You're overacting," he wrote. "Write again in a month's time and we'll see where we stand." Marlowe had not written as yet.

This image of himself, as an adventurer in the best sense of the word, was beginning to take shape. Buying his books and packing them in a small trunk, he had felt the real swagger in life; life which could drag him off, sans destination, into the blue, southward.

At dinner it was, unfortunately, much the same. A fresh rumour had started. The planters vowed that the evening boat would sail: that official permission had been received from Athens. The waiter corroborated the news, and when Marlowe suggested that it would be revoked again (as it had been for the five previous days) the man shrugged his shoulders from the waist upward and said no more.

"You like the environs of the town?" asked the banker over the heads of the Franciscans.

"I have not properly seen them," said Marlowe wryly.

Mrs. Sardanapalus, fortified by a siesta and huge tea-time meal of Turkish confectionery, was impressive in her familiarity. Ringless, her hands yet retained the shape of her rings embedded in their flesh, as a reminder, no doubt, of her indecent wealth. Watching her as she wound damp spools of spaghetti upon a fork, Marlowe found himself wishing that she would hang herself in the stuff. He watched the disappearance of each writhing forkful with a vague excitement.

"Tell me again," she crooned, "to where is it you go?"

Confronted by the bare question, Marlowe had to admit to himself that he did not know. He simply did not know.

"Patras," he said, "or Corfu. I'm not sure."[14]

With the same incredulous fascination he watched the manipulation of her fork and spoon. What a superbly gross performance! His mind metamorphosed her to a blackbird on an English lawn, tugging forth worms with its bill.

"But, My dear sir," said one of the inter-indistinguishable parsons to the journalist, "you can't get away from the Holy Writ."

"So it appears."

The writer, who had become rather weary of conversational shock tactics, felt impelled to attempt another breach in the ramparts of this clerical Philistia.

"Have you, my dear sir, ever read *Lady Chatterley's Lover*?"[15]

"Well, really," exclaimed the pink man indignantly, levering his neck up from inside his celluloid collar, "*really*, you know." He gazed round upon his fellows.

"Exactly," said the journalist with unction.

Mrs. Sardanapalus made a face and tormented another forkful of spaghetti. An inclination to consider the question in extremely bad taste was corrected by a glance at Marlowe's amused face. Like the chameleon, she took colour from the objects around her. Now, with a gesture and a wide smile, she declared cosmopolitan sophistication everywhere.

"A good book," she said soberly, "for the English to read. They are so stiff and puritan, no?" A raised eyebrow insinuated the delicate question.

"Well, indeed," said the pink man, who had not heard, "I refuse to mention THAT BOOK in the same breath as the Bible."

The Greek Revolution, if it had little purpose, was certainly beginning to have a definite effect. The journalist was slightly drunk and magnificently pugnacious: the writer was prompting him whenever he was at a loss for a retort or an allusion. The atmosphere was getting strained.

"Damn bad form," said one of the foxhunting men.

The writer hummed a few bars of *John Peel*[16] and was silent. The journalist opened his mouth to speak, hesitated, and finally filled it with food.

"I think perhaps most certainly the boat will go tonight," erupted Mrs. Sardanapalus of a sudden, positively exuding oil upon the very troubled waters.

"I think perhaps it will."

Marlowe drank a whole bottle of the local white wine and felt better for it. The don took advantage of the silence to become expansive; leaning over from his table by the wall, he expatiated on the gravity of the situation. Greece was poor enough as it was, said he, and here she was spending a couple of million on a new revolution.

"It looks pretty ticklish for the Government."

"The drachma will go flying."

"Ah yes, we'll get good money for the pound."

The old man winced sideways, as if a sudden convulsion had seized him. He was laughing. Actually, he said, in a new vein of sobriety, it was an even chance that the rebels would get in yet, and then what would happen? After all, they had the whole navy with them. They could smash up Athens if they wanted.

"And if they wanted, it would take more than a verse of the Electra to stop them," said Marlowe, and pleased the old man.

"Ah yes, you're right," he said: and then, with regret, "those days are gone for ever, I'm afraid."

After dinner, suspecting that there would be an acrimonious evening for them all in the crowded lounge, Marlowe took his coat and hat and left the hotel.

Outside, on the dark quay, whose heavy darkness was splashed here and there with pale bulbs of light, there was the faint but growing hurly-burly of men and wagons. The Italian boat was in, and its single funnel towered above the town with an utter disregard for congruous proportion. From the fourth-floor rooms of the hotel it would be possible to look out directly upon the first-class deck. Once before, he remembered, he had woken from sleep to find a ship anchored at his window.

He turned aside and, crossing the narrow unlighted square, turned down one of those dark streets whose mouths opposed him like caverns, disposed at regular intervals facing the quay. His coat was huddled loosely upon his shoulders. It was warm and heavy.

Looking up he could see a piece of the night sky as if from the bottom of a huge coffin. The darkness was enormous. There was a faint noise of voices from the houses on either side, but no lights showed in the window; a gramophone suggested hitherto but dimly suspected depths of bathos in *Madam Butterfly*;[17] a child moaned, or sang – which, he could not tell. Once, in the darkest part of the way, a whole crowd of children rushed past him, chirping like bats, intent on some game of their own. Fingers whisked at the hanging tails of his coat, and an exclamation of fright and surprise came to his ears in the gloom. Then they were gone, and the wind of their passing came up to his face in a short gust; the dwindling clatter of their footsteps gave place to the sound of singing in the Jesuit seminary – a faint and chary benediction at nightfall. After the warm contact with the children in the darkness the noise was distasteful: a plaintive appeal against poverty of spirit.

"Like thin porridge," he said aloud, and turned off from the square to where St. Benedetto hung, like a folded bat, in swathes of tranquil blackness.

From the open door of a wine shop escaping light contributed a warm lambency to the cobbles; the faint but rhythmically even rise and fall of language was a sound welcome enough after the singing of the Jesuits. From the door-jamb swung a twirling bottle of yellow wine.

With a sudden affection for the warmth and liveliness of it all, and for the melodious resolving of language, Marlowe turned into the doorway and, walking across the uneven red brick floor, seated himself in a corner upon one of the wooden trestles. The grimy forefinger and thumb of mine host[18] placed a thick tumbler before him and decanted some wine into it from a lean bottle. Marlowe drank deeply: and drank again, washing the dust from his mouth. The wine was the colour of cinnamon, tepid, and stinging for all its sweetness. It warmed the back of his throat and sent little threads of heat tingling down into his chest.

Leaning his chin on his fists, he contemplated the half-emptied bottle very much in the manner of a philosopher contemplating Abstract Truth.

A group of Italian sailors and dock loafers argued vividly in a corner under the steady swinging of an oil lamp; a grey puppy, with one ear crumpled, scavenged for scraps among the feet; a rank red dust rose from the brick floor and settled on the wet rims of the glasses and on wet mouths. The bottle hanging in the doorway twirled and twirled, winding and unwinding its length of rope, like a felon on a gibbet.

Now, with the warm shoots of liquor pushing their way along his veins, he felt that the wine had begun to make his own despair, as it were, plausible to him. It was no longer a daemon, something to be cast out by incantations and exorcism, but a thing of little dread – a mere matter of song, or noise, or weeping....

Marlowe grinned and poured himself another glass. Mine host (abominable phrase), observing the success of his wine, decided to deliver a short address upon the subject. Joining the tips of his fingers together, as one who plucks a grape in a sedate way, he made a series of curious passes at the bottle. While being unable to understand a word the man said, Marlowe felt compelled to acquiesce, profoundly nodding; and ventured upon one of the half-dozen Italian words he knew.

"*Bono*," he said; and, after thought, "*Molto bono*."[19]

He was gratified to observe the effect of so simple a remark. The cluck and cackle of language broke out anew, and now mine host, with the aid of his hands and shoulders, began what Marlowe at first suspected to be an opera. He rolled his eyes. He spat quaintly and rolled up his lips in disgust. He crippled himself with an attack of rheumatism and hobbled up and down, holding his back. Finally, with a supreme gesture, he returned to the bottle and made as if to pour himself a glass of wine from it.

One draught dispersed the rheumatism; another reduced his age from a senile seventy to a sprightly twenty-five; his eyes rolled no more; instead of expectorating he swallowed, magnificently clicking the glass upon his teeth. Then, as if to signify that the performance was at an end, he blew his nose heartily in his apron, wiped one eye with the corner of it, and bowed.

"Magnificent," said Marlowe with real feeling, "*magnifique*," and lit another cigarette.[20]

It was exactly at this moment, I think, that Christ emerged from the press of men sitting at the tables, and made his way slowly but surely to where Marlowe sat. He was a small man, dressed in dirty blue stoker overalls, yellow sandals and the conventional seaman's cap. Later, when the latter was removed, it became noticeable his head was exactly the shape of a sugar-loaf – the shape of the divine Coryat's head – and that his features were defined uncertainly on it by three tiny arcs of bluish hair: a pair of eyebrows and a dim suggestion of a moustache.

One got the impression that, were it not for these barely noticeable landmarks, it would be difficult to believe that his face – that expanse of swart skin – possessed any features at all. They acted, so to speak, as indicators: with the help of the eyebrows, one detected the mauve eyes, set too close together; with the suggestion of hair above it, one hunted for and discovered the thin drawn line of his mouth. Certainly the man was no beauty.

He hesitated at the end of the table for a moment, as if uncertain what punctilio was to be observed on an occasion like this, then, lifting his cap with a certain shy ceremony, he said:

"English? I think so – No?" and settling down gingerly upon the bench propelled himself along it on the seat of his overalls until he was leaning against the corner of the wall, immediately opposite his victim. Having arrived at his destination, he replaced his cap, somewhat at an angle, and coughed behind both fists.

"Please to excuse," he said, and shouted for some wine in high, rather melodious tones.

"Now," he said firmly when that was done, "I make a little exercise with my English? Yes, please?"

"Yes, please."

"Good." He furled his eyebrows and sniggered archly.

Marlowe drank some more wine and nodded encouragement.

"You like Italy?"

"Yes."

"You like Italy very much?"

"No."

"Good."

The wine arrived and Christ (subsequent history revealed the fact that his name was Christos Kasapikos) poured himself a generous drink. Then, raising the glass, he lapped at the yellow liquid daintily but persistently until the glass was empty. He drew a long breath.

"You leef Italy soon?"

"As soon as possible."

For a reason not then apparent Christ winked and nodded. What a perfect conspirator the man would make, reflected Marlowe.

"You go to England?"

"No. I go to Greece."

Eye-sockets widened until the mauve eyes swam in moisture.

"Aha," said the little man with triumph, as if the confession he had extorted were of supreme importance, "*aha!*"

"Yes," said Marlowe, "aha." He was getting a little weary.

"Where to Greece you go?" demanded Christ suddenly. "Corfu? Patras? Piraeus?[21] Athens?"

Again, confronted by the question Mrs. Sardanapalus had hurled at him, Marlowe found himself at a loss; but this time it was easier to confess that he did not know – or, for that matter, very much care.

"I don't know."

Leaning back against the wall – as a judge would lean back at the conclusion of a difficult case – Christ said, his voice mild, yet thrilling with some curious pride, "I will take you to Greece."

Marlowe stared at him, and said with his sleepy incredulous smile, "You?"

"Certainly," said Christ querulously. After a pause he added with shrillness: "I am a Greek boat come from the Island just to-night. To-night again I go."

"Are you indeed?"

"Indeed I am a Greek boat," protested Christ with his hand clapped to his solar plexus. It was impossible not to believe him.

Marlowe did not give way to the impulse which suggested laughter to him as a possible solution to these perplexing phenomena, for laughter in the face of Christ was somehow impossible. One could only nod and confront the incredible with a face of wood. He asked the price. Christ suggested a thousand drachmas as a good basis for discussion, hesitated and, looking Marlowe full in the eye, came down to seven-fifty. Rapid calculation on Marlowe's part deduced the fact that this was cheaper than the fares on the Italian boat. The island could not be very far away.

"But where?" he said at last, as though this, the most important factor of them all, was a negligent afterthought – almost a conversational gambit – "Where is this…this island? Supposing I come, that is?"

Christ indicated its position roughly with a sweep of his hands. It was near Kephalonia,[22] he admitted: nearer Corfu: and of course it was within full sight of Santa Maura[23] and the mainland. As if to clinch the bargain he leaned forward and whispered impressively: "Very exclusive, dear sir. Very unknown and exclusive."

The rolling mauve eyeballs seemed to express an almost diabolical delight: Christ's small brown features contracted in an effort to express the magnificence of the island. After a slight convulsion, however, he gave up trying to express what was palpably beyond all expression, and hunched limply over his tumbler.

Marlowe knew that it was in the humour of the evening that he should go; already he had visualised it – apart from the more irritating and trivial of official formalities – as something that was definitely to be, but he teased his companion by pretending to have difficulty in making up his mind. What a sulky waif the fellow was! He demanded more particulars.

If the wind was favourable they were to reach their destination about daybreak on the following day; he, Marlowe, could lodge ("very de luxe, sir, for very small prices") at an inn; the island was more beautiful than Xante and less damp; the sun shone all the year round.

"Very well," said Marlowe, repressing a chuckle, "I'll go."

As they stood in the doorway paying their bill, Marlowe noticed the feet of his companion for the first time; stockingless, they were aligned in his sandals like diminutive brown grapes. The feet of an ape or a child.[24]

In the hotel lounge Mrs. Sardanapalus, still laced firmly into an evening gown of faded purple satin, dotted and dashed with winking sequins, hurtled up and down, leaning forward on her toes: her movements were the ponderous, irresistible movements of a human landslide.

"Permission is given," she trilled as she caught sight of Marlowe. "I know," he said, breathless, brushing past her, "I know."

Once in the security of his room, he performed the routine he had set himself, with calculated slowness. He packed his meagre outfit of clothes; repacked his trunk of books; rang for his chambermaid and, having paid the bill which she brought up to him, tipped her.

Outside, in the dark street, Christ stood waiting, a lighted cigarette spluttering its little spots of saltpetre away between his lips. He had undertaken to attend to the official side of the business. Inside, Marlowe, who had by this time completed his arrangements, began the most hazardous part of his journey – that of crossing the lounges without detection, hat in hand and overcoat on arm. He was unlucky. Mrs. Sardanapalus saw his attempt to sneak out of the hotel unseen, and foiled it. Taking a short cut across the floor, she bore down upon him on another tack, and, when he was least expecting it, swarmed out upon him from behind a tubbed palm. It was most distressing.

"You are going already?" she questioned, with an expression of terrible concern spread evenly across her vast face. "So soon you are going?" She seized his right arm and made as if to climb it.

Marlowe disguised his instinctive recoil from so suggestive a gesture, by implying that, as permission had been granted for the boat to touch Greece, the Revolution must have ended. Anything, *anything* to keep her at bay.

"So they all say," she replied, "so they say."

Her lips had begun to loll forward on her face, and there was a distinct sadness about the tones of her voice, and in the tilt of her pouting head. Perhaps she was sorry to relinquish the idea of them all being captured by pirates; perhaps it was dismay at being parted from her shy Marlowe: but she succeeded in being damn embarrassing.

"Well," said he at last, since punctilio must be satisfied, "good-bye, Mrs.

Sardanapalus…er…for the present." He realised suddenly that she was expecting him to travel on the Italian boat that night, and added, with relief: "For the present."

Mrs. Sardanapalus bowed her head to the inevitable.

"For the present," she agreed. "Later on board we meet again?"

And Marlowe, like the traitor he was, agreed.

It was getting on for midnight before officialdom received its full recognition and Marlowe was once more equipped to leave this land for another.

In spite of the serenity of moonshine overhead, here, on the stone dockside, the industrious robots had contrived a dark world of caves and Calibans.[25] The long ellipse of the quay bloomed with a border of pale lamps. Cranes and gangways, trolleys and bales and stevedores – a surly confusion raged around the flanks of the Italian steamer; while from the cauldron-like vent in the tin roof of the station bubbled a riot of escaping engine steam.

It was strange, this confusion of voices and actions, in a night which seemed to hold room only for the majestic moonlight, and the rise and recession of waters; it was stranger that the dwarfs who prowled the quays, each attended by a taller shadow, should have lowered their voices, as if in awe of a world dimly visible from their world, but beyond it. Ineffable serenity and security of the moon, above a world of men!

Marlowe hardly noticed the small companion at his side, who picked his way so nimbly and delicately among the litter of straw and paper and the spilth of the gutters.

There is perhaps one more fact worth recording in that evening of unimportant facts. The boat drawn up flush with the dock flaunted for a second (while the swell lifted her nose into the radius of a lamp's light) the incredible name: BUMTRINKET. To Marlowe the impact of the round English was almost physical – like an unexpected blow on the back. For a second he was at a loss, and then his mind threw up the picture of Dekker's incomparable Simon Eyre,[26] the master shoemaker of an older and happier London; and this time the customary torment of laughter was too much for him. It seized him like a quiet fit. Sitting down on one of his own battered suitcases he laughed long and quietly to himself: and in the laughter there was an element of supreme comfort.

"The name," he said at last, "the name of your ship?"

Christ appeared in the hatchway, his face puckered with surprise and delight at such notice.

"Yes. The name."

"Where did you get it from? The name."

Small horizontal furrows appeared on the man's brow: for a minute he could not remember: the name was on the tip of his tongue: he snapped a finger and thumb with irritation: then, remembering, he turned up a widely grinning visage and said:

"Missa Francesca. She give it. It is a good name, sir. Yes?"

Marlowe said that it was one of the best names possible. Who "Missa Francesca" was, it seemed pointless to enquire.

"Leave the little boxes, dear sir," added Christ, as Marlowe stooped to a suit-case. "Please to leave them suet-cases. My men will bring them."

Jammed snugly into his barely adequate bunk, hovering between waking and a limitless sleep that seemed like death, Marlowe damned and dismissed those vague fears which suggested that he might be trusting Christ without reason. Once he was awakened by the sight of his friend's face, coffee-brown in the dim light of the lamp, leaning over him to whisper that there was a strong and favourable wind; and once to hear the engine in the station (which had been the merest hulk of inert metal when he had passed it) come to life and squeal a piercing hysteria to the sky. After these nothing but an insensible lulling: a consciousness of water sliding by underneath him, and the boat leaning deeper and deeper to the water, as if for comfort.

## Chapter II

# Blackdaphne[27]

LATE morning found them crawling tardily through a roughish sea, with a bright horizonscape of mountains and cliffs ahead. Christ, blear-eyed and blue about the jowls, operated a hissing spirit-lamp, and at intervals abused his minions through the open hatch; apparently their seamanship left a great deal to be desired.

Marlowe, however, awoke to an infinite content, and sitting up in his nest of blankets assured himself that his suit-cases had not been tampered with during the night; with gratitude he accepted the food which Christ had prepared for him: dry bread and Attic honey, Turkish coffee[28] and hard-boiled eggs – altogether he made an excellent meal. Then leaning back lit a pipe, gently sucking its black stem, drawing the smoke into his lungs and throat and nostrils, and fell into a mood of gentle apathy that was more than half sleep. Somewhere overhead a sail drummed lightly on wood; the close smell of oil, the smell of tar and wood, mingled with that of his tobacco; the square of light almost directly above him teased his eyesight. But the delicious apathy was tempered with discontent: soon he would have to get up.

On deck it was different. A watery sunlight, diffused by the low cumulus, covered the waters with smears of brown and gold light. The inner troughs of the waves which rose so steeply against them glinted steely and inimical. Christ stood for a while in the heroic posture of a Columbus scouting the too-nakedly-visible Albanian[29] horizon through an antiquated telescope. He pronounced the weather warm for the time of year. Soon, however, the *maestro* would begin to blow and then things would take a turn for the better. Conversation was somewhat difficult; even an exchange of trivialities was slightly ludicrous when the wayward tilt of the deck sent them leaning away from each other one minute, and decanted them into each other's arms the next. Marlowe gave a series of nods which suggested unconditional assent to anything that had been said or implied, and pointing his pipe-stem indicated his intention of going below.

Climbing stiffly down the hatch-stair, he unlocked a suit-case and removed his stained little English translation of Molinos from among its fellows; and squatting to the floor on an improvised cushion of blankets spent the morning in an uneasy word hunt among the nests of small black type for the place from which his eye had been distracted by a lurch or tilt of the vessel under him. It was not much of a success but he persevered, and the passing of time was reward enough for the effort, even though concentration and peace were lacking.

A lunch which consisted of bread, duck-eggs, tomatoes, Greek champagne, and a cube of sour grey village cheese was eaten in ceremony at the filthy wooden table; the ceremonial part of the business was indicated by the fact that Christ carefully covered the impossible table with selected pages of *Le Journal*,[30] and by the fact that his tiny feet had suddenly flowered into a hideous pair of square-toed patent leathers, each sporting a large cracked grin across its instep.

The Captain crossed himself with reckless prodigality before falling to the food, and Marlowe wondered whether his intention was a grace or a prayer for internal protection: whatever it was, the mauve eyes, weakly puddled in water, accused him with their dilute piety, and he too crossed himself, albeit a trifle self-consciously. Then Christ, his face carved in a fascinating rictus, broke the spell by helping him to champagne and a tomato.

In another half hour, he said, they would be in the sheltering channel between Corfu and Albania. The sea would be calmer, and if the wind did not swindle them they would most certainly reach their island by three or four of the clock.

"Mavrodaphne," he added as an afterthought, "which in your language is it not 'Blackdaphne'?"

"Black laurel," said Marlowe literally, "but the other sounds nicer. Blackdaphne it is."

Then the sun came out of its sheath of cloud and blazed on the changing tones of everything.

The long spinning tides had gradually become pressed down into a uniform flat quilt of cobalt water by the walls of the sheltering channel. To the right, the gilded snout of Pantokrator bulwarked the horizon like a hippopotamus sunk in mud, trailing the last anatomical dislocations of the Corfiot mainland; to the left, sunk in their own mystical communion with infinities of rarer air, the Albanian mountains brooded.[31]

By the time the point of Lefkimo ran outward to meet them the Captain protested that Blackdaphne was in sight. The swoop of his telescope had positively awed the horizon into yielding up the ghostly vision of the island. And...yes. There it was. Marlowe, discerning the tiny float of black ahead, was perplexed by its extreme triviality; a blob, a macula, a mere atomy in a landscape carved and squeezed into heroic forms and suggestions of forms, it invited neither speculation nor comment: barely interest.

But Christ's enthusiasm was not lightly to be put aside. Feeling slightly ridiculous, Marlowe accepted a loan of the telescope, and clapped it awkwardly to the right eye; through the cracked and crooked lenses he detected an approximate image and, adjusting it to focus, glared long and fixedly at Blackdaphne, wondering if he would be expected to indulge in enthusiasm for its natural beauties from such a range. A misty headland, upon whose flank and top gleamed green boles of vegetation, baulked the present direction of their course; they would have to round it. What lay on the other side he could not tell.

They drew gradually near across the lovely waters, and Marlowe, seated cross-legged on the scorching deck, his eyes in the deep shadow of his hat, watched the growing form of things. Beneath his thighs he could feel the oily throb of the engine that drove them on in regular pulse-beats across the languor of the afternoon tides.

Suddenly, far ahead, he sighted a long flight of racing sea-gulls that had climbed from the water to meet them; the splendid trajectory of their path led his eyes to the figure of Christ, standing square-legged on the stern, scattering powdered bread with wide sweep of the hands.

Looking round at that moment he gave Marlowe the full impact of an almost imbecile smile, grinning his red gums wide in a sort of communion with the birds: gawkily leaning and scattering the bread, with the gestures of an ecstatic.

The air was become full of the soft explosions of flight, and the keen tones of the gulls, sweeping and diving, swarming and migrating, freckling the sunlight with their shadowy manoeuvres; angels whose flight across the sun sent a dozen shadows scurrying over the deck and Christ's small figure. Marlowe was almost afraid of their delirious screaming as they settled upon the food.

No description in words of their magnificent progress from this moment until, having rounded the headland, they finally stole into the bay of Nanos, could be anything but hyperbolical and inadequate. There were no dolphins leaping to be sure. No sleek vine tendrils wreathed the mast. There were no solemn dances trod to the flutter of Attic flutes.

Only the long arc of gulls acclaimed them like an aerial bunting. Otherwise everything was as still as death. The sudden cessation of their engine left a crater in the air that took the silence a long time to fill. Drenched in sunshine, and a silence in which the least movement or sound – the noise of feet, or voices, or the shriek of a gull – became a fearful sin, the bay drowsed, in a perfect hypnosis, a trance of fire.

If ever afterwards he chose to reconstruct from memory the very moment of their anchoring, the hundred images of things would leap out at him, dazzling.

The place lay, like a toy, in a sort of hard shining trance. The shelves of sand, white in sunlight, blue in the shadow of the rocks, against the lip of which clung the mercurial waters, now lapsing, now advancing their blue inches of distance. The jetty, bright in a new coat of paint, and stinking of dry seaweed.

As they stole in (but there is no word to express the breathless, the timeless gradations of their progress) the floor of the sea sloped up towards them, softly visible and comprehensible. Marlowe's eyes explored the forests of moss and water creepers – saffron and mustard and cinnamon coloured – whose motionless languor was tempered from time to time by a voluptuous frivolity of gesture. A noiseless opera of gestures in the bed of clear water. Silver, red and brown, the senseless fishes haunted the reflection of his white northern face with its grey eyes built into the skull.

Now the gulls were dropping to the water about them like feathery bombs. And as they came alongside the jetty Christ skipped ashore and, turning to Marlowe with an outstretched hand, remarked: "Here is the place, dear sir."

In silence they marched down the blistered wooden planking, Marlowe first, Christ a pace behind, and two following men with the suit-cases.

A tortuous stony path led them up the face of the scrubby cliff in the comparative shade of the olive trees; Christ, panting by reason of the gradient, attempted another essay in topographical appreciation:

"Very beautiful (pant) dear sir (pant)....Very nice and good to cheap (pant) living…. The house of my cousin (pant) very clean, sir (pant)…. *British Subject*, sir (pant)…" and so on; holding his tubular pants hard against his loins as if he were afraid of losing them, and clenching his eyes open so wide that Marlowe was afraid they would drop out.

At the top of the path they waited a moment to allow the men who were carrying the suit-cases to catch up with them. Dead, absolutely dead in a dead universe of sun and blank shade, the landscape drowsed. Through the frieze-like agony of the olives shone the motionless carpet of sea. Dead and inert. On the topmost crags of the headland snoozed the white Villa Pothetos (of which more hereafter) whose white-washed walls reflected the glare like a minor sun, whose green window-shutters peeled their new paint profusely in the warmth. Dead, all dead.

Great poppies raved in the weeds at the edge of the roadside, and the brittle earth had put out a riot of flowers upon the hillsides. There was not a soul in sight; only a grave faced, dusky child sat in the shadow of the bridge-parapet, curling and uncurling its toes in the deep dust. It did not even look up as they passed. On the left as they walked a splendid lemon-grove passed them like a procession of torches, and the blank door of the church retained its distinguishing cross in the face of the sun. It seemed to Marlowe as they walked that they too had become part of this death, this sun-paralysis, and that their progress along the white road between the lemon groves was some mechanical destiny.

It was a few minutes before they reached the village that the voice sounded. A gentle yawn from behind a vast hedge of prickly pears (whose Mexican profusion almost completely hid a small pink villa)[32] was followed by the sacrilegious tones of a tenor voice, lifted on the heavy air like the sound of a distant earthquake, singing a song, whose words were these:

> "I wench as well as others do,
> I'm young not yet deformed,
> My tender heart, sincere and true,
> Deserves not to be scorned.
>
> Why Phyllis then, why will you trade
> With forty lovers more?
> Can I (said she) with Nature strive
> Alas, I am a whore...."

Then, in a voice of the most lachrymose agony:

> "Alas, alas, I am a WHOOOORE."[33]

Christ offered no explanation of this phenomenon: and Marlowe demanded none. Even the robust voice could not shatter the mood of apathy that had fallen between them; they hurried on down the road to where an inn lay asleep in the puddle of shadow cast by an elm.

In the vast cool room, floored by flags, and as dank as any dungeon, their voices sounded very loud; too loud by contrast with the deadly stillness outside.

Christ's cousin shuffled slowly towards them, a woman of immense girth and corresponding depth of voice. Had she not been so filthy, she might have been considered "homely." Vast discoloured brown eyes peered at everything they could see from under the sandy scrub of eyebrow. She said that she spoke French, but one or two brief essays in this direction convinced Marlowe that she had made a slight mistake, and he was content to let Christ arrange everything for him. A gabble of Greek was a prelude to his being shown into a large back room furnished with a large bed, a three-legged footstool, an exceptionally ugly eikon,[34] and a fly-swatter.

"Bella," said the woman, using coercion. Perhaps she saw his reluctance. "Très très bella. Nay?"[35]

She bowed until her sagging breasts almost hung at her belt.

"Bella," agreed Marlowe dubiously, confronted by the soiled linen of the bedclothes. He turned and looked about him. Christ had disappeared. For a moment he was angry, and then the anger gave place to a hopeless laughter. He sat down on the bed and grinned: and the woman, scatching her hair out of her eyes, set up a smooth musical crackle of laughter. The suit-cases had been left in the bar-room. The road was quite empty of people.

The furnishing of the outer room was no less remarkable than that of the room in which he was to sleep. From the stone floor to the whitewashed ceiling climbed row upon row of wooden shelves, which housed only a large quantity of dust. In a glass case at the bar-counter, faintly odiferous and mildewed, the immediate stock was on view: three eggs, a tough strip of bread, half a sour sausage, a putrescent olive, a cube of cheese the colour of a decaying molar, and a small enamel tea-pot full of black wine. Visited by a desire to eat or drink something other than any of these relics, Marlowe asked politely if he could have tea; and while he waited for it to arrive he retired to his room and began to unpack his clothes and books, regardless of the fact that there was nowhere to put them. But one forgets. There were six small nails standing insecurely in the soft plaster wall, obviously destined for the unpacking guest, and on each of these he suspended some article of clothing. The books, appearing to him infinitely more valuable than the clothes, he left in the trunk, after a cursory rearrangement of them. It was really beginning to look as if he would have to live "from his suit-case" – a prospect which was irritating to contemplate; but being somewhat philosophically intentioned in mind he produced the illusion that such a life would abound in small opportunities for self-discipline; and these were more or less what he enjoyed. Either he did not know, or he had forgotten the Shakespearean adage concerning the philosopher and toothache.

Certainly one would have imagined that life between these four crumbling plaster walls, whose surface yielded a great quantity and variety of insects (from great hairy centipedes to mere thumb-sized cockroaches), was a field more fitting for an entomologist than for a mere contemplator of things spiritual; that life between sheets whose soiled and stained surface did not disguise the pullulation of fleas, and other entomic curiosities, was more conducive to the exploration of the body than of the mind. However, as it turned out he was never tried (for against the trials of one night one must place what-might-have-been): and in a few short hours Kostas Rumanades had effectively altered, if not his destiny, at least his domicile. Indirectly, that concerns the fantastic Vassili, and an even more fantastic whorl of bunting that gave a rakish colour to the bar room ceiling; and a small pile of festive eggs (painted crimson) which Marlowe had not previously noticed. Such gay phenomena in surroundings so dankly dismal seemed to demand recognition. He asked the woman, partly by mime, what the meaning of it could be, and she, after a moment's deep thought, replied in her best French:

"Festa. Grando festa. Mangiare. Pouf!" and with a sudden agility skipped across the floor in a wildly facetious dance, drumming her tongue on her lips and humming to indicate, no doubt, the imaginary presence of mandolines. Then, abruptly cutting the dance short, she fell on her knees and became suddenly immersed in her devotions. It was very curious.

To Vassili, who lounged splendidly against the door-post, the mime seemed something more than curious; it was terribly suspicious. So suspicious indeed that he drew himself up to his full height and allowed a sharp bark to emerge from between his red lips. Marlowe swiveled round to glare at the intruder, and connected with a withering stare from the brown eyes with the bloodshot rims, whose accusation seemed to suggest uncomfortable and unnameable things. Vassili was the policeman. He had run half a mile buttoning himself into his uniform as he went. His manner was closely modelled on a film actor's conception of what a detective should look like; that is to say, he tried to look like a pontiff, and merely succeeded in looking hungry – almost ravening. Hunger and a certain dark significance were the alternating expressions on that bald face, flowering on a tub-like body like a gigantic polyp. He had no eyebrows and no hair, but as if to make up for this his moustache (which smelt as did his whole person of pomade) looked as if it had been sculptured in coloured stone and attached to his pouting upper lip. He was quite the most impressive policeman Marlowe had ever seen. He smelt quite extraordinary. When he spoke his voice had the fussy rasping quality of an insect. A rough approximation of his speech would seem to go thus: "Erm…erm…Vous êtes erm erm FRANÇAIS?"

He searched the pockets of his uniform long and diligently, extracting thence a tin-hilted pencil and a quantity of forms and questionnaires which he dropped on the floor as he spoke, and which the woman kept picking up and handing to him. Then he wrote and wrote and wrote, leaning heavily against the wall as he did so, and looking up now and again at the subject of his examination with an expression of horrifying hunger on his face. He had exhausted his stock of French.

Perspiring freely at the neck, he tried both Italian and Greek without any success. Each time Marlowe said that he did not understand, Vassili moistened his pencil-tip by inserting it in the pink recess beneath his archway of sculptured whisker, and wrote something down, lolling his little pink tongue out at the labour of it all. The woman was no help at all. Gradually the process became slower and slower, and the pauses longer and longer, and the policeman so hot that his splendid uniform stuck to his uncomfortable flesh. Then a deadlock was reached.

The three of them stood there, in the merciful shade of the great bar-room, and stared drowsily at one another: Vassili, the woman, and Marlowe. Silence. One could almost feel the putrefaction creeping about the food in the glass case. The tea which the woman had made for him lay forgotten and cold in a giant peasant teapot. Even the merciless flies, normally so tiresome, had hung themselves on the white ceiling and were asleep. Silence.

And in the immensity of the silence the woman began to laugh, holding on to her breasts as if she feared they would become detached by the puffing of her abdomen, and the gushing of the laughter in her lungs; and Marlowe, watching her, felt the whole trial and tedium of the cross examination dissolve and become part of that universal solvent – deep laughter. And he too contributed his gentle chuckling to swell the noise.

Perhaps the most significant thing was the effect of such an action on the policeman. For a minute his hunger (or was it his dignity?) was outraged: but only for a minute. Leaning back and closing his eyes as one about to imitate the languor of the sleeping beauty, he allowed half a dozen precocious shudders to rack his stomach underneath the leather belt; and, while not a muscle or fold of his face was disturbed, from his parted lips emerged a faint popping. He was laughing. Marlowe found it delightful; curious, too, that no matter how his chest hopped, no matter how his lungs wheezed, the bland polyp-face behind its sculptured moustache retained its impassivity.

The gradual disintegration of common laughter prompted them all to assume postures of greater relaxation. Marlowe subsided gently on one of the wooden trestles. The woman, still in the grip of her seismic convulsions, retired behind the counter and poured three measures of black wine. Vassili, whose methods of expression were those of extreme subtlety, merely undid the hinges of his collar, and winked a filmy brown eye, thereby indicating with extreme accuracy that he too had relaxed the stringency of official attitude.

With a certain pomp they drank, solemnly toasting their hostess and then each other; and, while the police-man and the woman kept up a long and obviously quizzical discussion about him, Marlowe contented himself by smiling encouragingly at them from time to time.

It was only when Vassili caught sight of the sheaf of questionnaires he had put down on the table that he was reminded again of his official status, reminded that the safety of the island (perhaps of all the Ionian Islands) was dependent on him alone; the responsibility harrowed him. With the same look of unearthly hunger on his face he made it clear that he was going to fetch an interpreter; he gave a brief but impressive mime, plainly cautioning his victim not to disappear. ("As if I could," said Marlowe indignantly.) Then, lounging to the door, he gave one fierce glance over his shoulder, and set off down the road at a gallop, holding on to his hat. They watched him disappear in a cloud of dust down the hot road with as much listless apathy as if they were witnessing the disintegration of a ghost; perhaps, thought Marlowe, he was a ghost, called up by the heat of sun and who knows what other quirks of essential matter. But the faint smell of pomade remaining in the room insisted on the reality of Vassili.

The lapse of an hour was as casual, as uncompelling to the notice, as would have been the lapse of a minute; the siesta hour is always like that – timeless, beyond all mere reckoning, as life might be, suspended between worlds out of all space and time. Marlowe, lying still on his verminous bed, shielded his eyes from the merciless penetration of sunlight through the throbbing square of window, and dozed on towards death.

When he did wake from the half insensibility of inaction and peer from under the heavy lids of his eyes, it was to see the figure of Gordon standing over him, apocalyptic,[36] like the figment of a dream: his body full and brown in its scanty bathing slip, and burnt to the colour of cured meat. There was something brutal about his nakedness in that shabby room.

"I was asked to come and help you," he said simply, in the deep rusty tones which Marlowe afterwards knew to be a sign of his shyness. His chest expanded and contracted easily under the pressure of breath, hooped like a barrel by the curve of ribs under the skin. His forearms twinkled in their covering of hair, which the sun had bleached against the flesh. Had it not been for the sight of the policeman lurking in the doorway, Marlowe would have had difficulty in believing his eyes.

"You'll excuse the general wetness, I hope," said Gordon, "but I was bathing when this creature found me."

He combed a large hand through hair that was matted and wet with salt water, and grinned.

"It's kind of you," said Marlowe. "I've been worried to death by him."

The policeman grinned ingratiatingly from the doorway, and coyly waved a sheaf of paper.

In the cavernous bar room the three of them settled down to grapple with the curious examination paper officialdom had set them. Gordon, standing in his own wet footprints, switched adroitly from English to Italian, occasionally scratching his rump and giving subdued bursts of laughter at the imbecilities of the policeman.

"Your name," he said, "Your father's name, date of birth, date of death, your mother's name."

"But, damn it all," said Marlowe, "I don't know."

"He says you look most suspicious."

"Well, I can't help that."

"I tell you what to do," said Gordon. "Make the whole thing up. It won't matter. No one bothers. When I came here there was exactly the same fuss. I told them a whole pack of lies. It doesn't matter."

Marlowe, after a brief mathematical calculation, deduced a set of imaginary dates and facts which would roughly coincide with the real ones. Under the heading *Profession* he lingered for some time, and under the inspiration of Gordon's light heartedness wrote: "Traveller." "That seems to cover it," he said, "and I'm really very grateful to you for the help. We might have gone on for weeks."

Vassili gathered up the papers and placed them piously in one of his bulbous pockets. Then, with a sharp bow, he turned about and marched away through the sunlight.

"The end of a chapter," said Gordon, "Do you feel like a drink?" and without waiting for an answer ordered some more of the red wine. Smiling across the brimming red crater, he sipped and said: "So you're a traveller?"

"More accurately a liar," said Marlowe. "I've not been out of England before. And you?"

"I?" Gordon seemed surprised at the indelicacy of such a remark. "I? I'm a creature of circumstance entirely without distinction. I have spent my life perfecting the art of loafing until I have almost succeeded in formulating a philosophy from it."

Marlowe said nothing but sipped his wine and stared at the glass case with its mouldering relics. Exchange of casual witticism and banter with someone he did not know came hardly from him. With the easy candour of the young man who sat, all but naked, on the bench opposite him, he did not know how to deal. Curiously English and shy in the heat of the room, he was still dressed in his worn blue serge suit, which now stuck to his flesh like sodden paper. His fingers, he noticed, were very dirty.

But, if he was uncommunicative, Gordon was neither worried nor affected. His own casual remarks had the slight turn of flippancy about them which went well with his information. One or two positive facts he ventured. That he was staying on the island indefinitely; sharing a villa with a friend of his; that he had once been a copy-writer in an advertising house, as well as a journalist. He considered himself an old man at twenty-six.[37] The last item of news he delivered with a cocked eyebrow, adding that he had chosen Mavrodaphne as a place most suitable for retirement.

"You must come and have tea with us," he said. "Preferably now, if you like. It will be better than this place."

To the woman, who had reappeared when she heard the scrape of their moving feet, Gordon expressed, in limping Greek, his intention to carry the visitor off to his villa. Paying for the wine, Marlowe noted that it cost three drachmae each: threepence altogether, which was a pleasing thought after the Italian exchange. Commenting on it, he put on his hat and prepared for the impact of the sun on his limp body.

They walked out into the sunshine of the road, and down the knotty path, to the dazzling stone promontory where a pink villa hung above the sea. And as they walked Gordon talked quietly and enthusiastically about the peasants: their eccentricities, their superstitions, their personal filthiness; and above all he talked of their marvellous imbecilities – their utterly magnificent idiocy. That to him was their salient characteristic – the splendid unreason which characterised life on the island.

"I envy them," he said more than once. "They still manage to keep that wonderful sense of *gesture* which we bloody northerners have lost. Now take old Rumanades, for instance: you met him?"

"No," said Marlowe.

"That's queer," said Gordon. "He owns the place."

"What?"

"Yes. He owns the island."

"I had no idea."

"Well, it's of no importance," said Gordon, "you'll meet him at the fireworks to-night. Mind the steps. They're a bit loose here and there. Pity you missed the procession. Vassili was a treat to watch. He kept his composure in spite of the heat. Behaved like a pontiff even when the little boys made rude remarks about him."

In the small garden, screened by a hedge of prickly pear, they stumbled upon a lean, dark-haired young man, who lay sun bathing on a narrow concrete plinth. He did not open his eyes at their approach but murmured: "Fee Fi Fo Fum, I smell the blood of an Englishman."

Gordon, by way of waking him, scratched the sole of his foot with the nail of his own big toe.

"Come, come," he said. "The *leit-motiv* to this is genteel courtesy and a certain olde worlde charm. Cast off sloth, boy, cast it off. Defy the fiend."

To which the impassive corpse replied: "I am a million revolving suns."

Gordon led the way into the villa, and in the deep cool shade of its rooms they brewed strong tea. On the cool red tiling of the floor a puppy scavanged for food, pausing from time to time to lick its master's feet. The afternoon was slowly mellowing to hallowed evening. The long curve of the land held the water in its grip like a dish. Far out, a forgotten petal, a fishing boat with lemon sail scouted the edge of the night.

As they sat on the terrace under the lattice of vine, the conversation petered out into long comfortable silences. The smoke from Marlowe's pipe hung in the still air; palpable blue against the blue of the water. The shifting tones of the sunlight slanted in a profuse fickleness about the mountains of the mainland, and the olives each became a sundial, projecting lean shadows one way.

Walsh sat beside them on the grass of the terrace, clad in a red dressing-gown, gravely teasing the puppy with a stalk of celery, and talking quietly to himself from time to time. Once a brief wind shuffled the vine tendrils above their heads, and a plump lemon in the groves at the side of the promontory snapped its stalk and fell, like an extinguished sun, to the beach below.

"Tell me about England," said Gordon at last, with the trace of a sigh. "Who are the heroes of the moment?"

"Is poetry still Communism?" asked Walsh.[38]

"And is there honey still for tea?"

Marlowe pondered and sucked his pipe before answering. Then he said abruptly: "I don't know much about that side of things, really, but the world seems pretty full of dreariness at the present time."

In the silence which greeted these words Gordon yawned hugely, and stretched his strong arms up towards heaven. The span of his ribs expanded with breath and then suddenly was deflated: his body curving away forward laxly until, his arms on his knees, he leaned forward with his face touching his thighs.

Walsh, grave of face but speechless, rolled the brown puppy over on its back and thumped its small heavy belly until it produced a sound like a toy drum.

"You see," said Marlowe, with a hint of apology in his tones, everything is built on a foundation of nihilism and nimiety. Hence the whine of the young. Communism, like a gigantic Procrustes, is just beginning to take a hand. America, with her cinema, her hot jazz and her dreadful idiot-mind has virtually conquered the world....Oh, it's fantastic." His vehemence surprised himself. "Fantastic!" and his hand involuntarily sought the place where the long scar had split the skin across his ribs, and rolled up its puffy red furrow of flesh parallel with his heart.

"You must really forgive me," he said at last, "but I feel so strongly about these things."

Walsh drew up his long legs and subsided gently on to the ground, putting his arms behind his head, staring up through the lattice of vines at the darkening sky. Gordon got to his feet heavily and strolled up and down the terrace once or twice, saying: "England, my England, can the news be true?"

"Of course," said Marlowe, whose sudden burst of annoyance was lying heavily on his conscience, "I'm no judge. My job was a purely sedentary one. I didn't have much time to see things as they are."

The final stages of contemplation, he was thinking, should be interesting as a solution for problems economic and domestic: that last state of devotion with its physical self-immolation, its concentration on the finest trivialities. The old saints, for instance. Anthony, with his temptations. He said, half humorously: "There's still the monastic life, thank heavens, we've still got that."

"But then it's merely the choice of evils," said Gordon, "one anaesthetic against another. The cinema versus the Trappe. For my part I'd choose the cinema: one is rotted in quite a painless way. But the idea of getting up at two every morning and sleeping in my own coffin..."

"Me too. I can't stand all this gnawing away at honest Christian bones."

"Yes, but the Trappe is not softening. You missed the point of that. It's hardening. It gives you armour. If you have a capacity for suffering, or if you happen to be suffering, what could be better?"

"That's true enough," admitted Gordon mildly. "But all the same it's a choice of evils." He sat down again in his chair, hands in lap, and stared out across the sea in ambiguous silence. "I was just thinking, myself," he said slowly, "what very thin air we were creating. Also that it's getting on. Would you care to stay and eat supper with us? The inn won't give you much besides bread and olives."

"Very much," said Marlowe. "And if you'll let me I'd like to help in the cooking. I'm quite good at it."

They sat on for a while in silence, watching, the light dropping softly across the terrace, and slanting round the immature grapes. Somewhere, from among the trees at their back, came the brisk talk and laughter of the peasants around the spring; soon their servant would come down the hill, swaying under a yellow pitcher of water: and it would be time to start cooking.

Gordon yawned heartily and pitched the stump of his cigarette over the low parapet into the sea; the puppy turned over on its back and began to dream of chasing a kitten across a treeless countryside. It gave small barks and squeaks in its throat, and wagged its paws convulsively. Walsh sighed and whistled a few bars of a tune.

The evening drew gently on, oblivious of the mere doubts and fears and opinions of mortals, concentrating, like a true mystic, on its own quintessential loveliness, holding and devouring its few remaining hours of day-time life as if this were the final evening of the world.

*Chapter III*

# Rumanades

KOSTAS RUMANADES, if he had not made history himself, was the kind of man with whose help history is made; and since history, they say, is no longer a question of conquest, but merely of what political science calls "economic penetration," it is as an economist that he takes his place in the history of Greece.

To say that he was a Greek, is to insist on those qualities which made him what he was materially: a man of judgment, of perception, of natural thrift, soaked in the politics of his day, possessed of an almost infallible prophetic sense. He knew which way the cat would jump. Yet the track which his career cut across the financial world of his time was not meteoric; it resembled rather the careful, continuous marks left by a large tank on a wet tar road. Slowly, with a care that made the final effect of his life more grandiose, he had built up his financial barony until it was impregnable.

He was born in the islands some twenty years before the end of the century. His father was the moderately wealthy owner of a trade in currants, a snob, and profoundly religious. His mother was without significance. Kostas at the age of sixteen spent most of his time beating up and down the coast, on the currant boats, or making longer trips abroad, to England and Holland. His life was spent in the company of seamen, and with those dreams which even at that age he nourished with regard to a fortune. He learned English, French and Italian, and read widely in all three languages. His reading always had a direct bearing on the economic problems of the time, and laid a foundation of knowledge

33

which afterwards proved invaluable to him. At the age of nineteen he had developed the economic penetration of a rifle-bullet.

By this time his father had died and his mother retired to a nunnery in Xante. The field was clear.

The nineteen-year-old son, lean and swarthy, bright and alive to possibilities, took over the business and made it work as it had never worked before. His father, who had possessed neither vision, nor what our American cousins call business ethics, would have been amazed at the changes of policy which his son instituted; his delight at the increase of business could hardly have equalled his disgust at the shifts which were made to achieve it. The money rolled in, and Kostas collected it thoughtfully, and tucked it away in his sock. For his own part he was not interested in the currant business. It was, to him, merely a stepping-stone to things even more wild, exciting, and lucrative. He was waiting for the necessary diversion, and when it came, he was ready for it. The Turks provided it.

During the war with Greece he plunged all his available resources into the manufacture of boots for the conquering Greek armies, regardless of the fact that he was no judge of shoe-leather. What interested him was the growing lists of figures in his ledgers. As far as he was concerned the armies could (and history relates that to a certain extent they did) march to victory on cardboard. Again the money rolled in, and again he collected it – thoughtfully. This time, however, his gains were more than amazing. They were quite frightening.

But it would be a misstatement to call him unscrupulous, or any of the other names which come to mind so easily in contemplating people of his kind. No great financier has ever been unscrupulous. Merely dis-eased. Like art, finance becomes a drain on the vitality, and absorption a vampire, which makes demands one can only satisfy by disregarding the laws of an envious and less demon-possessed society. No, he was not unscrupulous. Merely a financier devoured by his own passion, not so much for the actual money, as for the power it gave him over himself and mankind.

And his art, after all, was as tireless in its demands on him as ever the creation of music or painting could be. Ledgers, books, signs, figures, letterheads, machinery, workers, ships – these were all part of a technique which he set himself to master. Business on a large scale, controlled by himself, the fruit of his own brain and fingers, was an ideal epic enough to flatter his ambition. Money, too, as a symbol, held the real quality of sugar icing romance. Drachmae, sterling, dollars, naps, Guatemala quetzal, Honduras, peso, krone, balboa, escudo, rouble, dinar, cordoba, Peruvian libra, Polish zloty, rupees, yen, Hungarian pengö, Slav dinars, Salvador colons – with these mystical symbols, their fluctuations and interrelations (to most of us, alas! how esoteric) he built for himself a new Zodiac; in it he moved, happily remote, as sure footedly as an astronomer among the symbols of a universe which is incomprehensible to us.

It was a strangely aloof, strangely reticent and gentle Kostas Rumanades who confronted the economic world in the years immediately preceding the World War. His happy opportunism had already placed him in a position of wealth and eminence. He was the prosperous owner of a big house outside Athens, land in several islands. His taste in dress had developed along the approved lines. Impeccably dressed, he was to be seen lurking on the outskirts of the crowd at desirable functions. His lean body even showed signs of taking unto itself a roll or two of fat. But none of these distractions could blind him to his real purpose. The lean young man who had squatted over his ledgers in the poky offices of his island had not altered appreciably. The svelte financier, stripped of his provincial airs, still forbade his interests to flag for a moment. Rumanades still pored over his ledgers, occasionally pausing to cast a careful eye over the world and estimate with that rock-sure judgment of his, what its changes were going to be in the future.

Strange pre-war world, now so remote, so lacking in actuality for us. Whiskered Imperial England, with her gout, claret, port. So splendid the isolation. Money being coined, and more money. Queen Viccy still on a pedestal. Willy and Edward distrusting each other. Bismarck's insane robot machine still working, still building. Robot out of control, which no one could stop. The key had been lost or thrown away. The Balkans smouldering, smouldering, like a train of brown paper. Russia powerful and unafraid. France uncomfortable with the memories of Metz. The King of Greece trying on his German uniform. The calm eyes of Venizelos watching, watching, assessing chances.[39]

Needless to say, Rumanades had anticipated trouble, located roughly the quarter from which it was most to be expected, and made his preparations accordingly. To his interest in boots he added another interest: arms.

When the war swept over Europe like the Flood, he quietly built himself an ark with his ledgers, and sailed away, well out of harm's reach. His profits were enormous: his prestige amazing.

The post-war world found him one of that select band of European dictators, now casually turning aside to help one country out of financial difficulties, now being summoned to the council tables of another. He was hymned, honoured, starred and gartered to a degree which mildly puzzled him. His presence at Geneva was indispensable. Every Balkan crisis found him somewhere in the middle of all the tangle, definitely involved, however remotely. He made a triumphal tour of America, visiting two newly opened shoe factories, and lecturing in his precise, well-pronounced English to gangs of polyglot salesmen, workers, etc. His evening waistcoats were thick with emblems, stars, ribbons, medals.

But inside all this multicoloured bunting, somehow remote from these exterior manifestations, the statue of the real Rumanades had not altered very much. Even with his downy moustache, his sleekness in clothes, you might have seen traces of that long armed, gawkish Greek boy who had sat (how many centuries ago!) over his ledgers, checking figures by the light of an oil lamp. His vague puzzlement, his dim alarm at his own success, persisted. Staring at his own delicate signature at the foot of important documents, he would wonder for a second at the name; somehow, below the saurian plating of business, commerce, documents, deeds, treaties, there was a vague doubt as to his own identity. Who was this ghost of himself – this sleek-moustachioed, soft-hatted, dapper financier, with his beautiful leather shoes bright in polish, who travelled in luxury from one corner of Europe to the other, attended by a secretary and a long thick satchel of paper? Who?

From Dijon to Paris, from Amsterdam to the Hague from London to Berlin, in trains, in luxurious Pullman sleepers, in cars, in restaurants, he wandered. Speeding across the sun-gold Italian countryside he pondered the question; in the deep French nights, when the countryside flashed by them like a continuous strip of black silk and the stations banged and hummed by, he would stand for a moment in the rocking compartment, before undressing for sleep, and consider his own features in the mirror. Who was this important ghost? He was destined never to discover.

It was inevitable that the law of diminishing spiritual returns should begin to prey upon him after a while. The value of his money dropped in his own eyes. He found he was getting less and less for it. The ark of his ledgers on which he had floated so safely and with such comfort for so long, began to oppress him by its utter indestructibility.

Of late he had become damnably lonely, lonely with that dreadful isolation which great wealth seems to carry with it; and behind the loneliness he was aware of the lack, that spiritual want, which is the mark of a man who has not lived near enough to his fellows.

To a great extent and for a time, Manuela supplied that want.

Perhaps it was unfortunate that he should have bought her, very much as if she were a consignment of some marketable commodity; for the ignominy of the business preyed heavily upon her. But the slight Spaniard said nothing, nothing at all; she merely gazed at him from under her eyelids (always they seemed pressed down by the weight of her boredom) and stared her contempt, for an infinity of seconds.

It was useless for him to protest his slavery, his abject surrender. She knew which of them was enslaved. Standing with her slight body rigid and arrogant, she would say, slowly, with the contemptuous silence creeping in between her words: "Well...what do you want me to do? Tell me." And she would walk with the insolent swing of her narrow loins across the cool floor of her bedroom, goading and enticing him. But that was afterwards.

For their marriage he bought Mavrodaphne, and on the small square plateau overlooking the sea, commanded the palatial white villa to be built, with its cool tiled floors and sun balconies, and the sloping vine trellis radiant with hay coloured tendrils setting off the beautiful white walls. "I will make you a princess...a princess," he said, delighted with his own fancy; and certainly her estate would have made Cleo feel the sultry drab she was.[40]

But Antonies are not made of money; and if the body of his princess was lean and delightful like a young girl's, and full of sensualities and secrets, he was never allowed to forget that he had bought, and not conquered it. The barrier of her secrecy and silence he could never penetrate. For a time he suffered her cruelties, and she his clumsy adoration; and then quarrels began to disturb the dangerous quiet of their intimacy – a series of wars in which she was the conqueror, and he the conquered: and the great hollow rooms echoed to the sound of his voice, pleading, cajoling, reviling, while she dispassionately stood and smiled under her heavy eyelids. She never raised her voice above its customary husky whisper. After he had said his say she would go to the long black piano and play for hours. Sometimes she sang, in a smooth icy voice, peasant songs of Spain and Morocco.

Once, when he had goaded her almost to fury, she snatched up a paper knife from a table and, without word or expression, ran it into his forearm; but only once. For the rest she contrived to be absent from him (even though the shell of her body stood in its characteristic poses of insult), dreaming of he could not tell what, behind the façade of a smile or a sneer. It made him fear her.

"You are a cat," he told her once, and the trite epithet stayed fast in his mind, reminding him of her in those more lonely hours of the endless blue night, when he lay on their vast marriage bed and stared down across the moonlit bay, most pathetic of despots, unhappy of victors. Yes, she was a cat; and in his overshadowed mind he could see her as the symbol of all that was delicate, cruel and rapacious.

Sometimes from bewilderment and self-pity he wept, but never from anger. Never from a rich primary cause. And she? Sometimes in the deep silence of summer nights she would get up from her bed and walk about the cold tiling of the floors, radiant with the moonlight, smouldering away the slow hate in her, her hands hugged in her arm-pits, desperate;

or she would sing the weird crooning flamenco songs on the terrace, leaning forward to the shining sea, with a strange animal satisfaction. There were anxious times of the moon.

But when the end came, he could not say he was unprepared for it. One morning she had disappeared, taking with her the motor launch, and nearly all her clothes. She had driven up the straits to Kerkyra where there was an aerodrome.[41] In the whole of the neat letter pinned to her coverlet one phrase wounded him, so that he grinned as he read: *"You bought me like a mare and like a mare I have broken stable."* So that was finished.

The sense of finality, of loss, did not reach him until long after, for his mind was snapped off short, like the imperfect foil it was, and the merer trivialities hedged him in, breaking down his control. But somehow he knew that inside himself the essential man had crumpled and perished; and like a beachcomber he set about gathering the rags of interests and affectations to hide his naked disfigurement.

He still lived on in the palace, but its name was changed from Villa Baucis & Philemon to the more sombre Villa Pothetos.[42] That was the only trophy of his defeat offered up for the world to gloat over. The rest was left to time, and the mercies of oblivious age.

From the dazzling summit of Leucothea[43] to the small nameless village which lay in the shoulder of the northern headland, there was not a peasant with a grievance who had not been treated with fairness and courtesy, gently reprimanded for his or her inherent tendency towards theft, or consoled in the approved manner during a time of bad harvest. If their condition was little better than feudal serfs', they were treated with the respect due to venerable landowners when they brought their troubles to the white house, for a discussion with Rumanades. Gravely punctilious, he heard them out, with the air of an emperor humouring his subjects, drumming his long fingers on the glossy wood of his desk and sniffing benignly through his nose.

Yes, all these once negligible duties (which had been evaded or dealt with through a deputy) began, as time went on, to assume a definite place in the quotidian routine. He extracted a grave and gentle pleasure from them, the pleasure of a long, enjoyable monotony; and if ever the past did intrude, then it was no more painful to him than was the daily intrusion of a sailing-boat, petal-sailed, in the straits of blue water which he could see from the windows of his villa. His life had started upon another cycle.

At fifty-seven he was already an old man, dry, fussy and pedantic, but with a queer humanity peeping from him, and shy delight in his eyes at most familiar of human marvels. Watching him as he walked the dusty roads, stooping his head and shoulders forward as if intent on following a scent, lean-shanked in his black clothes peppered with cigar-ash, one would have found it difficult to believe in him as a once spruce and immaculate young financier, with the world in his hands; or, for that matter, as anything but what he seemed – a touchingly human black-beetle, whose humour and credulity were those of a child.

Like a child, too, he was avid for fairy stories. Locked in a bureau, somewhere in the Villa Pothetos, was a card-index file, which contained the results of several years' arduous research into the origin of the local legends, together with a large amount of personally collected evidence written in his sprawling hand. If he was eager to discover and document legends, the peasants were no less eager to supply them; their only desire was to please, and there was no better way of putting him in a good temper than by inventing a new and startling legend. So they paved the way for every request by crossing themselves, gazing fearfully around, and whispering some awful tale about Maria's washing being stolen off the line in full view of twenty people, or Vassili's cow being struck with the pox. Inevitably they were rewarded by the gleam in his eye, and by the alacrity with which he unlocked his bureau and produced his card-index.

"Most curious," he would say, "most odd," and peer up at them through the wilderness of beard while he clipped his glasses carefully on his nose. "Most odd."

Latterly, too, it had seemed a pity that so few people ever got a chance of seeing the natural beauties of the island: for the laws of privacy sternly forbade the casual entry of foreigners. It seemed a pity to keep this pleasure to himself. So Christ was given permission to bring back with him anyone sufficiently interesting and interested, when he returned from his weekly trip to Brindisi.

To old Rumanades the arrival of a new visitor was a source of great happiness, implying as it did contact with a world he had rejected and which had finally denied him through the person of Manuela. More than that, company of any sort was welcome, not merely because he found a chance to show off his private pet – Mavrodaphne – but also because he could assume the natural prerogative of royalty on such occasions, and reinstate himself in his own eyes as something of an old conqueror.

Along the crater of the bay there were one or two dilapidated villas of various sizes, relics of the days when the island was a little-known but exclusive summer resort for Southerners. These were repaired and painted in their bright pristine colours, and visitors, as they arrived, were requested to reside in the one of their choice. But if Christ was a diligent fisher of men, his catch was small, though various.

First to arrive had been that nameless dithering old Frenchman, an entomologist with the appearance of an itinerant musician, who lived by preference on the western slope of the island in a damp peasant hut and spent his days hunting for a rare species of wood insect. Nothing was known of him except that he talked endlessly about an injustice done him by the University of Padua – and carried a walking-stick as thick as a tent pole with which to guard himself against lizards. On the whole he had been disappointing.

Then came Francis, who declared that she was on her way to Mistra and Constantinople, and could not stay more than a week. But the heat and luxury of one summer, and Rumanades' entreaties that she should stay until the village church was built, and glorify it with a fresco, were sufficient to melt her resolve. She stayed on, even though the church showed no signs of being so much as repaired, let alone rebuilt. The fresco she painted round the walls of her bedroom instead, to the horror of the priest and the vast amusement of the peasants.

After her came Fonvisin, a sluggish, heavily built Russian doctor whose politics had not found favour with the Bolsheviks.[44] A pale, rather brutal man this, with a bald head and tufts of red hair, like tiny horns, at his temples. His manner, which was a source of distrust and alarm to old Rumanades, was one of quiet, occasionally punctured by an outburst of hard forced laughter, or a brusque question (implying disagreement) propelled up from his throat with a violence that seemed beyond his control. Particularly disconcerting was his habit of demand-ing a definition in terms during the course of an argument; at least this was disconcerting to the old man, who was in the habit of referring to God, or using phrases like "the Classic Perfection of Greek Art," in a comfortable casual way, without bothering much about their exact meaning. "What do you mean...*God?*" Fonvisin would erupt suddenly, bristling into the middle of some pleasing flight or felicitous generalisa-tion; or "What do you mean...*pure art?*" And as often as not, he was uncertain what he did mean.

For some reason or other, however, Fonvisin stayed. He refused the of-fer of one of the smaller villas with a contemptuous rudeness that wounded the tender susceptibilities of his host, and lodged in the flea-ridden back room of the wine shop. He spent his days lying on his back in the garden, or walking the dunes of seaweed at the foot of the cliffs, talking to himself soberly but vehemently. He drank great quantities of black wine, and it was rumoured that several of the more beautiful peasant girls had been dishonoured by his attentions, but Rumanades preferred not to take any notice of rumour; besides, as he always told himself, even if the rumours were grounded in truth, what business was it of his?

So both Francis and Fonvisin stayed; and after some time came Gordon, followed by that strange waif, Walsh – enigmatic, but given to uproarious fits of flippancy and horseplay, nursing a private dejection of which only Gordon knew. Like Fonvisin he lived a strange numb life, divorced from everyone save, perhaps, from Francis with whom, as with Gordon, he shared the savagery of laughter, moods and silences.

The Ritual of the Fireworks, as it was called, had been Rumanades' own idea.

In the old days, the annual church procession in honour of the patron saint, led by the village priest and two senile deputy-acolytes recruited from the monastery on the top of Leucothea (of which they were the sole inhabitants), had been enough to satisfy his national and personal sense of honour. But with the arrival of foreigners he had begun to feel that something more was demanded of him; something more in the way of entertainment which would reflect favourably not only upon himself as the owner of the island, but also upon the patron saint. Hence the fireworks.

More than this (since any fool could buy a box of fireworks and let them off on the beach for the entertainment of foreigners), it was necessary and fitting that the whole business should receive, as it were, ecclesiastical sanction. It was the Punctilio, the Large Gesture, that the old man was after.

The village priest was asked if, before the ceremony, he would be good enough to give a short address, offer up a brief prayer – in short, indicate in some way that a definite connection existed between the bona-fide ecclesiastical ceremonies and this informal one. And here was the rub.

The priest, who was conscientious, crawled up the precipices leading to Leucothea on his hands and knees, and was hauled up the sixty-foot cliff-face fronting the monastery, in a basket to which a rope was attached; which itself was attached to an antiquated windlass propelled by the two senile, perspiring, verminous old gentlemen who were his acolytes in times of ceremony. A grave conference was held; the priest wondering all the time whether he would live to announce its results to Rumanades.

The two monks, who were jealous at being excluded from the invitation (this was a grave tactical blunder on the part of the old man), spent the whole day arguing the matter backwards and forwards, stopping for a glass of wine and a rest at five-minute intervals, during which the question was pondered with a grave silence.

"Let us not be in a hurry," one of the old men kept repeating. "We must consider the question from every angle." With the air of hardened medieval Sorbonnières they settled down to resolve the tangle of opinion with a wealth of dialectic that did them considerable credit, when it is remembered that neither could read nor write. At sunset, when the priest was finally deposited with a crash at the foot of the cliff, they were still at it, primed with wine, and really grateful to have something which they could discuss for an indefinite period of time. Looking up indignantly, he caught sight of one of them leaning over the terrifying drop, waving genially at him with one hand and unsteadily clawing his vast beard with the other. As he stumbled down through the dusty woods he caught the sound of an aged voice blithering: "We must not be in a hurry. We must consider it from every angle."

That night he presented himself at the Villa Pothetos, and informed Rumanades that the procedure demanded of him would not be seemly in the eyes of either God or man. By "man" he implied the two garrulous anatomies be had left behind on the cliff top; God, even after twenty years of diligent search, still withheld a single clue to His identity.

Rumanades sighed, raised his eyes, and drummed his long fingers on the glossy wood of his desk. He would have liked to accomplish the business with tact and diplomacy, but in the face of refusal so blank he felt called upon to exert what pressure he could still apply.

The church, he said, after a long and stealthy silence, was in a very bad state of repair. The priest agreed. There were holes in the walls, the damp had rotted the painting off the walls, and the woodwork of the altar was rotten. The priest agreed. Did he (the priest) think it was fitting for services to be held for the glorification of God in a temple which was only distinguishable from a stable by the bleached cross on its door? At this point the priest opened his mouth to speak, but the old man with a gesture silenced him and continued quietly. Did he (the priest) not realise that they could be of great use to each other, and between them assist in the general advancement of worship, to the glory of the patron saint and all concerned? The priest knew he was beaten.

In the silence that followed, Rumanades scrutinised him closely, from the top of his grubby stove-pipe hat, to the uneasy black shoes that peeped nervously out from time to time under the soutane. Then meaningly he said: "Would it not be to the glory of us all if I were to restore the church?"

He knew only too well that the priest slept on a straw mattress behind the damp altar: and that he suffered from rheumatism; that another winter in the dank, unprotected barn was more than even the most practised ascetic would stand. Accordingly he drummed away at the tabletop and smiled: and called for a bottle of wine to seal the pact.

And it was so.

## Chapter IV

# Phaon[45]

THERE are moments in the intercourse between men, when those qualities of ease, silence, content become, not the jealous property of one person, but the common pool of all; and it was in such a silence that the three of them, Marlowe, Gordon and Walsh, set out to walk down the road to the bay. Food (and Gordon's cooking was really excellent) had put new life into them. They lounged down towards the beach, lazy and comfortable in knowledge of their companionship, talking triviality with the zest of veterans in friendship.

In the electric hush of twilight which preceded positive darkness and followed the quenching of the sun, the high-road had become peopled with peasants from the mountain villages who had come down to watch the fireworks. The throb of donkeys' hooves in the thick dust, the voices, the bright passing of coloured clothes, the curtain of drifting dust – all contrived a soft, orderly pageant of colour and sound, through which the hush of twilight contrived to break. Then, lingering, trembling, like a new lover for the world, the night slipped down upon them, and the pageant was swallowed up, annihilated. In a moment they were marooned on the stony cliff-path, groping for sure footholds where a minute before they could walk upright and at ease. Gordon stumbled and swore with fervour. Somewhere to the left on the darkened beach a maroon stormed up to the sky and, after the preliminary crash, loosed its five or six pattering yellow flares.

"Good God," said Marlowe.

"I know," panted Gordon between blasphemies. "Seems to go off between one's teeth up here."

"We're late," said Walsh. "The priest's beginning."

A beautiful bass voice like a gong now took up the tale. Slowly and with infinite relish it began what seemed to be some sort of liturgical incantation, dwelling on and tasting the lovely syllables of language, rising and falling in the perfect expression of the sense. From the terraces of olive-trees came an occasional muttered response. Soft shapes moved like pieces broken from the darkness, and the humid silence was penetrated by worshippers, and girls' quiet laughter.

"Look," said Walsh suddenly, "do look."

To the left and above them, in broad silhouette against the sky, a ledge of rock curved out sheer from the level of the cliff-face, and on it, sculptured in black, fixed in a rigid sitting pose, the figures of the two old monks were visible. Leaning forward in a vain attempt to see the palpably invisible, their bodies were clenched in scornful anger. They seemed the very substance of rock carved into a caricature of scorn. Gordon chuckled.

"The poor old dears," he said. "They're as jealous as hell."

Walsh, giggling as he stumbled down in the chasmic glooms ahead, turned up his face to Marlowe and explained that they lived on the top of Leucothea, in the ruined monastery. "How they both manage to get back into the nest is a mystery to me," said Gordon. "It's bad enough when one stays behind to work the windlass."

"Oh, I saw them doing it once," said Walsh, "through the old man's telescope. Quite by mistake. They both got into the basket and started to pull the rope. Like a couple of demented prophets, with their old beards flapping over the side. Crashing against the cliff at every pull. And ducking down, too, as if they were afraid of bashing their craniums on the sky."

"Do they do anything?" asked Marlowe. "I mean, besides just winding themselves up and down the cliff?"

"Hold hard, the path turns here," said Gordon. "No. I don't think they do much. Pray a good deal, I suppose. And they love considering things. Simple things for preference. It's their own brand of work; that and drinking white wine. They're perfect medieval relics. If only they could write I'm sure they'd spend their time composing long tracts determining the exact number of camels that could pass through a needle's eye, or ditto angels stand on the point of a pin."

"Rubbish," said Walsh. "They're too simple-souled to be casuists.[46] Christ! The old man's started blasting."

For a second the darkness was broken by one tiny flare: a match: and in its flapping light the domed face of Fonvisin was visible, puckered about a cigarette. Then a flight of saffron rockets fizzed wildly up into the night, and the bay of Nanos rocked in a wild sheet of colour; a pungent cloud of smoke fell to the level of the water, and lolled drunkenly inshore. A rapturous murmur of applause greeted this effort, and from the higher terraces a sharp burst of clapping. In the few seconds of light Marlowe caught sight of the little band of privileged sightseers grouped round Rumanades: Vassili hopping with uncontrollable delight on one gaitered leg; the priest, lounging in an attitude of resigned boredom, chin on breast; Fonvisin supine on a rock, motionless and somehow contemptuous; and Rumanades himself, with Francis and Christ at his heels, fussing about among the mounds of seaweed.

Any introductions at that time and place were bound to be cursory. Rumanades was for a moment nothing but a handshake with darkness, until a shower of gold rockets gave him a lean, bearded face, shyly arrogant in expression, and a lank body clad in fusty black; a shower of white light for the grave face of Francis, with its deep eyes, and sleek, unplucked black eyebrows; red for the bony dome of Fonvisin's head.

"This is Dr. Appolyon Fonvisin. Mr. Marlowe."[47]

In the red glare their eyes met, and Fonvisin's smile belied the sober stare of the eyes, considering, criticising, assessing....

"You must really forgive," said Rumanades nervously, "my preoccupation with the ceremony. The day of our Patron Saint, you know. If you don't mind..." and he fussed off.

Fonvisin lay back on his rock, and his nostrils gushed cigarette smoke. Pillowing his head on his arms, he stared fixedly up at the sky. Marlowe sat down near him and presently Walsh came and joined him with a casual: "Hullo, Fonvisin. You still alive?"

For a minute the Russian smiled grimly up at him. "I am alive, he said. "Yes. I am alive. If you want to know."

"So am I," said Walsh with a sigh, perching himself on the rock and swinging his legs.

Yellow, green and red, flight after flight of rockets fumed up to the dark ceiling of heaven, and loosed their showers of coloured rain. The hollow bay flung back tremendous echoes in the face of the still water. The roar of applause swelled with the crash of clapping from the olive-covered slopes above them. A great throbbing pall of red smoke wavered among them, and with each successive flash, the bright silhouette of the priest, standing with his chin on his breast, was lit with a bright phosphorescent outline.

Flight after flight of rockets. The darkness which, undisturbed, gave the illusion of being limited to the small radius of sight, bulged elastically in all directions. Each new comet plunged its colour, like an avenging knife, into the black. Great, lovely, faltering trajectories were carved out above the cynic impassivity of the sea; and from the natural amphitheatre terraced upon the cliff-top round after round of applause seeped into the vacant seconds of silence, demanding more and yet more.

Francis danced up from the confusion, her face an unholy cipher of delight in light, a shadow against shadow in darkness.

"Isn't it lovely? Oh, isn't it miraculous?"

For a long moment their eyes met and she stared down upon Marlowe's small, rather fine ascetic head, lean and pointing away to the chin: his eyes were small but very bright, a clear salt blue, and seemed to be built deep in under the heavy ledges of bone. They were full of that evasive anguish of his generation; and the evasion in them made her smile and counterfeit ease.

Through the reek of gases the voice of Rumanades called vaguely: "Nearly over now. Nearly finished. Finale."

There was a moment's lull. Then the last fuse began to giggle and splutter, and, gathering impetus from the fiery commotion in its vitals, lurched up into the night with a wheeze, splendidly bound for heaven in defiance of all gravity. Up it went to the top of its curve, unfaltering, and then, after a preliminary stutter, shot a loop of gold stars outwards towards Epirus[48] and the hills. Neatly and cleanly the stars lapsed, waned and were extinguished and only the reek remained, and the faint slap of a discarded stick on the dark water. Then a grudging applause broke out, disturbing the night.

There was a sudden gap at the heart of things. Speech, which had been keyed to its highest pitch to carry in the inferno, sight, which had been tormented by alternating noon and midnight, hearing, which had been well-nigh blasted – these faculties were suddenly restored. Quite what to do or say they did not know. The applause from the olives, gradually growing in volume, gave them their cue.

"Finished. All over." Rumanades lowered his head and peered in their direction. "All over," he said, "my dear Mr. Marlowe. Please forgive my bad manners, but I am a sort of high priest to-night. "Marlowe made the appropriate reply, in the appropriate voice.

"Bed for me, I think," said Walsh, yawning and knuckling his eyes.

The peasant audience were on the move. Laughter and animated talk, mingled with the fresh scent of flowers, came clearly down to them; the priest bade them good night in his rich voice and swept off into the darkness; the ledge on which the two monks had sat was empty. Fonvisin yawned and stretched with insolent ease, and picked his teeth with a matchstick. "And I'll" he said in his careful, exact English, "have a little adventure waiting for me before I go to steep. Eh?" He smiled vaguely around him and unknotted the handkerchief from his bald head. "A little adventure."

"You and your conquests," said Francis, with a certain contemptuous emphasis.

"Conquests!" he mocked, twinkling with glee. "What a Puritanical woman. 'Your conquests,' she says." His imitation of contempt was delightful. Puffing out his lips, he gave a snort of laughter.

"Er…Mr. Marlowe," said old Rumanades nervously, "if you will take a little walk please, there is something I want to speak to you about…"

When they were out of earshot he sighed and shoved his thumbs into his waistcoat pockets so that his fingers dangled down across his abdomen. His jaws moved slowly as if he were chewing his tongue.

"I would consider it a great honour," he said at last, "if during your visit you would live in a little villa which I have empty. It is called Phaon, up there on the Cliff, among the trees. It is a nice little place…"

Marlowe, who had been coached in his part by Gordon, stopped and protested that such generosity was more than he could allow. "I am already in your debt," he explained. "I have landed on a private island, and you have given me permission to stay a while…"

Rumanades became exquisitely nervous, stabbing his pocketed thumbs downwards, and hanging his head.

"Nevertheless," he said doggedly, "I would consider it a great honour if you would accept my offer. It is really not very much to ask…" and Marlowe, taking pity on his embarrassment, accepted the offer with a gratitude which he expressed as delicately as he could. The gesture had been achieved. They shook hands with grave formality. "I can only hope that some day I will be in a position to return your hospitality," said Marlowe, and Rumanades thanked him as solemnly as any owl. "I am sure you would," he said. "My dear Marlowe, I am quite sure you would."

When they returned they found Francis and Gordon alone, talking. Walsh and Fonvisin had gone.

"Marlowe is going to live in Phaon," Rumanades called out excitedly.

"Bad luck, Francis."

Rumanades clicked his tongue against his teeth, and bade them all good-night. "It's long time past my bedtime," he said, dragging out a large watch.

"Well, good-night," said Francis, and held out her hand.

As he shook it he wondered whether the gesture was significant of anything beyond mere formality. As he smiled back into the dark eyes, he seemed to discover again that enigmatic silence which they had shared during the fireworks, but less approachable now, less certain.

"When will you be moving in?" she asked.

"I'm not sure; perhaps to-morrow."

Their voices as they called good-night sounded strangely loud and uneasy on the silent beach.

Turning aside, they made their way over the tussocks of dry, wholesome-smelling seaweed and began to climb the cliff; Marlowe, to whom the geography of the place was as yet unfamiliar, glad of Gordon's company.

The cliff-top was silent and deserted when they reached it, but away to the south, on the road among the olives, there was still the beat of donkey's hooves, and the sounds of laughter and talk.

"Lucky there was no moon," yawned Gordon. "It would have been an outrage. The fireworks, I mean."

Marlowe grunted non-committally, and stumbled on beside him. "Fonvisin," he said suddenly, as if the thought had just occurred to him, "he's a queer fellow."

"Absolute puzzle!"

Gordon yawned again, and made an indefinite gesture with his arms. "I used to think," he said, "that the whole trouble with him was that he had a shortage of emotions. Perhaps I mean half emotions. He reacts violently to anything, not normally. It's either laughter or anger. Nothing in between. Nothing at all."

"Is he a doctor?" asked Marlowe, and Gordon nodded.

"That's another amazing thing. He's a brilliant one. Without exaggeration. Mind the stump. Just there. Two steps more."

"I shall think twice about going sick while I'm here," said Marlowe soberly.

## Chapter V

# Moving In

THE move from the inn to the Villa Phaon fulfilled all the necessary conditions of a musical comedy finale. It was infectious with gaiety, and Marlowe, to whom ceremony – even such well wishing and spontaneous ceremony – was anathema, was a trifle dazed by its extravagance.

He awoke about dawn to the brief sight of sunlight topping the olives and moving across the sea, and was puzzled by the unfamiliar scent of flowers in the little room. Before he could bring his mind to bear on the subject, however, he had dozed off, and it was only the familiar roar of Gordon's laughter that shocked him into a sitting posture, hands to his head. Embarrassed by the intrusion of faces in the low doorway, he stared about for signs of their laughter, still half asleep; and was aware that he lay couched in an absolute nest of flowers, fruit, vegetables, and eggs; orchids and anemones, cherries and wild strawberries, beans and giant tomatoes – the room was swarming with them. On his trousers lay a pyramid of red festival eggs. A bunch of vermilion pomegranate blooms sprouted from the pocket of his coat.

"Gordon," he said, "what is all this?"

The wrinkles crowded about Gordon's laughing eyes, and crawled upwards across his forehead. Leaning sideways against the door-post, he answered: "Bribery."

Marlowe soberly crossed his arms over his chest and stared.

"It was Magnificent," said Gordon: "you lying there sleeping, surrounded by a harvest festival."

A dado of grinning faces bobbed around his head in the semi-gloom of the passage-way, corroborating the laughter. Marlowe was suddenly filled with a shy annoyance. He huddled down in the clothes and frigidly requested privacy. The faces vanished like snuffed candle-flames, and Gordon, serious of a sudden, apologised fervently and closed the door, leaning his broad back to the wood as a safeguard against intrusion.

In silence Marlowe began to dress, carefully examining his clothes for signs of the ubiquitous vermin which had tormented him all night. Pausing as he lifted his shirt to his shoulders, he half turned, and caught the eye of the young man. Gordon smiled mildly and apologised again. "It was thoughtless of me."

"My dear man," said Marlowe, "*that's* not what worries me – it's all this." Standing there, between perplexity and annoyance, he swung his arm wide, indicating the tumbled bed, with its load of market produce, the chair, the floor....

"It's all this," he added, and smiled gradually.

Gordon crossed to the bed, and cleared himself a place to sit on. Elbows on knees, he said: "It's bribery. You'll find this stuff useful, though, if you're moving into Phaon to-day. Save you a trip down to Christ's place."

"But, good Lord, do I accept it?"

A brief examination proved that the donors had left no clue whatso-ever to their several identities; fruit and vegetable, as Gordon remarked, could hardly be traced back to their owners.

"It's pure formality. I imagine they want to bribe you to buy fruit and vegetables and stuff from them. Anyway, we'll see."

Breakfast for Marlowe was purely an affair of coffee and a cigarette; and the duration to-day was determined by the perplexity caused by these agricultural phenomena; yawning lethargically from time to time, he sat beside Gordon on the bed, and puffed smoke up at the dingy ceiling.

"Tomatoes and broad beans."

"Even, my God, a cauliflower. I must have had my head on it."

Prodigiously yawning, he followed Gordon out, to where the crowd of suitors talked together in the hollow echoing bar-room, and shuffled their bare feet on the flags. The room was swimming in colour against the vivid sunshine of the doorway. Christ's cousin, more blowzy and drab than ever in contrast to the gay head-dresses and the swirling skirts, dispensed equal quantities of black wine and garrulity, making the best of the time and the trade.

At the moment of their appearance they became the focus of all inter-est, the pivot upon which the whole gathering circle of humanity turned and whirled, in its swarming and squeezing towards the door.

Voices fluent with necessity beseeched, cajoled, insisted. Scarves danced and swayed, profuse with colour. The heavy dresses twirled and snapped at their ankles, instinct with a disturbing life. Heavy and sickening, the smell of garlic rose on the air. Gordon, head and brown shoulders above them all, laughed in the fresh laughing faces of the women, and shouted for them to make way. Maria, Chrysanthe and a horde of others shouted him down, beseeching him, with a familiarity that horrified Marlowe at the time, but which he recognised later on as a natural trait of the peasants, to intercede on their behalf.

Down the road they went, hedged in by the women and followed, at a respectful distance, by the men who carried the suit-cases; a cavalcade of noise and colour centred round Marlowe, pale, blue-eyed, and nursing his northern reserve. Only Gordon was laughing unfeignedly, and bargaining noisily. The fine dust of the road rose in a cloud about their ankles, and the sun, as yet not uncomfortably hot, warmed their backs.

"Chrysanthe will bring you eggs and milk."

Marlowe nodded perfunctorily.

"Maria wants to be your servant."

"Which is Maria?"

A broad figure, electrified by the mention of the name, pushed nearer to them, leaping across their path on a pair of stodgy brown legs. Leaning towards them and repeating her name, the woman smiled in a sort of humorous anguish of speechlessness, and drew her green head-dress back from her black hair. Her white teeth were set evenly in a broad, kindly mouth, devoid of almost everything but laughter and a certain casual sensuality.

"Maria?" he said, and she, nodding her head in recognition, twinkled her brown eyes at him.

"Malista."[49]

Talking, and chattering, the women still followed them, across the path to the road, and down beyond the ruined stone bridge and the iron spring, from where Phaon was visible, glittering on the hillside.

"It looks as if it were carved in salt," was Marlowe's comment, when Gordon pointed it out to him.

"That," said Gordon, grimacing, "is a poor compliment in this part of the world. They use sea-sand sometimes in the building, and in the winter the walls of your house have such a large quantity of salt in them, they suck up the rain like a sponge."

From the parapet flanking the road a path had been cut, and a white concrete stairway mounted to the villa's porch. A trellis of vine, Marlowe noticed, shaded the cool green porch; and at the back of the little place a deep volume of colour, dashed with bright gold spots, receding to a pure sky, established the identity of the orange-groves – green freaked with gold, already dusty and tremulous in the heat.

The procession followed them doggedly to the very terrace in front of the house, the men groaning under the weight of suit-cases. In the shade of the vine-lattice, Marlowe turned to watch the womenfolk, brilliant in their colours, mounting the long flight of steps, casually conscious of their own kinetic beauty, direct and assured. An hour of negotiation followed, during which Gordon, with his mixture of lame Greek and fluent Italian, did the talking.

Chrysanthe was to bring him eggs and milk when he wanted it; Agathie and Sophia romped off in delight at the thought of having a regular customer for their vegetables; Maria made a point of beginning her job at once, swaying off to the spring with a pitcher on her head, to get them a drink.

Marlowe and Gordon sat down on the uncouth wooden bench under the dapple of sunlight.

"By the way," said Gordon, "what books have you got?" and Marlowe, kneeling on the ground, unhasped his battered suit-case and groped among his treasures. Molinos, Guyon, Bossuet and a crowd of others he lifted and placed in Gordon's brown hands, smiling up a trifle diffidently.

"Mostly quietist people," he said, without further explanation.

Gordon was silent, turning the books over, opening and shutting them. Long slants of sun picked up the sheen in his head of unkempt yellow hair and his heavily marked eyebrows.

"Oh! dear," he said slowly, "I want something to read, and I can't stomach metaphysical pinpricking." He smiled up suddenly and leaned back so that the sun shone on his great gold thumbs.

At that moment Maria reappeared with her pitcher and they followed her into the house to find glasses. It was small, but very clean and cool: a mere two rooms and kitchen, with a lopsided house or office added, it seemed, as an afterthought. It was scantly furnished for one, with good shaggy unpainted wood – a table and a single book-shelf – and sturdy peasant chairs. On the low bed lay a pile of utensils and odds and ends which Rumanades had sent down from the Villa Pothetos: a pair of sheets, some dusters, a saucepan, several earthenware pots, a tin oven for the charcoal fire, a kettle, and a bundle containing a knife, a fork, a spoon and a tin-opener. These Maria took immediate command of, refusing positively to leave them where they were until Marlowe had made an inventory.

"They don't understand a conscientious soul like you," remarked Gordon, and laughed at his glumness. "Never mind."

Pacing the bright tiling of the floors with a fine sense of ownership, Marlowe busied himself with the opening of windows, the throwing wide of shutters.

"Good heavens, Gordon," he said dramatically, "the Sea!"

"It's always there," said the young man negligently, asprawl on the bed, "and it's never the same."

Marlowe's eyes followed the long line of the coast, laid out, it seemed, for his inspection, like a relief map: squared in colours that were bright and positive in sunlight. To the north there was a giant growing ruffle of tides, being pushed round the point of Lefkimo. Otherwise the long slab of water was immobile, impervious, it seemed, to the single lateen-rigged fishing boat which rested upon it, showing no sign of trough or flaw. Eastwards the misty, mountains brooded. Very faintly, as if doubtful of its powers, a wind, whose path had somehow missed the water, tested the suppleness of the two dwarf cypresses in the garden, rocking them.

"I suppose it's always like this," he said at last, with the uncomfortable feeling that he had broken the silence stupidly.

"It's taken for granted. For my part I'm sick to death of it…"

Turning, Marlowe saw the smooth abstraction of the brown face, and for a moment was himself filled with a gust of nostalgic yearning for greenness. The North, at that moment, as he gazed out from the vine-porch to the pure flamy landscape, ripe and positive in tone, seemed an inconceivable distance away, tucked down under obscure landscapes, misty and wet and remote in its forests and marshes: a land of gnomes and shadows, which could produce no vivid memory here, where the fruit burned ripe on the trees, and the glossed green of the olives achieved a hundred subtle gradations from green to green. No, the North was unthinkable, and as yet the South was barely comprehensible in its vividness.

"It's funny," he said, "habit."

Sombrely Gordon agreed, his gaze fixed unwinkingly on the slender tips of the cypresses, which moved in a grave rhythm against the sea-line. In his imagination (the heroic deception of memory!) he was confronting a wide English prospect, lush and delightful undulations chequered with crop and arable and fallow. Wheat like gold foam; the ashy rectangles of oats, the mustard crop, spittle-bright: these were tantalising images of coolness and ease focused against the blue water and the distance that hid Epirus.[50]

*Chapter VI*

# The Portentous Pattern

"IT IS curious and instructive to examine those processes by which the character of the place is made manifest; through the simple necessities, the trivialities, the daily gains and losses it grows, unseen, unsuspected, quietly creating its impact on the receptive mind: until, in retrospect, the form emerges cleanly, comprehensible, having become a coherent whole, a spiritual entity.

"The quotidian manifestations, which are, so to speak, separate tesserae, contribute to the final mosaic, the contemplative pattern. The Pattern emerges through a routine; and the routine itself is the frame upon which the practical realisation of the modern Quietism is built."

Thus Marlowe, painfully trying to detach the dictum of Molinos,[51] disentangle it from the confusing polemics of later disciples, and adapt it to a personal need: to build upon it a personal philosophy of passivity and contemplation.

Pausing at the very turn of a sentence, he leaned forward with his elbows upon the rough table, and, staring out of the window, reviewed the month that had just passed, with as much detachment as he could command. Then, rereading the words he had written (albeit anxiously, since Gordon, to whom he had shown the first few pages of "Quietism Rediscovered," had said: "The prose rather smells of stylishness, doesn't it?"), he pondered their significance and their truth.

Certainly the preceding month in retrospect yielded nothing more than a succession of confusing and vivid images, conforming to no fixed pattern. He supposed, however, that he was too near to them – too near to events – to co-ordinate them; to assemble them as components of a whole. Was it true, then, as he had written, that the final pattern could only be gauged and appreciated in long retrospect? And was passivity, "the soft and savoury sleep of nothingness," the key to that vision?

He stretched his small hands out before him on the table and stared out upon the yellow afternoon landscape, letting the pen slip idly from his fingers. It was very hot.

He could see the figure of Francis, lying effigy-still upon the roof of her villa down the hillside; tranced, and as brown as a coffee berry. For hours every day she would lie thus, naked and still, with her arms folded upon her small breasts and her sheeny nigrescent hair spread under cheek fan-wise. He wondered what she thought about, lying there alone, with her sleeping face turned to the sky. Perhaps nothing at all: perhaps her mind, drenched as her body was drenched, in sunshine, had become inarticulate, leaving her nothing but the consciousness of her own body slowly growing ripe and warm in the heat.

The season was crawling through its infinitesimal stages of heat toward the final inferno – summer. Gordon had bought himself a large straw hat in which he strode about, looking like a South American gaucho. Of late he had become a regular visitor – "almost a resident critic," as he himself said, adding slowly, "than which nothing more foul can be imagined." Together they had argued over the whole field which Marlowe's essay was to cover, disagreeing violently on almost every point. But if Gordon was dogmatic, arrogant in opinion, and forthright to the point of cruelty, there was a certain natural vividness and candour in him which made friction – serious friction – almost impossible.

"You're hopeless," he said on one occasion. "You're a lineal descendant of the medieval *parvipontani*.[52] You want to split hairs."

"And your hair wants cutting badly," said Marlowe. "You simply cannot see that people are not all temperamentally alike."

They were lying side by side on the wide doorstep, sunning themselves after a bathe. Gordon was puffing huge clouds of tobacco up into the roofing of vines, and grinning.

"The whole of your contemplative scheme seems to be built up on a sort of spiritual asceticism; mental celibacy."

"Rubbish. I don't deny life – immediate life: sensation, or whatever you like to call it. I merely use it as a foundation for contemplation. You merely accept the impact of things, sensual, intuitive, physical things, for what they are. What I want to do is to relate it all to thought. To fit it into a scheme."

"You mean that you want to reach thought through the direct appetites."

"Exactly."

"That to me," said Gordon, "is a sort of idiocy. Life is too great in itself to be chopped up for spiritual firewood."

"I'm not chopping it up. I'm merely enjoying it in a different way, that's all."

"You're filtering it. You're weakening the juice."

Sitting up, Gordon threw back his head, and grinned challengingly. He said: "I think you're denying the very things you want to enjoy. The purgatory and pistols, duty and dungheaps, tarts and trombones, corsets and Christianity, women and water-closets – the lot of them. They're not catalysts. They're themselves."

"I think," said Marlowe, "that you are an infinitely tedious young man. You will not acknowledge the difference. The fundamental difference is simply emotional and temperamental."

"Oh I see all that," said Gordon airily, helping himself to another cigarette, "but I just think that the people who idealise and complicate life by their own emotional diseases are indecent. Indecent, my dear sir."

"Just for that," said Marlowe, "I shan't ask you to dinner."

"Well, whatever you say," said the young man, pretending not to have heard the last remark, "who can deny that it's all a good deal removed from the original Molinos?"

"No one denies it," said Marlowe, with a touch of irritation. "I've merely adapted the central idea of the Guida Spirituale,[53] disentangled it, and related it to a sort of retrospective quietism of my own.... I refuse to be blamed for that. Damn it," he added vehemently, and was suddenly silent.

"Oh well," said Gordon, giving, as always, the first sign of weariness, "what in hell does it matter? We live differently, that's all. Only I'm sure you don't get the direct, hairy, steaming kick out of life that you should. You can't enjoy an orgasm in retrospect, you know."

That was as far as their widely divergent opinions took them; and Marlowe, remembering their arguments, was forced to admit that they were not exactly enlightening.

However, there were other visitors at Phaon during that time. Rumanades himself wobbled up on an ancient bicycle and concerned himself about his guest's welfare, inviting him, rather nervously, to come up to the Villa Pothetos one evening for dinner. Marlowe, who relished the idea of the company of someone who neither probed nor challenged, presented himself at the Villa Pothetos, and was shown into the magnificent tiled hall by a man-servant who requested him to wait for his host.

Rumanades was not a long time, but when he did come, clad in his black mourner's outfit, his apologies were out of all proportion to the time he had kept his guest waiting.

Dinner was a quiet flawless affair, taken at sundown on the long stone terrace overlooking the sea, banked by a hedge of olives. The talk turned on the subject of Fonvisin.

Of late, said Rumanades, there had been a rumour that the blow-hole in the bay, below Phaon, was inhabited by an octopus of vast proportions. A poverty stricken fisherman, driven by hunger and the promise of reward (to say nothing of the actual cash value of octopus meat), drove his boat in under the ledge and explored as much of the cavity as he could with his iron-shod trident. Assuring himself that the octopus was a myth, a mixture of curiosity and stupidity prompted him to further exploration. With astounding temerity for one of his profession (for the Greek longshore fisherman is a timid creature) he dived into the cleft of the blow-hole, and disappeared for the space of about an hour: to return to his alarmed brethren with some yarn of a crystal cave, glowing with precious stones.[54] So vehement were his protestations, so incredulous his audience, that a fight had started which overturned the boat and threw the three quarrelsome fishermen, and two small boys who were with them, into thirty feet of water. Two of the men were unable to swim. They were gradually drowning when another boat appeared and picked one of them out; Walsh, who had heard the noise from the villa, swam out and brought in the other. He was unconscious and full of water.

Artificial respiration applied for an hour or so by Fonvisin pumped most of the water from his lungs, and brought him round sufficiently to clamour for his share of ouzo, which his luckier fellows were about to drink between them. Then Jani repeated his story of the cave, which was again greeted with shouts of derision, and a mutual bout of oathing. One of the fishermen drew a knife from his sodden rags and made an attempt to carve Jani into pieces; unluckily, Fonvisin, who interposed, managed to get an inadequate grip of the menacing knifehand, and had the ball of one thumb sliced neatly off: which put him into a white rage that even the fisherman's bloody temper could not match. Roaring, he released the hand, and snatched up a thick bamboo staff that lay near them. Two tremendous blows on the top of the skull spun the man round and he slumped crookedly on the ground. Meanwhile Jani, whose temper was still growing, had been seized by Walsh, who held his head in the shallow water until he became unconscious again.

This time, however, Fonvisin refused to treat either of them. Jani came round again in about an hour, but the other man was carried up to his hut, suffering from serious concussion. Nothing could be done without Fonvisin, and Fonvisin refused to do anything – "which makes it very awkward," said Rumanades, "because the man might die, and that would mean an enquiry."

Marlowe said nothing; indeed, he barely listened, but sipped his coffee and stared out across the darkening landscape. In a little while the moon would be up, soft, trembling, and the great tract of silver would spread across the sea, dimming the hills of Epirus.

"I envy you this lovely house," he said quietly.

"Yes," said Rumanades sharply, "yes."

He was rolling small pellets of bread between his long fingers and flicking them down the terrace. Leaning heavily forward in his chair, his pointed face had assumed an expression of vacancy, of pathos. Vague regrets shifted and vanished in his mind as he, too, watched the vanishing light, and the shifting tones on the water: old aches and fears, whose origin he could barely remember, crowded upon him.

"Let me show you the house," he said, with a sudden eagerness. "Will you?" There was still enough light.

The beautiful furniture lay, still as death, in the long shadowy drawing-room. The long polished bulk of the Bluthner glowed faintly in the dimness: absently Marlowe lifted the lid and pressed down one or two chords, which grew up in the quiet room, rich and mellow, and were absorbed in the silence and dissolved by it. He had the sudden illusion of moving in another age, among the *débris* of lost lives and desires, whose warmth and reality had been suspended in death. He was a mere archaeologist who could reconstruct from given data, but not re-create the age, recapture its more intimate sensations. Only a poet could do that. And poetry was as far removed from him as it was from that leaning figure which stood silent, head bent to the sound of piano-chords, lost in some bottomless abstraction of his own.

The suite of rooms which had been Manuela's was untouched. They had been left exactly as they were while she lived in them, not for sentiment, or by design, but merely because, when she had gone, there had been no further need of them, no necessity to convert them. The bed was stripped, but covered in the same vast cover, with the design of the phoenix worked upon it. On the glass surface of the dressing-table stood a row of pots and bottles, half empty, still holding their face-creams and cleansers, and a box of rice-powder, backed by more lotions and unguents. To the right, giving a half-reflection to the mirror, stood a framed portrait of a woman, who stared at them with large eyes.

Rumanades unlatched the long French window and opened it, as the moon came up, to chequer the coloured tiles of the floor and warm the cold brown tones of the photograph with a fictitious life. Tilting the portrait to the light, Marlowe said: "She is beautiful. Very beautiful."

Rumanades, staring out at the terraces of dark olive trees, nodded vehemently.

"Yes," he said with positive emphasis. "Yes."

Who was she? Marlowe wondered. A sister? A lover? An unhappy rich man's concubine? He stood and stared curiously at the stooping back of Rumanades and said nothing, replacing the photograph on the dressing-table.

At this very moment, leaning back in his hard chair and closing his eyes against the hot afternoon sunlight, he could see the scene in tableau, objectively. He could see the figure of Rumanades standing before the light, gaunt in silhouette, could see himself furtively replacing the photograph and glancing curiously sideways at his host; could hear, at the same moment, the silver cloudy chime of the clock upon the mantelpiece, which seemed a signal to end the mood of silence that had fallen between them.

That night, when he left, Rumanades had shaken him hard by the hand, and smiled with a curious pride.

"You must come again," he said, "as often as you like."

"The piano is seldom touched," the old man had added, "except for Walsh who comes occasionally and does his work here."

A momentary shadow of doubt – perhaps perplexity – crossed his bearded face. Lifted half sideways to the moonlight, it assumed a strange wistfulness.

"If you care to play you are welcome," he added, and turned away, tugging at his beard.

Walking down the hill path by bright moonshine, Marlowe pondered these phenomena, with the sense of something lost in himself.

To Gordon he tried, uncomfortably, to express these things, in words which would be casual, easy, void of emotion; but the attempt was a partial failure. Gordon merely recounted, in a matter-of-fact way, all that the priest had told him of Manuela and Rumanades, and their life together at the Villa Baucis & Philemon.

For the last day or two Gordon had not appeared, and Marlowe had escaped happily into a routine of loneliness and thought. He could sit for hours quietly staring at the bright landscape, listening to the local sounds of life on the hillside above Phaon the chirp of cicadas, the gaseous giggle of a donkey, or the rhythmic *milch milch* of the sheep as they nibbled the hot spikes of grass and be aware of nothing but the sunlight on his fingers, and the luxury of abstraction.

Life was, at such times, like a landlocked lagoon without a ripple on its surface, without a disturbance to its continuity; but how imperceptibly it passed, how soon the delight in its images was swallowed up! Slowly the almonds ripened, slowly the ripe medlars tumbled from the trees, slowly the flowers shone out of the sconces of the prickly pear. All day long the Greek shepherd girls lolled under the olives on the hillsides, like snipers, singing their songs or talking; in their vivid headcloths and with pomegranate flowers in their teeth. A hundred sights, sounds, sensations created their momentary impacts and passed on. They would recur, he knew, in retrospect, become luminous and whole in relation to the Pattern; and the flavour of them would be purged of any discomfort. Enjoyment would come with assessment. For the present, passivity inside the narrow cage of immediate routine and work was enough.

Chapter VII

# Walsh

GREY days in the south of England. Autumn with the long mounded fieldways in a crush of rotten, sweet-smelling leaves. Prodigious quilts set for the feet of winter. Down by the lake, on the damp margin of hummocks, pitted and perforated with old mole burrowings, the decomposing stubs of horse-chestnuts indiscriminately littered, like the relics of feasts, significant of feasts to come. The lupins in the cottage garden were burnt out. Their colour heavy and patched with decay, sodden brown patches with the stumps rotten. Why is it that lupins burn up heavenward from the feet, like martyrs? How fine it must be, she said once, to feel the flame of life eating one away upwards, out into space: burning up the body from the toes to the face, and short life flowing electrically upwards. Baucis and Philemon should have been changed to asphodels, so that their mouths could meet finally above the flame that swept up their bodies. Trees are clumsy in death.

Autumn, I give you late Autumn, like a once bright playing-card, now softened and blurred with the damp: its painted significance now indistinct. The bright inks running wet, with all the hard outlines gone. Late Autumn like a bedraggled parrot, moist in the declining season. The popjaye royalle. Smoke from the cottage chimneys, from the farms, lifting and merging across the hill slopes where the sodden grass lay crisp all summer. Now we have a sopping scalp of green to the earth, easily peeled, easily torn by heavy boots or the brute feet of the cattle that crowd the gateways. Southward, if you look from one of those hills among the farms where all night long the dogs tug at their chains

63

and bark at nothing, you will see the long grey form of the sea stirring through the mist. Uneasy grey patrol of waters round the coast, eternally vigilant.

And then Ruth. Dozens of pictures of her: dozens of shapes and lights which were her. Ruth, particularly, under sentence, like the lupins and those lissom early flowers that flagged the April hedges. Ruth smiling, elbows propped on the wood window-sill of the cottage, staring down across the slopes, seaward. Ruth angry. Ruth in quiet nakedness beside him in the heavy bed upstairs. Ruth shaking the hair out of her eyes, smiling again – the red oval in her face, fringed with teeth, and the bright soft rim of lips about it. The eyelash, particularly, fluttering in soft terror against his skin. The terrific interchange of gestures, the great flux of lightning that swept them, drinking them up, while the eyelash beat and beat. The tides, the recession, the final music of nakedness. Yes, but he had seen her face turn back, folded in painful crying, half laughter, half tears, and her mouth actually moaning. Surely the lupins had voices for the final fire that consumed them, surely the last spasm of life shivering in them made them moan like this, upwards?

There were so many images that it was no use to apply method to them, to go back step by step, stratum by stratum and reconstruct them: memory was a sudden gift out of nowhere, as if a child should turn and hand one a bright playing-card of himself and Ruth, static and fixed in the eternity that was two years by the calendar reckoning. Two years in which he could watch the progression of a million springs, summers, winters, for time itself, all continuity, had utterly vanished. The one big division in the pattern was Ruth dying; her lapsing like that into quietness, like a gift of faithlessness. There was only time before that and after it. An infinity in which her going was the one clean partition.

Before the events it was nothing but bright colours to remember, crowding in on him, without method or progression. Ruth, for instance, in summer, her hair wet and salt from swimming, shaking down the apple blossom from the tree, standing in the shower of petals shouting with laughter. Apple blossom. And then himself – how unreal that dead self – breaking through the wet fringe of hair at the nape of her neck with his mouth. Or himself again, as they lay on the clean hard sand of the cove, naked, filling her sleeping nostrils with fine sand. How unreal themselves, laughing and tangled in each other's arms on the warm sand! But we are talking of Autumn, and the last fruit.

They walked in the rain together, among a torrent of wet dead leaves, wind tugging their hair back on their scalps, rain in their mouths and the smell of dead earth.[55] Little splashes of mud coming up on to the rim of his corduroy trousers, and congealing hard. Rain falling from the elms. The vicarage with its damp red stone sweating water and the limp trees smoking round it. Her icy hand stuck inside his coat for warmth, burrowing like a mole through his red pullover, his shirt, his vest. Icy contact with skin![56]

They walked together in the rain, across the long meadow, in heavy grass, their footsteps cutting a long trail of fallen rain-drops, until they reached the long last lich-gate on Trimmer's Hill. Crouched on the wet gate, hooking their heels in the bars to keep them balanced in the wind. He spread his mackintosh over them both, and under its shelter they smoked cheap fags and sat silent. Below them, half a country curved away to the sea, laced with lines of road and hedge, toned here and there with long tracts of woodland. Cars spinning along the shining black lines in a flutter of water, like wild geese dragging their toes along the surface of a lake. Small cars like uncouth baby bears, and coloured monsters as well, but all in a flutter of rain-water.

Then the long race back to the cottage. The gate with the latch that stuck. Ruth dancing about impatiently while he wrestled with it. Indoors, Dolly, the rosy farm-girl, had built up the big log fire and laid tea. Fresh bread from town, butter from Dail's farm, icy milk with three fingers of cream on the top. Honey, muffins, toast. Stampede in the great flagged kitchen, slipping out of their sodden clothes and shoes into dressing-gowns and slippers while Dolly poured the tea.

Rain again, lashing the windows, scuttling in the gutters. The fire smoking blue and crackly. Sparks, goldstarred, flashing along the tough forest wood. Drops of resin, burning blood bright, falling from the wood in a pother of smoke, hissing among the embers. Butter and resin, warm slippers, toast, the rain falling outside, and Ruth. Oh quick, draw up the long couch to the fireplace, and put the tea-table beside it. Pull the curtains across the big-bay-window to blot out the rain and the closing darkness. Ruth gobbling the muffins with the melted butter running at the corners of her mouth. Kiss the warm buttery mouth and slip your fingers inside the warm blue dressing-gown at her breasts. The slow even bumping of her heart at your fingers. Capricious metronome. The delicate mechanism faulty; quiet heart ticking itself away into the silence, consuming itself, consuming him, consuming this rapt world of toast, wood-resin, warmth in slippers, butter mouths, breasts, loveli-ness, stars at night, and the wake of liquid nightingales which sang in the elm all summer. Everything being poured out and consumed by just this inexorable movement. Systole, diastole. The dance of life in the imperfect body. And her rich mouth and breath, fit to blow in the nostrils of an aeon of lovers.[57] O God, O God, I know that my Redeemer liveth. Kiss the yielding mouth again in silent panic. Squeeze the small breasts again until they hurt.

*Perilous and woundable frail flesh....*
*O to forget this gnawing memory*
*That where I have invested love is only*

And Ruth, for the moment not thinking, not noticing his fear, not allowing her own perpetual fear, saying: "Tell the girl to light the candles, will you? The bitch always forgets." And the wrinkles that ran along her nose, drawing up the fine mockery of her smile.

Soft lamplight on them both now. Candles in a long iron stick, and one softly radiant oil-lamp. Feet spread in luxury before the fire. The infinite quiet, the infinite rest. Mouth to mouth it was no good in the silence; they would be masks moving each to each. The torsion of subcutaneous muscles, the shape of the eyes set back against the brown forehead. The mouth as senseless to his want as the rubber lip-mask of a dentist's gas apparatus. Only that chill, half-second's pause before orgasm, when the skins trembled and tangled like a pouch of snakes together, when the voice broke haunting in among the summer nightingales and the dogs, rattling their chains and barking at nothing, only that moment, above all others, held the mystery. Then she was lost in himself. Not the daily and imperfect osmosis of ordinary life. Feeling percolating through a membrane. In that moment the walls were broken down, and the fluid rushed together, like the meeting of seas.

But what did she know of these fascinating abstractions as she sat, trying to pretend that she did not know that he was staring at her: with her stockinged toes curled under her, reading herself into a doze? For himself, in an amputated world, there was only the slow crumble of toast in his mouth. The warmth crawling over his feet on the coloured carpet and up his legs. Little draughts and eddies of air in the room behind him. Dust on the shelf of books. A cheque for thirty pounds on the mantelpiece and a letter from Garland saying: "Do you mind selling your soul? You do it well. This last tune of yours is good. As I see it you'll be rich before long. *Ecstasy to be in Love* is still selling mildly. But I anticipate bigger things from this one, *Never Come Back*." Does one mind selling one's soul? Does one mind anything when she is trying to pretend that she does not see me looking at her with grave eyes? Why can't I weep? And his diary.

"So many abstractions in that one brown face, and the eyes moving like synchronised insects along the lines of black type. So many faces in one face. If I sit down and try to write of her the thoughts fly into splinters, and my brain numbs, while the images of her fall across my body like burning rockets. These very white, senseless, bloodless typewriter keys refuse to chatter of her. They become so many dissimilar white faces of her. Let me count them. Thirty-two keys to her, and all lost, all sterile and lost by words. Yet one goes on, for no discoverable reason except this insane desire to make oneself real, to understand the splintered mirrors in oneself, and through oneself to reach out for that twin world, whose discovery is lost in a single second of two bodies in friction, heeling over like toy balloons whose strings have snapped, heading for the spaces among the planets.

"Forget these dreary milestones, the commas, the hyphens, the exclamation marks, the colons, the full stop which lies at every sentence whether it has the flux and ecstasy in it, or whether it is some drab and meaningless cliché, down-at-heel, sucked dry like old orange skin, and tossed into the mind's limbo as soon as comprehended. Open and close the inverted commas, though the words of her mouth can never reach another mind except through perhaps some turn, some artifice, which another's words place over them. Reality of her, I suppose, must run like a thread in a worn carpet, here and there bright, visible and new. The carpet slippers of old men, the dust of ancient ankles have blotted out most of it, will blot out the rest. Even these banal lines can only blow across the mind like a casual scent of March flowers, soon lost, soon disseminated, and the breath of a lover's mouth in darkness on your tongue, becomes for an instant her breath, significant. Otherwise we meet across acres of ink, of paper, of corrections, ink blue, red, green, violet, vermilion, ink running in the veins of the head, the mouth gushing ink in poetry, the hearts of our lovers filling, pausing, gushing ink again into the body to complete the endless circuit. I think if I took a bright knife to you, my darling, and split the artery which bulges above your elbow, your arm would spout ink like a tiny fountain, running across my wretched papers, across the wretched type-heads of this machine which tries and tries to hammer out an image of you; one hard medallion of you on to the senseless paper. Perhaps when I kiss you, your mouth is only wet with ink, where I have pressed shapes in you, printed my own longing indelibly across your body, hammered these dancing type-heads into your very pith...."

But the playing-card of their last Autumn had more than one face on it; or rather, the faces changed, merged, swapped. Dolly, with the red cheeks and the hefty loins, Dolly the dour potential baby-maker who could not marry until old Vole skipped into his coffin. What a four-foot tyrant the old man was, hovering on the edge of the grave! And the big stout harness-maker's son, with his blue eyes fixed longingly on the old man's second daughter. They courted now. One could see them on Sunday, holding raw red hands, dressed in their best (he in a black suit, she in a red dress), standing like rooted stumps by the cornfield gate, immobile, gazing with a queer gentle puzzlement on the earth bursting into life. The atmosphere would go thin some time, and cut them like knives, and goad them to action. So gentle they were, so puzzled, with the mud sticking to the soles of their heavy shoes. Their desire, one felt, if it ever got hold of them, would submerge the whole household, would sweep away all the furniture of old Vole's life; all the gimcrack paraphernalia which helped him to maintain his autocracy over the female.

The kitchen range, with its stirring pots and pans over the bright fire, the mantelshelf with its two sere photos of an ice-age, Mr. Vole and his big-fingered, now-dead wife. The little tea caddy, with green and gold patterns on it, in which he kept his shag. The guns hanging up on the wall. The cherrywood stick behind the door. The sink where the thick cheap plates were washed up. His innumerable soiled waistcoats in the bedroom. *Whitaker's Almanack*. A shovel. Boots like iron, whose toes had curled upward with damp, and to whose soles hung the dry mud of a hundred winters. His little insect hands, finger and thumb dredging his waistcoat pocket for loose matches. His feet on the fender. Dolly herself, standing for an aeon over the sink, staring numbly out of the window across the farmlands, with a plate in one hand. The warm cattle, whose breath stirred one with its sweetness and volume: the loose black mouth of a foal she could take in her rough hand and kiss with great winsome smacks. All of this, one felt, would be swept away giddily, loosely on the torrent that waited to break forth from their stony bodies. Yet the flood never came. Old Vole, oblivious, could think of nothing but his crops and his bitter beer. Ruth would have liked to see him playing Noah, sailing away on the wrathful flood of his daughter's life. But the flood never came. To-morrow, I think, if it is spring or summer when you read this, you could go down and see them still there, Dolly and the red-faced youth, rooted by the edge of the cornfield, quite dumb, quite still, puzzled by the silence and calling of cattle. They will stay there until the first midges begin to bite her red arms. Then they will say good-night like wood-carvings by the edge of the corn.

So much for Dolly. But a half turn of the card in the light will give you the Rev. Richard Pixie, the parson. Here was a six-foot pixy, bowed down by the cares of religion, who called and was drearily friendly, in the name of our sweet Saviour, etc. He insisted on calling Ruth "your wife"; though he knew they were living in sin, he still had some vague idea of helping them to avoid sinning in life. He would come so dreary, so weary, so lax, debile, anile, frustrate, gnawed, and unwind himself into a chair by the fire, stretching out his wretched black boots, and accepting cigarettes with both bony hands. He stank faintly of all the mouldering relics of his caste and occupation, much as the brick church smelt – of damp vegetables and flowers – after the harvest festival. He was a confirmed reader of the sporting page, supporter of the party policy, subscriber to conventions, coloured bathmats made of cork, mothers' meetings, lads of the village brigade, football on the green. He did not even preach his own sermons and give one the chance to have some fun at his expense. He read them out of a book. He had never heard of Donne, piles, the Reformation, Duke Ellington, the cosmic ray, Remy de Gourmont, Henry Miller.[58] The top of his head was flat, matted with light red hair, the shape of a snake, or some reptile. Sometimes he brought his wife, sometimes he came alone. He seemed happier when he was with her, perhaps because the endless rushing of her conversation completely obliterated him, allowed him to take refuge in a corner by the fireplace. She was a thin woman, with a body like a pencil. Her mouth was a purse of solecisms which was continually tearing and allowing the clattering, bouncing stream of old pennies to run out among the company. Such a stream of coins, and every one old, with the face rubbed off it by long handling. Not one bright bronze newly minted coin in the collection. Nevertheless out they all flowed, in the drab stream, rolling across the floor, hitting the legs of chairs, the wall. Stunned, one bent down and groped about for them, collected them. Handed them back to her and hoped for the best. Alas! within a moment, bang went the mouth of the purse, and out rolled the stream again, intolerably tedious.

She had big rough hands and slack breasts, long since laid up against her, useless: stacked like late autumn windfalls. Their only child, which had been named Maud Alexandria Helen Pixie, died when it was four. Since then they had had five dogs, Rufus, Whisky, Bill, Rufus and Whisky; two cats, Betty and Annie; and an Austin seven, which she had called Victor III, after her now deceased father, and on whose faulty tin bowels she spent her most cherished maternal treasures. She decarbonised it herself, cleaned it herself, mended punctures, recharged the batteries, fitted new rings when necessary, boasted about it, added up its insignificant mileages, painted the wings, corrected a slipping clutch, knitted it a radiator cover, and only used it when she had to. In spite of this, however, the bloody thing only went about once in every five times.

Besides this occupation of hers, there was nothing else worth noticing. She showed a clear inch of petticoat under her dress when she walked, and left cigarettes in her mouth until they fizzled right away up under her nose, without touching them. But she once said to Ruth, looking significantly at her, as she got into the car: "You'll regret all this one day, dear. Believe me, I KNOW."

Now what in the name of heaven (as Ruth said) could that mannish, tubular parson's wife know about "all this"? Walsh was sure that the answer was one of the largest zeros ever drawn. Nix. Nothing. He had a good eye for the symbols of private tragedy, and once, when the vicar was showing him the excellence of the interior architecture of his home, he had penetrated the fastness of the bedroom, and let his eye wander across all those signposts to domestic decay.

Pixie obviously gargled in permanganate before going to bed. On the shelf above the wash basin were two identical tooth mugs, each holding a spare set of witty false teeth. An atomiser for Pixie's tonsils. A corn cure. Embrocation for the lady's rheumatism (probably the result of lying out all winter on the damp garage floor under the Austin). A prayer-book; a cheque-book; a bank-book; a *Daily Mail Year Book*; a Bible, and a collection of unpleasant male neck-refuse – collar studs. A photograph of a Herculean maiden aunt suggestively flanked by a print of the Colosseum. Two pairs of worn slippers. In the corner, with the dust thick on them, a pair of fantastic skates. Obviously the domestic ice had never been firm enough for him to skate on. Perhaps the way was effectively barred by the shelf full of preliminaries – permanganate, Milton, Sloane's, and the atmosphere of Swift's lady's dressing room.[59] Over the bed-head, on the wall, was a text, such as one sees in hiker's hostels: *The Lord is my Shepherd*.

At any rate, then, the Pixies were honest enough to admit each night, as they went to bed, that they were sheep. The Good Shepherd protect them, and keep his fingers out of the mincer, and his wife out of the mangle, for I have done with them.

Trigger, I suppose, was much the same – but in a different way. He was the village doctor; very large, heavy, with a face full of pores the size of pin-heads, and a fan-shaped ginger moustache which seemed an absurd Edwardian relic fixed on a face that was medieval in its obesity. The face was the face of a Renaissance prelate, the voice was the voice of Gargantua.[60] One could imagine him eating pilgrims with the salad and not noticing them. His laugh was infectious, rousing, under the fan of whisker. His great paws were always full of chilblains, and smelt, (*a*) of absolute alcohol, or (*b*) of *embrocation*. The folds of his tweed shooting-coat swung wide as he walked, spreading a faint damp whiff of tobacco, lint, spring onions, and damp dead pigeons.

His life was built on two passions: killing and curing. When he was not indulging either of these he was bored with a terrible annihilating boredom. When there was a long spell of saving life ahead of him, he would go out with his gun, and shoot the stuffing out of every man, woman or child in sight, by way of compensation.

Trigger was majestic. In the simplicity of his tastes; in the crudeness of his ideas; in the sparseness of his opinions; in the profound singleness of his purpose. While the philosopher was meditating; while the fakir was sitting on a trolley-full of pins; while the poet was fulminating, the painter daubing, the pedant, like an elderly hen, scratching around the barren mud of his natural backyard – the letter page of the *Times Literary Supplement*; Trigger had quietly and with system arrived at a simplification of life which defeated them all.

They used to go out a lot together, he and Walsh (the latter with an old twelve-bore he hired from Vole), and rough-shoot across the park-lands. The squire had given Trigger permission to shoot where and when he liked. Explaining this, Trigger said significantly: "I once treated him successfully for constipation, y'know." Quite seriously, with his discoloured blue eyes fixed fiercely on a hedge from which something might be put up by the sound of their boots in the mud, or his own loud voice.

Walking across country, stopping for a rest and an occasional cigarette, one could find out a lot about Trigger's passion for medicine; in the consulting-room, at the sick-bed, in the surgery, one could not get him to talk of anything but shooting. His mind hinged into two watertight compartments, which functioned, as it were, inversely.

"And look'ee, my lad," he said one day, as they skirted the long meadow by Dail's Farm to get to some rabbits, "don't go expectin' any bills from me, 'cause I won't be sendin' you any, see?" He cleared his throat loudly and hawked. "Young Ruth is worth mints to me in a dead practice like this. Mints. Nothing but greenstick fractures and scarlet fever to keep me busy. And old Verey's piles. I ought to be paying you."

For all his adoration of Ruth he could never quite see her as a person or, for that matter, imagine anyone else doing so. She was a "dooced interestin' case." One felt that he could see her only through the transparent walls of a test-tube. But it would have been intolerable had he been one of those grave, sententious, mourning cockroaches, which batten on death.

No, Trigger was some sort of gent, in a peculiar way of his own. A mixture of rube and gent which it would not be difficult to find anywhere in England. Tact, as far as he was concerned, was non-existent.

"Know anything about surgery of the heart?"

"No. Nothing at all."

This, while they were sitting under an elm on the further slopes of Trimmer's Hill, in the grass of a long meadow, with a dead pigeon beside them. Walsh squinted along the black barrel of his gun, turning it now on this target, now on that. He held a cartridge to his nose and inhaled the fine smell of a past explosion. The pigeon had a strange green membrane over its eyes. Its beak dripped eloquent bright blood.

"Dooced fascinating game. I read of a case the other day of a fifteen-year-old. Mitral stenosis and regurgitation. Bloke laid open the heart by a flap job. Clamped the bottom of the appendix. Couple of sutures shoved in, appendix incised and pulled over his finger like a glove. He found he could poke around inside the auricle as much as he liked.

Amazing, what? He found that stenosis wasn't too bad, valve wasn't as thick as he thought, so he just stretched the damn thing with his finger. Ligature, and there you are. Chest-flap closed. There you are. What do you make of that, eh? Amazing, what?"

"Amazing."

"But, I mean, really amazing what they can do to one these days, what? I mean, it's amazing when you think of it?"

"Amazing."

Trigger contemplated infinity with his cigarette burning away under the tabby fan of moustache. His paunch rested comfortably against the inner wall of his plus-fours, his hands were plumply spreadeagled to support the weight of his body thrown back. The grass was very damp. Sideways, Walsh could see the slight prognathous starting of his underjaw, fixed in an attitude of concentration. The whites of his eyes were discoloured by fine veins such as one sees in those rich Blood Royal children's marbles.

Several times he called with his car to take Ruth into town to the laboratory of a friend of his. His gallantry was profound and a little embarrassing. His laughter set up pin-point answering vibrations in the elms, in the dead leaves along the ditches, in the trembling nerves of the girl herself, in his own hanging suit of clothes, heavy with damp tobacco and pigeon smells. His big teeth shone their yellow film of cigarette-stain, and the veins twinkled around the circular blue vent of meaning, the iris in each eye. Trigger was being tactful. In the cold his laughter clouded into jets of uproarious steam as it left his lips, ringing like a spade on the frosty earth. His hands were blue meat, heavily chilblained.

The girl in her rough tweeds and black beret, perched beside him on the front seat like a substantial bird, could feel the cold thrill of leather run along her thighs; could smell the warm engine smell; and could smile between red cold lips as the car gathered way down the lane, among the plundered trees – cold algebraic patterns on the dark sky – across the shivering countryside into winter; into the winter which closed on her like the cold black wooden lid of a coffin. Sometimes, as he turned his head and looked at her, hunched and queerly male in the seat beside him, he was flushed with a queer bright emotion that was half fear and half pity. There she was, after all, beside him, with her brown socked legs stretched out under the dashboard, smoking his cigarettes. How strange the eyes of the girl when she turned to him! The light fell slowly, deeply into them; they showed strange moods, half flickers, dyings of colour. The moist lips shaping themselves about a cigarette. The broad thinning curve of eyebrow, hooding the secret nose, evasively wrinkling its laughter upward.

Ah well! It was a different Trigger who could stand, in white X-ray guards, watching the ray turn her bloodless; a spindle of bones in a white jelly. He was admiration itself for her afterwards. I think, if he had been able, he would have put her into a little test-tube, labelled it, and contemplated her with reverence and adoration for the rest of his days. Men have strange goddesses. Ruth as Ruth only existed in pieces: minute spaces of feeling in acres of objective vision. She was only real to him thus, as a marrowless framework of transparent bones, swimming in jelly, a machine which symbolised the only mystery which was real to Trigger. To his own way of thinking this was Love.

Walsh would never go on these expeditions, though the girl pleaded with him once or twice to go with them. He knew that his own lack of composure would startle them both, would annihilate that reticence between himself and Trigger on which their relationship was based. Trigger might come awake with emotions too barely uncomfortable, sentiments too threadbare to stand his vocabulary. He would go instead for a walk, dropping in on his way home at Tarquin's cottage. Tarquin[61] was the schoolmaster.

Sitting in the threadbare armchair, puffing his pipe, with his feet crossed at the wide fireplace, he would be again amazed at the huge, bald, gentle cranium of his host; the twists of silver at his ears. The mild eyes, almost olive purple, with their fine lashes. The ease with which one could escape, as it were, through Tarquin, to ages long past, to traditions, pomps, splendours, colours, pageants, against which his own age appeared shabby, bigoted and mean. Tarquin was interesting because he was a splendid medium: through him one could reach history. No, it was more than that, for Tarquin *was* history. The perfect refugee to whom any age was more immediately accessible than his own, he lived between the fireside and the long shelves of dusty books, which fed his insatiable taste for the living death. The ghosts of Greek boys, more real to him than ever Walsh could have been, haunted the low windows of the cottage; sandalled strangers from the dusty Ionian waited in the porch, respectfully alive in the precious music of his voice. Tarquin had drifted for centuries down the vivid Nile, among a pageant of barges, with his attendant Nubians, black shining midnights, while the long spokes of moonlight cartwheeled the still waters and sunk in the smoky flare of torches. Women more delicate than Cleopatra had been his abstractions, with the shift of light along unguents, resins, salves; the fume of balsams hung in his nostrils. His feet had been laved in lotions more purely astringent than grape-juice or the rank liquid pith of olives. He had been disembowelled by Ptolemaic embalmers, cured and mummified, and had risen again on the third day. The colonnades of white Mediterranean villas had heard his slow footsteps, pausing in peripatetic meditation; Lucretius had bathed with him; Epicurus kissed him as a brother. The long blue Ionian nightfall, splintered by lights among stone columns, had given him the vision of Greek women, ripe as marble, natural as fruit to be plucked, lingering among the shadows of the waters, laughing upon the mouths of the young men. The high-riding disc of full moon showed the leaning, falling torsos of young men, swerving down into the spray, with the laughter drifting up on the spice-ladened air: mimosa sweetening the still air across the bays and islands, and the girls with pomegranate flowers in their mouths. Tarquin kept these images of his life stored in that deep, shining cranium of his. As he talked his long hands released the stem of his briar, and built up the cool breathing statues for you – bodies of the young men now dead, and Greek girls.

Quiet and precise he was, while his language was as sure and cold as the technique of a lapidary, as he snipped away at the cold pebbles of thought. But the light shone in and through him, in a shaft of clear thought illuminating lost ages. His talk had the quality of some ancient and unhappy epigram, written by an anonymous lover to a lover as anonymous, holding all the bright and eloquent pain – eloquent as the bright blood dripping from the nose of the dead pigeon – of an age dead, but still strong enough to wound us. His Love was different from Trigger's, but as poignant.

December came in that last year like a long breath of cold from one of the poles, settling frost along the farm-ways, the pumps, icing the bare trees, leaving a white finger under the dripping taps. The fruit was all laid up in the lofts at Dail's, snug with straw, and a log fire blazed all day in the little hall. Dolly's arms had become red and raw with cold as she walked among the steamy breath of cattle. At night, lying with Ruth beside him in the bed upstairs, watching the cold distant flicker of head-lights on the arterial road tinting the raftered walls, he could feel the season closing down on them like a suit of ice; could hear the ringing stamp of hooves on the rimy track which ran behind the cottage. The strawberries were laid under straw. At night the candles beside their bed winked and smoked in the cold draughts of air from the tiny window. The season was gathering its forces to sweep them both away in a whirl of snowflakes, into an eternity. The blood was slow in their veins, black arterial rivers congealed along the body's canals, now viscid and almost still: like the desire. Laid up under straw like the scented apples in the loft, whose fragrance drifted down from time to time to them as they lay in the stupor of half sleep. Why had they need to make provision for next year's cider? All this was a remote world, in which the real poignancy was numbed; a world of ice, spiked crowns of thorns, dead rotten leaves, shadows of bare trees now innocent of birds, fires guttering below the chimney-pieces, candles in raftered rooms, cold breaths on their cheeks. In the darkness, in the pale shadows of winter along the walls, in the light of lanterns, among the scented steam of animals' breaths in byres, sheep moaning beside fiery thorns, what room, what feeling was there left for the sharp spikes of death or desire or loss? In darkness their breathing mouth to mouth (so far between bodies, so distant the space between planets of flesh! ) was the breathing of white cadavers already, laid in the velvet-lined caskets of a remote charnel-house. No longer they had electric lips, eyes, knees, loins: but only the cold mesh of veins, running cold and heavy with the dark blood. At night she would read to him in that clear voice, ringing like a shadow of truth among the truths and falsehoods of other ages; while he, with his hands folded across his still body, his eyes closed, saw too deeply into the mysteries of her personality ever to weep, or grudge her the natural deceptions she held before him. The candles burned away on the pages of their books. The voice of winter was vague with warning. For his own part, beyond deception, evasion, beyond the talk and trembling, the lies and happiness, with a hard serene conviction he knew the end: with a conviction as cold, stern, as the rim of ice which had formed across the lake, he knew it all. He could hear her reading without emotion now, while the candles beat down their tracks of gold across her throat and her moving lips, and the small breasts in her dressing-gown.

"Every revolution which the sun makes about the world divides between life and death; and death possesses both those portions by the next morrow; and we are dead to all those months we have already lived, and we shall never live them over again: and still God makes little periods of our age. First we change our world, when we come from the womb to feel the warmth of the sun. Then we sleep and enter into the image of death, in which state we are unconcerned in all the changes of the world: and if our Mothers or our Nurses die, or a wild boar destroy our vineyards, or our King be sick, we regard it not, but during that state, are as disinterested as if our eyes were closed with the clay that weeps in the bowels of the earth."[62]

The heavy blankets which covered them so warmly might have been the layers of sod, cut finely and shaped by the patient spade of the old sexton. In the dark the walls of the great upper room shrunk down to the dimensions of a six foot coffin. Yes, raising the pads of his fist he could beat and beat on the polished walls of the blackness that was obliterating them both, until there was no reason or sense left in his breathless, stifled mind: only the doom hung over him like a curtain, and he was inarticulate.

For a time the frost scouted for the season. A St. John the Baptist time, with bright berries on the hedges, robin vermilions fluffed on every paling, like financiers puffed with wrath at an economic winter. A St. John the Baptist time, minus scrip, locust and wild honey, but vivid with berries and hungry sparrows crowding for food. They walked together down among the crisp spikes of grass, by the lakes, and watched the ice crust over. A blue membraneous scum first over the eye of the water: then green, muddy black, like a gangrened wound. And then the steel surface upon which the feet of the wild duck found no purchase. All night long the wind ruffled the woods. The noise of stones flung on the ice by passing farm-boys squeaked away, diminishing, into the further woods, across the iron-bound fences, northward. The winter had been announced.

One night when Dolly went into the yard for wood it was snowing in large velvety tufts. Ruth and Walsh watched from the upper window when they went to bed. All distance had vanished, had been broken down by this manna. Columns of turning, tossing, leaning whiteness drifted out of heaven like feathers out of a sack, settling easily upon the cowed world. There were no stars, no planets, no signs, no wonders, no orange comets, not even shapes material evolving laboriously through this soft pile. They were quite alone now, in a sunk world of snow, penned in a little house among woods and hills which existed only in their memories. Four hands over a dead fire, and all the candles low.

Episodes of decay. Numb feet in boots on the snowy road. Sunlight so watery that when Ruth breathed across the window a rainbow sprang from her mouth across the light, a slanting prismatic portent in a deep curve. Perhaps a pot of treasure at the end of it. Largesse as gold as urine. Hands, bright hands and flushed cheeks nestling in wool. Hands kneading snowballs. A parcel of dribble-nosed schoolboys on the way up to Tarquin. One orange-haired imp with bloody knees, pressing bruised hands in his armpits, blowing on his nails to warm them, after a fall on the frosty road. The snow put deep shadows on the world, in the corner of the bedroom, across the walls like webs. Looking out across the garden, like seeing a negative of a known photograph. Christmas card December. Signals of ice hanging in delicate fingers from a tree. The voice of birds quipping, a little shrill with cold, a little anxious with fear. The racket of milk churns being loaded on to a six o'clock lorry. Episodes of decay. The old thumbed notebook of Ruth's which held all her poems.

> *I am so plunged in you, God knows,*
> *There's no redemption but the falling,*
> *Spirals of terrible water, my princeling,*
> *Snatching the life of me, cold,*
> *Colours of water about me, calling...*

Wretched stuff,[63] with here a line, there a line, skip a page, skim a page. Then suddenly,

> You are my only logic in the cold world.
> I, a graft to your tree, following, merging,
> Fruiting as you, flowering as you.
> The thorns of winter spike us both.

Poor bright pages with their tributes fluttering past under his thumbs like successive kisses. Out of one's mouth came the words. The frost made a witty steam of them.

A letter from Gordon, Ruth's brother, with a beautiful Greek stamp, and a pen-drawing of men drawing a boat up a sand-beach.

> It's silly to wish you a merry Xmas, isn't it? When the oranges are ripening slowly on the stalk, I mean, and the tangerines sport a green and yellow glaze like the finest porcelain. Occasionally the old man of the sea gets up, wraps the north wind round him and prowls down these coasts, havocking. Old man *maestro*. And then I think it's winter. But the olives aren't fully gathered yet, and the fishermen still skip barefoot into the water. Sun, life a long coma. No, I can't think clearly or continuously about you two. Are you happy? Please be happy as long as you can. Why don't you make a dash and come down to this Island? Coral and sea-gulls, sponges and octopus, and a patron saint who's represented by a decayed tibia. Please darling Ruth bring Walsh down south. I haven't seen you for such ages I don't know what you look like. Yes, it was a Greek girl in Athens, but it didn't last. We strained the litany of sensualities until our voices cracked. I don't care. I recuperate in a long sun-convalescence from a disease more lovely than T.B. Chastity like a pure dream, for ever and forever, as long as one sun lasts. And then? The rest is silence.[64]

Episodes of decay. Dolly proud of a ring on her red finger. Her mouth broad with slow, amazing laughter. Old Vole had consented. A robin found dead on the path. Pompous even in death, fluffed out its red stomach. Lying in Dolly's laughing hands. They put it on the fire and stoked the wood. The fiery bird. Robin into Phoenix. Would it be born again and vanish in a red tuft of flame up the wide chimney?

Then one night a snow-storm came down out of forests, with a big insane wind to guide it. Past midnight. The slow clock from a steeple sounding foggily through the blanket. Wind at the shutters, at the oak front door.

Something had happened in the field outside. Cattle trouble. Something dead in the long swirl of snowflakes. Lanterns shining out in a dim parade, and men's voices.

Inside it was so still he could hear himself thinking. Dust sleeping along the books. The oil lamps sleeping yellow. The yawn rising up in his throat. Feet sleeping along carpet slippers. The fire sunk to embers. The dead body of a book in his fingers.

Then the silence became so profound that thunder, or artillery leaping into action from the hills, could not have been more utterly paralysing. For a minute he was afraid to look at her face, as she lay on the long sofa, a book folded between her breasts. His breathing, the dim noise of voices, water-music from a tap in the kitchen, insects moving in the musty wood of the rafters, all insisted on the silence.

Looking, then, he saw Ruth staring away heavenwards, quite pleasantly remote, but terrifically motionless. Snap went a crazy spring inside the mechanical brain, quite cleanly and perfectly, without pain, but something like relief. His own fingers on a book, his cold thighs against the chair, his own breath flushing the lungs, infinite processes along the nerves coming into play. Light scorching his eyeballs. The mouth hung open from his face in concentration, dribbling. Casually, without urgency, formed the desire to urinate in his mind.

Episode in numbness. Standing in the stern of the big liner as it loped southward across a heavy sea, smelling the wide smells of salt water, scourged by the March winds.

People passing at his back. Talkers. The drive of the engines under his shoes. The clean sand-scrubbed deck. The long beautiful arches of spumy water, slipping away under them.

Off the shores of Portugal a flight of brown, queer-billed sea-gulls pulled out to meet them, ravenous, curving with a splendid velocity to the wash of peel, sticks, cardboard, bread, peelings, offal, soup, fish, meat, ham-fat and big-eyed potatoes.

When they were off Cadiz a wind swept the white horses out from the land at them, deploying beautifully. At night on the gusty dark upper deck you could swear you smelt the warm South coming nearer, ever nearer.

One night the wind, like an offering, brought them the smells of apples, guitars, neck-cloths, donkeys, dust, mimosa, jonquils, voices, garlic, desire.

Nevertheless the great ship, undistracted, nosed down Gibraltar way, through the neck, into the blue Mediterranean.

## Chapter VIII

# The Mummy

ONE moonless night Marlowe was waked from deep sleep by the sound of a voice, and the yellow smears of torchlight on the slats of the shutters by the head of his bed. Leaning up drowsily, he pushed aside the obstruction and found himself staring into the smooth face of Walsh. Instinctively he said: "What is it? Is anything wrong?" Walsh switched off the torch and leaned upon the window-sill, saying: "Nothing at all, only it's a good night for fishing. I wondered whether you'd care to come out."

"Fishing!" said Marlowe, and grinned with relief, drawing back the warm covering of a sheet from his naked flesh. "Fishing! God, but you gave me a start. Yes. I'd like to."

As he stood barefooted, dragging on his shorts, he was again aware of the alienness of the boy, the abstracted tilt of his head as he stared down upon the dark water. "A dash of torch," he said quietly, "I can't find my shoes. Thanks." With precise fingers he tied the laces. The light slid across the chequered tiling of the floor and was snapped off. Said Walsh: "I'm going on to get the boat ready. Come down in a little while, will you?"

Outside the house, all was as still as death. He paused for a second and listened for some familiar sound, some indication that he was not alone here, marooned upon a mountain-top, above an invisible sea. But there was nothing to be heard. Down in the crater of Nanos, by the jetty, however, a faint point of light punctured the integument of darkness, flickering about the rim of the boat. It was reassuring; and, thankful for it, he set off down the road, treading warily in the dust. The path down to the sea from the road was a blank tunnel down through the olives, narrow and dangerous to use when there was no light, but he struck out bravely upon it. Once he lost his footing and nearly fell, and once a snake swung from under his feet into the cover of the hedge, but that was all. As he stood, panting, at the foot of the cliff, on the soft carpet of seaweed, and peered about him for direction, he heard the voice of Fonvisin near at hand in the darkness, raised in a small owlish hoot of laughter. Unnameable things seemed to spring up in the darkness at the sound of it; the ghosts of an antique world – satyrs with insolent mouths, and sirens, the archaic gods – those things which in sunlight are no more than savage fables of a lovelier world, became, in the tunnels of gloom behind him, plausible realities, instinct with life. Above him, somewhere among the trees, a heavy fruit fell to earth, crashing among the foliage. He put out his hand and touched cold stone.

"The soul," said Fonvisin clearly, "is a cheap abstraction. Don't for God's sake speak of it as a reality."

Again the little laughter, and he could see the broad mouth drawn back across its small teeth like a wound. Stiffly, as if he were sleepwalking, Marlowe crossed the strip of beach. His footsteps rang out on the wood of the jetty. For some unknown reason his knees trembled under him, as he approached them. Walsh was saying, between grunts, "But what about identity, personal identity?"

"Hullo!" said Fonvisin to the darkness, arching his back in a great yawn, "Hullo there!" and Marlowe's response came in a voice so low and hoarse as to be barely audible. They hailed each other across gulfs. In a painful silence he waited while the final preparations of the boat were made. The heavy carbide lamp was fitted to its bevel in the bows, and swung down to an approximately accurate level. Afterwards its direction would be corrected. Three long tridents and a sharp boat-hook were flung anyhow into the boat; food – cakes, bread, and wine – followed. Meanwhile, Fonvisin seated himself by a long branch from which hung a dozen oranges, and, with a scalpel, made long single incisions in the rind of the fruit. The branch he tied to the stern, so that it should trail in the sea and flavour the ripe pith of the fruit with salt.

"Ready?" said Fonvisin, and without waiting for an answer skipped aboard to take the oars. Walsh made room for Marlowe on the narrow seat, and the latter climbed in.

Fonvisin rowed with a quick maniacal twist of the shoulders and loins, uncouthly but powerfully, grunting at each stroke. Under the impetus of his driving oars the boat turned, hesitated, and slid away quickly towards the headland, gathering impetus as it went, lifting its nose a little from the sea. Behind them the cliffs hovered out of the darkness, insinuating their outline on the sky. Turning back to shield a match for a cigarette, Marlowe noticed a light shining in the Villa Pothetos, from an upper window, and commented on the fact.

"It's the old man making out his list," said Walsh. "The boat goes off to Brindisi to-morrow." Fonvisin grunted.

Walsh produced an old briar pipe and a pouch, and began slowly to shred the tobacco between his fingers and fill the bowl. Practice and experience had made this a job of extreme nicety, and Marlowe, watching him from the corner of his eyes, admired the skill and method of the business. With each addition to the three-quarter-filled bowl an adjustment of the binding was necessary; the stem was placed between his teeth, and he drew gently at it, testing the closeness of the packing, the strength of the draw. Only one match was used to complete the job.

"Right," he said at last. "Easy on. It's somewhere around here. This cove, I think."

Fonvisin edged the nose of the boat in and stopped rowing. He sat in a glum silence, his head fallen a little forward, his mouth in a pout. Imperceptibly the cliffs menaced them, growing taller. Walsh, in the bows, scouted for landmarks.

"Yes," he said at last, when the nearer ravines of rock had become more or less defined, "this is the place. It was thick with *barbuni*.[65] Let's light up, shall we?" The carbide lamp began to fizzle and give off its nauseous stench. For half a second it lay back and blazed at the sky like a searchlight, and then it was caught and swung down to the water, adjusted and fixed. "Right," said Walsh with a queer note of triumph in his voice.

They were in a narrow channel of low-lying rock, down the centre of which ran a long rib of pure sand, dotted here and there with patches of weed and sea-ferns, among which the coloured fishes scouted.

Marlowe, leaning curiously to the side of the boat, saw the deeper water come into clear focus under the steady spray of light from the flame; he could see, defined in a radius of a few feet, the runnels in the grey central field of sand; the rocks with their coat of mosses and weed; the blue cavities under the side walls where the fishes lodged.

Fonvisin, still silent, impelled them slowly forward with tiny beats of the oars, which did not break the surface or disturb the loitering fish as they nosed about in search of food or of a safe resting-place. Walsh stood in the bows, tense and upright, with the nose of his murderous trident tilted down towards its victims, giving orders in a voice of deathly quiet. "To the right a bit. To the left. Easy."

The dark figure bunched itself and the trident was lowered, then flicked down at some unseen object outside the radius of the light. The boat rocked slightly and the dank water came up from the floorboards and wet Marlowe's naked feet. For a second the lamp stuttered, and then continued its uniform whisper.

"*Barbuni*," said Walsh. "Missed it."

Once a small octopus materialised from what seemed a floor of simple sand, and skidded grotesquely to the cover of a rock, like an obscene foetus, soapy and bloodless. The boat hook nosed down, the refraction seeming to break it in two, and dragged it from cover on its barb. Wriggling, it was brought up, wringing its small tentacles to-gether in a convulsion which combed back the water from the side of the boat. As it lay in the sheets, grotesque and malevolent, Fonvisin turned it over in his fingers, examining it with a quiet preoccupation: the detachment, thought Marlowe, with which he could fumble among my tripes or Walsh's. His own viscera seemed to coil away inside him at the thought. Nevertheless, he watched the broad beautiful hands as they busied themselves about the creature, turning it this way and that, manipulating and exploring. The quiet voice of Walsh, when it came, was a sound alien and disturbing, so deep was the silence, so profound the detachment of the man.

"I thought the index of refraction was fairly constant," he said.

A plump, coloured *barbuni* came up, triply crucified, and running threads of blood from the gills and belly. Then a long, coloured fish, brown with a red stripe, which beat out its life on the wood. Thump, thump, thump, like the weakening pulse-beats of death. "They call it The Englishman here. The fishermen, I mean. God knows why."[66]

The tall figure sank down to a sitting position and puffed the final mouthfuls of smoke from the dottle of the pipe.

"Take a turn," he said quietly. "It'll be a miracle if you hit anything on your first trip. Go ahead."

In silence Marlowe obeyed, bracing his knees to gain purchase in the bows. With his trident presented at approximately the correct angle, he searched the water keenly. Walsh lectured him quietly.

A procession of green fish, dismayed by some purely submarine event, executed a panicky half turn and dithered out toward the deeper water. For a minute the channel was empty, and then, slowly scouting the rim of rock with the delicate tips of their noses, came three bright silver fish. Marlowe lunged twice, inexpertly, and missed. The fishes flicked themselves into the outer darkness and safety, and Walsh suppressed a desire to chuckle.

"You'll turn the boat over," he said, and spent a happy quarter of an hour demonstrating and advising. "See? I should stand more forward. That's right. Now unless you do the trick correctly you'll fall on your face in the water. Sort of deterrent."

The time passed very quickly. Quietly absorbed, Marlowe grappled with his difficult job for over an hour, lost in the greenish subaqueous world which the light defined for him. In the quietness his mind, as it were, sprouted fins, and he became, not so much an avenger from the upper world of dry land, as a fish himself, pale and delicate, loitering down the shafts of light, in the glooms and rocktunnels, staring and starting at each new manifestation of light or shade in the world of mud and moisture around him. At any moment his life might be stabbed out; from anywhere above the surface the wicked trident might swim down and fix itself upon his horny flesh, might pin him to the sand. His little eyes were zeroes of wonder and fear. His mouth hung back on its hinges, boggling at destiny. What did fish feel or know?

"Here," he said at last, handing his trident to the boy, "I've had enough for the first lesson."

Fonvisin yawned and looked at the luminous face of his wrist watch, saying: "Let's try farther out. We may get some bigger stuff." Guided by Walsh, he nosed the boat into a narrow cross-channel with overhanging rock on each side and made for the open sea. Marlowe lit a cigarette and watched the diminishing size of the black rock-escarpments behind them, drawing the warm smoke easily in and out of his lungs. The night was very warm, and the sea utterly flat and silent, a small plateau of silence and emptiness, fading into the mist which hid its ultimate boundaries.

"The moon may swindle us yet," said Walsh, as the little man began to prepare his line without a word. (Three atoms, Marlowe was thinking, three maculae, three spots of sentience, similar and dissimilar, in a wooden shell, drifting upon a vast elastic surface under heaven.) Fonvisin sat humped over his rod-reel, a fleshy monolith, with terrible patience. (An idol, something of wood or stone, not flesh, intent on the methodical procedure of murder.) Walsh sat cross-legged on the sheets and rubbed his thighs with his lean hands. ("This sensible warm motion to become a kneaded clot.") The fish lay in a moist pile at his feet, and with them that wet parcel of tripes, the octopus.

Suddenly, he picked up one of the fish and held it before him, twirling it round and round, examining it. "The final abstraction," he said clearly. "Fish!" He smiled up at them as if inviting comment. "Fish, oh Fish. So little matters!" Marlowe lit another cigarette and said nothing. "The final abstraction," repeated the boy more quietly, "incomprehensible, secret, remote, beyond understanding."

Fonvisin half turned and gave a dry snort of derision. For a moment he stared full in the eyes of the boy, and then he turned his glance to the fish, which still twirled like a dervish in the long fingers.

"Put out your hand," he said at last, savagely; and after a moment, imperiously, "Go on. Put out your hand."

While the fish still rotated from the fingers of his right hand, Walsh laid the left, palm upwards, on his knee. For a moment an uncontrollable fury seemed to contract Fonvisin's powerful muscles. But his voice when he spoke was as dry as cork. He coughed once.

"Look at it. Look at the mechanics of it."

"Yes," said Walsh, with queer humility.

"Look at the disposition of the flexion folds."

"Yes."

Leaning forward jerkily, Fonvisin drew his nail across the skin, indicating the relation between the folds and metacarpal bones. "Otherwise when you gripped anything the skin would come away from the skeleton like a glove." He explained the method by which the skin was tied down to the dermis, the intricate system of pads to facilitate grip, and as he talked his face became strangely alive and vivacious, strangely young. Still the tireless fish twirled in the fingers of Walsh's right hand. And now, concluding, Fonvisin was shaken by little gusts of laughter, a sort of inner relief. He had made something clear to himself, though what it was Marlowe could not tell.

"You're so familiar with it, that's the trouble," he said. "You cannot see it objectively. But if you cut it off and set it swimming in the sea," his face clouded for a moment, and he drew his hand across the dome of his head, "if you set it off swimming and I caught it…"

Infectiously his laughter echoed out across the water. He leaned back against the gunwale and nodded his head as he laughed. "You see what I mean?" he managed to say at last, "you see what I mean?"

"Yes," said Walsh sombrely; but his fingers still held the fish. Chilly cipher of another creation, it hung down, lank, and the thin blood ran slowly from its snout to the wood.

They might have sat there for ever, the three of them, so deeply did silence fall, so inert was the night about them. Symbols, thought Marlowe sadly, symbols of mortality. He could stare down upon them, all three of them with himself among their number, as they sat in that small boat on the Ionian water, and see them as three symbols of three lives, of three directions. Himself, he knew, was a symbol of all that was past. His life was drawn from the old dead ages of traditional simplicity, faith, civility. He was a living past, drawing his nourishment from the memorable antiquities of lives that were ended, not from the disturbing transitional present; and the boy lolling indolently at his feet could not choose, could not define his own path in the wilderness of paths. The old and the new drew him to them, and between them he could not choose. Only Fonvisin, only he, could honestly look forward, without fear, and greet the new age; could rejoice as he saw the bare cold spars of the new thought on the horizons. The rejection of all that was finished was sincere and complete. He had said, more than once: "I am glad when I think of the new age coming with its collective sanities. I am glad to kick all the old totems and bugaboos into the muck-heap. I am glad to destroy all the traditional attitudes and create the new values of scientific thought." And on that occasion Gordon, with a burst of derisive laughter, had quoted the lines:

> "With laughter on their lips and with winds blowing round them
> They record simply
> How this one excelled all others in making driving belts."[67]

The supreme bathos! The ultimate idiocy! But Fonvisin had merely turned from the laughing blue eyes with a shrug of the shoulders, saying: "That's something you won't understand for a long time yet. But it'll happen surely enough."

Yes, it would happen. Of that one could be sure. And perhaps there would be men and women in that time who could give the authentic stamp of life to it; make it more than this chilly currency of thought. The reign of the great throbbing white intelligence. But, for his part, evasion was necessary. Oh, to escape utterly into the past, to taste the forms of its life and thought.

Then the moon began to shine, purely and steadily, from the diminishing wrack of clouds, and in its soft incandescence lit up the features of his companions, shining on the great dome of Fonvisin's head, and on the smooth face of Walsh. The dead fish, touched by the same alchemy, winked and shone, like a vast heap of silver coins. In the silence the boy lifted his arms to the sky in a gesture mockingly heroic: "O Artemis O Selene O Diana."[68]

"And answer came there none," said Marlowe sadly.

"Who wants an answer?" said Walsh. "Are we scientists? Do we want the equation of desire, or the mathematical index of coition? Will you have surds instead of sensation?"

Fonvisin, who appeared not to have heard, quietly drew in his line, and stowed it away.

"The peasants still believe in the old gods," he said at last, without challenge or contempt.

"I know," said Walsh, "and I love them for it. I love to see these trembly Pan-like old gentlemen in velveteen skirts, long white stockings, and shoes with coloured pom-poms on the toe. I like to think they're true believers. I love to think of them sneaking off to the tumble-down fanes and temples in the woods in their scarlet nightcaps."

He clasped his long arms about his knees and laid his head back, a little on one side, so that the moon shone full on the broad nose, and the severe smiling mouth.

"I think," he said at last, brushing the long hair from his forehead with the back of his hand, and speaking as if he had some vast contribution to make to the thoughts that crossed and re-crossed the minds of the two men, "I'm hungry."

Laughing, Marlowe agreed, and leaned down to help Fonvisin unearth the food from the leather satchel in the cupboard. Cakes and wine and the first of the green figs – heavy green gourds plumped full of soft red fruit – they handed round. The bottle which held the wine was the only available receptacle from which to drink, and they took turns with it, punctiliously wiping the mouthpiece of it when they had finished.

After food, naturally, tobacco; Fonvisin accepted one of Marlowe's cigarettes, while the boy produced his pipe and pouch and conducted his methodical ceremony. He lay back, puffing silver clouds up, past their faces, into the moonlight, sleepy and content, snuggling his neck into the folded pile of towels which they had brought for bathing.

As a sort of final delicacy the oranges were brought up from the sea and broken from their stalks. The fruit was beautifully cold and flavoured sharply with brine. The skins were tidied up and rolled in a paper bag, as were any other crumbs left over from the feast.

"Later on," said Walsh indistinctly, crushing the yellow flakes between his teeth, "we'll have grapes. They taste superb after they've been lashed to the stern for an hour or two."

Fonvisin had broken a large fig in two between his fingers, and was examining the halves, holding them away from his face, minutely pressing the green walls this way and that, cocking his head first on one side, then on the other. Quite seriously, cocking a mournful eye at his companions who watched him he said:

"Look! Here is an exact resemblance to the anus of an embalmed mummy. See when I move it. Look!" He began to laugh quietly, moulding the suggestive fig between his fingers.

"More like the —— of a ——," said Walsh.[69]

"Yes. Or the original yoni of Eve. I always thought there was something wrong with the forbidden apple."

Walsh set up a guffaw and took the stem of his pipe from between his teeth. He sat up.

"No, but I am serious," said Fonvisin plaintively. "Embalming is my subject. I wrote a book on it once. In Paris."

He stared moodily ahead of him, still ingeniously moulding the fig. "And there was a very rich Pole who made me embalm his wife when she died. He was a very clever man."

He tossed the figs over the side of the boat and humped himself more comfortably on the seat, drawing out his flat leather cigarette case and placing it on his knees. In the flame of the match his face was sombre, enigmatic – the strongly marked eyebrows drawn up on his forehead, the big mouth distorted about the cigarette. The horned tufts of red hair at his temples quivered ever so slightly as the movement of his jaws contracted the muscles under the skin. His ears, Marlowe noticed, were small and pointed, and pressed back to his head; the hair almost hid them.

"Yes," he said at last in silence. "He was a very clever man. A very clever man."

"How old was she?" said Walsh. "The wife, I mean. How old was she?"

"Thirty." Fonvisin looked up with a queer tenderness in his mauve eyes, and added: "He was nearly mad. And he made me make a mummy of her. He loved her. She had been a prostitute once, but he loved her. She was an excellent wife for him. So the two of us did it. He helped me. It was in the winter in Poland. In the snow it was very cold. He was very rich, and from all over the place he fetched spices and ointments. We had two big earthen jars. Big ones, with blue glaze on them. She was a Spaniard, very small and dark."

He reached down and picked up another fig, breaking it in half between his accurate fingers. Holding the two red faces up to them he smiled and said evenly: "That is why I remarked on them. Evisceration per anum."[70]

Walsh beat out the dottle of his pipe on the side of the boat, and the noise was prodigious. Then he picked up an orange and began slowly to peel it with his fingers, staring out across the moonlit water, saying nothing. Far out, by the smudge that was Santa Maura,[71] a wind was born, which wrinkled the dark water, pushing out a long tentacle towards the island. In half an hour, perhaps an hour, he calculated, it would reach the boat. The moon was waning.

If the story itself was compelling to the fear and the imagination, Marlowe found Fonvisin's voice doubly compelling. It was flat and toneless, and the sentences followed one another with the inevitability of clockwork. Yet the picture grew and became vivid, was burnt into their minds; positive and clear in its casual detail.

Clear, beyond the ordinary clarity of imagination, he saw the heavy figure of Fonvisin moving about the huge rooms of that mansion among the snows; the candles dripping and fluttering, clenched in their sconces; the puddles of consumed wax on the floors; the shaggy dogs drawing before wide fireplaces piled high with logs from whose joints the resin trickled, burning blue and acrid; the tall, blond man who walked, with his eyes cast down, like Hamlet, and with the palms of his hands held stiffly before him, numb with loss.

A strange blond man who could watch the evisceration with wide eyes; whose hands could move steadily about his accomplice's limbs, disposing, aligning, holding, without a tremor.

"We injected a solution of cedar-oil, as a solvent, and emptied her guts out" (Fonvisin, stolid and methodical, with a cigarette in his mouth, and his eyes screwed up against tobacco smoke, working by the imperfect light of candles). "The brains were difficult. From inside the nose we broke through a part of the ethmoid bone – a place called the cribriform plate – it's a sort of bone full of holes like a sieve. He used an iron probe. Hooked the brains out. Then we washed her out with spices. The brain cavities, all washed out clean and sweet, and the body too. She was all flat and like an envelope, without her stomach being in her. We slit the skin over her nails and tied them down with wire, and then filled the glazed jar with a solution of crude natron, and doubled her up and stuffed her down into it, all except her head which was out."[72]

After that they put out the candles and left her, kneeling in the jar, with the liquid up to her neck, among the pungent scent of the extinguished wicks. The vigil was a long one; seventy days and nights she had to remain in her chilly bath. "We could have taken her out sooner, but I wanted to be sure that the whole epidermis had peeled off, and all the fatty stuff melted off her. So we left her the full time."

But in the interval they were not idle. In the woods quite near to the house was an old family vault, from which the bodies had been removed to the village grave-yard, some miles away. When the house had passed from the hands of the ancient family who were the owners, it seemed hardly fitting that the bones of their forefathers should be left in the grounds whose possession they had forfeited. So a newer, more imposing vault had been built, and to this the mouldering remains had been removed with all fitting ceremony. It was in the vacant vault that the two of them set to work, Fonvisin and the blond man. The great stone bunks, lidded with slabs, they broke down with pickaxes, and the rubble they carried out and threw into the snow. By the light of lanterns they scraped the festering walls clear of fungus and those obscene growths which spread upon the monuments of death, and the damp earth floor they covered with great garish tiles tom up from the hall of the house itself. With icy hands they mixed cement and in the very centre of the vault they built a wide shallow bath, smoothing away its parapet with their trowels. They worked on it with such perseverance that it became as smooth as marble, and fit for the body of any king's Jezebel: and they coloured it brightly, and the blond man drew a phoenix at the head and at the foot a nightingale; the former was a bird vividly depicted, bright

and arrogant on its nest of fuming twigs; the latter was softly and delicately coloured, as something of an old world, long since passed. Its beak
was wide with singing. And all this time the blond man hardly spoke a
word, but worked feverishly, as if his time was short, and he impatient
to complete the work. Once the winds rose in violence and came up out
of the woods, blowing out the lamps: and in the darkness he could still
be heard, like a mole, filing and scraping the cement to make it smooth,
and blowing the dust away. Once, too, he took a fine brush and, dipping
it in vermilion paint, wrote on the clean walls of the vault the words:

> O mes baisers peureux,
> Nous ne serons jamais une seule momie
> Sous l'antique desert et les palmiers heureux![73]

That was the only decoration to be found in the place; that and the
paintings of the two birds.

After that only one thing remained to be done to the vault to make
it ready. Gradually, in jars, in vessels of all kinds, they mixed the spices
and resinous liquors which the blond man had had sent to him from
many countries by his agents – cassia bark from China, myrrh from
Arabia, and Persian spikenard; balsams and sweet resins they dissolved
in various liquids – alcohol, turpentine, and pure linseed oil; and out
of all these they filled the shallow cement bath with shifting, melting
liquids; coloured liquids which mixed and shone and threaded among
each other, sliding glibly around the basin in which she was to lie. Then,
as a valediction to the tomb, they kindled a fire, and on to it piled
frankincense, which set up a wild spluttering, burning now blue, now
green, and giving off its sharp fumes, until the humid air of the place
was made warm and healing, and great whiffs of sweetness hung in it,
waiting to settle about the bath in which *she* would lie. As they turned
at the top of the snow-covered flight of steps, and the blond man turned
the great key in the wincing lock of the iron grille, he said, with the ghost
of a smile on his mouth: "I suppose it is all finished. One cannot sleep
with a mummy, my friend, can one?"

Fonvisin said: "Listen! What was that?"

"Only the wind," said the blond man wearily.

"It sounded like wolves."

"Perhaps it was."

But the cry did not come again, and they continued on their way to
the house, huddled in coats, from the snow. Upstairs, in the still air of
a sealed room, the prostitute knelt in her cold bath, her body peeled
and ready for the tomb. The snow made no noise drifting against the
shuttered windows. There was no sound.

"We pulled her from the jar and I examined her. The work was perfect. She was just ready. We dried her body carefully until it was quite dry and packed her brain with spices and resins. The stomach we washed out again, and cleaned, and then we packed it out with the same things. She became quite full and heavy again, and he said to me: 'Make it look as if she was pregnant, will you, my friend? Give her a child in her dead womb.'"

They laid her out on the long oak table spread with a red curtain that the blond man had plucked from its rings, because he had been impatient to begin the ceremonies: and Fonvisin plugged her body full of clouts soaked in resin until it seemed that she was pregnant, and bound coloured metal sheaths to the nails of her fingers and toes, while quietly, with a sad relish for the particularities of his delicate practice, the blond man farded[74] her small face, and enamelled the lips crimson on it, and rouged the nipple of each breast. He chafed the narrow wrists and on her left cheek he put a black spot such as the Regency ladies wore.

All the while the prostitute lay, limp and passive, with her belly puffed out with clouts, and her face turned to the frescoed ceiling where nymphs and dryads pursued their painted delights, and the wicked fauns stood, hand on shaggy hip, tittering. And downstairs the dogs lay about the fireplace dozing, or occasionally lifting an ear to the thresh of the wind in the heavy trees outside. Slowly, like white lives, the candles consumed themselves, and filled the whorled silver of the sconces with shapes and puddles in wax; or ran, like mercury, to the floors, and to the fingers and clothes of those who carried them. It was the worst part of the winter season, and the snow lay in mighty drifts on the path to the tomb, and on the broad drive-way of the house; and the ice clung in spikes to the iron grille of the vault, and the very water congealed as it ran from the gutters. It was at that bitter season when the souls of old men cringe and huddle in their shaky bodies, fearful of departure, that the work was finally completed.

They bound up her legs with clean white bandages, soaked in pre-servative, and the blond man combed out her black hair and set a wide clean bandage under her chin, to keep it up: then he passed the ends of it over her temples and fastened it over her sleek hair with a flat brooch, so that it looked as natural as any woman's head-dress. Then they wound the bandages about the rest of her body, except her face, and bound her up tight and simple. Then she was ready for the journey.

While the wind cried outside the walls, and the dogs fretted down-stairs by the fire, they made a rough stretcher of wood and canvas on which to carry her. And over her swaddled body they flung the great curtain to keep off the snow.

Then, huddled in coats and great caps, and carrying lanterns, they staggered out of the great front door and began their journey to the tomb, with the stretcher on their shoulders. The blond man walked slowly, with reluctance that his task was so soon finished; and as he walked he thought that a progress to Hell would be more welcome, more facile, more quickly concluded, than this short and difficult passage to the vault; and the prostitute, rocking gently on the canvas, with her pursed mouth kissing the curtain, was snug and content.

The blond man picked her up in his arms and carried her to the basin, and leaning down, gently lowered her body into the liquid, holding her up from underneath so that the backs of his wrists were plunged in it, and soft stains spread up the arms of his blue silk shirt. While Fonvisin rekindled the fire, and piled it high with knobs of frankincense, his companion stood, moodily watching the body as it gained equilibrium in the bath. The bandages sucked up the liquor, as lump-sugar sucks up coffee, and in a little while it seemed that she was not the mummy of a woman but a real woman, clothed in long garments, shot with threads of colour, lying passive and exquisite, waiting for life.

The fire had burned up, and the great fumes of frankincense curled up about them, blurring her form, resting in great visible balloons of smoke on the surface of the oil. As they stood staring, rapt in contemplation, the door was forced open, and a gigantic wind snuffed out the lanterns and set the smoke curling from the vault into the snow. As Fonvisin leapt to the door and forced it back, he heard the blond man cry out in a loud voice some words or sentences which, in the confusion, he did not catch. When the lanterns were lit he saw him kneeling by the basin, with his chin propped on his arms, and his wide-eyed face within a foot of the mummy's, lost in contemplation. He was smiling.

Fonvisin took him by the arm and, wrapping him in his coat, led him from the vault, himself locking the iron grille behind them. But if the man had been reluctant to reach the vault with his burden, he was more reluctant still to leave it and return to the house. He pleaded gently to be allowed to stay in the vault for a little while; pleaded in tones as meek and submissive as a child's.

But Fonvisin only gripped his arm and hurried him on.

All that night they did not sleep, but lighted the biggest candles and sat in the great entrance hall of the mansion, with the dogs at their feet. The blond man broke open the door of the sealed cellar he had laid down many years before and staggered up the steps, panting, his arms thick with ancient bottles. Blowing the dust and cobwebs from them, and polishing them with the wet sleeve of his shirt, he smiled and told Fonvisin to fetch glasses; cracking the wax seals with a knife, and holding the beautiful bottles to the light, he appraised their shape, reciting the age and quality of the wines which were in them.

As they sat in silence, sipping the choicest wines in the world one after another, without method or consideration for their exquisite quality, the polished wireless in the corner called up the voices of half the world to mock them in their loneliness. From Germany, from Spain, from England, from Russia, from the New World, the voices of men and women, of singers and entertainers, of politicians and professors, came clearly through the shining wooden box. The blond man was never content with one, but turned and twisted the knobs and handles, calling up more and more voices from differing continents.[75] Among other things, he filled a blue saucer full of wine and gave it to the dogs to drink, so that in a little while they were drowsy and a little tipsy.

So there they sat, Fonvisin and the blond man, saying nothing, but moodily drinking and staring into the heart of the climbing fire.

Once, towards morning, the latter leaned forward in his chair and said: "These things do not surprise me. I have been warned." As he drained a full red glass he held out the palm of his right hand, with a quick gesture: "See, my friend," he said, holding out a beautiful white hand, "I am a creature without a destiny. I have no past, no future. Only my despair tells me that I exist."

Fonvisin took his hand and examined it. True, there were lines in the deep folds, but where the palmist can trace those minor grooves and curves whose significance is destiny, the skin was as smooth as an egg.

Shortly after, they composed themselves to sleep, as they were, sitting in chairs before the fire; and Fonvisin knew nothing more until he woke to the sound of a terrible crying outside, in the night. The dogs woke too at the sound of it, and the fur stood up on their necks, as they bayed by the great front door. The blond man had his back turned to him, and was dragging wide the doors of the gun-case; snatching up a shot-gun and slipping a handful of cartridges into his pocket, he whispered the one word: "Wolves," and was gone, whipping the door shut behind him.

Fonvisin was not slow to follow, and arming himself by the same means, he too made for the door, around which the snarling dogs bristled, too afraid to venture out. As his hand touched the iron latch he heard a shot, and then another. After that silence.

Once out of the house, in the deep snow, he ran as fast as he was able in the direction of the tomb, hampered by the heavy gun, and by the lantern he had snatched up on his way out, from its hook in the porch.

The iron gate to the vault was wide on its hinges, and in the snow which lay deep on the steps were the foot-prints of the blond man's boots.

As he stood in the doorway and raised the lantern, he saw the figure of his friend leaning sideways across the basin with his arms about the mummy of the prostitute. The tears were running down his face, but he made no sound. His mild eyes were wide open.

"She was alive," he said, "she was alive."

Fonvisin's eye fell on the mummy. It was mutilated. The cartridge had riddled one side of the face, and split open the jaw. From a deep hole in the chest a twist of stuffing protruded.

The blond man stood up slowly and faced him. Threads of liquor had discoloured his shirt and ran down to the floor from his delicate finger tips. He pointed quietly to the doorway and tried to speak, but his mouth curled up in a grin and the tears started in his eyes. Very slowly he said: "She was standing there, outside the door, waiting for us. The gun went off in my hand as I ran down to meet her. *She was outside the door.* My friend, do not think I am mad. At the shot she fell down and I ran to her and held her. She was alive until I fired. *But alive!*"

Fonvisin put down his lantern and gun and went to him; taking him by the arm, he said: "Come. You must get out of here. Do not imagine things."

But the blond man only shook his head from side to side, and pointed to the floor.

"Look there, then," he said steadily. "If you do not trust me, do you trust your own eyesight? Look on the floor and tell me what you see."

And Fonvisin, looking down, saw for the first time that a single set of footmarks was printed on the tiled floor in liquor; a single set that went to the door but did not return from it. The feet were small and bare: the feet of a woman or a child.[76]

Telling the story, in the bare moonlight of that summer night, as he sat in the angle of the wooden seat, he seemed again perplexed by the speculations and doubts which this phenomenon had roused.[77] Marlowe could imagine him, turning fiercely from the tall weeping man to that parcel of ruined meat, the mummy, as if it could rise up and explain, in the cold language of the sciences, how this thing could have been. Yes, the enigma of the living man in the blue shirt, with the wine falling from his finger-tips, must have been as great as that presented by the swaddled figure, gross in mutilation, gently rolling in the odorous basin of spices and liquors. Had he invented, faked, swindled? But the details were so perfect, so without flaw. The very spacing of the footsteps indicated someone, whose shins were bound, walking with the utmost difficulty.

For these and kindred perplexities his even voice found a place; as though here, at the very core of the story, he himself had begun to doubt its essential truth.

"But the other shot," said Walsh coolly. "You heard two."

"Yes." With the most casual of movements he drew the cigarette stub from his mouth and pitched it into the sea. "Yes, I asked him and he said that he had fired at wolves. As we went back to the house there was one part of the path I noticed which had a wide sweep of tracks across it in the snow. A pack of wolves quite certainly had crossed the path. That was true."

"You know," said Marlowe after a long and painful silence, "that the Egyptians believed in a very definite connection existing between the mummy and the survival of the dead man's identity after death? I believe they even had a ceremony which was intended to bring it back to life.[78]

"Yes," said Fonvisin, "I know."

"If only it were true," said Walsh quickly.

Fonvisin sneered and said: "Personal identity!"[79]

"I don't care what you think," said Walsh wildly.

Death! thought Marlowe. And in that still night, under the bland Mediterranean moon, of all things which were compelling to mind as possibilities, death was the most powerful, the most plausible. Pondering on it, he could see no reason for those fears, those despairs, with which humanity has been tormented at the thought of death, and whose outlet has been the sonorous meditation of poets and musicians. Surely the clean break with events was not so horrible. O eloquent, just and mighty death.[80] For thine is the kingdom.[81] How cleanly and subtly one passed from time into history. One's identity suspended with one's breath: suspended, caught, as a strip of cinema film is caught, showing a still image. And yet beyond death was thought, the only positive value, the only constant in flux. Why stuff the viscera with rags and ceremoniously feed the cold mouth, why breathe into the dead nostrils? Thought was the phoenix.[82]

*Ay but to die and go we know not where;*
*To lie in cold obstruction and to rot.*[83]

As in a dream he could see the eager leaning face of Walsh, fronting the ancient dome in the Russian's head; he could see the flicker of light in the mauve eyes. Uncomfortably, as if from a great distance, he could hear his own voice saying:

"Thought is the phoenix. Thought goes on."

The mystic phoenix, he was thinking, remembering the phoenix painted on the wall of the tomb. The phoenix of pure contemplation persisting through aeons, beyond the mere temporal damage of body, beyond good and evil, beyond time and the vagaries of circumstance.

"The mystic is the phoenix," he heard himself say.

In the pale face of the boy turned to him he could see rage and a certain contempt.

Fonvisin had slipped off his clothes and stood, his squat gorilla body naked and luminous in moonlight, dangling his feet in the water. He sniffed soberly and lowered himself into the water. The hair on his forearms glinted in the light. He gave a sniff of pure pleasure to feel the rushing tide take him by the loins and come sliding up his body to his chest. Turning, he kicked himself from the boat and paddled away quietly, swimming like a dog.

"Heads," called the boy sorrowfully across the water, "here I come." He cut a long figure in the air, and tore up the surface of the water with a shallow dive, beginning to swim in long racing strokes, beating his toes behind him. The two heads diminished, passing across the great silver bar, moving towards the open sea. Marlowe watched them for a moment, and then slipped off his own clothes, and lowered himself into the water. It came sliding up around him, plunging his nerves in its coolness, but he did not let go of the gunwale. Rigid and supported he thrust himself under, and pulled his head above surface again, panting, knuckling the water from his eyes.

For a long time he stayed there, and the small fish came up curiously to look at him, to nibble his legs and to prod his navel and flanks with their noses. The boat drifted round in wide circles, and he with it, attached, in a dream of ecstatic luxury.

After a time Fonvisin returned, and both men got back into the boat. They had drifted back into the entrance of the lagoon when Walsh swam up to them, finely swimming with his long stroke.

Marlowe was aware that the light had changed. It was early morning; the sand beach was pale lemon in the cold light. To the east the tips of the mountains were alight like soft tapers, and the sky behind them was vivid with colour.

Yawning, he watched Walsh climb into the boat. He felt suddenly very tired.

Chapter IX

# Francis

TO FRANCIS the phenomena presented by the casual behaviour of
the islanders were, exactly, not astonishing. Her world was one utterly
removed from theirs, subject to different values. In a sense, too, she was
shut away from them all, being absorbed and pinned down by the sight
of ordinary feelings actuating the motives of people.

Marlowe had stumbled upon her several times, as he crossed the
hillside, sitting on the grass under the olives, gathering coloured anemones and plaiting them into chains. He remembered the way her throat
curved down, white by contrast to the coaly black hair; the purse of her
small mouth, and the thin shreds of melody coming from her lips; her
long legs, ochreous with tan.

"Early anemones," she had called, and he went across the path to her,
a little shy of his home made short trousers, and his pale, rather bony
knees. For a few moments they made scraps of conversation. She asked
him how she managed to live, and he confessed that years of bachelorhood
had equipped him to deal adequately with most domestic troubles. He
even showed her his trousers with a sudden reckless confidence, inviting her to admire them. She was vague then, with a gentle vagueness,
but she had the grace to make him stand up and turn round. Yes, the
trousers were excellent: and their excellence was a source of delight that
seemed to bubble up, like laughter, in her eyes.

He remembered also the ardour, the fury of her painting. She would
stand for hours on the hillside, in a torn straw hat, trying to build up
the form of a landscape by an interrelation of its colours; angrily as-

sociating and reassociating her groups of colour, with a self-immolating dissatisfaction: screwing up her face, and swearing softly under her breath, as she tried to express herself in this difficult language. And when she became disgusted with the fatuity of her attempts she would produce a colourprint of some landscape, a Cézanne or an El Greco, and, propping it up against the bole of an olive tree, stare at it for hours on end, slowly crunching a dwarf-pear between her teeth, or peeling an orange; she would stare and stare as if to draw every secret from the cheap print, the secret of its composition, the secrets of its author's practice. And more often than not she ended by kicking her easel, with the offending canvas on it, down the hill....

To Walsh this profound disregard for her own productions was nothing short of sacrilegious. The hillsides, he said plaintively, more than once, were simply littered with half-completed canvases. Every time he and Gordon went for a walk they brought back one or two.

"I can't understand it, Francis," he said. "After all, even if you loathe your own stuff, why shove your boot through a whole day's work? It's indecent."

Fonvisin who happened to be there had sneered and said: "Artistic conscience. You wouldn't understand that, Walsh."

The comment of Francis was somehow characteristic and complete. Shy and remote, beyond the broader interplay of banter or cynicism, she had said: "When Cézanne couldn't get what he wanted – some frightfully subtle relation of colours – he left a blank on the canvas. Just a gap in the colour. That was real conscience. If mine were half as strong I should produce nothing, but a series of blank canvases."

And that was that. The casual sentences, without affectation, seemed to measure her personality against theirs; and even against the bitterness of Fonvisin her defence was complete. She was invulnerable, and Marlowe, watching her as she lounged home across the hill, was aware that her invulnerability was simply detachment. She was dependable only on herself: that rather unsatisfactory and vague self which puzzled him.

Precisely why her relations with Rumanades should have been more satisfactory than with any of the others, one is at a loss to determine. Perhaps there was something in her which was attracted by his qualities of silence and his evasion of personality. And he, the old man, was still too near to emotional damages of his own, to risk fresh ones. But the casual friendship between them matured; a friendship prepared by gallantries on his side, which were only a shy preliminary to offering her the red stone villa at the lip of the headland. She had been sufficiently interested in the economics of the place to let herself be taken on a complete tour of the island to see the olive-crop being gathered, and inspect the orchards and vineyards which flourished on the farther slopes; even to call on the goat-like entomologist, who lived in a ruined hut on the windy western headlands.

Her enthusiasm and, better, her approbation, were warming things in a cold life, and the old man became almost jaunty under their influence. When one day she announced that she was leaving to continue her interrupted pilgrimages to Mistra and Constantinople, he was quite shaken by the thought.

"But…but that's impossible," he heard himself saying. He was so thunderstruck, and withal so incredulous, that he upset his tea down the trousers of his new duck suit. Mopping his thighs with a coloured handkerchief, and wagging his bearded face at the alarming idea, he repeated: "But it's impossible." He was dimly aware that the frightening world of emotional attachments which had opened with Manuela, and had closed as suddenly behind her, was still as painful and as possible a reality for himself as it had ever been. In the grip of a curious panic, which he was at a loss to account for, he poured himself a second cup of tea, indignant that his hand should waggle as he did so. He was almost angry with the girl, as she sat there on the edge of the vast drawing-room sofa, looking coolly at him across the rim of her cup. Inside himself he was fulminating vaguely about the irresponsibility of the young, and the impossibility of knowing exactly where one stood with them: and yet, the idea was preposterous….

He caught himself enumerating all those minor changes in his life which dated from her arrival: domestic trivialities – such as, for instance, this afternoon cup of tea taken English fashion in the drawing-room – this very ceremony in which they were both participating. Latterly, too, he had taken to having his beard trimmed every other week; and then there was the new suit he had ordered from Paris – the dinner-jacket with the broad lapels, and the soft silk shirts to go with it. Confound it, he had got into the habit of dressing for dinner on Sundays and feast-days! Benedictine and Marsala: he had become almost fanciful in his tastes; and English books and periodicals to leave about in the drawing room.

"This is very sudden," he said primly, trying to behave as though his trousers were not wet through with tea and stained from hip to ankle, "very sudden, indeed."

"The merest whim," she said quietly, putting down her cup, and turning over the leaves of a book. "Hadn't you better go and change your trousers?"

He stood up like an obedient animal, and made for the door. Pausing with his hand on the latch and his back turned from hers, he said: "It seems a great pity. Are you fed up of Mavrodaphne?"

"Good Lord, no."

"Oh!" he said inexpressively and left the room.

The exact significance of her remark did not occur to him until he was clothing his hairy legs in a clean pair of trousers. She was not tired of the island. He sat down on the corner of his bed and repeated the phrase in his mind, reproducing the exact tone of the original. No, she was not tired. With his head cocked on one side he made a rapid diagnosis of the case. A touch of restlessness, he thought. Perhaps a touch of loneliness.

As he stood up and made the final adjustments to his dress he recalled that one evening some weeks before the village priest had called, to tell him that gossip was getting busy among the peasants. Francis was reputed to be his mistress. It was extraordinary how the news fired him; so great was his elation that he had pressed the priest to accept an expensive cheroot and a glass of one of the better wines. Now, as he remembered the incident, the same elation was tempered by the fear that her departure would not be delayed for long; he stood, rather sadly, and stared out across the beautiful grounds of the Villa Pothetos.

From the tangles of this ambiguous friendship, one thought emerged, clearly and emphatically. She must be persuaded to stay. The bait would have to be tempting.

That night, over the coffee-cups and the liqueurs, he asked her, with a diffidence that was not all craft, if she would consider doing a fresco in the village church, when it was rebuilt; and she, with the casualness that was characteristic of her, said she would love to do one. That was, more or less, that. Up to a point he felt confident of the success of his ruse: but the vaguest of doubts persisted, the most shadowy of fears haunted his mind when he thought of the business. After all, the restoring of the church, even with Greek labour and a Greek mason, could not last for the rest of his natural life.

Little by little he found himself in the position of making little presents to her, paying attention to her wants and interests. Though he did not know it, he was using the most dangerous of persuasions, the most unsubtle coercion. Canvases, for instance. She ran short of canvas and paint, and, hearing of it, he sent Christ to Brindisi with instructions to obtain a gigantic roll of the stuff, and to call in at Corfu on his way back, and collect the paints which he had ordered from Athens. The village carpenter was commissioned to make wood stretchers of various sizes, and the two of them spent a whole morning crawling, about among the sawdust and the chips, fervently explaining (with the aid of diagram both on paper and in the dust) the exact manner in which the canvas was to be attached to its frame.

On another occasion, when the spring was merging into summer, she had suggested that he take up sea-bathing, an exercise in which he had not indulged for years. He was both tantalised and agonised by the invitation. For what would be said if he spent his days in a state of semi-nudity with an English girl on the beach? What, indeed!

His trepidation had increased almost to a panic when an idea occurred to him; in some vague way it was all muddled up in his head with pre-war English etiquette, and the grave question of male decency where women were concerned. The carpenter was summoned to the house and commissioned to build him a bathing-box: one of those Victorian contraptions, whose appearance suggest a compromise between a tabernacle and a wheel-barrow. This work was to be undertaken on terms of great secrecy.

With industry and a touch of fear the peasant completed the work in record time. It stood, an incongruous and haphazard affair, painted green, in his backyard; and to Rumanades, poking round and prying open its door, it seemed to be a thing of great excellence. From its pleasant privacy he could indulge himself, he felt, without fear of gossip or the malicious wagging of tongues – even though a rumour had already started, to the effect that it was an elaborate devil box.

It was wheeled to the beach (its creator had given it a couple of heavy wagon wheels) one dark night, by a dozen fishermen, and run down to the edge of the water.

The next day Francis, on the way down to the beach at the usual hour, was stopped dead in her tracks by the sight of the bathing-box. But more – Rumanades himself, in a woollen bathing-suit covered in bands of mauve and vermilion, and very long at the knees, hesitating coyly on the steps, one toe in the water, peering round nonchalantly from time to time to see if she was coming. She sat down in the grass by the side of the path in a small convulsion of laughter. She pondered the reason for this sudden excursion into Edwardian conventionalities. The bathing-costume, my God. The bathing-costume was almost more astounding than the bathing-box. It formed a daring ellipse in front, and the opening was heavily piped all round. It exposed a segment of collar-bone, but as if to atone for this frivolity it covered, not only his knees, but his elbows as well. It was almost insanely decent. It was so decent that it was positively pornographic.

For a moment the sight of him, standing there, poised like a nymph, with one toe in the water, was so astounding that its only response could be this explosion of sounds in her throat. But seeing him, and continuing to see him there, she was filled with such a desire for outright laughter and affection, that she crashed down the slope, shouting and laughing, with her sleek black hair flying behind her, and her arms above her, bellying out the folds of her rough towel like a sail.

With the sight and sound of her, however, the customary panic was too much for him, and he fell sedately into the water, disappearing with a profound crash from sight.

Coming to the surface he found himself laughing, yes, shouting with laughter. As he stood, with the water running from his beard, and squeezing from his eyes, looking like some comic Edwardian Beowulf, she dashed in and seized him, still tittering, by the hand. Crashing hip-high in the cool water she danced him round in a circle, laughing and exclaiming: "How wonderful of you, how wonderful of you, how wonderful of you."

"Wonderful?" he said, puzzled. "Wonderful?"

"Yes. It's wonderful," she said, laughing.

"But how?" He released his hands and stood there, suddenly, staring at her. He was utterly at a loss to comprehend the motives of this affection. Was it, he wondered, something a tiny bit funny about the business? And how could one be subject to laughter and affection all at once? Laughter to him was inseparable from ridicule, and the idea of ridicule painful.

"Is it something wrong or silly?" he said anxiously.

"No. No." She was still laughing, deeply. "It's fine, it's wonderful." And her enthusiasm, If puzzling, was heartening enough.

"I don't understand," he said simply. But he was happy.

If the subsequent history of the bathing box was varied, for the time being, at least, it served a purpose. Francis painted a large canvas – a formal decorative affair – which included it; and included also the figure of the old man, hesitating coyly on the steps with one foot in the water. But she did not show it to him.

The arrival of Fonvisin, and of Gordon, altered a number of things. It altered, firstly, that delightful and ambiguous friendship which had become almost a flirtation of minds. The old man retreated into himself a good deal; the invitations to tea, to dinner, to the local fêtes became less frequent, and himself less eloquent and open in conversation. It also altered, to a remarkable degree, the history of the bathing-box. Fonvisin's immediate reaction to it took the form of a wild bout of laughter – this time unmistakably the laughter of ridicule.

When he was told that if he cared to bathe it was always at his disposal, he went.

"You don't mean to say," he said, between howls, "that you bathe from *that thing?*"

"Good heavens, no. I should think not." Inwardly trembling, the old man denied the accusation: "It's simply there for the entertainment of my guests," he said primly, "that's all." But he was sick with dismay; angry too, at the remembrance of Francis' laughter. If she had only warned him against the monstrous error of taste. If she had only warned him.

But instead she had said it was wonderful. And now this boor could giggle at him!

After this betrayal he never quite trusted her again. From that time their relations were tempered with a watchful suspicion. He on his side was determined to prevent the repetition of such a mistake; and she, on her side, hardly gave the matter a thought.

One day, when Gordon was walking down the road with Rumanades, he caught sight of the bathing-box, and asked what it was. Braced against the inevitable laughter, the old man replied according to formula. And by some fluke the spark of laughter was slow to light that day. Perhaps Gordon himself noticed the slight shake of his host's voice, the nervous gathering of his hands over his watch chain. At any rate he looked gravely at it for a moment and then asked if it were used a great deal. Never, was the eager reply. "Never used at all."

"I was thinking," said Gordon slowly, with a blessed solemnity, "that it would make an excellent diving board if it were pushed out a bit farther into the deep water. Just up to the roof, I mean."

Rumanades' gratitude for such a suggestion was almost embarrassing; indeed it was as great as his gratitude for not being ridiculed. That very afternoon a gang of villagers propelled the devil box out to sea, with great efforts and shouting, and succeeded in covering all but a couple of feet of it in water. From that time onwards it was used as a diving-raft, and Fonvisin's references to its original function became fewer and fewer until finally they ceased altogether. The past, one hoped, was done with.

But, in spite of all the shames and panics, the old man had overlooked one thing: the bathing-costume.

This article of wear reposed on a hook inside the bathing-box, its existence forgotten even by its owner. When the box was pushed out into the sea, the costume went with it and, for a period of weeks, stayed with it. But the laws of a whimsical chance are always producing things from hidden places to serve as evidence against us.

Perhaps it would be far-fetched to suggest that Constantine Paparrhegopoulos had any connection with the spirits of chance. The only claim he could possibly advance to such a title was that both his birth and his upbringing had been handicapped by his parents' taste for liquor; spirits, one must confess, of a very different kind. Constantine, *le pauvre*, was the result of chronic alcoholism, undernourishment, rickets, and a life of lounging. Paparrhegopoulos senior, his father, kept (or rather was kept by) a small wine-shop in the village. He had found an adequate escape from the financial worries that torment smaller minds. Every morning he would lay himself down on his bed again (if, indeed, he ever happened to get up) and shout through the fly-swarming door at Constantine: "Bring a bottle of wine for your mother, like a good boy." And Constantine, that misshapen, white moron of a son, would bring the usual six bottles and leave them to it. In a way, of course, it was useful, this habit. It consumed stock which would otherwise have rotted on the shelves.

If Paparrhegopoulos senior was a scandal in the village, Constantine too had his niche. He was the village idiot. And what an idiot! No one, when teased or ridiculed, could gnash his teeth and spit and quiver as Constantine did; no one, moreover, could have fits; he was unique.

For Constantine everyone retained a genuine affection. After all, he was an epileptic. On feast-days he was dressed in a white sailor suit, whose cap and vest were piped in gold braid with the name "Averoff,"[84] and forced along with the procession, clutching a bunch of flowers in his large, white hand.

Now Constantine was a keen and enthusiastic swimmer, unlike most of the other villagers. He bathed several times each day, whenever the tedium of hanging about in his father's tavern became too much for him. Sneaking down to the beach, he would slip out of his verminous clothes, pitch his cloth cap on a rock, and wade stubbornly into the water. It was on one of these excursions that he stumbled upon the bathing-costume.

As he stood on the roof of the bathing-box, gathering himself for one of his sprawling dives, lie suddenly noticed that the door of the box was ajar. He lay on his stomach to verify this, and it occurred to him that it would be a pleasant idea to open the door and explore the interior of the devil box. The prospect of finding it tenanted by an octopus did not appall him in the least.

He embarked on the attempt, and after a time succeeded in opening the door and insinuating his body into the cavity. Even in that dim underwater light the costume, still attached to its peg, shone like a beacon. For a moment Constantine thought it was a big and curious fish, and was afraid, and then he noticed that its shape and movements were not those of a fish. Snatching it up he made a victorious lunge skyward, and, consumed with curiosity and delight for its colour, he sat for a whole hour on the roof of the box, turning it over and over in his hands, grinning. He held it up against his naked body and observed that it would suit him. And the colours were ravishing.

As he sneaked back with it under his coat, to the tavern, desolate in its little square of dung splashed cobbles, he planned a début.

For two days he waited, curbing his vanity and delight at his find, until, on the afternoon of the third day, he heard that they were all down on the beach, Rumanades, Gordon, Fonvisin; then, judging the time ripe, he got the costume out of its hiding-place, and rushed down the slope.

They were sitting about the flat central rock, talking desultorily. Francis and Gordon had just bathed. With a false nonchalance, extraordinary to watch, Constantine undressed, pretending that he had not seen them. Then he sneaked behind a rock and swarmed into the costume. As he reappeared, the effect created by the sight of him was as great as if a bomb had been dropped out of the bland sky on to that peaceful strip of beach. Gordon gasped, Fonvisin knuckled his eyes, and as for the old man himself, he sat, turned to stone, with the trembling palm of one hand clutching the rock behind him. In that half-second's flash of surprise, he had recognized the lamentable relic as his own, and in the same moment tried to devise some way of disowning it. As Constantine entered the water, he realised that Francis knew: more, Francis had seen him in it: more still, she would be sure to allude to it at this moment. The effort required to prepare himself for the onslaught was considerable. Crossing his hands on his stomach, as he always did in times of stress, he gripped his heavy watch-chain so hard that it nearly snapped in two. But his guardian angel was with him that day.

While the comments and speculations of the two men ran their course, Francis merely looked at him, and quietly smiled. She did not mention the thing again, either then, or ever afterwards. The same evening he cycled down to the village and bought his own bathing-costume from Constantine for five hundred drachmae, and sent Francis the largest bunch of flowers she had ever seen. She had redeemed herself.

But if the redemption was complete by her forbearance on this occasion, their friendship never recovered its first delightful intimacy. It was due perhaps to the constraining presence of Gordon and Fonvisin, and later of Walsh. With their arrival things had changed a good deal. But the system of gifts continued, though modified, mercifully, by the presence of the others. Through them, he complimented her.

There was the question of music, for instance. Finding that both she and Fonvisin were passionately fond of music, he carefully sounded Walsh on the subject of gramophones and records. On the latter's advice he procured, at a great price (for the Greek Customs laws are as greedy as they are stupid), a Ginn horn gramophone from England, and from time to time gave a concert of records on the small plateau which overlooked the sea, in the grounds of his villa. At first, so successful had been the idea, so grateful and enthusiastic the visitors, that hardly an evening went by without a small party arriving at the Villa Pothetos, with the request that a concert should take place; but later, owing to the vast attendance of peasants, who, though caring nothing for the music, considered an evening spent watching the foreigners enjoy themselves an excellent diversion from the tedium of village life, the custom was only kept up about once a month; and while anyone was quite at liberty to go to the Villa Pothetos at any time and play the gramophone to himself, nevertheless, the public concerts had a status which no amount of secret music-playing could ever have achieved. In this matter again, as in most, Rumanades could not resist the temptation to invest something which of itself was nothing more than a social gathering with some of the trappings of ceremonial. The tormenting desire for gesture was present in his least actions.

With the concerts (which, be it noted, were known simply as "The Music") he indulged his talents in a sweet deception of the priest. Perhaps the desire to place ecclesiastical sanction on yet another of his treats for visitors was due to the fact that he feared the malice of tongues: which might insinuate that, if he was capable of driving a hard bargain with the most poverty-stricken of his own countrymen, when it came to the question of maintaining what almost amounted to a foreign court, no expense was considered too great, no effort spared. But whatever the reason, it is a matter of fact that he took himself to the priest on the occasion of the second concert, and informed him, gratuitously, that the music was sacred, and was given in honour of the patron saint.

The natural consequence of such a move was that the priest felt himself called upon to represent the Greek Church at the function; and subsequently the two gap-toothed old monks from the Leucothean monastery on the cliff-top considered *their* presence necessary for the preservation of the properties.

With a gravity against which mere laughter is powerless, some sort of ceremonial was evolved. Chairs were provided, where formerly the ground or the bole of an olive tree had been considered seat enough. To the left of the gramophone the two skeletons in Christ would sit, sleeping profoundly, with their beards on their laps. To the right, Rumanades and the priest, unconscionably bored, grinding their yawns between their teeth; in front, across the tiny plateau, or on the edge of it, among the olives, the heterogeneous collection of peasants and the foreigners (who refused to sit) arranged themselves. The effect was an impressive one. Gordon on one occasion said that it reminded him of nothing so much as a meeting of shareholders, enquiring into the causes for the total ruin of their company. The expression on the faces of Rumanades and priest, during the more felicitous passages of a Beethoven sonata or a Mozart symphony, were the expressions of a gigantic boredom. Frankly, like little old children, the two monks slept. They slept; and only the shuddering concussions of Wagner's lighter lyrical work could wake them. As for the peasants, they could sit by the hour, uncomprehending, unappreciative, simply watching the foreigners or the gramophone; their dark eyes moving from the polished wood to the faces of the old man or the priest.

Though the five foreigners were punctilious in attending the public music, only Marlowe and Francis ever availed themselves of the privilege to play the gramophone in the Villa Pothetos itself. For reasons best known to himself, Walsh, although as interested, never did. His attendance at the Villa Pothetos was purely a matter of business.

Rumanades had given him permission to use the piano, and once a month, with unfailing regularity, he and Gordon would indulge their imaginations in the composition of a song – a jazz song. This, amazingly enough, constituted business for Walsh. When Marlowe was first told that the boy made a living, more than a living, by composing these ball-room tit-bits, he was frankly incredulous. But Walsh convinced him.

"We get nearly all our ideas from the Elizabethans," he said. "We touch them up, bastardise, sentimentalise, bowdlerise the damn things, and ram them down the throats of the G.B.P. Not the tunes. The words."[85]

Slightly indignant, Marlowe had turned away, with some casual remark about having sufficient conscience to avoid doing things like that. "It's useless being scrupulous these days," replied Walsh in a flat small voice. "Surely you've found that out?"

It was Gordon who produced another point of view on the matter. To him, there was something violently funny about their imaginative reconstructions of Elizabethan and Jacobean lyrics. "It's the thinnest possible edge of satire," he said. "It's beautifully ironic. For instance – last year I wrote the words, and Walsh the music, of a song which we called 'To Be or Not to Be, That Is the Question.' It was a whacking success. Every time the old man plugged in the wireless set it came moaning through. Whenever possible I listened in to it. It gave me a really grand sense of tragic idiocy whenever I heard it and thought of those strange dark moods in *Hamlet*. The tremendous language of *that* strapped into two-syllable words for the mumbling, sweating sons of bitches to croon. Perhaps you don't see it."

"I'm afraid I don't," said Marlowe coldly.

"Why, it's really destructive satire in its way. Though for the life of me I can't explain how," said Gordon.

And to Marlowe no explanation would have been sufficient to condone what to him was vandalism – vandalism pure and simple. What was more puzzling still, when he mentioned the subject again to Walsh, he found him not so unscrupulous as the times seemed to demand. "I could understand you taking music, phrases and things, to work into jazz songs, but it seems a bit...a bit queer...to take poetry." And Walsh's reply was: "Poems don't matter. They're all part of language. To bastardise music would be the final sacrilege."

One day, as he was sitting in the bare upstairs room of the Villa Pothetos with Francis, during a recital of music, he mentioned this curious display of scruples to her, half inviting comment. When he had finished, she said: "I don't think either matters, do you? After all, nothing is original. All art is copied in some degree...even *Hamlet* was.[86] Why should it matter to what lengths people go? People who are keen on life, any kind of life, don't mind. It's only antiquarians and philosophers who feel tender about the past, and they don't really count." To which rather muddled piece of thought Marlowe produced what seemed to him to be the correct response: a long, reproving silence. As the music began he found himself studying the grave face of the girl, with its sombre preoccupation, and he wondered why she should present such an enigma to himself; was it, perhaps, a sentimental fiction on his part? Yet the quiet tone of her voice, the lift and fall of beautiful apathy in her body, these forbade the thought. Perhaps, he concluded lamely, for he was never beyond the reach of malice when it concerned the generation which was not his, it was all part of a semi-romantic self-abandonment to languor; the modish pallor, the almost Keatsian fading....

But the actual story was a different one, and he was told it on just such an evening, when they were sitting in the wide balcony-window of the room, playing music and talking: Francis herself told him, in the bare syllables of a language which divested it of drama, and left the grubby trifles of reality bare and without comment.

The only child of a country parson and his wife, the first ten years of her life had been spent in the north. The memories of that part of it were vague, with here and there sharp lights, definitive sights or sounds or smells. The gloomy stone house in which they lived, with its narrow fireplaces: she remembered that. The drawing-room with its ugly furniture, vast lumpy sofa, cretonne covered in roses. The photographs of grandpapa and grandmama, and numerous relations, rusting and fading in their cheap frames. The little shaggy dog, her only companion, which they had named Andrew; the rows of dusty books in her father's study whose smell was enchanting; father himself, sitting alone with a pipe in his mouth, soothing his bald head with his fingers as he wrote his sermons, and telling her to go away and pray to God to make her a good girl and prevent her from talking to the grocer's boy in the road again; father again, gesticulating and raging from the pulpit in the damp church, making her sick with fear of the Lord of Hosts; Communion: this is the body and blood of our Saviour: gnome-like little girl with black hair, rising to her feet at the horror of the thought, spitting and spitting and wiping her mouth on her long sleeves: the deep note in father's voice as he said: "I have taken the trouble to get you admitted to the sacred mystery of communion with our Lord Jesus Christ before most children, and what thanks do I get for it?"

"But the blood and the body?" she was crying.

Afterwards her mother soothed her and said: "Silly, it's only an idea.

It's really wine and bread." But she would never take Communion again after that. It made her sick to think of it. And they did not dare to try and make her.

Lying in bed in her tiny attic room, next to the maid's, with Andrew, curled like a warm ball of life on her feet, she would listen to the rain beating exuberantly among the apple-trees in the orchards at the back of the house, and remember that moment when warm blood of Christ cloyed on her tongue, sweet and sickening. She was a very solitary little girl. On fine days she would walk across the moors with Andrew to watch the Girl Guide practices. She envied them their uniforms and their extraordinary hats; loved the ragged discipline of that mob of girls, blue with cold and with dew-drops trembling at their noses, as they manoeuvred and tramped the wet moor-land grass.

The Guide Mistress had stopped and spoken to her once, and she had at once fallen madly in love with her. Her name, she knew, was Hilda Clagg, and she lived in the big house at the end of the village road to Madly. She was twenty and lived at home with six brothers and her father, who was on the Exchange in London. She was a bit fat in her guide-uniform but otherwise utterly ravishing. For the whole winter the child Francis had been absorbed in this passion, in which Andrew was her only confidant: and for a whole winter of chilly days she trudged the frosty roads in the hope of seeing her beloved.

It was very melancholy to stand thus, afternoon after afternoon, outside the wet wall of the cemetery, waiting, while the yew trees shivered in the wind and dropped rain. Sometimes at home, sitting in front of the mean little coal fire, when everyone else was out, she would take Andrew into her arms and pretend that he (poor fellow) was Hilda. She would make impassioned speeches to him and hug him, but it wasn't very much fun. And he only looked faintly reproving and embarrassed. Then one day, from boredom, she had crept into her father's study and stolen a book from the shelves – just any book, it didn't matter which – so that she could pass the time until dinner. Opening it at random, under her fingers she found the very poem which for ever afterwards was to remind her, heaven only knows why, of Hilda: remind her of the way Hilda had turned to the solemn little girl standing in her goloshes in the moor grass and said: "When you're old enough, dear, will you join my troop? We have such fun. You'd love it."

> *Season of mists and mellow fruitfulness,*
> *Close bosom-friend of the maturing sun.*[87]

She had caught her breath with sudden pain at the flowing lines, and the lushness of it all. And through it all she could see the round face of

Hilda, with its blue eyes, and the dimples cleft in each cheek. She was almost crying with the pain of such loveliness when her mother came in and said: "Wash your hands, dear. It's nearly dinner time."

Cold meat with strips of white fat; cold greasy potatoes; and green pungent pickles.

On the sideboard, waiting, were three portions of cold rhubarb tart and some condensed milk in a jug. Father took condensed milk with his tart, and they put up with clotted custard. It was always the same.

That night, as they sat down to dinner under the reproachful ticking of the grandfather clock, her father had said, priding himself on his shrewdness: "What was the book you borrowed from my little library to-day, Francis? I noticed one missing when I came in. Was it the Keats?"

She choked on a mouthful and said: "Yes, daddy," without lifting her eyes to his large benevolent face.

"Ah! So it was Keats?"

"Yes, daddy."

"Whatever could the child want with Keats at her age?" asked her mother.

"What were you reading, my dear?"

"I don't know, daddy."

"Come, come, you must know what you were reading." She gulped the noisome forkful of pickles and gulped: "Something about mellow fruits."

"Ah!" he said with pleasure, "*ah!*"

"Season of fruits and mellow mistfulness," she was thinking, consumed by panic. The words were going round and round in her head: "Season of sweets and misty mellowness."

"Season of mists and mellow fruitfulness," began her father, kindly giving her the benefit of his pulpit voice. He continued vibrantly to the end of the poem, his voice lifting and falling beautifully to the flow of the words, his right hand making small illustrative gestures with his pickle-fork.

She listened with a cold potato poised and ready to put in her mouth. When he had finished he said: "Well! That was it, wasn't it?"

"Yes, daddy."

She did not raise her eyes, but she knew he was sitting there, his bald head pushed over on one side, his dark eyes bright with unction.

"Now, dear," said her mother, "do you remember what it was all about? Tell us in your own words. Let's see if you understand the poem."

What did it mean? With her eyes cast down on her plate she suffered the poem again. Trees, yes: the rain threshing in the orchard; but above all, Hilda's face with its enticing dimples, and the provocative look in the blue eyes.

"I don't know."

"Oh, come, come," said her mother mildly, "surely you know what it's all about."

"Autumn," said the child Francis, flashing up her eyes for a moment, "and the fruits getting ripe."

"Good," said her father in a large way, packing pickled onions away in his check, "*good!*"

But it was more than that, much more than that. It was all those dreadful rainy days she had spent, standing under the wet cemetery wall with Andrew, her feet wet through her goloshes. It was the frost on the road, and the shrunk winter hedges. But above all it was Hilda, and the tears and loneliness of winter evening. Yes, it was Hilda.

She had been glad to escape from the draughty dining-room that evening, to sit over the small coal fire with Andrew on her lap, wondering why she should feel afraid of Keats. The book she put back, sneaking into the empty study at a propitious moment, and never took down again. The next day, as if, it seemed, Fate had chosen to warn her in advance, she heard that Hilda Clagg was to be married.

She was marrying a young officer in some regiment or other, and a month or two later Francis was at the wedding. Her father was performing the ceremony, and she and her mother were plunged into the thick of it.

Hymen[88] managed things in a peculiarly clumsy way that day. It rained from early morning until night. The church roof leaked loudly throughout the service. The bride fell down the slippery steps of the church and put her heel through her veil; the bridegroom, who was a small, shiny, black little fellow with a faint tracing of regimental down on his upper lip, and a fearsomely nervous air, had contracted a cold the day before, and supplied the necessary answers in a voice which creaked and wheezed with catarrh. The baker's dozen of brothers were driven into a wall by the local taxi-driver and arrived on foot, soaked and breathless. It was the most miserable of faces.

But to Francis, who stood against the cold stone wall, it was a tragedy of gigantic proportions; each new irritation only served to deepen the general sense of gloom. Hilda looked bulbous and red in her veil; and her wheezing little polecat of a bridegroom looked as if he were going to die of influenza at any moment.

Walking home through the rain, she felt numb and dead herself, as hard and bleached as a marble tombstone; she did not even bother to answer the remarks which her mother addressed to her. Cold and desolate was the damp vicarage with its circle of dripping rhododendron bushes. The fire had not been lit. The photographs of her relations and ancestors, dead and alive, slowly faded on the mantelpiece.

Her attic was cold, too. Sitting on the bed, tucking her knees under her, she stared out bitterly on the long flights of rain sweeping down on the landscape beyond the orchard. The windows clicked faintly in the wind.

Somewhere, at this very moment, Hilda Clagg was sitting in a Daimler, being whirled up to London with her husband, for a short honeymoon. London!

Over there, beyond the purple smudges that were hills, somewhere over there, was London. At that moment London seemed to her to be a New Jerusalem; never did philosopher desire Utopia more fervently than she, that day, desired London; it was a long time before her wish was answered.

After that, she went away to school: a modest school, but of a high tone. Here she was undistinguished in her achievements. Prize Day always found her among the audience, Sports Day was much the same. The only thing she could screw her interest to was the drawing lessons. At drawing she was reputed to be quite good. She drew until she was eighteen.

By that time daddy was getting on, and mummy was a little bit worried about the money. Would she (Francis) consider taking a job as secretary to some Church Society or other? If she would like to, her father would only have to say a word to the dear bishop.

Her father wrote her a series of charming letters, tactfully insinuating that, though he had promised her a year in London at an art school, she would by no means have to renounce drawing if she took the job which the dear bishop had mentioned. She could draw in her spare time. The scenery around there was very lovely if she wanted to do rural scenes, etc. And anyway, he didn't think there would be enough money to give her an allowance to go and live in London by herself.

Francis, who suspected the real reason for this tightening of the parental purse-strings, wrote back and asked if they would consider letting her have a year or two at the Varsity. She could get a degree in economics (or some such useless subject). Father, falling heavily into the trap, wrote back and said that he would like nothing better than that his girl should get a degree and equip herself for the game of life. If she really wanted to go to Oxford (what a pity she was not a boy: she could have gone to his old college), he thought he could find the money somewhere.

In order to make perfectly sure, Francis wrote and solicited full particulars from a mildewed lady don, whom she had once met in a seaside boarding-house during a summer holiday; and passed them on to father.

Reading the letter in which he repeated, quite definitely, that he could find the money for three years at Oxford, she smiled quietly to herself.

The matter was allowed to slide for the rest of the term; she answered neither her father's importunate letters, which demanded whether she was to take Responsions,[89] or to try, instead, to get five credits in the Oxford Locals, nor the angular blandishments of the don.

On her arrival home she immediately stated her intention of studying art in London for a year. That began it. Father, protesting that he could not afford it, was told that it would cost less than the amount necessary to send her to Oxford; cornered, indignant, feeling as if he had been swindled, he backed into the open and said that, whatever happened, the money was his and he could spend it in exactly the way he wanted. Then Francis: "But where is the objection to my going to London?"

The objections were numerous, and based, for the most part, on fear. Father produced one of the prettiest lines in mission talks she or anyone else had ever heard, while mother knitted, sucked her teeth, and contributed an occasional mite of reproof and sweet forbearance.

"Of course we want to do the best for you, my dear, and we wouldn't think of making you do what you didn't want to do, but really, there's no knowing what might happen to an innocent little schoolgirl in London."

Father, fortified by what remained over from a niggardly morning Communion, launched a fleet of objections and blazed away for an hour or so. He began with the trials and temptations of Bohemian life, and ended with the exact statistics of the White Slave Traffic ravages in the larger cities.

Then he locked himself in his study and wrote an sos to the bishop, asking him to lend a hand. It was all very puzzling, he said; and where did young girls get such ideas from? And exactly how many beans made five?

The bishop, poor old cadaver, came down for an afternoon, swathed in an atmosphere of snuff and Quaker Oats, and lumbered about the house like a patient mastodon, trying, as he put it, "to talk the girl out of it."

"Ai have known yar father, mai dear," he repeated again and again, "for a long long taime naowe, and Ai am grieved, mai dear, grieved and sorely perplexed for him in his dilemma."

But neither his perplexity nor her mother's recriminations could get anything out of her but a sulky: "Well, after all, you've got the money. Go ahead and tell me what you want. I've got to obey you."

That was the only weapon she had in her inadequate armoury, and she used it hard, despite those frequent pangs of contrition which insisted that she really was an ungrateful little bitch, and that her parents were sweet, and were trying their best to help her. Some instinct of self-preservation, some god-given gift of guts (unusual quality) insisted on her facing up to the issue.

The bishop, poor old thing, was really very sweet, apart from his clack about purity, and the lily-white innocence of country girls in a large city. He had a large muffin-like countenance, a great crooked boss of a nose, a vast and bulging body on the smallest pair of bandy legs ever seen. He drank his tea with a relish that seemed not quite ecclesiastical, from the saucer and not from the cup, blowing violently upon it to begin with. And, as he devoured bread and jam, shortbreads and iced cakes, he talked in a vague and rambling, manner about things parochial; when occasion presented itself he managed to stroke Francis' head or arm, shining his loose mouth and bright eyes at her with a debonair and provocative lasciviousness. At odd intervals too, when it occurred to him, he impregnated not only himself but the whole company with snuff, piping, and blowing, into a red handkerchief after each bout, with a really delightful catharsis. It relieved his catarrh, he said, blandly.

The snuff was carried loose in a waistcoat pocket, and each fussy insertion of his fat finger in the flap caused clouds of the stuff to rise around him.

"Well," he said at last, with a sigh, looking round and noticing that there was not a scrap of food left to eat, "Ai see that there's nothing to be done with the lassie. Ai reely don't know *quwhat* to advaise in the circumstances."

He beamed round and wagged a finger at the object of the family's despair. The job he had offered her, he said, was still vacant. He only hoped that her good sense would reassert itself before she caused her dear parents much more pain and anxiety. Swarming up to his full four feet six of height, he shook himself free of crumbs and brushed his paunch with a fat hand. He said it was time he was leaving. "There," said her mother as he passed out through the front door, clasping her hands, and registering conviction, "there goes a really *good* man. A GOOD man."

No doubt. No doubt. The pity of it was that, good as he was, he was not prepared to be helpful. Ah! well, thought Francis, standing in front of the fire with her hands at her hips, the clergy! What did one expect of them anyway?

Meanwhile the bishop was being helped into his car. He turned a carbuncular red face up to Francis' father and said, with an incredible leer and a wink: "Laugh the girl out of it. Make her see the silly side of herself. Make her laugh." And, laughing himself, he crawled into the car, and was driven away.

The family skirmishes began again that night, after dinner, and continued over a period of days. In one way, she had them by the short hairs. She would not admit that, if she did take the clerical job, she would do it willingly; in fact, she lost no opportunity of telling them that, if she *did* take the job, she would take it unwillingly, and under compulsion. Of course all this nearly "broke poor father up": he was pretty "seedy" as it was: his sermons were getting shorter and shorter: his congregation was getting fewer and fewer: and what was the upshot to be? What indeed?

Francis continued to the very end, with a desperate and sullen determination. True she was conscience stricken at times, true she wept a good deal to think how much she had loved dear mummy and daddy before all THIS happened; but only in private. To the world in general, and to her parents in particular, she presented an unflinching face. In itself this was no mean feat, especially as her mother indulged in hysterics whenever possible in order to melt her resolve, and insinuated that if she didn't give way soon her father (who, be it remembered, was "pretty seedy") would be sure to have a nervous breakdown. Francis looked the other way, swallowed the mawkish lump in her throat, squeezed the tears back into her eyes, and whistled the dog out for a walk across the moors.

Season of mists and mellow fruitfulness.

One can be horribly lonely at eighteen. Even old Andrew, who was quite a passable companion for her youthful ecstasies, was getting on now. The vicarage was utterly dull, damp and depressing, with its narrow fireplaces and smudgy coal fires. In the village she knew nobody. At home there was no privacy, not even in the attic room which was nominally her own. She tramped the wet moorlands with a savage desperation in her – the desperation of tears which in some way was an equivalent to the moods of the misty countryside, to the long slants of rain, or the frost on the moonlit roads. In the woods sometimes she experienced the real despairs of youth, to see the trees, soaked and limp, dripping water, the pulp of rotten loam on the fieldways; and sitting down she would weep, pressing her pale face into her fingers, and saying, in a trembling agitation: "Oh, Andrew, Andrew, what can we *do? What can we do?*"

All her money was spent on books. Sometimes she took a bus into the nearest town and bought all the cheap edition novels, or second-hand cast-outs, she could find. The comfort of books! They were one escape from the importunities of the bloody vicar and his spouse. Sitting on her bed with a rug over her cold knees she would devour them, thankful that they could drive her into worlds beyond the reach of ordinary people. So intensely did she live in them, that for days at a time she would feel, as she would have put it, "half seas over,"[90] living in the shape and colour of another's thought.

With Lawrence's eyes and mind, she explored Sardinia,[91] pin-point in definition and vivid, like a flame among those cold bleak days; every page of the book shook and warmed her like wine. For a week she was so gorged on it that she read nothing else; was content to sit and let the memory of it play upon her like a jet of fire as she drew and drew in her cheap sketch-books.

On the shelf of her room grew a line of books, which her mother noted with disapproval every morning as she superintended the ministrations of the maid: *Sons and Lovers*[92] (which she found, for some reason, unreadable); the Georgian Anthology[93] of two years back; books of poems by Yeats, Drinkwater, Blunden[94]; a few shilling books of Artists and Their Work: Monet, Van Gogh, Titian, Botticelli; a History of Art; and a backless copy (perhaps the most precious thing in the room) of Aldington's *Dream in the Luxembourg*.[95]

"The girl is getting queer," said her mother. "She's moping over a lot of old books in her room day after day. I think we ought to do something."

Father sneaked up one afternoon when Francis was out and cast a Christian eye over the pathetic little collection of treasures on which his daughter had spent all her pocket-money.

He started when he noticed that there were two books there by that immoral fellow Lawrence.[96] The situation was one that called for gravity, and heavy treatment. Sitting down on the bed, he made a professional examination of the books, picking them out one by one, glancing through them, and putting them on the bed at his side. It was ghastly, he was thinking, ghastly that a daughter of his…. He wondered what sort of action would be suitable to the occasion. The punishment must be made to fit the crime, by Jove. He thought perhaps it might be advisable to have a talk with her in his study; but then, in his mind's eye, he could see her, that beautiful, rather gawky school-girl, challenging him with her dark eyes and her sullen mouth.

He picked up the *Dream in the Luxembourg* and read it through, his eyes bulging. "The idea," he said aloud, holding it between finger and thumb, "THE IDEA!"

The course of action which he finally decided upon was perhaps only too characteristic of a Christian and an incurable fingernail-biter. The offensive books he put under his arm, and, having replaced the others carefully in their original order, he tiptoed downstairs and burnt them in the kitchen stove.

Francis did not notice the loss that evening, but the next morning, waking early, she ran her eye down the line of books and saw that the most precious were missing. Heaven only knows what premonition told her to hunt in the grates. The maid was about to empty the kitchen grate when she reached the kitchen. Sure enough, there at the back lay a vast wad of ashes: layer upon layer of crinkled black paper. Quietly she raked out the remains. A single page had escaped the fire. She turned to the early morning light which feebly penetrated the grimy kitchen window and read:

*Shall I ever be happy again?*
And I began to kiss her mouth
*Until we were both dazed and trembling...*[97]

If there was any doubt at all, that settled it.

Haggard with rage, and shrill of voice, she tackled them at breakfast, and was met with a cooing response. What books did she mean? They hadn't seen any books.

"I found the ashes in the kitchen grate," she said wearily. Her father soaked a finger of bread and butter in the boiled egg and said that perhaps the maid had done it by mistake.

"Agnes," he called bravely, "Agnes."

"Yes, Sir."

"Did you put any of Miss Francis' books in the kitchen grate?"

The maid, sturdy and bandy-legged, was not going to be blamed for anything she hadn't done. She put her hand on her hip and said, "No, Sir. You did, yesterday afternoon. Just before tea-time."

"So you did," said Francis, "and deliberately."

She burst into tears and ran from the room, climbing the stairs three at a time. In her own room she lay down on the bed, trembling from head to foot, and turned her face to the wall.

Downstairs, sitting in his study, pen in hand, father racked his brains for clichés and truisms with which to garnish his Sunday sermon; the text he had chosen was, curiously enough: "Blessed are the poor in spirit: for theirs is the kingdom of heaven."[98] As he drew idle little faces in the marginal of his blank foolscap he planned yet another exquisite bombination: another fustian rampage from the parish pulpit. In his mind's eye he could see himself, large, grave, and woefully impressive, banging the wood and striking the fires of hell from the flinty souls of his congregation. In the intervals between the orgasmic ardours of invention, however, he thought of Francis weeping upstairs, and felt a little annoyed and ashamed of himself. It was really most annoying the way the young behaved. He began to feel aggrieved, almost as if he had been himself the victim and not the author of the trouble. Yes, if one looked at it logically, she was to blame. It was all this silly business of refusing the bishop's job. And he? He had only wanted to do the best for her, to help her. He sniffed indignantly and added a man in a bowler hat to the other marginal annotations. Yes, that was the truth of the matter. It was he who was betrayed; he had wanted to help her, to make a chum of her, to let her confide in him, to advise her, and finally, he supposed, to marry her off to some nice upright youth.

By the time he had added a tremendous rhetorical question to the existing paragraph of prose, he had begun to feel quite a little Jesus himself, with mother and the bishop as apostles in ordinary, and Francis as a sort of she-Judas.

It was a betrayal, that's what it was, he assured himself. Throwing down his pen with a gesture, he indulged in a sound which in late Victorian novels, was represented thus:

"PSHAW."

Stepping meekly upstairs (he could still see himself as a saviour), he tramped down the passage and knocked on the door of the attic. No answer came. Opening the door, he peeped in.

Francis lay, stretched out on the narrow bed, asleep, her head in her arms, clutching her black hair in her fingers. From his angle of vision he could see that her eyes were swollen with tears.

"Francis, my dear," he said gruffly.

"What do you want?"

He was so surprised at the immediate response, and at the natural bitterness of the voice, that it quite put him off his stroke. So she was not asleep.

"I came up, " he said loudly, "to implore you to listen to reason. Things can't go on like this, you know. You're only making things worse for yourself. I only want to help you."

She began to weep again soundlessly, gripping her teeth on her wrist. Pleased to have her at a slight disadvantage for once, he went on rather more quickly: "This job, for instance. It's not a thing to be sniffed at, you know. You ought to be grateful for a chance to earn two or three pounds a week. At your age I would have been only too glad. And the bishop has been such a brick. Why not reconsider it, old girl?"

Walking up and down the small room, he composed his face in an appearance of deep humanity and consolation. The books he had not burnt, he noticed, had disappeared. She had locked them carefully away in her school tuck-box.

"What do you think?" he said.

There was no answer at all. Only her shoulders clenched and un-clenched under the soundless weeping. He could see a segment of white teeth as it gripped her wrist.

"If you loathe it," he said gently, "after a year or so we could talk over this business about London. What do you think?"

Turning her body sideways, she said in a voice so choked with disgust, rage, fear, and despair that it was a mere whisper in the silence of the room:

"Anything. *Anything to get out of this morgue.*"

The next day she went to live in the cathedral town, with the blessings of daddy, mummy, and the bishop, and earn her own living. She took with her a little money, a trunk of clothes, and the books.

For a time the blessed quiet of that provincial town was more wonderful than even London could have been. True she had little money; true she had no friends; but, on the credit side, she had a room of her own, enough food, and an occasional shilling or two to spend on books, on cartridge paper for sketching, on cheap books of reproductions.

At her job she worked like a fiend. In the evenings she went to night classes and learnt typing and short-hand. Once a week on the sly she attended a life class at the local art school. Any time that was left over she spent lying on the frayed carpet of her room, in front of a tiny coal fire, eating apples and drawing: or reading. In this time she managed to do several things; among others, she wrote an impetuous, arrogant, formless novel about village life in general and village parsons in particular, which no one would publish. She did a vast luminous fresco on the wall of the local R.C. church (the commission for this she got by pretending that she was of the Faith) and received the munificent sum of three pounds seventeen and sixpence (after deducting the price of paint, size, etc.) to crown her labours. It was exhausting but inspiriting. She went out into the street with the money burning in her purse, and ate a really gigantic meal. After which she bought herself a bottle of Old Tawny port, a virgin seven and sixpenny book – *but a new book!* – and went back to her room, exultant and weary. What did it matter if the trams wailed outside, if the streets were moist in drizzle: she could let down the shutters, and light the tails of paper at the bottom of the grate, and be quite alone. Alone! She lay down on the floor, snug on cushions of her own making, and sipped the belly-wearying, diuretic stuff, feeling more lordly than ever Cleo[99] felt, drifting on Nile waters in her barge.

Once the bishop called for tea. He crawled up the seven flights of stairs to her attic, for the most part on his hands and knees, and burst into her room, puffing and snorting with fatigue. He had come, he said, to see if everything was going along all right and if she was happy in her new job. He was heavily avuncular for an hour or two, and quite filled the room in snuff. It is true he took every advantage to lay his hands on her hair, or stroke her arm, but all with such a delightfully debonair lasciviousness that she was quite warmed. He produced a set of pocket chess and, sitting on the floor in front of the fire, they played a rousing match which he easily won. Altogether she liked him very much, and was quite sorry when he left; leaning from her high window she watched him didder across the road to the car with his pre-natal stoop, turning round from time to time, at his own peril, to wave gallant good-byes to her. But that was the last she ever saw of him, for the following week her long chance cropped up, and she took it in her stride.

*Wanted*:

A young lady of good appearance and education, some knowledge of business, shorthand and typing, etc., for Sewing office in London. Enquire BXXCZ.

Mr. Emmanuel Glanders was a bright Jew. He sized her up the moment she entered the room and, having received proofs of her ability to type, take shorthand dictation and book-keep, explained the job to her.

"The job," he said, "is not one that requires a great amount of energy. You will merely spend your time going out and keeping an eye on our two branch shops in the West End, and booking enquiries and orders through to us. It's a slack job but a responsible one. It's worth two pounds ten exactly to me. Mind you, I have a regular under-manager up there to report to me if you get slack. If you do…phut!" He made an expressive gesture and snapped his finger and thumb. "Well, what do you think?"

"I think," said Francis nervously, "I'd like three pound a week for a job like that. I've got to live, you know, and look decent for interviews. Two ten is the borderline."

Inside herself she was trembling, scared of her own bravery.

"Well," he said, "that's fair enough. I tell you what. Leave your address here. I'll interview all the other applicants first, and if I can't get anyone educated and all that, I'll consider your proposal."

With her heart beating uncomfortably loud she swept out of the offices. That, she thought, was the end. She would never get the job. She had missed her chance. Almost she was tempted to run back into the inner office of Mr. Glanders, past the formidable rows of secretaries, and accept. But she hadn't the courage to do that.

The next day, with her breakfast, she got a postcard.

Would you care to talk over my proposal again. Saturday afternoon as you are in a job?

Yours truly,

EM. GLANDERS.

The result of the business was that she found herself accepted on probation for six months under Mr. Glanders' professional eye; after that time, if she proved capable and proficient, she was to go south – to London.

The probation did not last as long as that, however, for Francis, getting her teeth into the job, found out nearly all there was to be known about it. Mr. Glanders was delighted with her. The time went by so quickly that when, in the third month, he suggested that she might as well get started, she was surprised at the amount of her probation which had already passed.

Nevertheless, as she sat in a third-class compartment of the south bound express, she looked out over the flat, knobbly country she was leaving with a pang of something like regret. There is always a Hail and Farewell left in us, even for the places and the people we abhor. Mother and daddy had made a special trip into the town to see her off. They really were quite decent about it all, and quite a bit annoyed that their daughter had actually learnt to drive around a bit in the world under her own steam. The old man produced a cheque for a fiver, and intimated that if she was hard up for money at any time…. Mother, slightly more practical, sneaked open Francis' suit-case while the train was still standing in the station and slipped into it a little book of warning essays about the great city. By some fluke or other she managed to avoid stumbling upon the small yellow contraception manual which Francis had herself (partly from curiosity, partly from a feeling that she would need it at some time) added to her collection of books. As the train yanked out of the station, she leaned from the window, smiling good-bye and waving. Father held his hat forlornly out to her, as if engaged in making a really fruitless collection.

Mother began to sniff into her handkerchief, and then, struck by an idea, dashed forward, caught up with the carriage, and said: "You will remember to be *good*, dear? Promise me you'll be *good!*"

"Yes. Yes," said Francis. "Good-bye," and the metal wheels took up the refrain, with a gathering "Yess. Yess. Good-bye. Yess. Yess. Good-bye," getting faster and farther as they drew away across the fields.

> *London, thou art of townes A per se.*
> *Sovereign of cities, seemliest in sight,*
> *Of high renown, riches and royalty;*
> *Of lords, barons, and many a goodly knight,*
> *Of most delectable lusty ladies bright;*
> *Of famous prelatis, in habitis clerical,*
> *Of merchants full of substance and of might:*
> *London, thou art the flour of Cities all.*[100]

It was rather a pity that London proved to be none of these things. For nothing had she read *The Oxford Book of English Verse*. After a month or two at work, living in an expensive room in Theobald's Road, she found that London, like the lilies which fester, smelt far worse than weeds. But it had a wild rancour of life which seemed authentic at first, and whose influence took some time to wear off.

The job, however, was by no means as easy as the cheerful Mr. Glanders had suggested. It absorbed a good part of her time – from eight to one every morning, and from two to seven. But, for all that, what did it matter? She was near enough to her picture galleries to see the latest exhibitions. She could go to life-classes at night.

She could see the latest films from France and Russia.[101] But the loneliness of being isolated, with no one to share her enthusiasm, was beginning to tell on her. It was difficult to bottle her delights up for her free hours.

More than once she let herself in for future trouble, by committing small errors of tactics in business hours. She turned up occasionally with a book under her arm that did not quite meet with the approval of the lecherous little Mr. Rollins; once she dropped a casual remark about free love and marriage which was quizzed. She befriended Millie: and anyone at the office who befriended Millie couldn't be quite decent, for Millie, quite happily and unashamedly, was living in sin with a sailor whom she was too poor to marry. Francis rather admired her for the casual way she talked about it; the utter consternation in the office, when Millie ingenuously produced some trifling anecdote about the connubial felicities, was very splendid.

"It's nice," she would say, "to have a boy to get into bed with. Makes you all warm." Then, with a giggle, "You don't need no blankets either."

The superior typists and virginal stocktakers would sniff, powder their noses, and stalk out for lunch with the most crushing posterior-action. They were waiting for her to arrive one day in (the felicities of jargon!) A CERTAIN CONDITION. Then they could snarl round and say: "I told yer so, didn't I?" It was a mystery to them why she didn't get the sack. Mr. Rollins himself had remarked darkly, chewing the voluptuous words hard among his false teeth: "The girrl's little better tharn a common whoore." Only her obvious poverty and efficiency at her job saved her.

But if Millie was splendid as a personality she was no use at all as a friend, and it was not until Francis met Reuben that she found the need satisfied.

Reuben was a young man who arrived one day at her boarding-house, armed with a tattered suit-case, a type-writer, a bundle of dirty washing slung from a stick, and a terrier under his arm. He was dressed in a baggy brown suit, bulging at the knees, a black hat of alarming proportions, and an Austrian briar pipe; his nails were clogged with thick black printer's ink.

Francis was sitting in the lounge at the time, and through the open door she heard his arrival; heard his calm assured voice telling the landlady that her attic room was not worth more than twenty-three shillings a week, plus breakfast and washing and baths. And what is more, heard the old lady climbing down in price, until she grudgingly accepted his terms.

The lift of the young man's voice as he spoke was almost insolently assured: "Right," he said, flinging his hat on the communal rack; "done. Now, Mrs. Fleming, will you send this bundle to the wash, and let me have a bath before dinner. As you see, I'm filthy." He *was*, she noticed, pretending to be absorbed in her book, but stealing an occasional quick glance out through the lounge door. He was utterly filthy. His face was clothed in a mild ruff of coppery hair; he needed, not only a shave, but a hair-cut. But he was warm and lively to look at as he stood there at ease in his shabby clothes.

At dinner, which for some reason he ate in the boarding-house that night, he stared at her a good deal in an interested way, and when they got up together to go upstairs he followed slowly behind her. With a curious feeling of panic she reflected that there was only a flimsy wood partition between their respective attics. As she sat down on the bed, wondering whether she could afford a visit to the cinema that night, she could hear him moving about clumsily in his battered shoes.

For a few days, however, she lost sight of him, being busy with work and amusements of her own. One night, when she got back fairly late from the cinema, she heard the typewriter going in the next room; and once she heard his cracked voice raised in song. He was singing something in a queer time, and beating out the bars with his hand on the wooden table. But he did not eat another meal in the boarding-house, with the exception of breakfast, which was always taken up to his room in the morning.

One evening she heard him entertaining. There was one other voice besides his own in the room, and through the partition she could catch snatches of tales and songs. It was obviously some sort of celebration, and it continued, to her exasperation, until four o'clock in the morning. She got no sleep at all and was too panicky to knock on the wall (that hoary boarding-house dodge) and tell the two of them to shut up. Afterwards, when his bibulous companion had crashed down the stairs and out into the street, she heard him being violently sick.

"Serve you damn well right," she whispered angrily to the darkness, and drew the blanket up to her chin. "I hope it damn well hurts." And, to judge by the noise of retching, it hurt quite considerably.

But the evening of their meeting did not arrive until a few weeks afterwards. She arrived home late from the office, in a pouring rain, and by the time she had had dinner it was too late to go out.

Outside, in that mournful hinterland of lamp-splashed blackness, the trams soughed and crooned, moving up and down the shiny roads like pillars of fire, thick with crowding humanity. A heavy wind flicked the rain up off the pavements to the ankles of the passers-by, and lugged at the passing umbrellas. She put on a mackintosh and ran down the urchin-squalling length of Devonshire Street, and bought a few pennyworth of fragrant fish and chips in a cone of newspaper.

As she climbed the black staircase to the top landing, she noticed a light under his door, and heard the patter of the typewriter. Easing off her sodden clothes she lit the gas fire, and sat down on the divan bed, trying to read. But the effort of concentration was a failure. She threw down the book, and lay back, wondering what it could be the young man in the next room was writing. Probably an earth-shaking first novel. Having written one herself, she felt disposed to smile with tolerant superiority. How dismal it was to hear the rain flicking at the walls, and the water lisping down the gutters by the window. She felt utterly tired; tired beyond mere physical fatigue, with a weariness of life and everything that moved in this great iron-bound city. Slowly, imperceptibly it was eating her alive, devouring her. She was becoming a unit.

The gas fire ticked out its little measures of shilling warmth. The rain, now in light bursts, now in heavy drifts, squirted along the window-panes, striving to wash out the image of the wet street, shot with gold points of light. London, thou art of townes *A per se!*

The same pall of rain that was sliding to the artificial ground – the concrete crust of a county – the same rain was falling in the south, in Lee Green, in Dulwich, in Camberwell; in the north, in Finchley and Hampstead. The trams still skirled in Lordship Lane and Tulse Hill. The hurdy-gurdy throb of the eager electric train hung in the air like a doom at Streatham. And out of London the beautiful counties lay, hushed in darkness, while the trains set out trailing their noisy streamers across England, foaming sparks in the rain. If she could have conquered the apathy of that moment she would have wept.

Then, in that moment, she was aware that the type-writer in the next room was silent. Everything was drenched in a local silence; only the rain and the trams, and the gas fire ticking.

She heard him push back his chair and get up. Lying on the narrow bed, she was shaken with fright to hear his footsteps cross to the partition that stood between them.... Her bed was level with the wall. He was so near now that she fancied she could hear him breathing. She was lying on a bed within six inches of him, but out of sight, thank God, out of sight.

As he stood there, so close to her, she began to feel afraid. Was he staring, at the partition behind which she cowered? In the absolute silence she clasped her hands together and pressed them to her forehead, waiting. Waiting? For what? What would come out of the silence? Would he speak to her like a ghost out of an empty wall? He stood there for a long time, not moving, not saying a word. Then he banged once on the wood, so heavily that she feared it would fall down.

"It's ridiculous," she heard him say gruffly, as if half to himself, "it's utterly ridiculous."

What, she wondered, was ridiculous? She wondered whether she should answer, whether she should call out to him, feign anger or indignation. But she was past primness.

He banged again, more loudly, more imperiously.

"What…what is it?" she asked in a shaky voice.

"It's ridiculous," he repeated angrily but more loudly, "going on like this day after day in this bloody tenement."

She said nothing. She lay still on the bed with her eyes closed. She could see him clearly as he stood, menacing fist raised at the wallpapered partition.

"Do you hear me?" he said.

"Yes."

"Well, why don't you answer?"

"There's nothing to say."

Nothing, she thought, nothing at all to say. They felt drugged by the inertia of the hot room and the gentle insinuation of the gas fire. There was nothing to say.

"It's the rain and all these trams," he said, as an afterthought, more gently. "Can you hear the trams?"

"Yes."

"And the rain?"

"Yes," she said; and more angrily, "Yes!"

"Does it make you feel mad with anger?"

"No."

There was little anger in her for all this; only that tremendous apathy, that inebriation, which pushed out its sluggish tentacles into her body and constrained her to lie laxly on the bed with her hand over her eyes.

She heard him walk away from the wall, and stand, rustling papers at the wooden table. At last, with infinite slowness he came back to the partition and tapped gently on it with his knuckles. In a low voice he said: "I suppose you wouldn't care to share a quarter bottle of gin with me?"

She sat up and looked dully round the room. She said nothing, drawing the hanging locks of black hair on one side of her face behind her ear. The silence rose up like a sea and nearly stifled her. With a catch in her throat she said: "All right. I'll come, if you want me to."

She crossed her room and stared at her own pale face in the glass for a long minute. Then, abruptly, she turned off the fire, snapped off the light, and went.

His room was a chaos of untidiness. Everywhere, on chairs, on the bed, on the floor, lay clothes, books, and hundreds of tumbled sheets of music manuscript paper. The terrier was not there. Afterwards, he explained that he had had it put away because it limited his choice of diggings.

He sat in the centre of the room at a gate-legged table, on which the reading lamp cast a cone of bright light. In front of him he had arranged two thick tooth-glasses, and a small bottle of gin. He sat, with his elbows on the polished wood, and his chin in his hands; the light, flung directly upward to his face, showed its leanness and heightened the faintly rufous tint of the skin. His eyebrows were drawn down as he stared into the gloom where she stood, beyond the radius of the lamp's light.

"Come in," he said. "Do come in."

She closed the door behind her and stood, her back pressed to it. Her mind was wholly occupied with an estimate of his face as he sat there, with his smile tilted up to her, his nervous, rather beautiful-fingered hands twirling one of the tooth-mugs. He was older than he seemed, and his face was delicately lined, as if with the first signs of a telling debauchery.

"For God's sake," he said, half humorously, as she did not move, "either come and sit down, or say something to me."

She sat down, rather nervously, at the table, and he poured out a measure of gin, edging the glass to her.

"Can you drink the stuff neat?" he asked, "because I'm afraid there's only tap water to add to it."

"It's all right," she said, and tilted the first sip of gin down her throat. It scalded her.

"In order," he said, "to dispense with all the formalities, I shall tell you all about myself. And then you can do the same. And then we'll know each other."

Reuben was twenty-eight. His parents had died and left him a pound a week and a gift for life and music. In order to supplement his inadequate private means he had become a literary hanger-on in Bloomsbury: there was no devil's job he had not undertaken in his erratic desire to earn a living. "A Johannes Factotum,"[102] he said gravely, "an uninspired hack. Even at times a pimp – a *souteneur*, and what-have-you to elderly ladies." He had done hack research in the British Museum for historical novelists; he had been a personal bodyguard to a conscience-stricken satirist; a chorus-boy; a printer's minion; a publisher's reader; he had even, as he said, tided over the more barren times of life by accepting the favours of elderly Bohemian ladies in exchange for a cash return. Sipping his gin, he smiled gravely across the table, and told the tale with a look of quiet humour. Evidently he had got beyond being appalled by the grubbier vicissitudes of existence; or else they had simply not touched him. He was absorbed in music, and during these years had managed to do two little books on the Elizabethans, and a shilling biography of Berlioz. Of course the returns were in no adequate proportion for the amount of time and energy he had spent, but the job itself was what mattered.

"I wanted to do a book on European folk-music,"[103] he concluded quietly, "so I went abroad with a woman novelist, and while she was hammering out her miserable trash, I collected all the material I could for it. Used to spend all day and night sneaking off to village dances and fêtes and things and writing down tunes."

They had travelled through Italy and Greece as far as Constantinople, and from Constantinople back through the Balkans, Southern Russia and Germany.[104]

"I've got it all here," he said with a rising excitement in his voice, "all of the material's here. In this very room. Look at them." Impetuously he jumped to his feet and walked about gathering up the wads of manuscript in his fingers and scattering the pages over the bed for her to see. "Look! From all over Europe I've got little songs and tunes and things. Isn't it funny?" He put his hands to his hips and gave a quiet ripple of laughter, putting his head back on his shoulders. "Funny to think of all those little European dance tunes being stacked up in this bloody little room." He stood limp for a moment, staring at the litter of manuscript on the bed, in a sudden apathetic concentration which seemed to sharpen his features, make them more haggard, more hungry.

Then, with an impulse of contrition, he sat down again and said: "Sorry. Are you bored by all this?"

"I was wondering," she said coolly, "whether it was worth it – all the things you've been telling me, I mean."

"Worth it?" he said, flushing, "worth it? Of course it's been worth it. The only thing to do when you've got no money, no prospects, no food, is to go in the direction you want to go as hard as you can. One can't afford sentiment these days, you know. It's a privilege of the rich."

She put her sixpenny packet of cigarettes on the table and invited him to help himself.

"Thank heavens," he said. "In another second I should have asked you for one. I knew you smoked. Sometimes I could commit murder for a Woodbine."[105]

"What are you doing now?" she asked coolly; in the sick moment of suspense between her question and his answer she heard her heart ticking over quietly, evenly.

"I work by day in a printing place off the Euston Road. At night I try and get on with my book. I've done very little to date because I'm so tired and dirty at night. I'm still trying to fix up an index for these things."

With the hand, whose long fingers were shaped about the cigarette, he made a wide gesture, whose comprehensiveness reminded her again that not only the bed, the chairs, the cup-board top, were littered with manuscript, but also the floor.

"And now," he said, "tell me about yourself, please, without missing any of the details. I'm interested."

Puffing clods of grey smoke to the sooty ceiling of the room she told him: of daddy and mummy, of the bishop, of Glanders...and, in the telling, felt a deep anger for the whole succession of trivial annoyances; for that great expenditure of energy in a waste of gain.

"My God, yes," he interpolated from time to time, "what toads. What utter toads. What happened next?"

He was the most enthusiastic of listeners. When she had finished the tale he leaned back in the uncomfortable chair and drained his gin. "Guts," he said crisply. "I didn't know girls had as much guts these days." And she felt excessively proud of herself, grateful for his approbation.

"That's the lot," she added, "except that my under-manager paid me a delicate compliment the other day. He ran his hand down the back of my neck and said would I consider living with him if he made me an allowance, and rented a flat for me in Camberwell. I declined the offer, though for a moment I felt so fed up at the thought of working for three pounds a week, when I could earn five or six by doing nothing, that I almost said yes.

"My God, yes," said Reuben, smiling with quick sympathy, "I know just how you felt. Misplaced heroism, though; you should have accepted. In a year you could have had your own studio and done a lot of work."

She made a grimace and shook her head at him.

"Not with this particular person. It made me feel pretty desperate for a day or two, though."

The logical development of friendship between Reuben and Francis takes their history into the field of the literary commonplace; for what is more commonplace in the world to-day than love? And yet, what is more rare? For if the cinema, the Sunday paper, the novel, the dance number, deal almost exclusively with the subject, they are incitements to a manifestly inferior form of this unique disease. And the peculiar distortions which civilisation has imposed upon it, through its own derangements, have given rise to a confusion of terms. There should be two words with which to express the two conditions of this malady; for men have died from time to time and worms have eaten them, but not for the love expressed in jazz tunes, in fashion advertisements, not for the love extolled by bishops, prostituted by society novelists, not for the penny journalist's cipher, the advertisement magnate's index to success. No, not for these.

Francis and Reuben joined that great band of lovers whose acts are played out in a thousand furnished rooms, and tenements, behind soiled curtains, among the dusty furniture of town life; among the bric-à-brac which countless generations of other lovers have passed over without comment. Their desire, too, took colour from their surroundings; from the intrusion of yellow street-lights at night; from the sound of single policemen on patrol at morning, and the shriek and clatter of carts pulling out into the city; from the laughter of prostitutes in the dark streets; from the thousand sounds and smells of the town.

Often lying in bed in the small room they had rented in Millman Street, while Reuben slept fitfully beside her in the darkness, Francis would wonder how it could be that here, in this single little lair, they had built up a world which matched the world outside; that here, in this single cell, they had discovered something which discounted the activities in those millions of cells which made up the gigantic honeycomb. Lying there, staring at the ceiling on which the grimy pattern of light from the corner street-lamp played, she would, in her mind, tunnel those million labyrinthine nooks and coigns,[106] seeking out the other lovers who, like themselves, were trying to make something bright and keen from the mud and despair which surrounded them.

She would take Reuben's sleeping head in her white arms and cherish it, whispering, "Reuben, my darling, my darling," while devotion and tenderness poured out of her trembling body, as water from a fountain.

And if the world outside had its bondages, its infamies and betrayals, they too had their little totems and charms to pit against it; they had their few books, their enthusiasm, and the shaky bed they could creep to when night came. Only the telling need of money was an enemy they could not fight, and one which was quietly to wear them down.

It hurt her to see his lean body when he undressed at evening, grimy and weary; the ruff of hair which grew down the nape of his neck; the ink deeply engrained in his fingernails. Sometimes, too, when they quarrelled, she saw, with fear, how much his control had been worn down; with murderous contrition she would watch him as he lay, face down on the divan, shaken with a small painful fit of weeping. He was ill once, and had to have the doctor, and for a whole night she sat by him while he struggled back from the altitudes of fever to comparative normality.

"Undernourishment," said the doctor calmly. "And you don't look too well yourself, young lady. Are you married?"

"No."

The doctor shook his head kindly, and snapped his bag shut. "He should get away to the country for a holiday."

But three days later, still a little groggy from the after effects, he was back at work.

The first stifling summer days came to the dusty street, bringing the regular white hospital ambulance, which fitted down the length of their street like a death-butterfly

They came to dread the luxurious purr of its engine, and the insinuating tinkle of the bell, as it stopped outside the houses. The stretcher-bearers would hurry in at the wide front door. At all the windows opposite the neighbours would crowd behind curtains and peep out, fascinated by the apparatus of death. They would stare hungrily at the open front door, the damp crumbling plaster walls and the strip of threadbare lino showing: until the men came into sight, scrambling down the stairs with something on the stretcher. And then the old women watching would begin to weep, quietly, into their handkerchiefs.

It was during the stress of the summer that she first felt that dour necessity to fight the enemy that was wearing them down; felt the need, in the face of their own shabbiness, to try and make life a decent thing, and their attempt at love worthy of its enemy. But it was not much good. Physical dirt, weariness, ennui, weather, insomniac nights – all contributed their mites of disgust and despair. By an ironic coincidence their fortnight's holiday fell at exactly the same time in August. They would have a fortnight's freedom together, she thought with wild excitement, when he told her the news; but then, looking at his pale face – the doll-like set of it as he puffed a cigarette – she realised that they would have no money to go away. Out of their weekly money they had saved none; anything that had been left over after paying for food and rent and so on had gone in little things like a new pair of shoes for Reuben, and a twelve-and-sixpenny summer frock for Francis. True they had bought a few books as well, and once Reuben, in a fit of brittle anger, had bought a half bottle of gin.

She sat down slowly on the bed, feeling numb and hopeless, and clasped her hands in her lap.

"Well," she said, not looking at him.

"I've been thinking that too," he said quietly. "Oh, God, Franz, wouldn't it be lovely…."

"How much money should we need?" she asked suddenly, looking up.

He yawned and pitched the stub of his cigarette into the grate. For a moment he stood very straight and rigid, yawning, and then dropped to her side on the bed. Putting one arm round her shoulders, pressing his fingers under her breast, he said evenly: "I've been sweating blood to try and find a way out. We've got nothing we can sell or pawn, have we?"

The time drew on, in stages so slow that she could hardly bear it, so protracted seemed their misery. She wrote and asked daddy if he would let her have five or six pounds for a trip to Cornwall: and received an answer by return of post saying that just at present he was afraid he couldn't quite manage, but they were looking forward to seeing her that summer, and to sharing their holiday with her.

Reuben tried for a little while to persuade her to go, but she would not hear of leaving him alone in Millman Street in that furnace-like little room under the leads. She was angry with him for suggesting such a thing.

In the evenings when they were not too tired they worked feverishly to try and earn a little extra money. He did a small book on folk music and submitted it to a publishing firm which kept it, regardless of his daily visit, for six months. (In the late autumn they awoke from their deep dream of peace just enough to reject it.) Francis, for her part, spent the evening on the couch designing book-covers which were to secure her commissions, and trying to dull her ears to the fiendish prattle of his typewriter. They quarrelled a great deal.

"Just one book-cover," she would say. "If only I could sell just one, darling, we'd be all right." But she was unsuccessful. The publishers were very kind: they were afraid that just at present they could not see their way to accepting…however, if she cared to call back in a few weeks, perhaps…. The dear publishers! She even got the tattered typescript of her old novel out of her trunk and tried to sell it again. She submitted it to a firm and waited until the following winter for an answer to her importunate letters. Meanwhile the humiliations of failure were increasing. Poor Reuben made a selection of the treasured songs which were to form a vast appendix to his book *The European Folk Song*, and tried to sell them to music publishers. In vain.

London, thou art of townes *A per se*.

It was in the middle of July that things worked themselves up to a crisis. Reuben came home one evening, made the dinner omelette, and sat down to work. When she came in she found him busy. He was, it seemed, a little shy and tired.

When they had eaten he suddenly came across to her and, taking her roughly by the shoulders, kissed her mouth, and made her sit down beside him on the sofa.

"I've got an idea," he said, with little frightened glances at her face. "I've had it a long time, but I didn't have the nerve to speak to you about it. Francis, dear, don't be angry with me. Listen to what I have to say, and don't be upset. If I went off on my own for a day or two I could raise the money for our holiday."

"Yes?" she said stonily.

He put his knuckles against his cheek and tilted his head on one side. "If I went off," he said very gently, "and came back with the money, would you want to know where and how I got it?"

"Reuben," she said wildly, "Reuben, don't," and the tears came slowly up into her dark eyes, "darling, don't."

Putting his arm round her shoulders, he shook her gently, and whispered: "It's quite silly for us to feel bad about it. It doesn't mean anything really. Not a thing. Don't you see we must go in a dead straight line for what we want? Let's be opportunists for once and get out of this miserable place for a fortnight. Franz!" He shook her gently as she began to cry. "Francis, for God's sake let's have a little control when we talk it over. Let's. Please stop crying."

She got up and took a handkerchief from the cupboard.

"I'd rather," she said at last, standing over him. "Reuben, darling...I can't bear the idea of either of us...."

She walked slowly up and down, dry-eyed, watching the dust crush up out of the carpet with each tread. "Yes," she said at last, "why shouldn't it be *me* this time?"

"There are reasons," he said quietly, relieved to see that her tears had stopped; that she was capable of actually contemplating this project calmly. "Lots of reasons, Franz."

With a kind of fierce gluttony he stared at her back, noticing the curves of her shoulders through the cheap cloth, the fine loins, and the long, but powerful legs. With the familiar gesture that wanted to make him cry aloud and catch her shoulders in his hands, she turned, hooking the strand of smooth black hair behind one ear, and said, in a voice suggesting nothing but deep pity and gratitude: "Reuben, make up your mind. I won't be silly any more."

That night, lying in the single bed together, he noticed that her body was rigid, unyielding; and much later, waking, that she wept.

He was up early the next morning. When she awoke she saw him, quietly moving about the room, selecting clothes from the cupboard and from his trunk, and packing them neatly in a suit-case. She got up immediately and helped him, saying nothing. He had already put the kettle on the gas-burner, and while he made the coffee, she took out the rolls and butter and marmalade from the cupboard. They sat down at the gate-legged table, and he pretended to eat with great heartiness, stuffing his mouth and chewing the stale rolls, exclaiming from time to time: "Excellent coffee, this." Or, "Damn good butter you get from this new place."

When he had finished he stood up and brushed the crumbs from his only good suit.

"Well," he said, with heartiness, "time I was off."

She got up meekly and brushed the hairs from his coat, and ran a shoe pad over his new brown shoes.

"Right," he said. "Well, Franz——"

She put up her hands to his face and, pressing his cheeks between her fingers, pulled his mouth down to her. He began to tremble as she touched him, but he suffered the embrace without remark or movement.

At the door, he said: "I suppose you couldn't let me have a pound out of this week's earnings? Sort of investment." He grinned with great facetiousness as she opened her bag and handed him a note. He turned with a great swagger to the door. As he was closing it behind him, he turned back and put his tense face to the aperture, and looked at her.

"Good-bye, darling," he said hoarsely, and was gone. The morning passed with a calculated slowness: almost, it seemed, with deliberation. From the little hutch on the first floor of the office she stared out bitterly on the sooty buildings in sunlight; the splashes of vividness on the coloured trams and buses as they passed revealed that even here in this wilderness of concrete and steel, of soot and musty stone, the sun still retained its power: it was not quite blotted out by factory smoke. The dust dried and powdered on the asphalt; flags of soiled paper made a few slack attempts to move on, and then subsided languidly about the ankles of the passers-by.

From inside the office came the drilling of typewriters and the sharp tone of voices; a tiny core of noise against that deep melodious hum and whirr of street-traffic.

Millie, typing blind with her long fingers, carried on a one-sided conversation about "fellows" with the blonde trull[107] from Tooting; she was afraid, she said, that her sailor was going to leave her and run away with a woman he had met at the Astoria. She could dance much better than Millie, it appeared. Millie had been left alone Sunday while her "fellow" went to Brighton with the dancing woman. She paid for the trip. She didn't think it was quite right, like. Going to Sherry's with a woman paying the bill.

Rollins came up that morning and insinuated himself through the doorway of Francis' little glass hutch.

"'Ere, miss," he said genially, "look at this telegram just come from the factory."

Francis turned the telegram over in her fingers. It was a request for the London office to hurry up with the designs for some advertisement posters which, it appeared, had been ordered a week previously.

"What posters?"

Rollins scratched his head and eased his hard collar from his neck, pressing a blunt finger against the inside of his moist collar stud. "Mr. Glanders wrote and said they were doing an advertisement series in the windows. Holiday posters. He wanted designs for them so as they would be ready for the summer sales."

"Well," said Francis, "where are the designs?"

"There aren't any," said the little man with great simplicity. "I asked the agencies but they wanted about fifty quid for the series of twelve." He scratched his head and added piously, "I wasn't going to pay out fifty quid of the firm's money and get the sack probably for paying too much. I suppose you don't know a cheap artist, miss, to do them?"

"What will the firm pay?"

"Mr. Glanders said he wanted between five and ten posters. He didn't say what price, but you know what he is!"

"Twenty quid for ten," said Francis crisply. "You won't get them cheaper to print in four colours. I can arrange all that. Wire him at once, will you, Mr. Rollins, and I'll find you the artist this afternoon."

By lunch time they had received a wire from the factory to say that the terms were accepted, and would they hurry the order through.

Francis put on her hat and coat, drew five pounds from the firm, and announced that she was going to Hendon to find the artist; that she would not be back that day.

She bought herself a great roll of cartridge paper and a number of pots of good poster colours, and, having ordered them to be sent up to her room, ate a large and expensive lunch, drank four iced lagers, and went home.

For the rest of that day she was so busy that she had no time to think of Reuben. She cleared out the room, and, pinning up poster-size sheets of the cartridge paper, set to work on them, having first mapped out her lurid, stylised designs in little. By eleven o'clock that night she had completed four of the ten posters. Lying back on the divan, she puffed cigarette after cigarette and stared at their magnificent, their garish imbecility. They were holiday posters right enough. In each was depicted some form of holiday amusement – hiking, bathing, riding beach-donkeys, petting on the pier; and in each the figures of her human subjects were adorned with a pair of luminous feet. Shoes being the subject of the advertisement, it was only natural that every pair of feet in her posters (being clad in Slumber-Sewn Shoes) should shine like a beacon. The posters themselves were linked by a connecting chain, a story; in each was represented the adventures of the Slumber Sewn Family. At the Seaside, In the Country (among the rural scenes of rest and quiet), On Donkeys, On the Pier. They were extraordinarily quaint.

Waking to the sound of the alarm, she turned in bed, putting out her arms to find Reuben's body, and came sharply awake at the lack of him. Then she remembered and began to weep, quite naturally, and without much real pain of mind. She felt weary in her very soul as she dressed that morning. Oh, if only it were possible to send him a wire, or a letter, and tell him to hurry back. Her heart gave a leap when she thought of their good fortune. Twenty pounds! She got breakfast, and as she did so, cast quick, humorous glances at the posters. Three would be dry enough to take with her to the office.

"Bless you," she said extravagantly, raising her hands to the stupid loutish Family that stared fixedly past her, radiantly proud of their luminous feet, "God bless each and every one of the Slumber-Sewn brood, and may they increase."

Mr. Rollins' eyes swam in pools of wonder and approbation when he saw the posters unrolled before him and spread across the office floor. "*Gor!*" he said, confronted with art. "*Gor!* but they aren't *half* good, miss." Even the typists stared approvingly at them.

Francis, bursting with self-satisfaction, feigned a magnificently airy nonchalance. As Rollins himself remarked later, "Anyone could see she was *used* to pitchers."

"The rest won't be done quite so quickly," she said, "because the artist has got other work on hand. Perhaps by next Tuesday."

But it was a fortnight before she was finally finished with the Slumber-Sewn Family, and during that fortnight there was no news from Reuben. She had begun to worry and to feel the lack of him; already she had the habit of him so much that it was painful to be alone for more than a day or two. The weather had become fiendishly hot, and the district, if possible, more dusty and sooty than ever. The very air she breathed seemed to have a thick taste of soot in it. But Reuben – her mind was full of him; she could not put him right out of her mind even for a moment. Once she startled the office by bursting into tears while she was dictating a letter. Mr. Rollins, having been told of this remarkable fact, relieved himself of the following dictum in tones of sombre despair. It might have been Hamlet speaking.

"Ar!" he said slowly. "It's *Ro*-mance, that's what it is."[108]

The days passed, and still there was no word. The landlady's son developed a temperature which alternated between 106 degrees and 103; and a great blue lump behind his right ear. He was taken off to hospital and operated on for mastoid. A discharging ear which had not been looked after had rotted away the bone. He was not expected to live.

She sat in her room trembling, as the ambulance men staggered downstairs with him, and whispered over and over again: "Reuben, Reuben, Reuben. Where are you? Reuben...."

Meanwhile Reuben sat, shivering with fear, on the bench in the lock hospital, waiting his turn. The glazed tiles of the wall sweated mildly, and on the hot-water pipes the dust had collected in a fine coat. One by one the men disappeared into the sound proof box, dragging the door shut behind them: leaning over the counter to the bland, weary-faced man who wrote down their particulars in a book. One by one they came out with their book, filed and numbered, and joined the long waiting line, sitting on the cheap wood benches.

His turn came. He entered the box and shut the door behind him.

"Name," said the weary voice. The man did not glance up at him, but wrote, painfully, with method.

"Occupation."

"Student of music."

"Can you pay any money?"

"About half a crown a week if it's any use."

"Half a crown a week," repeated the man, and wrote it down with the other particulars. "All these facts," he said parrot-like, "are divulged on conditions of the strictest privacy."

"Yes."

"Here's your book. Wait with the others. Next."

Reuben took his book and left to seat himself humbly among that crowd of waiting men. Through the angle of the doorway he could see men going to and fro, ridiculously, in their shirts. A group of Indian medical students passed, chatting and talking. There was the prolonged hiss and gurgle of the urinals.

Staring sideways along the line of sombre faces, all cast in moulds of varying sombreness and despair, he could see bitterness and disgust uppermost; Jew-boys, ponces, pimps, schoolboys, undergraduates, navvies, policemen – they all sat, waiting their hour. Some, however, were jocularly talking, confident of themselves and their familiarity with the place. An aged man, with bald spots in his hair, talked animatedly to a great blond navvy whose eyes were circled in rims as sore and red as a cock's comb, and whose eyebrows were a mere line of fluff.

Presently a man in a white coat came in and shouted: "All right. This way," and the crowd of men rose to their feet and filled the narrow doorway.

"Season of mists and mellow fruitfulness."

She was aware, as an anaesthetised patient is aware,[109] of the dark movements of men and women around her; of the significant shapes and colours of dream. Her head was swollen with fever: swollen, until she knew that at any minute it would burst. She struggled back from time to time from the rare air in which she floated like a spirit, detached from her substantial body.

The pleasant hawk-faced doctor had called several times. When she first saw him, moving through the hot shimmer of fevers which fell across her eyeballs like rain, she had shouted: "Go away. Go away. I can't pay you. I'm saving for a trip to the country." He had said nothing, but sat down at the bedside and stuck a thermometer with a bulb as big as a lemon in her mouth.

Later he had listened carefully to her breathing and said: "Look here, my young lady, this kind of thing can't go on. You're frightfully run down. Where's your young man? "

"Reuben?" she said, her teeth chattering, and remembered the letter he had written her. "Look on the wall," she said, "up there, to the right. To the *right*. There."

After reading it she had pinned it with great care on the wall, beside one of the Slumber-Sewn posters which had got smudged and had to be done again. The doctor steadied the slip of cheap blue notepaper with his fingers and read it slowly, moving his mouth as he spelt out the words.

"Mumph," was his only comment. "Would you go into hospital?" he said at last, putting a cold hand on her forehead.

"No," she said loudly, "no."

Closing her eyes she saw the white ambulance flutter smoothly down the street. The filthy death-butterfly! She heard the chime of its bell and saw it stop at her door. The ambulance men were on the stairs now. They were coming for her. She remembered that the landlady's son had died after his operation.

"No," she said again.

"Well, unless you get better you'll have to," said the doctor. "I'll come back to-morrow morning. I've given the woman the prescriptions. Now be a good girl and don't worry."

The landlady was as long-suffering as she was good-tempered. She came in every hour or so to see the patient and gave her the prescribed febrifuges. By morning Francis was bathed in sweat and her fever had dropped a bit. She could talk quite coherently to the doctor when he called.

"Mumph," he said, "Your temperature's down. But not a great deal. And it's always less in the morning. I'll come again to-night."

She had several nightmares, and in all of them she could see, clearly with the sharp images of her dream, the faces of Reuben and Hilda. But the ambulance did not call.

When she was better several of the girls from the office called, bringing flowers and fruit for her, and Millie came with a pack of cards and her great red, hairy, sweating uncomfortable sailor, to spend an evening with the invalid. Francis was very touched by these favours. Even little Rollins made a ceremonial call, holding a bunch of flowers in one hand and his wife's rough paw in the other.

"Well," he said with gruff jocularity, "it *is* a fine way for to spend your holiday, miss. A fine way to be sure. I want you to meet me missus."

She was nearly well when the doctor insisted on examining her again. He spent twenty minutes prodding her, listening to her breathing through his stethoscope, and making her turn round in bed.

"Mumph. I thought so. Just wanted to make sure."

He strapped up his bag, and, sitting down again by the bed, said: "Now, look here. One of your lungs is a bit wonky. You can't stay on here in London. You must get away, either to the country or, better still, abroad."

"Impossible." Francis shook her head slowly. "'Fraid I haven't any money, doctor. I'm tied to my job."

"What is your job?"

"I'm in an office."

"Where do your people live?"

"I haven't any. I'm an orphan."

"Well, you certainly don't want to stay here. You must go off somewhere and build up your resistance."

As he got up to go, his eye was caught by the great poster of the Family disporting themselves on the too yellow sand of some Margate. Turning with a half-smile on his brown face, he said: "What about all those things?"

"Those?" she said, and shook her head, smiling. "There's no money in those."

The doctor took a closer look at the poster and seemed impressed. He smiled quickly and shrugged his shoulders.

"Mumph. I don't know much about painting, but one of my patients told me he was on the look-out for young artists. He makes mats. Very rich man. Silverstein. Know the name?"

Francis shook her head listlessly. Her eye had been caught by Reuben's letter.

"Well, I must be off. But I tell you what, I'll keep my eye open for you. Would you take a job as a governess if you could get abroad?"

Francis nodded.

"Splendid. Well, good day to you."

"Good-bye."

Lying, back in bed, she tried to read the words on the sheet of blue paper. "Dear Franz," the letter began; but it was not quite fair since she knew it almost by heart.

DEAR FRANZ,

I've failed. Not the money, I've got that, but something else has happened. Franz dear, please be a comfort and try not to worry....

For perhaps the first time since she had received the letter she contemplated its contents, faced the issue squarely. Before, this had been impossible; the most natural of states – that of mental numbness – had forbidden her to think connectedly. She was aware of what had happened, but not directly, not with the immediate stab to which tears or wildness could be the only answer. Now, very slowly, the receptive mind was coming awake; and the thought of Reuben came nearer and nearer to her sentiment. Why, she wondered, did he not come to see her, to talk to her? The thumbed phrases of the letter answered her, question by question:

I'm not coming to see you because I wouldn't know quite what to say to you. There wouldn't be anything to say or do, Franz dear, except weep – and you mustn't do that. O damn the staleness of these words, it seems an insult to write them when I know you so intimately. A pity isn't it how things have got worse and worse for the last month or so? One might almost have foretold it. The final slap in the mouth for you. For us both, in a way.

So Reuben himself had seen it as the final blow to their self-respect; the peculiar and final triumph of events! What a grubby thing it had been, she thought, shuddering with distaste for their life together. Honestly, objectively, what a grubby and unsatisfactory thing. It was not their fault, they had tried – heaven knows they had tried!

She was well enough to spend the remaining week of her holiday in the country. She was still emotionally unstable, still given to quick fits of weeping which puzzled herself. But she returned to the office on the correct day, despite any qualms she might have had about this weakness.

Everyone, from Mr. Rollins downwards, was kindness itself. She was given very little work to do, and was told that she must "go easy on herself" until she was well again. Rollins, for his part, was burning to ask her a very special question. One day, during the tea interval, he did so:

"You know the day I came to see you with the missus, miss? When you was ill?"

"Yes."

"Well, I saw you had one o' those Slumber-Sewn pitchers up on the wall. And me missus told me she saw heaps of li'tle po's of paint all around. I thought to meself then, perhaps the young lady painted the pitchers herself."

"Yes, I did paint them."

Mr. Rollins expressed concerned amazement by drawing a chair up to the desk and studying her countenance for a full minute. Then he erupted: "Gor," and was silent as one in the presence of holiness.

From that time onward he treated her in a very curious manner. He would always be on hand if she needed anything. But she often caught him looking at her in a queer way; as if he expected her to start barking, or have an epileptic fit.

Time passed very slowly. But at the end of September, when the summer holidays were finally over for everyone, when the office had settled down to its autumn routine, when the newspapers had begun to print fewer pictures of bathing beauties on the English beaches, the doctor, whom she had completely forgotten, called again.

She had just got back from the office when the land-lady showed him into the room. He shook hands briskly and sat down. "Just came in to see how you were getting on, he said. He cast a furtive glance up at the letter which was still pinned to the flowered wallpaper.

"Will you have a cup of tea with me, doctor?" she said, and he accepted with thanks. "Dusty work at this time of the year." As she took another cup from the cupboard, he said: "I've got a little bit of news for you."

"Oh," she said dully, trying to sound enthusiastic. "What is it?"

"That man Silverstein I told you about. He's come back from abroad. I saw him the other day and had a chat about you."

She put on a pert little smile, which was intended to represent enthusiasm and interest. "Do tell me."

The doctor tilted a large mouthful of tea on to his tongue, swallowed loudly, and mopped his mouth with a handkerchief.

"He controls a huge textile industry and is a very rich man. Any number of well-known artists work for him."

"Well," she said, with sudden gladness, "well, that lets me out. I'm neither very good nor well-known."

"Why not have a try?" said the doctor quietly. "You never know. He might give you a roving commission or something. No harm in trying. Now, which evening would suit you, because I've got to let him know?"

Noah Silverstein was one of those happy mortals who combine a small amount of business with a large amount of pleasure. He had been clever enough not only to inherit riches, but to hang on to them and, when he felt like it, to add to them. In the textile industry there was no giddy peak he had not scaled, no financial Everest on which he had been unable to breathe freely. He was more than self-made; he was perfectly self-possessed. Even in the social industry he was known and respected, if not for himself, at any rate for his money.

Like other giants, however, he had his weaknesses. Among these, and greater than the others, was woman. Women were his life. In and through them he lived; one would not be pushing a figure too far if one likened him to the male bonellia, which, de Gourmont[110] noted, is a mere appendage to its female, living attached to the aesophagus. His life was this: whenever possible a warm, womby, soft, slippery attachment, unheeded by the female, but always there; always hanging on, like a vermicular appendix, to the life that fed him.

Noah Silverstein's world was made in the shape of a woman; woman was at once his master and his lure. He was never happy unless he was with women, attending on them, being commanded by them. Three wives had found his company unbearably tedious, his tireless attentions noxious, his proprietary jealousies infuriating to distraction; and two had threatened him with lethal weapons of different calibres. They had left him as he was when he found them, small, baggy, liable to fawn, easily humbled, but not easily shaken off; and at their going he had thrice produced a form of dramatic expression with which to make his desolation plain. He had solemnly removed his silver-rimmed glasses and polished them with a silk handkerchief, as if to mop up the result of a whole life-time's weeping.

But, if a few of the animals went overboard, the ark of Noah Silverstein still floated; and there were enough left in the menagerie to entertain him with their tricks. Again the simile is not unapt, for the women he chose were more various, more conflicting in physical, mental and temperamental characteristics, than the animals in a dozen Noah's arks. Crabbed age and youth together: Bohemians and Blowsies, Sirens, Savages and Spinsters, Tarts and Tight-Rope Walkers, Chinks, Wops or Woollies[111] – it did not matter very much.

Francis, when she called the first time, was shown into the elegant withdrawing-room of his West End flat. There, seated in one of the most sumptuously modern chairs, she was examined with care by the critical eyes of Noah. He had been sitting, appropriately enough, at the Bluthner,[112] tossing his small woolly head about and squeezing a Beethoven sonata out of air and ivory, with delicate fawning gestures of his fingers. It was most impressive, the whole cultural reception. He had been warned, of course, that a Young Artist was calling to see him, and, as he knew the value of young artists as well as anyone, he had prepared the event; perhaps, over prepared it, for Francis was not impressed at his absorption in the work of THE MASTER. Being a young woman, he had reflected, she will be pleased to receive signs that I, too, move in the most up to date circles of intellectual thought. Accordingly the works of Mr. Priestley and Mr. Golding[113] were removed from the drawing room shelf, and the latest poems of Mr. Eliot and Mr. Pound[114] substituted for them. This line was rounded off in a pretty catholic fashion by backing them with the latest publications of the Nonesuch Press,[115] and the calf-bound works of Jeremy Taylor.[116] A quarter of an hour before the appointed time, Noah, in all his glory (complete with dressing-gown and talcum-powdered jowls), sat at the piano, stroking Beethoven and listening for the sound of the bell.

His start of surprise when he turned and found, all unknowingly (so rapt had been his communion with THE MASTER), that a young lady had been announced, was so violent, that he all but precipitated himself into the modern fireplace.

"I had no idea," he said apologetically; "I had absolutely no idea, my *dear* young lady." He worried her hand for a while, and gallantly clapped a pair of moist large lips to it.

"Pray sit down," he continued effusively, "*pray* sit down."

Francis sat down and explained the subject of her visit; from her bag she produced the card of the doctor and the message he had written on it. Noah read both the name of the doctor and the message and sniffed with pleasure.

"Yes," he said brightly, "yessss," with a terrific sibilance, "this is he. This is the fellow. He told me about you. He said some very complimentary things about your work."

He pursed his lips and simpered.

"Do you know anything about textile designs?"

As he gazed at her pale face, with the dark marking of eyebrows, and the lank strands of black hair tucked under her cheap hat, he moistened his lips and blinked. She was ravishing. He had noted with pleasure the easy grace of her figure, with its strong back and loins. Yes, she was ravishing.

She said that she had done a good deal of design for various things and industries, and lied to him feebly for a moment or two, during which she could feel his eyes fixed upon her with that look of fawning desire. She disliked his large wet lips.

"Have you anything to show me?" he asked, and seemed disappointed when she said that she had nothing except a few book-jackets.

"Well," tossing his little head to one side and allowing the laughing wrinkles to tighten thickly on his forehead, "well, what does it matter? You can do some and bring them when you call another time."

He put a finger and thumb to the rims of his spectacles and studied her for a while, as if from a great way off. "Haven't I seen you somewhere before?" he asked, in a devastatingly male tone. "Now, let me see. Savoy? No? Mayfair? No? *I say*. You weren't one of the party that drove down to Charlie Brown's in Limehouse last winter?"

He wagged a finger in the air. "You were wearing a green frock, a red scarf and one of those funny hats – Robin Hood affairs, with a feather?"

"*No.*"

"Funny, I could have sworn – Ah, here comes Bodly with the drinks."

He skipped to his feet and busied himself with the making of a cocktail, the secret of which he guarded by keeping his back to her during the process. It was a deadly brew. Francis sipped hers slowly and felt her heart beat faster; felt the blood begin to warm and thaw in her veins.

They talked for an hour or so about design, and he obligingly produced several of his own fabrics, which had been designed by famous artists; and others designed by casual people like herself – mostly women.

"You know," he said, "a big organisation like ours depends for the most part on the artists. Until about six months ago I had one man on a retaining fee, whose job was to go about all over Europe and keep an eye on the designs of each country. The people at the factory thought I was mad, of course, but in the end it paid. We'd get simply *exquisite* designs from places like Persia and Greece – rugs and pottery and stuff made by the peasants. Hopkins – that was the name of the man – used to do free adaptations from them and post them back to us. It was a good advertising line, too; people are mad for anything that's foreign. Unfortunately the idiot Hopkins committed suicide and left us flat."

"Who's got his job?" she asked. The drink made her feel drowsy. She moistened her lips.

"No one: that's the point. You see, my dear young lady," he leaned forward and dropped his voice, "you see, I am a man of business. The fee I offer is a small one. There is no well-known or good artist who would accept it and devote his time to the needs of the factory. And the young artists are either too bad, or so keen on travel and copulation they have no time for other things. I must find someone I can trust. Someone stable, someone who is not going to spend my money and give me nothing in exchange."

"Yes," she said glumly, "I quite see that."

Noah produced a vast silver cigarette-case and offered her a smoke. She accepted, though her fingers were unsteady.

"When you bring me your designs," he said, with his eyebrows raised, his mouth pursed in a *moue* of delicate insinuation, "I'll be able to tell whether you are the person I've been waiting for."

When she did return, at the end of a fortnight, with a bundle of designs, Noah himself opened the door to her. Placing his hands, like pats of icy butter, on her shoulders, he said: "My *dear* young lady. At last. I was afraid you were not coming back."

As they sat down he added, with terrifying sincerity, pushing his underlip out with an expression of melancholy appeal: "I've thought a great deal of you these last few days, you know."

"Oh," she said. "Oh?" Her flesh had come alive and warm with disgust at his little hands touching her shoulders. And yet, inside her, something was numb, dead, but wary: watching the moves.

He crooned over her designs. They were excellent for a novice, he said, excellent. He was quite carried away by them. Of course he had seen better, but then, he had seen worse.

"This one," he said, "is something like the one I put on the bedroom rug. Here," and he skipped off to the bedroom. When she got there she found him on the floor on his hands and knees, crawling about the rug, and laying out the roll of thick paper beside it.

They examined and compared the two designs, walking to every conceivable point of vantage in the room. Finally he sat down on the bed and said: "Come here and let me congratulate you." Catching her hands, he kissed them loudly.

Rigid and wary, she waited. Something inside her had gone flat and numb; the essential her was not there, was lost in some infinitely remote speculation about Reuben, the Slumber-Sewn Family, or something else, utterly irrational. Only the husk of her body stood, rigid and alert, flinching from the buttered fingers of Noah. What did it matter, after all? she was thinking. What did it matter? Sickly, she was aware of his arms drawing her towards him.

"Would you like Hopkins' job?" he asked casually, folding his arms round her hips, and laying his woolly head sideways against her stomach. She had the momentary vision of Noah looking up at her, like a monkey, from between her own breasts. "Would you?" he repeated. "Would you like the roving commission?"

"Yes," she said. "Please I would."

"I'm very pleased with you," he said softly, rubbing his chin against her; "little girl, I'm very pleased with you." He was aware, annoyingly, that he would have to change his position slightly. He was getting cramp in the left buttock; and, curse it, if he moved he might destroy this beautifully cultural atmosphere of seduction. He must talk in order to cover the necessary readjustment of his limbs.

"Have you read *The Waste Land*?" he asked loudly.[117]

"No."

She was staring past him at the blank wall with its single tasteful etching. Thank heavens, she did not notice the move. Why, he wondered, was she so rigid? The doctor had assured him she was not a virgin. It was very curious. Still....

"You should," he whispered idiotically. "You really should."

He pressed his hand slowly into the arch of her back.

"Francis," he intoned with passionate fervour, "Francis, little girl, you must be kind to me."

She said nothing, but closed her eyes and thought, fervently, of anything that came into her head. Reuben, Hilda, Mr. Rollins – a procession of faces across her closed eyes. Reuben's shadow rose before her so clearly that she began to tremble. Raising his tumbler, he toasted the devil as he always had done: "Well! Skoal[118] to old Nick."

"You shall have the job," said Noah, "that I promise you." His voice came thickly through the spittle that had collected between his cheeks. He swallowed loudly and drew her down until she was sitting beside him on the bed. With a quick gesture he unlatched his glasses and put them in his pocket.

"Francis," he crooned again, "little Francis."

"Yes," she said harshly; "yes?"

She saw his transfiguring smile. Without his glasses his eyes had retreated back into his head, twinkling like jujubes of liquorice in their sockets.

"*Dear* little girl," and he snapped off the light.

For a long time after that, in the dark room, she could see the great wide smile of Noah Silverstein hanging above her, luminous, like the smile of the Cheshire cat.

When she reached her room that night she boiled kettle after kettle of hot water and sponged her body clean: she cleaned her teeth and spat, and spat again. But the job was hers.

Leaning on the window-sill, unable to sleep, she watched the occasional passing of a man or woman in the dark street. Reuben? No. The yellow street-lamps, dusty bulbs of light, illuminated the clothes of the late travellers. A prostitute sidled by, attached like a leech to the arm of a man. Reuben? No. They halted in the dark doorway opposite while the woman fumbled for her key. A policeman stared wearily at them, and then marched on. The street-lamps were suddenly snuffed out, without warning.

Over there, to the east, faint light silhouetted the chimney-pots and the parched trees of the Square. Morning.

# Chapter X

# The Music

THEY sat there together in the evening for a long time after she had finished speaking, while the music broke in long waves of gentleness and heartbreak across the air.

As she finished speaking, she had risen and put the needle to the record, and now the slow gathering and diffusion of strings broke in on their reverie. Out there, the bay had become molten, and on its brim, where the mists hid the mainland and the other Greek islands, a fishing-boat was delicately balanced. Across the sunset the bodies of the young cypresses moved, delicately, touched by a wind from the land. From the garden gusts of scent came up to the doorway, with the sound of cicadas. The music of Delius[119] continued its own tender meditation.

"It wasn't very good fun," she said at last, intruding on the music and his silence. "You see that?"

Marlowe sucked his empty pipe and stared stubbornly out on the garden. A man in a red shirt was spraying the olives. The music unfurled its shapes and patterns – made them almost visible things on that clear still air, in which the swallow and the martin exultingly dived and spun. Down on the road, below Phaon, a procession of mules and donkeys came into sight, treading languidly. On their backs, seated sideways in the uncomfortable wood saddles, were the old women who had been collecting seaweed all day. They were limp with weariness and their hands bounced, palms upwards, on their knees. Dead with fatigue and not caring if the heavens fell, they jogged onwards up the hill to their village.

"Yes," he said at last, with a sigh, "I see it."

Curious, he was reflecting, that no amount of mere explanation served to lessen the enigma of her personality; for to him it was still enigma. Furtively he studied the profile of the girl as she turned to look away across the garden, noting again the strong nose and the slight droop of the upper lip, the lean brown hands.

"Shall I turn the gramophone off?" she said suddenly. "I can't listen to the music properly."

He nodded. Sitting down again she cocked her head on one side and watched him critically.

"I hope that I haven't bored you with these schoolgirl confidences," she said, with a flicker of a smile.

He got to his feet and quietly brushed the ash from his trousers.

"Will you tell me something?" he asked, smiling back into the dark eyes.

"Yes."

"Exactly how do you hear music?"

She walked into the corner of the room and took up her packet of cigarettes, lighting one and putting it in the corner of her mouth. He could feel her moving about in the glooms behind him, but he sat still, staring out quietly on to the darkening sea. Then he heard her come and stand in the window at his back.

"Will you tell *me* something?" she asked nervously, at last.

"Yes." He was amazed at the smallness of his own voice, sounding as if from a great distance. "Yes. What?"

"Have you," she said coolly, "ever been in love?"

He sat there for a full minute, quiet, drawing at his pipe, and staring out at the sea. But his soul had gone suddenly small and icy inside.

"My dear girl," he said at last, with a small burst of explosive laughter, wrinkling up his nose and allowing the net of wrinkles to grow about his blue eyes; "my dear Francis, what a question. Really," and he turned his own small laughing face to her, persuading her to sanction his laughter with a smile or a word. She turned aside, however, and said: "Sorry. I didn't mean to sound as naïve as all that. I take it back;" but there was not a trace of a smile on her face. His own face became sober again, and he said: "Don't think me rude. I was just bowled over by the irrelevance of the thing. Out of the blue like that." It was easier, he was thinking, now he had put the subject on the casual level of banter. He gave a final small chuckle and added: "If you really want to know, I haven't.... I've not really been very much interested in the subject. I imagine I feel rather like Swift about the whole thing, or old Odo of Cluny...[120] besides, *Foeda est in coitu*...[121] you know? Doing, a filthy pleasure is, and short. No, there are so many other more interesting things."

Neat, he was assuring himself, to be able to fob off the tedious importunities of this young woman with a Latin tag and good-humoured laughter. Very neat.

"I wonder," said Francis, "if you are right."

He turned as he started to knock out his pipe. "My dear young woman," he said irritably, "it's not a question of being right. There's no such thing. One can only be true to one's temperament."

She looked at him for a moment, pondering.

"You're right," she said finally; "you're quite right there." She caught his eye, and turned away, wondering what processes of thought were shaping themselves in that small ascetic head, behind the blue eyes.

"It must be time for food," she said.

"Yes," he said mildly, and rose.

Rumanades met them in the hall and blinked up the staircase with a shy pleasure: "Been having music?"

"Yes."

"The boat's just got back from Brindisi, so I expect we'll have a concert to-night. Gordon wants to hear the new Beethoven concerto."[122]

"Has it come?" she asked; and then, looking at her watch, "You won't start for an hour. Time for a bite, eh?"

Marlowe and she walked down the hill together, casually chatting, and at the turn of the road they bade each other good-bye. Imp-like, for the sheer fun of seeing him wince, she said, on impulse: "Forgive the last attempt of mine to burst in on your male privacy. It was disgustingly rude and naïve."

"Not at all," he said, again laughing, waving his stick in the air, "not at all."

She watched his small figure swinging away from her down the hill with a curious perplexity that was almost remorse. Damn the male privacy, she thought rebelliously, damn the cliquiness, damn the evasions; and above everyone and everything else, damn Marlowe. Yes, damn him.

Marlowe himself, however, found cause to do a bit of swearing on his own, when he got back to Phaon. Maria had become bored by the tedium of waiting for him to return; and, having nothing else to do, had taken all his clothes down to the sea, washed them, thrashed them, banged the buttons off them, and spread them over all the neighbouring bushes. Having worked off her energy, she now sat, meek and placid as a cat, on the front doorstep, crocheting him a dish-cloth. She stared up with frightened eyes into his red angry face, crossed herself, and wondered what could be the matter.

"Damn it, Maria," he expostulated, pointing to his trousers which were rapidly shrinking on the bushes. "Confound you for a silly girl."

He dived indoors for the Greek phrase-book which Rumanades had lent him. "Here," he said, "come here," and laboriously he pronounced the nearest thing to an anathema which could be found in that polite manual of phrases. "I am very ashamed of you," he mumbled, "ντρεπεομαι για çας."[123]

She stood up and stared curiously at him for a while as he pronounced words with which she was evidently unfamiliar. Then she began to laugh; great husky laughter which shook her loins and her stomach. Putting her mudgrimed fingers on her hips, the girl roared.

He sat down on the bed, and hopelessly gave up. Later, when she had conquered the impulse to shake with fits of mirth, he managed to point out, purely by mime, that he was angry with her for savaging his clothes. Then she was contrition itself; great tears stood in her eyes. The transformation was alarming, it was so sudden. Her lower lip drooped, she began to sniff, and was shaken with sobs more deep, more painful than ever the laughter could have been. He began to feel rather a fool. However, as soon as he gave her something to do – in this case she was commanded to boil some sweet corn for his supper – she was happy again, absorbed and delighted with herself and everything else in this quickly changing world.

That evening, as he sat under the trees at the little wooden table, and was waited on, she was in magnificent spirits. The clothes, it seemed, were forgotten. When he told her that the sweet corn was too tough, she picked up the one he was eating, snapped her teeth easily into the yellow pips, shook her head as much as to say, "These foreigners are dainty-stomached creatures," and, tossing it over the hedge, invited him to wait while she cooked him some more.

He was quite relieved when she came to say goodnight, after locking the back door. As her strong figure strode off down the path among the olives, vividly swinging in its coloured skirt and vermilion head-dress, he rose and took up his stick, locked the front door and walked gently in the direction of the Villa Pothetos. He was already a little late: but what did it matter on an evening like this?

He whistled as he took the path up the hill, between the splendid avenue of cypresses.

Approaching Rumanades' villa, he heard the hubbub of voices which was soon to settle down into silence for the music. They were all there.

The great black gramophone with snout like horn had been set in the circle of trees which fronted the plateau, and beside it stood the rank of ceremonial chairs. The priest and the two monks were already in their places, discoursing amiably among themselves; Vassili, to whom fell the coveted job of winding the machine and changing the records, lay on his back in full uniform and stared at the clear sky, waiting for Rumanades himself who had gone up to the house to fetch the records.

In a wide half circle squatted the peasants, laughing and talking, and making a great play with their bright scarves and coloured petticoats; eating breakings of bread and olives, or cuffing their little brown children.

Fonvisin and Francis sat together, with their backs against a tree, talking quietly, while farther off Gordon, to whom ceremony meant nothing, lay on his back, arms behind his head, clad only in his customary slacks. Marlowe took up a position somewhere near him, and, choosing an olive-tree against which he could lean, began to fill his pipe against the time when the music should begin.

The old man appeared at last, hurrying towards them with the books of new records under his arm. He acknowledged the priest and the monks anew, nodding shyly and enunciating the conventional greeting, and settled into his chair, having handed the records to Vassili; who rose languidly from the floor, and yawned with the nonchalance of one, if not himself distinguished, perfectly at home in high places. The peasants tucked away their pieces of food, dusted crumbs from their skirts and trousers, gave their children a final cuff to impress on them the absolute necessity for silence, and settled down to watch everything with their dark eyes. Vassili took out one of the great shining discs and handed it to the old man, who announced, in English and Greek, the Fourth piano concerto.[124] His words were greeted by a rapt hush.

Marlowe, closing his eyes, felt the dusk sliding down across that delicate landscape. The mists were closing in on them. In the hush the sound of the waves grew up in volume, accustomed the waiting ears to their noise, and diminished to take their true perspective in the scheme of sound. The silence was a kind of limbo in which to prepare the soul for a new state. Closing his eyes fast, drawing at the stem of his pipe, he knew his brain ready and keen to leap out at the call of the music, and follow its forms wherever they might lead.

He opened his eyes, and heard the first piano statement detach itself from the silence and create its delicate impact on the air; the mind grasped it, recognised it as the signal of a form which was yet to be; and waited in sweet nervous anticipation.[125]

The strings had taken the statement now, and cherished it, languorously meditative, warmly deliberating on its development. The forces were gathering.

Glancing across the dusky plateau, rimmed with its silent olives, he could see the spectators as figures in some stiffly formal Byzantine frieze, fixed in the attitudes of silence and curiosity. The two monks (as near to blasphemy now, sleeping, as they would ever be in their lives again) might have been stylised representations of humility or prayer, with heads lagging forward on to their breasts. Rumanades smoked silently and evaded all eyes. The priest had folded his arms across his soutane and was leaning forward, staring firmly at his boots. Under his stovepipe hat his long hair, drawn tight in a bun, showed threads of faint silver. He seemed to be a symbol of pontifical detachment as he sat there, staring at the square toes of his mouldering boots.

The wide semicircle of peasants were very engrossed. Occasionally there was the faint shift of position or the turn of a face in one direction or another, but for the most part they remained immobile, while the light slowly drained out of their clothes, and left a ring of dark faces grouped about the machine.

Purely the theme developed and the second subject was stated. The music gathered itself in volume, filling out its proportions as it progressed. A slight tension of increasing interest and nervousness touched Marlowe, and he sat straighter, pressing his back to the rough tree, prepared.

Francis had moved away from Fonvisin, and sat, head cocked eerily on one side, as if busy with some purely superficial estimate of the recording, or the tone, or some such triviality.

Fonvisin gripped his arms about his knees and laid his chin on his breast, hiding his face. In the background behind the peasants stood Walsh, pipe between his teeth, leaning against a tree with the puppy asleep at his feet.

The music was settled and progressive now, throwing out its inevitable lines with a lift and stir of emotion. Marlowe, breath snatched from him again, followed the traceries of its sound, with the feeling of doom which Hamlet must have known, following his father's ghost along the vertiginous battlements of the castle. The music was a ghost beckoning them on across precipices of feeling, with sureness of foot that only a spirit could know which had crossed every division of sense and perception and sloughed its substantial body. And yet, in its progression, it threw in references to the first theme – mere suggestions which haunted the mind. The music was a doom, a new state of being.

In the gap of silence at the end of the first movement, he noticed that the darkness had come down on them; and out of the darkness grew the thousand fiery points of the fireflies.

The second movement opened brutally, with a dry snarl of strings across the darkness, and then the soothing piano statement.

With a sigh Gordon rolled over on his stomach and laid his face sideways across his forearm. Tense with fear – for if there is any magic in the world, where is there a more terrible statement of it than here, in the second movement of this concerto? – tense with the growing fear of this musician's mind, he heard the dry coughing of strings, insisting, compelling and then the sweet individual forms of the piano in meditation, dissolving the harshness of its enemy with simplicity. It was a duel or a game of cards in which each blustering advance of the strings was stemmed by the liquid piano-meditation. Trick for trick they played, and the listeners waited, in painful anxiety, for the moment of victory. Gradually it came. To Marlowe as he sat there, clenching his knees against his chest, and nipping the stem of his pipe hard, it was a mystery why the thing had not seemed inevitable from the beginning. Yet the exposition would have led him on, stage by perilous stage, with as much stress and accuracy, even if the end had been foretold.

The braying of the strings weakened, hesitated. The remorseless piano did not press them, did not add weight to its own form, but quietly, surely played trick against trick. The moment was one of profound tension. Marlowe had reached a stage of empathy, in which he himself had become the mystic piano-communion with quietness, curbing the fibrous vulgarity of the strings. It was the old question again, of passivity subduing the shouting and braying of life.

Imperceptibly at first, then with growing fear, the strings gave way before him; they became empty, powerless, while the piano arranged their doom and extinction. As the movement dwindled down to victory from the climax – that one whip-like treble note – he felt the power flowing into his body like a current; in his fingers and brain and loins it was generated. The conquest was purely his; and it was complete. The silence brought him awake with a sigh.

For a moment he saw the circle of faces, hushed and awe-still.

Then the faint shaving of a fibre needle on a record was drowned in the victorious plunge of music into space; with excited caution, children on tiptoe, the strings opened, dipping into the first subject with a hint of plangency and force to come. And the piano followed.

This time there was no escaping the remorseless hold of the music. The great trumpet of the machine brimmed with the noise and poured it out among them. It seemed to Gordon, then, that everything between the poles must be caught up and partially suffocated by the pressure of it. Everything, yes, everything knew this moment as an equivalent of infinity, timeless, indestructible. The fireflies were among them now, shooting spots of light among the absorbed faces, shining and winking on the dresses and brown eyes of the congregation.

Surely, Gordon was thinking, the impact of this emotion is not confined to a locality? The concussion of it must be a part of the emotion of every living thing. (Across Italy the trains were running, like strings of fireflies across the warm dark countryside; in the shrunken solitudes of the Arctic the seals were barking at nothing; surely, surely even there....)

He turned on his back and stared up through the foliage of the olive trees at the empty sky which the disc of the full moon would light in a little while. The music still poured over them, as if from a gash in the world's side; the flux was in him too, now, so that he felt his own life-force draining, pouring, for ever pouring in a passion of tenderness and exultation across the warm darkness of that early summer night.

So inevitable did it seem, so necessary every shade and implication in its continuity, that he began to think it would never end; only the faint shape of form denied him belief.

The trees were gaunt and still above them; their bodies knotted and twisted in supplication to the rising moon, which was already prowling across the mountains of Epirus. From the point beyond Phaon it would be possible to see the silver dazzle of the Lefkas cliffs, from whose top Sappho had jumped clean out of time into history.[126]

At last the music cast them up on a silence that was like a long deserted beach. Nerveless, trembling, they sat there, wreckage nosed up by the tides of sound.

Moonlight filled the olive glades. From somewhere down below the cliffs came an elephantine sucking in the mouth of the blow-hole. A faint clatter of clapping hands grew out of nothing.

The peasants began to chatter uncomfortably and gather their possessions together; the children recovered the use of their lungs and demanded bread and olives to eat. Fonvisin vanished, and Gordon, having slowly risen to his feet, made his way silently through the crowds in the direction of the path.

Marlowe went across to talk to Rumanades.

"Ah! Marlowe, there you are." The old man was busy taking a ceremonial leave of the sleepy monks and the priest. "Did you enjoy the piece?"

"Excellent."

"I myself even, though of course I know nothing of music, enjoyed it."

"Yes?"

Rumanades produced a case of cigarettes and they lit one each. For a short while, until the gramophone had been taken up to the house, and the last of the local peasants had tumbled drowsily down the slope to bed in the village, they chatted aimlessly of one thing and another. They were actually going to begin work to-morrow on the church, said the old man; two boats of building materials – good materials, mind you – were to arrive in the early morning; and the mason from the village above Leucothea was coming down to superintend the work.

"Well," yawned Marlowe, "I suppose it'll soon be ready for the famous fresco."

"Not for some time. That reminds me, I must have a talk to the priest on the subject."

"Well," said Marlowe, "all things being equal, I'll bid you good-night."

"Good-night," said Rumanades absently, "good-night," and walked slowly towards the house, staring at the ground.

As Marlowe went down the road he saw the silver dust climb up from the road in a column; the cavalcade of peasants had started on its way to the mountain villages.

Francis and Walsh were walking slowly down the hill, and quickening his pace he caught up with them.

"Hullo," said the girl, "I thought you'd stayed behind."

"I hear they're starting to build your church to-morrow morning."

"Yes."

They walked in silence, deliberately avoiding mention of the music. For some reason, not quite clear to himself, Marlowe seemed to notice a strain in the movements and expression of the boy. He walked with a strange jerkiness, and when they spoke, lifted his head to stare at the speaker with his dark eyes. The puppy padded behind them down the boulder-strewn path of the hill-side, sniffing at things and mewing from time to time with a strange plaintive insistence.

At the corner of the road Walsh suddenly stopped, clasped his hands together and said awkwardly, "Let's not go to bed yet. Let's not. I want to walk up to the Jump. Let's walk, shall we?"

Francis' eyes were dark with interrogation.

"All right," she said, slowly, watching him, as if at any moment he might betray something to her suspicion, "I don't think I want to go to bed yet." She turned to Marlowe. "Do you want to come too?"

"Yes," he said, "I shouldn't mind a stroll."

They set off up the hill, past the old ruined winepress, and the small chapel surrounded by cypress trees. Some sort of constraint had dislocated the relations between them; and speech at that time, in that place, among those gloomy olive glades, would not have been a strong enough medium to repair the damage. Francis whistled softly now and then as she stepped among the boulders and the patches of thistle. They struck the edge of the crater into which, forty years before, a whole village had been thrown by a landslide. Prowling round the rim of it which was scooped, like the rim of a goblet, between sky and sea, they stared down on the silent remains of that village. The white houses seemed to be like the tombstones of a dead race, shining a cold electric warning to the three prowlers who watched them from above.

"Up here," said Francis quietly, and took the single narrow path which wound away up the hill towards the Jump.

They went up in single file between the shin-high, prickly hedges. At the top of the hill they came across a shepherd-boy, asleep under a bush; his sheep had deserted him and chumbled loudly two hundred yards farther down the slope.

The Jump was simply a white cliff, which jutted out over the sea, rather detached from its nearest neighbours, and whose top – perched high above the hill-side with its tall trees – formed a natural pediment;[127] at the very top of the triangle thus formed was a flat surface like a small dancing-floor. The eye of a man, who lay flat on his stomach to stare down the precipice to the sea, could detect, at the base of the Jump, a pair of gnarled boulders, and between them, a clear forty feet of water. As a natural ornament, it was superb; but it was something more than an ornament.

Standing up there one day, centuries before, the future patron saint of the island had been impressed by the perfect natural disposition of the rocks at the base, and the flat dancing-floor at the top. It had taxed his ingenuity to the utmost to discover (more strictly to invent) an ancient and legendary function for the place. But he had done it.

To his dependents and familiars he declared the discovery of a legend: long ago, in time of war, it had been the custom to insist that suspected traitors and spies should prove the honesty of their actions by observing the ceremony of the Jump; and such persons were now required to pre-cipitate themselves from this natural pediment, before a representative collection of village elders and ecclesiastical dignitaries. If they managed by skill or accident to fall between the twin rocks, and were not killed by the impact with the water, they were acquitted by general consent, and handsome apologies all round for mistrust were in order. If they were killed, then they were judged guilty.

For some time after the saint's pronouncement, the function of the Jump was a strict one. It was only when Theseus, a local athlete, was called upon to show one good reason why he should be allowed to marry the daughter of a man of substance, that the whole thing took a romantic turn. At an early date which I[128] have forgotten, this Theseus, who was a man of determination, declared himself irrevocably possessed of the favours of a rich man's daughter, without the consent of the father. When called upon to show good and sufficient reason for turning the head of a woman who would one day be rich and powerful in the island, he declared that he could offer nothing in the way of material wealth: but that he could out-run, out-wrestle, out-hunt, any man from any island. Furthermore, said he, to prove the strength of his attachment, he was prepared to chuck himself off the traitor's Jump in the presence of an audience nominated by the girl's father. If he were a man of fitting abilities, the gods would preserve him; if not, he was content to die.

On the day appointed for this divine test, all the inhabitants gathered on the top of the cliff, weeping and bidding good-bye to a famous and handsome athlete. Theseus, for his part, very calm and collected, measured the distance with his eyes, took a firm diver's hold on the rough rock with his toes, and waited the word of command. Then he launched his body out into space and directed himself, with deadly accuracy, at the pool between the two rocks. Above, on the dizzy crag, the crowd moaned and wept. But the body of the athlete shaved the left hand rock and entered the water like a raging torpedo, to appear, triumphant, twenty yards out to sea. The gods had granted him his life and his lover.

But that night (so capricious are the ways of gods) the athlete caught a bad cold at the village festivities given in his honour, and after a short illness, unaccountably died. Everyone was annoyed and not a little mystified. Why, if the gods had considered him unworthy as a husband, had they not taken their chance and killed him at the Jump? The village priest was sharply spoken to, as if he, in one way, were to blame. In self-defence he produced some cock-and-bull story about the gods refusing to pass judgment on any but traitors at the traitor's Jump; the man was not a traitor, he pointed out, but merely a suitor. The gods had reserved judgment until a time which they personally considered more propitious. And the dissatisfied villagers had to accept this enucleation. The only person who enjoyed the flavour of the anticlimax was the betrothed's father. He had been expecting a natural end to the importunate suitor, and had been put into a real panic when he realised that the athlete had passed the test of the Jump. Now he was able to laugh freely.

But, if Theseus died an ignominious death, the memory of his heroic jump served as a popular memorial to his life. His tale was embroidered by several local poets, his spiritual aid was invoked by lovers to smooth the course of erratic love affairs, and his example was followed by disappointed suitors. Many men young and old had jumped from the rock after him, and one or two women. The casualties were fairly high, though no one seemed ever to stop and consider this. (There is a splendid quixotry about lovers that is wholly admirable.)

They toiled up the path, panting a little at the exertion, while the puppy alternately ran on ahead and entangled itself in their feet, or got left behind and raised the most piteous din.

The dancing-floor was reached by climbing half a dozen steps cut into the wall of stone. Once on top, having gazed around at the island lying below them, and the immense sea, they sank to the ground, as if by common consent. Up here there was a sudden lift and fall of wind that made walking a precarious affair; and a faintly ominous whining at the sharp corners of the pediment beneath them. Francis made three attempts to light a cigarette, and at each attempt the match was blown out by the wind. Walsh, lying back on the smooth rock, and clasping his hands behind his head, began to whistle softly, beating one heel on the ground.

"Wind," said Francis angrily, and borrowed the pipe Marlowe had managed to light, sticking the tip of her cigarette into the bowl and sucking the smoke into her mouth.

"What did you think of the music?" asked Marlowe suddenly, and drew his legs in until he was sitting with them doubled under him, Indian fashion.

"Superlative," said Walsh out of turn.

"Particularly," she said, "the *tutti*[129] bit and the piano. That was pure magic."

"Yes, it was good," he said, relieved that the subject seemed to come easily to them at last. "Though, of course – "

A gust of wind swept round the corners of the dancing floor. Walsh made a wry mouth at Marlowe, and getting up walked steadily to the very edge of the Jump. Putting his hands to his hips he stared down the dizzy drop without blenching, bracing his legs against the force of the wind. Smooth, the walls of the cliff slid away beneath him, straight down to the points of rock.

"You know," he said at last, cocking his head on one side, it wouldn't be so hard after all to dive between the rocks down there. A matter of judgment." He smiled at Marlowe and turned back to his contemplation of the drop from the very point where, centuries before, Theseus the athlete had stood, preparing his soul and body for the jump, arguing his judgment out of despair.

Walsh unlatched his sandals and stood there, trying for a good foot-grip, testing now this strip of rock under his soles, now that; with one eye always cocked in the direction of the plunge. The two juts of rock menaced his sight, while between them lay the deep natural pool, split as the rest of the sea was now split into long slivers, by the touch of wind.

Far out to sea, amid the procession of ruffles, a school of dolphins rolled, keeping perfect alignment and time, heading northward; from the areas of cliff below them came the roar of the deeper water exploring caves deep in the body of the cliffs. Walsh stood, with the wind on his mouth, filled with the sense of space and the elation of distance. It affected him at first with nausea, like an insidious anaesthetic, but that state soon passed and everything was dissolved but the pure sense of distance; the haunting, inescapable doom of travel, from which one must either turn back or be lost.

He stood there, and slowly the fright and instability in him was conquered by the sheer magnitude of the thought. It was in his power to launch himself into the most perfect of craters – pure space; it was an experience to be cherished, aspiring, as all deep states of soul aspire, to the condition almost of a music. Yes, a music of flight – the final travel. In himself he could feel the sag and pull of muscles, which would, after the first constriction, set hard against the impact. His hands would be held thus, one clenched round the thumb of the other, forcing a large double fist to break the water ahead of him. Taut and stiff the strings of muscle in his legs mimicked the dive. His toe curled about the sharp ledge. He was perfectly assured, perfectly contained, concealing the elation which wanted to break his lips open with a shout or a song. The moment was one of exquisite tension.

Marlowe saw him draw breath, bend knees, and pull his arms out behind in preparation for a dive: and himself, choking on a mouthful of raw tobacco, said: "For God's sake now – " Lurching to his feet, he was felled again by one glance over the rim of the precipice. As he groped on the floor on his hands and knees, he thought in his mind that it was too late. He felt at the same time irritation, rage, fear. Meanwhile Walsh, quietly preoccupied, was imagining the flight of his own body down towards the pool; the tension of nerves, and the shadow which would dive with him – only soundless and without destiny – down that toppling wall of stone, slipping from shelf to shelf with gathering speed. And in the moment when Marlowe opened his eyes and saw that they were still there, all three of them, Francis, who had been lost to their antics, craned forward and said: "What was that?"

Walsh looked far out to sea, and said: "Ship heading north."

"No," she said; "no," and Marlowe, watching her, saw that she was looking inland along the flat valley, lit in half-tones by the moon.

They listened, and very faintly there came a sound, floating and desolate, like the cry of some night-bird on the western uplands. Perhaps the cry of a shepherd, Marlowe thought, craning forward.

Before them, perhaps a mile away, the splendid shoulder of Leucothea rose to heaven, blanched as a skull. The monastery was indistinguishable from the white rock of the cliff itself, but its position was marked by the stiff, cultivated bristle of cypresses round the little courtyard in which the windlass stood.

"From there," she said suddenly, with conviction, and before he could reply the frail cry reached them again, echoing across the valley.

Cupping his hands about his mouth, Walsh shocked the night by the thunder of his voice. The echoes took the sound and flung it from rock to rock, until the hillside was alive with his voice's crying out upon the sleeping valley. Lights appeared in the windows of the village which lay beyond, and to the left of Nanos.

Again the faint voice cried out, and again. Walsh hooded his ears and listened. He turned a puzzled face to them. "Only get one word of it. I think it's one of the monks. Perhaps one's ill or something."

He called again, but this time there was no answer, though the three of them sat, for a long time, waiting. In the end Walsh gave it up and, putting on his sandals, lay down again on his back.

"Perhaps one of them has died," said Francis quickly.

"More likely to be ill."

Marlowe rose to his feet and said: "Well, I tell you what. I'll go down to the village and get Fonvisin out of bed. Maybe he can help." No one spoke, and he began to climb down the first few steps in the stone.

"There's no need," said Walsh at last, almost unwillingly. "There's no social obligation here, you know."

"Oh, well," said Marlowe, inwardly very angry with him, "I feel tired enough to go to bed anyway. It's not much trouble."

But he raged as he stumbled downhill; and to his rage was added the fear of falling down that precarious path and breaking his bones. Without doubt the descent from the Jump was more difficult than the ascent to it; time and time again he followed the cliff path out to the verge of the landslide, with the sensation of walking on a volcanic crater. Nevertheless, he whistled shrilly, if a bit off key at times, to quell his doubts as well as his annoyance. On the first uplands, where the going was comparatively easy, he left the path and struck straight across the groves of olives. Somewhere out of sight, a flute was playing: a monotonous melody in twirls and quartertones, which gave a very eerie flavour to his excursion. Perhaps one of the shepherds.

A steamer was driving up channel and he stopped for a rest, and to watch it. From time to time it emitted hoarse threads of sound and smoke from its funnels. Lights winked along its decks.

He walked down the village path in the dust, very tired and ill at ease as to how to wake Fonvisin. He prowled around the wine-shop, notic-ing that all the windows were open. From one came the slow, gurgling laughter of a woman, and the rustle of bed-clothes. Fonvisin's; but, if there were now more doubts added to his existing doubts, the thought of his weariness and Walsh's jibe was enough to spur him on. If there were a legion of women in there, he reflected grimly, it would not stop him; he had come to get Fonvisin and he intended to do so. Raising his stick, he rapped quietly on the open shutters, placing himself before the well of darkness, so that his face would be recognisable from within. A dog began to growl and whine somewhere at the side of the house. There was no answer. He rapped again, more loudly, saying with a certain primness: "Fonvisin. Fonvisin."

Deep asthmatic snoring was his reply, together with the uncertain sound of a woman's stifled giggling, and the crisping of sheets. Marlowe was convinced that the Russian was having a game with him. He rapped once more, and spoke through the window, telling of the voice which had called to them from the monastery. "We thought perhaps one of the monks was ill," he added.

The snoring broke for a minute, and then continued as before, rather too loudly to be convincing. The giggles continued also, implying heaven only knew what sieges and sorties, advances, retreats, coquetries, between the verminous sheets of that verminous inn bed. It seemed that Fonvisin was not at home.

Marlowe turned round in annoyance and stumped off down the road in the direction of Phaon. It was really most annoying the way people behaved, he concluded. He unlocked the door of his villa with definite pleasure. He was very tired.

Standing on the cool floor that night, naked and ready for bed, he stared out across the spur of hill behind which the crags, both of Leucothea and of the Jump, were visible, letting his curiosity run free on the subject of the crying voice they had heard. But he could offer his mind no solution to the mystery; and as he lay in bed it was at last lost, as all other problems are lost, in the common need of sleep. He fell asleep, drunk-tired, with the moon on his face.

Francis and Walsh, left alone, lay still and listened to diminishing sounds of Marlowe's progress down the hill. They could hear him whistling away in his absurd bravado for quite a time. The puppy, who had begun to find the rock cold, came and snuggled into the angle of Francis' shoulder for comfort. Walsh turned his face to the sky and set up an indistinct whistle that was no louder than a whisper. The bray of a steamer lifted itself from the silence and was swallowed up again. Turning on her elbow, Francis said: "You don't like him very much, do you?"

The boy turned his face to her for a second, smiling, and then resumed his staring at the sky, with an eloquent silence. He said drowsily: "All these people with a faintly pained look between the eyes irritate me. They're not positive enough. I can't stand this business of eating themselves in little bits, and working up a vast enthusiasm in raffia-work[130] or ancient history, and hiding behind their own pinafores. D'you see what I mean?"

"Yes."

She stroked the soft fur of the puppy and closed her eyes. Beyond his voice she could hear the heavy drive of the waves in the caves far down beneath them. Inside her was a deep peace which must end in sleep. She yawned deeply in her throat and was about to renounce life for this positive swoon of blankness, when she felt the firm pressure of his mouth close down on hers. It was so sudden that her nerves gave a great leap, and the muscles of her body tightened with an instinctive reflex of repulsion. But, holding her carelessly with one hand, he pressed home the kiss, as quickly and naturally as if by magic.

Opening her eyes she saw his face shadowy over her, and behind it the sky which held a single waning moon.

"Fool," she said sorrowfully, but not moving. "Fool, Walsh."

"Yes," he said, with a grin.

But, fool or no fool, his hold on her did not relax. Gently with his fingers he touched the round flesh of her arm, drawing them along her forearm until he held her hand hard.

"'Motley's the only wear'"[131] he said with a chuckle of intimate laughter, and began to kiss her mouth until they were both dizzy and trembling with the nervous delight of contact. She could feel his warm body, rather thin and fine, pressing elegantly at her side. Under the small mound of her left breast he put his hand, to feel her heart.

"Don't you see," she said at last, jerkily, sucking in mouthfuls of air to help her quickened breathing, "don't you see it doesn't matter a damn to me? Walsh, please."

"Of course," he said, lying back, with his arms over his face. "I didn't expect it to." She stretched out her body, trembling.

"Walsh," she said quietly, at last. But when he turned to her he was no longer Walsh, and she herself no longer Francis. The metamorphosis of the moon and place had made them, strangely, into Reuben and Ruth. His face hanging above her was all Reuben, so that she put an arm up to his throat and began to cry, in long painful sounds, her face puckered in the grimace of weeping.

"Let's go home," she said in a whisper, "Walsh, let's go home."

But for answer he turned her body over to him, and taking her head in his arms, kissed the uncomfortable mouth angrily, until the pain of weeping became inseparable from the pain of his bruising, and the night toppled backwards into a darkness of vertigo and swoon. It was something of the sensation Theseus had known on his vivid journey from sky to sea. But she found herself speaking in the quick tones of coherence and need.

"It's no use," she said finally, putting him gently from her. "Now for Christ's sake listen to me. I tell you it's no use."

"And why?" he said. "Why?"

He lit a cigarette with trembling fingers, and looking up at her with a smile, shrugged his shoulders.

"I don't understand it," he said at last, "but I'll believe it. Poor Francis!"

"Yes," she said.

"Poor Francis," he said more softly, himself hovering between brute laughter and compassion.

"Yes," she repeated numbly, like a child.

He leaned back and put one arm across his face.

"'Motley's the only wear,'" he said at last, and was silent.

It was a long time before she rose to her feet and said: "Let's go back, shall we? It feels a bit damp."

"Dew," he said.

They climbed the stone ladder down the side of the dancing-floor stiffly, Walsh carrying the snoozing puppy under his arm.

Eastward there was a faint light now; the sun was coming up behind Turkey and Constantinople. As they circled the brim of the landslide, a faint ring of hammers sounded from the valley. A collection of tiny red specks, like coloured beetles, were busy about a building, and beyond them, half in deep shadow, half in grey morning light, the river shone as it travelled westward. He yawned hugely and said:

"Look, Francis," pointing out the growing familiarity of the landmarks – Pothetos, Phaon, the village with its troop of mules jogging away down to the seaweed beach.

On the lowlands she crooked her arm in his and, laughing up at his face with the greatest affection, began to sing; and singing, cajoled him to join, until they were walking in time to their own music, cavalierly.

## Chapter XI

# World Without End

MARLOWE slept heavily until eleven the next morning; and his awakening was unique. He came drunkenly awake with the feeling that his head was about to part company with his body: and found that it was only Maria. She had taken his shoulders in her hands and was busy shaking and banging him awake. Mercifully for her, the step between mere coherence and downright anger was too large for him to climb that morning: so he coldly asked the reason for these frivolities, and was informed that Gordon wanted to speak to him.

"Come in," he called irritably, "for the love of Christ, man, and don't bother this girl."

Gordon came in and the girl in question departed. In his right hand he held a large bunch of black grapes. Seating himself languidly upon the chair, he cracked them singly between his teeth and chatted amiably until Marlowe felt sufficiently awake to go and bathe with him. As they trotted down the path to the sea he said casually: "Walsh crawled in at dawn dead-beat and said you'd been up to the Jump."

"Good Lord, yes," said Marlowe, and suddenly recalled the object of his speculations the night before. Gordon had more positive news. One of the monks had come down with pleurisy, and his fellow, after noticing someone on top of the Jump and shouting for help, had made the descent to the village in search of medical aid. He had arrived before dawn, and created such a din outside the wine-shop that Fonvisin had been forced to go up to Leucothea to see if he could do anything. Gordon, having been awakened by the general noise, had gone up with him to the monastery, and had only just got back.

"He's a game old bird," he said with admiration, as he stood ankle-deep in the water. "Lying there on a mattress of dry twigs and praying in all directions. It must have cost him agonies to come down for the music last night."

Fonvisin, needless to say, had been acrimonious to everyone, and particularly to Gordon. The peasants didn't need doctors, he insisted. If their natural resistance could not pull them through diseases, then nothing in the way of medical skill could do it.

"I suppose really their resistance to dirt and disease must be pretty high," said Gordon. "My word, though, Marlowe, you should have seen that old bird, sitting there like a winged rook and praying like hell. And his pal so pleased with himself for having got a real foreign doctor on the job. The patient immediately gained caste. And all Fonvisin did was to tidy him up a bit and tell him to lie quiet for a while."

The morning passed pleasantly enough for them. A bathe and breakfast restored to Marlowe his balanced mood of quietness. After the meal they strolled down the village and watched the boats unloading stone and materials for the church.

From the beach road to the small green in the grave-yard, a string of men and donkeys carried stone and yet more stone. This was stacked under the eye of the master mason, Spiro, who had come down from the furthermost hill-village in answer to the summons of Rumanades. Meanwhile, a small and languid demolition squad were stripping those parts of the wall which would have to be replaced.

The old man was there at the church, walking about in the dust from the passing donkeys, and chatting to the workmen. They could see his bearded face turning this way and that among the yellow hats flowering around him under the strong morning sun. The scene was instinct with vivacity. The village children frolicked like sparrows in and out of the dark church, laughing and chattering. Gordon and Marlowe strolled through the cool citron groves which flanked the road, and at their coming, the host of the tavern sent out a table and three chairs to the shadow of the great eucalyptus tree: here they sat with old Rumanades, drinking wine and encouraging the workmen by their example of sloth. The priest came up to pay his respects, impressive in his chimneypot hat and soutane, and holding above him an umbrella whose pitted, sieve-like fabric was the colour of a lemon-skin. In a little while, he said, he would be going up to Leucothea to see his monk. He did not think there was anything serious about the man's illness. He had been taken like this a dozen times before, and had recovered easily, without the help of anyone. He sipped a glass of wine with gravity, solicited their opinions of the weather, and then said a charming good-bye, puffing out his umbrella and taking the mountain path.

"Has Fonvisin come down yet?" asked the old man, and Gordon replied that he did not know, but he imagined him to have returned and to be sleeping his full quota in the wine shop; a hazard which was corroborated by the evidence of the tavern-keeper. Fonvisin, it appeared, was in the worst of tempers, so they put off their visit (a project suggested in pure malice by Marlowe) until a more suitable time.

Marlowe and Gordon lunched at Phaon, had a prodigious siesta (falling asleep in the middle of an acrimonious discussion on the exact definition of retrospect), and bathed at tea-time; after which Gordon took over the duties of host and supervised tea and supper.

To Marlowe the problem represented by their casual existence was one which was only too easily dissipated by the languor of sleep or exercise or eating; nevertheless, in the moments when he realised how, for all his contemplation, the sun was vaguely and pleasantly corroding his scheme, he was reminded that their existence there contributed really nothing to their lives. By their lives, of course, he implied a steadily rising line on a graph, plotted by ambition or any other of the actuating motives in life. But then, he reflected glumly, a positive up-curve on the graph represented more nearly what one owned, and not what one was. Spiritual growth was incommensurate: and the life of acquisition was dependent on time as much as on ambition and force. And there was the crux of the question. Time had ceased to exist, he realised with something of a shock. The shock of this realisation was increased further when he examined the calendar which adorned his walls. He had to strip a handful of paper days before he reached a date on which his birthday had fallen. It had passed three days ago.

Something of this mood he suggested to Gordon one day when they were lying, drunk with the sun, on the sand-beach below Phaon. Gordon's answer was excursive. "Not only time, thank God," he said, drowsily, "but they also keep distance under control here. It would be a good idea for tourist agencies. Ask anyone in the village how far it is to Nanos and they'll answer: so many cigarettes. To them all smokers smoke at the same speed. It gives one great courage if one's walking anywhere. You smoke like hell, that's all."

"But you yourself," said Marlowe curiously, "are you content to spend the rest of your life in a state of timelessness?" Gordon turned over and considered him. "I'm not sure," he said at last, slowly, and lying back in the deep ring of shadow cast by his straw hat, sank into sleep.

"It's an anaesthetic," said Marlowe, and for the life of him he could not avoid a touch of irritation creeping into the remark. Out of a deep drowse Gordon answered him: "You ought to be satisfied at any rate. It helps your scheme along, doesn't it?"

Marlowe's subsequent efforts to complete the essay on the New

Quietism were a sufficient if tardy answer to the question. So far from things being a help, they were a positive hindrance. It was impossible to construct the ordered and logical framework of his scheme, when a half turn of his head could show him the flawless gift of landscape; the boats rowing across his window like heavy birds, with the brown men standing at the oars; the sconces stuck with flowers around the flippers of the prickly pears; the peasants in their vivid costumes. Yes, it was impossible. The pen became a useless, intractable instrument, the papers began to swarm with drawings and tentative misquotations, while his mind itself became blunt and animal, unable to escape the sheer drugs of flesh-comfort.

Chrysanthe brought him a present of black grapes, and got into the habit of flirting mildly with him; a habit which he was too weak to destroy.

His carefully tabulated scheme of notes he put away at the bottom of his trunk, disgusted with himself. Instead of his plump, rather overlaid prose he found himself one day writing a poem.

In his crawling handwriting he read, with a genuine concern:

> What sweet white meat our bodies are,
> Who have no canon but delight:
> Such pretty devil's food,
> O daintier by far
> We triflers in a foreign night
> Than all those delicately tended meats
> That weight the tables of the rich.
> Angels have little meat in them
> But vague and evanescent shapes,
> Declare the elders wise
> Who hoard their comforts tip for Paradise.
>
> Are we then brutes, my dear, or hinds
> Who for refreshment can devise
> A sport so rich, a food so able
> That Soul, that gracious wedding-guest
> Waits at the body's table?[132]

He was scandalised by such poor philosophy, and tore the paper into guilty little pieces. But it was no good. The essay would not get moving. He sat for two hours every morning solemnly regardant, pen in hand, waiting for the afflatus. But the minor preoccupations delighted him so much that he would be lucky, at the end of that time, if he had so much as written the number of the page at its head. Curiously, too, it didn't seem to matter very much: and the moralist in him resented this sapping of conscience as much as the sapping of energy, force, direction. It was all tedious beyond words. However, the shreds of routine hung together and made a sort of covering for conscience. The needs of the flesh had lost none of their regularity, whatever the failings of the mind. Dinner time was as welcome after a morning spent in sunbathing as it would have been if he had walked twenty miles for it; supper time, with its following cup of sweet Turkish coffee, black grapes, apples, and a delicate Papastratos cigarette,[133] contributed a passivity, an ease, an unbuttoning which the wildest stretch of imagination could not relate to the cold mental processes of the mind. It was unfortunate, but there it was.

However, since conscience even the merest approximation to conscience – of which he was now possessed – demanded some kind of salve, he engineered something fresh with which to dress it. In the late summer and autumn, he assured himself, he would commence another drive in the direction of the philosophic camp. At present, it being too hot, what could be better than to lock his notebooks away, and give himself a holiday from himself? What better? He borrowed from Gordon a battered text of the *Odyssey* and a large lexicon and settled down to the heroic task.

If the tale had been moving before, it was now doubly so, having the authenticities of weather and situation to back it. He could delude himself, with real excitement in the fraud, that there, to the south-east, the fires still fumed stale smoke at dawn, from the Ithacan hearth of the hero. That grey-eyed Athene might, since even the immortals are subject to whim, suspend operations and pay them a visit; Chrysanthe herself, with her rough sense of humour, might be she in disguise. Droll speculations! And Francis? In the scheme of things Francis occupied a position roughly analogous to that of Calypso, binding the hero with bonds of magic to the sea bastioned island. The rôle of Odysseus himself he did not assign, but wisely left it open, confident that somewhere in the tale there would be a hero of his stature.

And so Marlowe played away his time with calculated deceit. If time had ceased to exist, then there could be no measure put against his playing; indeed, to complete the circle of paradox, there was no future when the present was so full: of the fruits ripening, of the peasants singing rich and melodious with plenty, of children being born, men dying. No, there was no future, as there was no past.

Occasionally, of course, there would be qualms; a nightmare or a fit of nerves would set him back to his defences, haggard with fear for a bit. But the medicine of casual life was too sure to fail him.

He grew a small fluffy beard which made him look like a gnome; and when Chrysanthe laughed at him, shaved it off painfully with Gordon's blunt safety-razor, because he was waiting for a relay of razor blades which the fortnightly boat was bringing him. With infinite difficulty he learned the crawl swimming stroke from Gordon. He spent a good deal of his time playing the piano in the Villa Pothetos; swimming; fishing; walking to the Old Temple for fêtes and trying to learn the complicated ancient dances which persist among the peasants in modern Greece. He went on a long excursion with the old man to see the fig crop gathered, dried and loaded for shipping in the tiny northern harbour. They visited the French entomologist in his bleak hut and found him hovering between rage and happiness; in one day he had broken two strings of his violin, and discovered a rare form of louse, which he kept religiously imprisoned in a test-tube, and on which he counted for fame. He offered them cold tea with a slice of lemon, and managed to turn the subject of conversation in the direction of university life: from thence to the University of Padua: and from thence (rising to his full height) it was easy enough to launch his familiar diatribe.

In addition to these, there were other distractions. There was a procession to the deserted chapel at the hilltop in honour of its own especial patron saint; a procession in which they all joined, even Fonvisin, and which was distinguished by the fact that Constantine had a fit and rolled about in the dust, foaming and snapping, until he had soiled his virginal white suit and sailor cap, and torn the fistful of ceremonial lilies (stolen from the grounds of the Villa Pothetos) into a mangled rag of grey pulp. Christ, who tried to lay hands on him, nearly had a finger bitten off.

With the first touches of real heat the peasants entered into their royalties. Baskets piled high with fruit and vegetables would arrive, mysteriously, at the door, and Chrysanthe would notify him of a present to himself from some fellow hillside-dweller, of whose existence he was not aware. The peasants gave for the sheer pleasure of giving, and did it well, with a graciousness that was touching. The fruit was a signal of their royalty, and the season of black grapes, apples, peaches, pears, was the season in which they expanded and, taking no thought of the winter, carried largesse in both hands. Old Avrili, for instance, riddled with consumption – whose house, uncouthly made from flattened tin torn from oil-cans, was a death trap in the winter – now carried his head high, and gave bunches of black grapes from his tiny piece of ground to all the foreigners, and to Rumanades, his master. It was difficult to imagine when one saw him, proud in a wide straw hat, chatting equally with his neighbours, that the winter would drive him back to his tin hut, and change him again to the small black wisp of wasted manhood shaken with that high cough. Yet it was so. In the winter, said Gordon, the peasants virtually starved. Now, in the first weeks of summer, Marlowe could not imagine these playing-card kings and queens suffering; could not indeed imagine that, for all the fruits, olives and bread remained their diet.

For the time being, the *Odyssey* gave him plenty to do. He even contemplated beginning a prose translation of it, but did not get farther than the first few pages. Time, or timelessness, had imposed too heavy a burden on him.

It was Gordon, again, who suggested a solution to the scheme, and defined the position which they occupied in it. Lying on his back on the tiles of Marlowe's little drawing-room, smoking one of his host's cigarettes, he said one day: "I can't understand the fuss and bother people create about doing nothing. There's Walsh down there wondering whether he's justified in ignoring civilisation and drawing his money from it, and you up here chewing your socks because you can't get any work done. It seems to me that Francis and I are the only ones who get any benefit out of sloth and inaction. Even old Fonvisin has qualms. I can't fathom it."

Marlowe, staring out with aching eyes on the morning landscape, tapped his teeth with a pencil, and decided that he, too, was at a loss to account for it. The sun had created a kind of vacuum for them, in which all action not connected with sloth or indulgence had neither weight nor significance.

"It's a sort of huge vacuum of heat," said Gordon, reading his thought almost word for word. "You can't do anything much inside it except live physically. And," here he began to laugh, "after all, my God, what more can a man want?"

What more indeed? Really, Marlowe was getting a little cross with himself for not being able to supply a coherent answer to any of these questions.

"It's an anaesthetic," he said again, almost plaintively, and this time Gordon laughed loudly.

"Which is what we all need," he said at last. "But then, why don't you leave?"

Leave? he thought; one could not leave. Even the activity necessary to face a change of place or time…. He was beginning to visualise them all as chained to Mavrodaphne, chained like Odysseus, by magic. But their Calypso was the sun. Waves of heavy scent broke across the garden, entered the room, and dispersed. The hum of the cicadas was a deep pulse beating in the silence. He turned the little tooth-glass which Chrysanthe had brimmed with flowers and placed on the table, round, and slowly round in his fingers. Soon it would be lunch time.

"What you ought to do," said Gordon, sinking into sleep, "is to shape your retrospection scheme out during the summer, and leave the writing of it to the winter."

He conquered the temptation to laugh. Shutting his eyes, he made a mental note of the fact that Marlowe was mad. Irrevocably mad.

"That's what I am doing," said Marlowe, mildly. To Gordon there was something a little pathetic in the idea of him sitting there, turning a useless pen over in his fingers and yawning.

"It's rather a good thought," said the boy slowly.

"What is?"

Gordon sat up and brushed the shaggy hair off his eyebrows. Having blown his nose violently in a red handkerchief, he said, eagerly: "You see, all our lives have a tendency to have flat spots in them. Drops off the graph if you like. Have you ever been in the state when you know you are just hanging between the past and the future? The present is a sort of null spot, a doldrum, what you like. Have you ever felt that?"

Marlowe considered the question with something very nearly boredom.

"Yes," he said at last, definitely, "I have."

"Well," said Gordon hoarsely, in articulo mortis,[134] composing himself for sleep with his hands on his stomach.

"In this state of waiting for the next bus after having got off the last, one only lives by virtue of the past, and is only interested in the future which is around the corner. For instance I don't consider all this real at all."

He indicated "this" by sweeping both hands in a wide arc and letting them lapse again to his stomach.

He opened his eyes for a minute and smiled beautifully at the ceiling. Marlowe turned in his chair, lifted his feet infinitely to the desk, and crushed the butt of his cigarette out under the leg of his tilted chair. Dusting his fingers on his bare breast, he blinked and said: "I don't follow you." He found the thought of the past unpleasant, the future, implying as it did a choice between Fred's Canterbury brewery and the pedagogue's desk, disquieting. Whatever the present did to one, it certainly presented enough immediate colour and life to disqualify it as a limbo – a gap in the continuity of things.

Gordon, in a drowsy voice, continued his parody of the schoolmaster's thought.

"It's a bloody limbo," he said robustly. "It doesn't exist for any of us really." His voice sank, huskily, to indicate that he was using large and portentous figures of thought. "A limbo," he said again. "I suppose you don't see that?"

Marlowe said that he did not.

"No," said Gordon, with satisfaction, "of course you don't. God but it's hot. Shall I try and explain?"

"Do," invited Marlowe, drowsily. "Please do."

"Well," said Gordon, making a great effort, "I begin by assuming that you know what I mean when I talk about 'all this'? Right. Well, if you examine it, you find us five people torn out of our environment and pushed up here for a rest. The limbo idea. A transitional vacuum for us all. I bet you if we five met in the civilised world, all doing our jobs, all the values of whatnot…thing…I mean our relationship would be altered. Do you see what I'm getting at? All our normal values are phut here. Washed out." He yawned and added: "Pause for questions."

"Go on," said Marlowe kindly, "go on."

He was picturing to himself the five of them; himself staring, away from the class of inky boys across the wet Kentish fields, waiting for the bell and the security of the common room; Walsh trotting from building to building in Charing Cross Road,[135] at home among those nests of Jew-boys and the visiting crooners who packed the professional departments; Fonvisin, clad in clothes less fantastically ragged, flitting from hospital to hospital, busy with carving and twisting the diseased flesh of his patients into quaint shapes; and Gordon? By no stretch of imagination could he imagine him in any other situation or pose than that which he occupied at this moment; clad scantly and asleep, smoking someone else's cigarettes. Gordon in relation to clothes, to bowler hats, to trains – to the whole structure of ordered civilization – was nearly as much of an enigma as Francis was – or appeared to be; for Francis would only fit into his picture of a world of typewriters and garrets with difficulty. Yes, he supposed there was some truth in it. Perhaps Mavrodaphne was some kind of limbo between lives, whose only furniture was the sun. He himself, he supposed, had changed as much as the others had. He said simply:

"It's not a bad idea."

"It's more than an idea," said Gordon loudly. "It's, it's…a Figure, that's what it is. Dash it, Marlowe, we might do anything here and it would be congruous. It would fit. I could cut you into pieces and boil you down for bootblacking without any trace of incongruous behaviour. We have no relation with the past. We're only interested in the future because it frightens us. It's more than an idea…it's a Heroic Reality. I would like to see you freeze up when you get bunged out of here some time. I'd like to see your reversion and readjustment to things."

Marlowe said nothing. He was busy trying to estimate to what extent he had been changed by events; and even as he screwed up his eyes to attempt an objective visual impression of his diminutive self sitting here, in spite of the glare outside the window, Gordon parodied his thought again.

"Look at yourself!" he said with humorous malice, "flirting old Chrysanthe off her feet, going about almost bare, and shaving under the arms."

Annoyed, Marlowe crossed his feet and said nothing. To banter of this kind there was nothing to say. He froze. But the idea, for all this vagueness and dependence on self-dramatisation, interested him. Perhaps, he thought, remembering that it would give colour to his reluctance for the hard work of writing, there was an item or two of truth in it. Perhaps there was.

"Why don't you leave," said Gordon at last, "and take a running dive into the stream again?"

Why did he not leave? And hearing the phrase repeated in his memory, he saw it take on a changed colour. As if a wave had broken over his mind, he saw the whole significant pattern of his present life, as it were, spread out and advancing on him like something he had long desired – the fruits, the flowers, the peasants, the smell and sound and above all the enviable nothing, the utter cleaning away of fear and desperation.

But the idea was not brought home to him fully until one day, when he and Francis had walked to the west coast of the island, and were standing on the great stone cliffs against which the African tides crushed and pounded. From the woods above a peasant came running down to them through the carpets of pine needles. He handed Marlowe a letter.

While the mighty wind dragged at his hat, and at the skirts of the girl, he turned the envelope over in his fingers, shocked by the English stamp and Fred's painful handwriting, smudged and thumbed by the various posts. With a feeling of remoteness that was almost a new despair in itself, he put it in his pocket, mumbling, and turned back to the cliffs, taking the girl's arm in his agitation. Down below, on a beach of powdered gold were the running, shouting figures of naked fisher-boys, as alone and self-reliant as those first small Minoans who had come here, to this very spot, in their crazy boat, and had beached it, laughing and chatting softly in the old languages.

It was utterly incongruous that here, on this final cliff of pitted stone, with nothing in view across the Adriatic, and Africa an imaginable speck over the horizon, men should come up and hand him letters from Fred, without so much as a "Doctor Livingstone, I presume."

One glance at the pawky handwriting, however, settled whatever doubts he might have had about its reality; no one but Fred would indulge in those twirls and flourishes. As he put it in his pocket he felt the whole weight of his England press down on him, like a sentence; the school, the common-room, faces, the Whitstable Road, the Brewery, the sea front under sheets of winter spray – the procession of images across his mind was endless. And the old tormenting decision which he had yet to make seemed as remote, and yet as tormentingly near to him, as had seemed the first rumble of guns he had heard across the Channel, from a Sussex hillside.

Below them the sun was slipping down across the bastions and ramparts of rock, glistening on the rock-pools and the wet bodies of the fisher-boys. The spray exploded in sheaves of coloured water among them. A couple of dolphins slipped westward into the night. There was such a deep loneliness in him, now, watching, at the thought of Fred's world waiting for him, at the thought of Fred's letter in the pocket of his trousers, that he wanted to turn quickly to the girl and take her in his arms; kissing her would be a kind of charm against the future, against age, against the importunities of life. But he would not. Only, in a kind of panic, he held on to her arm, pressing it tight in his fingers; and she, oblivious to his thoughts, only let the hair swing back across her forehead in the wind, laughing, turning her wet mouth up to him to make the laughter mutual.

That night, after he had read Fred's letter, and recalled the moment of receiving it, he was shocked at his own inclinations, and remembered Gordon's remarks on the subject of congruous behaviour. There was no precedent in his past for such distracting ideas. Yet he could not help imagining his mouth on the wet mouth of the girl, as they stood on the cliff, with her hair blowing over him. It was a thousand pities, he thought, in spite of himself, that he had not taken his chance. He examined his face very carefully in the mirror before rereading Fred's letter.

MY DEAR CHRIS,

Where you are, or what you're doing, I don't know, but I'm
writing to try and get you at the last poste restante address in Italy.
The point is this. When you were away a friend – do you know
the Englands (Major) – heard that we had a junior partnership
going and he came and asked me if his son could take advantage
of it (Eton and Oxford). I said I would have to consult you as
you have first option of it. He is a fine man and his son is a *real
scholar*. They have a Bentley and big social connections in the
county. On the councils, etc. So I want you to make up your mind
soon and drop me a line. If you still want to come in with us I
will be glad to have you, but if not I think this England boy would
be good for business. Emily sends her love and the kiddies too.

Ever your sincere brother,
FREDERICK MARLOWE.

Reading it three or four times, to get the full flavour of its banality, he realised that Gordon had been wrong in denying their present life on Mavrodaphne a reality. It was only too blessedly real; and realising this, he set out to impress its reality and comparative excellence on himself anew.

Perhaps he knew that his time was running short. He drowsed away the mornings with Rumanades, watching the church being built; sitting at a table under the eucalyptus tree sipping wine or *ouzo*.[136] He surrendered himself utterly to a life of eating, sleeping, bathing, fishing in the bay – and above all ignoring the menace of that letter which lay, pinned flat in derision, against the wall of the drawing room. Now that the possible end of his life on the island was in sight, he sought more than ever to enjoy its timelessness; to create a vacuum that would be proof against the future thin air of life. And for very comfort he would have liked Francis to share that vacuum. But his chance in this direction never came.

Francis herself had been filled of late with forebodings about her own future. Though she had no illusions about the comparative reality or unreality of life on Mavrodaphne, she did not feel equal to going back, and trying to sail the collapsible boat of her fortunes in the middle of the stream again. Walsh was another problem. She regretted having denied him. She was sick with the futility of her own mind and body.

But there were other signs of bad weather ahead. Noah Silverstein's letters had become increasingly infrequent, and less gallantly particular. Her designs, he said, in one letter, were becoming few and far between, and he had noticed a definite falling off in the quality of them. She replied that since Greece was flooded with printed cotton materials which bore the stamp, Jacob & Co., Wigan, 3/11 a doz., the chances of her finding a sturdy and original art among the local peasantry were small; however, if he could hang on until the winter, she would make a trip to the Turkish bazaars in Albania and see if there was anything amusing there. In answer to this, she received a huffy letter from him saying that Hopkins had already drained Albania dry of design. It was depressing.

If her preoccupations sprang from a different source, her reactions to them were much the same as Marlowe's. She too tried to impress upon herself the distractions of the glorious present, and began to prepare one of the walls of the church for her fresco. The work should be difficult enough to occupy her mind.

Marlowe would sit for hours in a pew, sucking his pipe, drowsing, and watching her begin the work. By the fortnightly boat he had sent off his letter to Fred, in which he had invited him to go ahead with the new junior partner. He was choosing, and choosing badly, he knew; but the choice had become to him less fatal, less actual, related more to the quixotry of this place where the peasants starved all winter, and gave the fruit of their gardens for presents in summer; where these softly chatting stone-shifters in their yellow straws and coloured baggy trousers moved with the swagger of buccaneers; above all, where this tall brown girl dabbled with the paint and brushes, whistling softly in the dark church.

Slowly the season advanced; the imperceptible marches of summer. The lagoon lay all afternoon, furled up by the maestro, like a great carpet of blue and green. The little steamers, coloured and puffing, which passed up the strait, seemed as local as toys upon the drawing-room carpet. He could reach out a hand and lift them up into the air; he could step out from the window on to this blue carpet and, in a couple of strides, overtake them as they fussed north for Corfu.

When the others slept he would go down to the shore, in the full afternoon heat, and walk in the surf, peeping under the awnings of the fishing-boats which were tied up, for the siesta hour. Once he came upon a boat stacked high with melons, beside which its crew, stretched out, slept. The sun shining down through the canvas awning produced lights, which ran like liquid butter over the flesh of the fruit, and the limbs of the crew. So tumbled were they that it was impossible to tell where the melons began and the bodies of the human beings ended.

But the policy of inaction did not quite dispense with the threat that civilisation held for him. Sooner or later.... When the next Brindisi boat put out he sent a letter to Latimer asking him if it would be possible to return to a school in the winter. That was one safeguard.

It was galling at this time, when his position had been threatened, to realise that both Gordon and Walsh were above the more grubby money-worries. Private means, slender but adequate for one, preserved the economic balance of Gordon's life, while Walsh, with his songs, was well off as people go. Marlowe was rather envious of that sort of proficiency; indeed he had always had a contempt for the natural prosperity of people to whom that prosperity was all but meaningless. From this feeling Rumanades alone was excepted. Perhaps that was because one could not help feeling that he had stumbled upon his wealth by mistake. So remote was that vanished dapper self of the financier, so unimaginable!

It came as something of a shock to him to realise that he was not the only one who was perplexed by the problem of the future. Francis asked him one day, with a laugh, whether he remembered the tale of Noah Silverstein. She handed him the latest letter from the mat-maker.

MY DEAR LITTLE LADY,

I am afraid that this will come as a bit of a shock to you, but don't be angry with me. In making the decision which I am going to tell you about I was forced to concede to the demands of my board.

At this point he noticed a cynical annotation in charcoal. In the margin, opposite the word "board," there appeared the query: (bawd?).

> Things have not been doing very well at this end for some time, and the company considers it a drain on their purse to continue paying your retaining fee. I would gladly have continued the fee out of my own pocket and let you carry on unknowing, but I felt it might injure your pride. So I thought I'd be honest.

Marlowe handed back the autumn yellow paper. "Well," he said, "you've got the three months in which to do nothing. Plenty of time."

She smiled at his remark and went on painting, saying quietly: "If I want to find a job, I'll have to get back to London by the end of this month. I can't afford to lose the fee while I'm looking round."

"No," he said, "I suppose not."

He was wondering, rather desperately, if there were no way of putting off these imminent changes, and re-establishing life on its old reckless basis of timelessness. Time, when they least expected it, had decided to set a very definite term to their activities. It was unfair.

That evening Francis strolled up to the Villa Pothetos and invited herself to tea. Sitting in one of the capacious arm-chairs, balancing a cup of tea on her knees, she announced her intention to the old man. To her surprise he took it fairly easily. Perhaps the former alarms had steeled him against the idea, so that now, in the face of its execution, he showed little fear, and less annoyance. He held his bearded chin in the palm of his hand for a time, staring sadly at the floor, and then said, in a small voice, whose rise and fall betrayed nothing more than casual unhappiness and a little interest: "Is it a question of money, Francis?"

"No, she answered. "It's just that the company I work for want me to go back to the central office."

For some reason her voice had a note of hauteur. In the silence she gulped her tea and prayed that he would not bribe her to stay on; that would be acceptable from anyone, curiously enough, but old Rumanades.

"It has made me very happy," he said at last, vaguely, softly turning the wisps of his beard in his fingers. "All my friends here on the island."

"They'll be here," she answered crisply, "all of them, except me." It was on the tip of her tongue to mention Marlowe's difficulties, but she did not. "They'll be here," she repeated, as though the thought would offer him some reassurance against loneliness. "And who knows? I might come back in a few months' time."

"Yes," he said, looking up at her shyly and smiling. "That's true. You might be able to come back again."

He poured himself another cup of tea, with a fatal feeling inside himself, that once she had gone she would never come back.[137] And she, watching him, drank her tea loudly, and cursed herself for a sentimental creature.

"Yes," he said at last, "I suppose it's true enough."

For a moment he had a wild desire to outrage his own sense of propriety: smash the tea-pot, or burst into peal upon peal of silly laughter. Instead he lit a cigarette and smiled calmly into the wide eyes of the girl.

"And what about the fresco?" he asked.

He was contemptuous, now, of his own subterfuge. Why had he ever imagined such an obligation would be strong enough to dislocate the machinery of life and business and set it out of gear for a term? It was a misjudgment. The fresco, at one word, assumed its place in the scheme of trivialities.

"The fresco?" she said, puzzled for a moment. "I can't finish it, of course, but I'll finish the west wall."

"Yes?" he said, showing no interest; only the abstraction which held his eyes to the floor.

He got up and walked across to the window, carefully opening it wide, to let the cool evening air, heavy with scent, come into the room. Turning to her he said, at last, as quietly as before:

"Shall we have a little farewell party here for you, if you don't mind? A day or two before the boat sails?"

She got up in agitation, putting her cup down on the tray. "If you like to," she said softly, and held out her hand to say good-bye.

That evening, after dinner, he went up to Manuela's room, and sitting on the terrace outside it, stared for a long time at her picture, turning it over and over in his hands as if it held some mystery to which he could not find the answer.

Below him the familiar seas lay, under the moon, holding, it seemed to him, something of the same quality of mystery as the photograph he turned and studied in the light of the lamp.

Down below, in the bay, was the familiar talk of the stone shifting crew; they had just brought in a fresh boat of materials and were debating whether to try and get it out of the hold that night, or wait for morning. Very rich their voices sounded to his listening ears, and their cheerful noise was the noise of another world, alien to him. It was only at night, he reflected, that the old hauntings and superstitions clouded the mind, and the spirit knew that there was no hope for it. I think perhaps at that moment he was seeing his own death, and understanding it as he had never succeeded in understanding the life of that little gang of chattering men in coloured clothes who stood on the stinking jetty and enjoyed a communion of banter and humour, each with his fellow. To-morrow, he knew, the sun would shine, and the peasants would come to him with their grievances as helots to their lord. The whole day-long preoccupation with common life and judgment would protect him. And after to-morrow there would be other to-morrows, no less full of quietness, while the fruit ripened and men died and women made more men to take their places. The church would have to be built and the saint glorified; the olives would have to be gathered, pressed, barrelled and shipped... life carried one along irresistibly.

Nevertheless, that night, standing on the balcony of his room, in his striped pyjamas, staring out to sea, he was shaken by a sort of grief: a pain which left no trace upon his composed features, called out no sound from his throat. Strangely enough his grief was not for Francis or for the vanished Manuela, but for something greater than both of them, which included them both; it was a grief for the life that was slipping away through his fingers, second by second, and which he was loth to renounce; for the garden and the stars, and the progression of days he had known, which could not go on for ever. Time was his enemy and his friend as much as Marlowe's.

## Chapter XII

# Atque Vale[138]

DURING the same week the weather, which had hitherto been so perfect, produced a few quirks and freaks from its repertoire. Waking one morning, Marlowe found that his bed was soaked in the rain which was beating down across the open window. An ugly wind dragged at the panes of glass and drove them chattering against their frames. Securing the window, he stood, his body glistening with water, and noticed that a great width of cloud hung above Leucothea, menacing the channel. Lightning slanted down out of the sky from time to time creating apocalyptic gulfs of blue light on the hillside, and the thunder followed it.

Below the villas the sea was piled up in furls of water, dashing now this way, now that, unable to decide upon which side of the channel to explode: while the seaweed in the bay was carried out in layers, like floating mats, and dumped on the end of the rocky headland. Such manifestations were inexplicable at this time of year.

The rain had ploughed gutters in the earth banks of the hillside. In the road itself were hundreds of puddles, spinning round and round in the wind, winking and bubbling. The air was crisply cold.

Breakfast that morning was a dull affair. Maria crept about her tasks like a whipped dog, muttering and crossing herself from time to time, when the lightning flashed. Her clothes were sodden on her and splashed with mud.

She served him that morning with an averted face, and a far away look in her eyes that seemed half fear and half concentration on some distant event – perhaps the next flash of light, or beat of thunder. He did not speak but ate moodily, staring out across the tossing waters whose end was chipped off soft by the curtain of damp mist which hung down, obliterating the mainland. When he had finished he remembered that Francis had promised to show him some of her canvases before she roped them up, ready to send back to England. Wrapping several thicknesses of newspaper round his head and shoulders outside a thin mackintosh, he tugged open the door and ran down the steps to the road, leaving the muttering woman to close it after him. The first drag of the wind nearly pushed him off his feet, and the rain rapped holes all over his swathed head until the newspaper was pocked like a sieve. He could hear the olives moaning and dragging at their roots as he scuttled down the hill.

Huddled in the doorway of her villa, he rapped long and loud before Francis heard and came to open the door. He flung off his pulp of newspapers and pushed into the hall, shutting the wind-swung door with his shoulder.

"Heavens, what a day!"

"Appropriate for the business," she said evenly, and led the way into a room where Gordon lay on the floor smoking.

"Hail to thee, blithe spirit," he said sombrely, pleased with the pun. "Is it still hailing outside?"

In the corner of the room stood half a dozen or so large canvases, loosely roped together, leaning against the wall. On request the girl undid the ropes and produced her productions one by one for his approval. They were pleasantly designed scenes from the life of the Island, for the most part carefully and cleanly painted. It was distracting, however, to attempt an appreciation of them when the light was so dull.

"Francis tells me she's going," said Gordon slowly.

"Yes," said Marlowe, still staring at the canvases; "so she says."

The girl stood by the window, expressionless, with a curious tension in her pose, turning now this canvas to him for approval, now that.

"Yes," he repeated softly, concentrating.

The flashes of lightning silhouetted her long body across the running window-pane, livid.

"When are you leaving?" she asked at last, deliberately forcing herself to the question.

"I?" he said, surprised; and for the moment he had forgotten the haunting decision which demanded fixed dates and times for his movements. "Not yet, I hope. Not for a bit at any rate."

"What about the critical intelligence?" said Gordon. He got to his feet and stamped out his cigarette in the fender. As Marlowe opened his mouth to say something he turned and cut him short. "Wait. Tell me something first. Don't you think there's a lovely sense of colour and design?"

"Yes," said Marlowe carefully.

"Thank you. I must be going."

From the corner, where he had flung them, Gordon produced a gigantic mackintosh cape and sou'wester in which he proceeded to imprison himself. Then he said, with camaraderie: "Well, you sods. So long. See you at the party."

"Party?"

"She'll tell you all about it," and he commenced his wrestling with the door. Putting a booted foot in the aperture, he inserted his face into the hall again and said, "Marlowe."

"Yes?"

"Try and convince her that she's got no feeling at all for the *form* of those bloody things. Not a trace. So long."

Marlowe turned slowly as the door crashed to, and the noise of Gordon's running feet diminished from outside it. He went into the room where Francis sat uncomfortably on the couch, staring out at the lines of rain on the window-sill. Very expressionless and stiff was her pose. He sat down beside her silently, disinclined to talk.

She said slowly, with a half smile on her mouth, turning her head to him: "Do you believe in omens?"

"No. Why?"

"Look at the rain."

Looking out of the window, on the panes of which the water squeezed and trembled, he had the sensation of looking into the glass plating of an aquarium. Dim and liquescent, the fringe of trees and the background of churning sea slipped across their vision. Their ability to stand there, on one side of the glass, dry and untouched by the weathers, seemed almost as much of a fiction as the dark landscape outside.

"Omens?" he said nervously. "What do you mean?"

"Gordon was at the wine-shop to-day and a peasant told him that bad weather at this time of the year meant the death of somebody. Everyone is awfully upset in the village."

"Oh," said Marlowe, compressing his lips in a prim line.

"Yes. And Fonvisin had to go up to Leucothea again to-day because the old monk had a relapse. I expect he's properly caught in it."

Somehow the darkness of that morning, the force of the storm, suggested something plausible and frightening about these beliefs. In the gulf of a thunder-clap his answer was swallowed up. He repeated his words as the noise rolled away:

"Do these things worry you?"

She turned to him with a smile. "Lord no. But this weather depresses me. Doesn't it you?" He admitted that it did; and, realising for the first time how weak and pointless it made his motives, his fears, his decisions seem, he was again cast down. On his desk he had left Fred's letter. The lightning would be flashing on it from time to time. He wanted to sit nearer to the girl for comfort; no longer to kiss her, for action so definite would commit himself; simply to sit nearer her so that their shoulders might touch, or their knees.

"What are you thinking about?" he said at last.

She was thinking of the vicarage at home, with daddy writing his sermons; the smell of damp; the cold rooms in which the fires had not been lighted. Mother sucking her teeth over her knitting. Andrew had died long since.

"Nothing," she said.

"Nothing!" he echoed and got up, walking over to the window to stare out of it.

By leaning his head forward he could see at an angle down the hillside to the right. It was very melancholy. The rain jumped a foot from the road, furiously, and little water spouts were snatched up off the sea and whirled hundreds of yards before they dropped. The village looked deserted. The trees heaved and shook above the cluster of coloured huts.

"What about this party?" he said, wondering how appropriate revels would seem in such weather.

"Oh, that," she said, almost contemptuously. "That's one of the old man's ideas. Seems a good day for the *Ave atque Vale*[139] business, doesn't it?"

Marlowe smiled and nodded. How dreadfully forced conversation seemed to be; how completely without motive.

"He might put it off a bit," he said, still staring down towards the village. A minute speck came down the hill from the direction of the jump, crossed the village road, and hurried down the path towards the villa which lay opposite them on the left flank of the headland.

"Hullo," he said, "someone doesn't mind the rain. I wonder——"

She got up and came to the window, pressing her nose against the cold glass.

"Christ!" she said. "It's Walsh, isn't it?"

Silently they watched the figure run down the narrow boulder-strewn path. There was a cape held above in the manner of a shield against the rain. Once it slipped and fell heavily down the bank of the path, but was on its feet again directly, running swiftly in the direction of Gordon's villa. "Yes," she said with conviction. "Wonder what he can be doing out in the rain on a day like this?"

"God alone knows," said Marlowe piously. "Well, I must be getting back."

Why he said that he hardly knew. Where could he possibly be going in weather like this? Nevertheless, he turned to the door and stood smiling at her, saying, "Don't believe a word Gordon says about your painting.

I think it's really good. In that one with the peasants on donkeys…you know?"

"Yes."

"Well, what more feeling you could want for form than that I don't know."

He circled himself in his paper cape and opened the door, placing his boot in the rift to prevent the wind shutting it again.

"This party," he said. "What time does it start?"

"God knows. I imagine about eight, after dinner. If you're wise you won't come. It's bound to be a ghoulish affair. Champagne and carefully prepared speeches. I shall want to break down and weep simply out of anger."

"Nevertheless," he said, gloomily wondering whether her prophecy would be correct, "I shall come."

"Good-bye, then."

"So long."

He accomplished the journey back to his villa in record time, stung by the hail-stones which were falling. Once safely indoors he felt the full weight of his depression come over him in a flood. Why the devil he had not stayed where he was until lunch-time, he could not imagine. He toyed with the idea of going down to see Gordon, but it was hailing really hard now, and even such a short journey would be painful.

He sat down slackly at his desk, got out his writing tools and began a new letter to Latimer.

DEAR LATIMER,

A line from my nowhere to that depressing somewhere you inhabit, viz. England, because I want to ask you again what the chances are if I come back. It's rather worrying. My brother, whose offer you know, has now decided, on my invitation, to take on someone who is young, keen, and worth his salt in the beer markets. That, as you see, lets me out; what I want to find is a plodding teacher's job in some soft country place where I can crust over quietly and end my days in sanctity and contemplation of my navel.

He put down his pen and stared out of the window, feeling disinclined to continue in the strain of flippancy which the thought of Latimer somehow made necessary. Latimer, so far away, vividly busy among his own business, could hardly grasp the essentials of his melancholy. But then Latimer had not sat as he had at this window, staring out across the lagoon through the rhythm of cypress-motion, at the plunge of swifts over the blue water. He tossed the letter into the waste paper basket and hunched forward in his chair, watching the lightning flicker on his fingers.

From the hall-way came sounds of Chrysanthe breaking up sticks with which to light the stove. The air was getting cold. He went into the bedroom and put on his old discarded coat, amazed at its heaviness and unfamiliarity.

He plunged his hands into the pockets and encountered a wad of tight paper. Drawing it out and unfolding it, he found it consisted of a great number of miscellaneous notes and references to his once-absorbing manual of Quietism. Sitting down at the table again, he sorted the notes and read them with interest, as if they, their author, and the subject with which they dealt, were things altogether new to him.

By God, he said to himself of a sudden, there is something new in this idea. There is something large about it. He wished he had read enough philosophy to discover whether he were busy enunciating principles and ideas long since dealt with and forgotten; but, as he could not know, he preferred to imagine that he had formulated something new. Perhaps the book would be famous. It would begin gently by converting, or at any rate amazing, the cultured minority. It would be referred to not only by philosophers and sociologists, but by mere novelists as well. After the first impact on the surface of thought the rings would gradually widen out to the more general public; editions would gradually sell out and be replaced by new editions. He would leave the school and live somewhere near Oxford, lauded and petted by everyone who was anyone…. He paused in full spate of imagination and wondered exactly where the book could have gone to. Then he remembered that he had shut it away in his trunk, cursing the obstinacy with which it refused to be written. Excited by these fancies, he went into the bedroom and opened the trunk. Yes, there is was. Carrying it back to his desk, he read every word he had written, and all the carefully chaptered notes which he had not expanded.

Admirably lucid it seemed to him. Delicate and yet in a sense strong; by no means as overlaid as he had imagined. Damn Gordon. He could see, through every line, the fine bare spars of the argument standing up, nakedly visible. He could feel the book shaping itself towards a satisfactory conclusion. There was not a superfluous word in it. He was delighted with himself.

Forgetting the rain and the sopping landscape outside, forgetting even the occasional flash of lightning on the paper, he sat down to it, and finished the sentence in the midst of which he had left off.

Marlowe worked like the devil all that morning. By lunch-time he had written two whole new chapters and begun a third. His moroseness during the meal matched Maria's fearfulness. He gulped his coffee angrily, and went straight back to his desk for another bout with the masterpiece.

At tea-time Gordon came in for a cigarette and a chat and was quite alarmed by these signs of industry.

"Really," he said, "You don't conform to decent psychology at all. On a day like this you should be in bed, not slaving away."

"I shall conform to whatever I choose," said Marlowe. "And as for you, when you've finished that cigarette you'll have to clear off and let me get in another two hours' work before dark. Great things are happening."

By six o'clock that evening the rain had decreased to a drizzle, and the sea was less violent in its hauling and flinging of seaweed mats across the bay and the headland. The landscape emerged from the mist, still lachrymose and feeble by reason of the clouds which hung above Leucothea and the deep valleys surrounding it on three sides. But Marlowe was so deep in the discovery of his own powers of exposition that he did not glance up; or, if he did, glanced outside the window with such abstraction, that he failed to notice these cheering items of weather.

The arrival of Maria at half-past six was an irritation. At the rate he was going he could have put in another four hours' work without a break. The noise of the woman's heavy movements in and out of the kitchen was distracting. Soon, too, the bad light would fail him altogether. He put down his pen and reread all that he had written, moving his lips as if he were delivering the prose to an audience. Yes, it was good. Pleasant, sinewy Anglo-Saxon, with here and there a touch of illuminating wit or malice, or a simile bright with irrelevance. Jeremy Taylor,[140] he felt sure, would have enjoyed every word of the book.

"*Etimo*,"[141] said Maria at last, appearing in the doorway. Now that the weather was putting a brighter face on things, she looked almost cheerful.

"All right, hag," he said in English, and began to put his things away. He had all but decided to sit up with an oil lamp and continue writing that night, when he remembered that there was another call on his time. There was the party. A party on a night like this was madness. Peering from the window, he was in time to see the darkness slide over the world· like a shutter. Vague and somehow ominous, the black stacks of clouds still lay across the mountain. Maria said, "Rain," and shook her head gravely. "Rain, to-night."

He ate his meal in silence, busy with his mind: planning the development of the argument in the next few chapters. At nine o'clock, when he had carefully reread and revised the day's work, he put on his hat and climbed the hill to the Villa Pothetos.

On the plateau the wind moaned quietly in the pines and olives. Mercifully the rain was still light.

The front door of the Villa Pothetos was ajar, and pushing it open he stepped on to the cold stone tiling of the hall, which was dimly lighted by candles held in rough wooden sconces. A servant appeared, took his cape and hat, and apologised in French for the dimness; the electrical gear had been out of order since that morning, perhaps because of the lightning. Everyone was upstairs.

He mounted the wide stairway slowly, noticing how much more soft and pleasant candle-light was than the hard defining electric light. Large shadows clung to the pillars and the staircase-well seemed swollen to twice its size by the darkness which filled it. The hall seemed to have more than ever the vast, hollow, echoing proportions of some feudal mansion. Threads of tallow ran down from the candlestick which was above the door of the music room. He rapped once, twice, and pushed open the door.

They were all there. Gordon, Fonvisin and Rumanades lounged in arm-chairs before an open hearth in which a log fire danced and fluttered. In the corner, leaning over the piano, in shadow, Walsh sat, as if about to play. Francis was curled up on the carpet, with a wine glass in her fingers, staring into the flames. So still they were, so rigid was their pose, that he had the sensation of intruding on the painted world of a picture, soft and complete down to the play of candle-light on the nose and throat of the girl, and the speck of blond hair in the old man's beard.

In the corner, beside the hearth, stood a small table with innumerable bottles on it, and plates of cakes and sandwiches. The red light slid along the surfaces of the bottles showing up their coloured liquors, and on the pure napery. For a moment the illusion of the scene being a picture, static in time, was almost alarming. Then the old man grunted and said: "Ah, there you are, Marlowe."

"Yes."

"We were wondering where you had got to."

Very softly Walsh's fingers explored the soft keys of the Bluthner, sending out little scraps of sound across the immense silence of the room. There was tenderness in his fingers for this great live beast over which he had power; the notes went down with the unerring precision of delicate machinery. They could answer every gradation of feeling which he might need to express.

Marlowe, on invitation, helped himself to a glass of wine and a sandwich and settled down on a stool near the fire. The atmosphere of constraint pervaded even such normal sound-producing movements as were necessary in eating. He held his sandwich stiffly in his fingers and sipped the wine quietly, wondering whether it was his presence which had caused the constraint. There was no hilarity in the mood of that circle of people.

The talk that followed was heavy with evasion and the discipline imposed on them by the silence of the room and the faint noise of storm outside. Fonvisin, it appeared, had just got back from Leucothea. The monk was very weak. He (the Russian) had been forced to tap the pleura for a pint of pus. He did not imagine there was a very good chance of recovery at his age, and with the lack of attention he got.

Occasional noises of thunder came to them in the dimness, as if far away, on the upper floors of heaven, furniture was being moved. The girl sat quite still staring at the fire, imagining the tremors of lightning that would be cutting up the sodden landscape outside the heavy curtains. She could imagine the terror of the animals, and the peasants as they huddled in their damp houses, drenched and afraid.

"On a night like this," said Gordon, "we ought to sneak up to the Jump and pour a libation to Thor."[142]

"You wouldn't be able to stand on your feet," said Rumanades reflectively, and added: "The wind must be terrific up there."

As by some prearranged signal they all raised their wine glasses to their mouths at the same moment, and drank. Slowly the conversation gathered way. After the fourth or fifth round of drinks everyone seemed to feel better. The thaw had set in.

As if struck by a brilliant idea, the old man suggested that they should turn on the wireless. It stood, this shining robot of chestnut-coloured wood, on a little table in the corner of the room, waiting for them. Rumanades bent over it, breathing loudly through his nose, and tentatively manipulating the knobs. The most plaintive whoops, skirls and caterwauling were all he could get for a moment or two; then the lift and fall of a Viennese band playing Strauss;[143] a German peroration about Aryan blood.[144] Finally, with an unexpectedness which was shocking to the point of being funny, there petered through the instrument the thin tones of some cleric, outlining the Protestant objections to sexual promiscuity.

"To you who have brothers and sisters," trickled the voice, "to you who have brothers, sisters, I would say this: that you must strive, by the grace of God, to preserve in them that chastity which we know is a sign of an upright life, lived nobly in the sight of the Lord. Verily indeed we may say a man has the strength of ten, not only because his heart is pure but his body also."

"Somewhere," said Gordon with resignation, "it must be Sunday." The wireless gave a couple of hiccoughs and lapsed into silence. Rumanades tried for some time to get something fresh, but the instrument refused to render sound distinctly. After a short session of screams and bleats, he gave it up.

"I had a brother but no sister," said Fonvisin suddenly, in tones so rankly lachrymose that everyone turned to look at him. They were surprised to see that he was drunk. He lay in his chair, humped over the frail circle of glass which he clutched in his right hand; his eyes closed and opened slowly, his breath came thickly from his lungs, as if hastened by the oncoming of tears. Blowing out his lips with something between a sigh and a hiccough, he repeated the words again, giving one quick glance round as he did so.

"A brother?" said Marlowe dully. The drink was sending fumes of warmth up to his brain. The firelight shone on his sweating face. He smiled softly as if at some very whimsical and private joke.

"A brother," corroborated Fonvisin stridently.

Walsh stopped playing for a moment to ask: "Where is he?" Fonvisin's answering voice broke out again, simultaneously with the pebble-cold piano-notes.

"He? Where is he?"

"Yes."

"He's asleep." The Russian dropped his voice to a whisper, and thrusting out his feet, studied his muddy boots with embarrassment. Gordon's mouth twitched, but there was no sound from him.

"He's asleep," said Fonvisin again after a long pause, casting his eyes down coyly. "He's been asleep for twenty years."

He stood up with swiftness, as if about to make an attack upon one of the company, reeled, and leaned back against the mantelpiece, dashing what remained in his wine glass down his throat. Bulked there, against the strong firelight of the room, he reached along the mantelpiece for a cigarette and a candlestick. Before he put the cigarette in his mouth he added: "Twenty years. I put him to sleep. I did. Yes. Completely to sleep. Ha, Ha." With a nimbus of smoke and flapping light round his domed head he stopped short, caught up in a seizure of laughter. He dropped his head back on his neck and laughed scandalously until they thought he would vomit. The candle-flame under his nose bobbed and winked and shone on his trembling uvula, and on the fillings of his back teeth. Then he stopped, completed the lighting of his cigarette, replaced the candlestick, and stood, hanging his head, quite silent like a chastened child. He peeped up at them from time to time from under his eyebrows, and smiled with great cunning.

"My brother and I," he said at last, whispering, as a child whispers in telling itself a story, "we were medical students together. We worked together. We did research together. We loved each other. D'you understand, we loved each other?"

"Yes," said Gordon, bored and depressed by these antics. "Yes, we understand."

"I loved him and he loved me," insisted the little boy with the Rip Van Winkle eyebrows.

"Yes."

"I had a wife. Very fine strong girl. I loved her and she——"

"And she loved you."

"*No*," said Fonvisin emphatically, striking the air, yet with triumph in his half angry smile. "She *said* she loved me. Perhaps she did. Perhaps she loved us both. But I don't like to think that. She *said* she loved me."

Marlowe tiptoed across the room, like an usher at a wedding, to fill his glass again. He was chuckling to himself unsteadily as he did so. Walsh sat at the piano, no longer playing, staring at the face of the Russian. Only Francis had not changed her position. She sat at Fonvisin's feet, staring past him into the fire.

"Go on," said Gordon with a yawn.

"My brother and I were doing an important work. We worked and worked and worked at this work. It was very important. Finally we were successful." Bending down with his lips pouted, he wagged a finger at the wall behind Gordon and whispered: "We succeeded in isolating the germ of sleepy sickness. We made a culture from it. You understand? But we kept it secret, while we wrote our treatise. Dead secret. Dead secret." His voice had in it something of the lift and fall that the wind had had in the trees on the plateau. Marlowe, listening dumbly, felt the sudden tug of fearful things at his heart. He gulped his drink for warmth and lit a cigarette.

"We had the germ there. We found it. We had agreed to share our results without favour. My wife was a fine girl, you understand? She was fine before that."

"Go on," said Walsh evenly.

"I can't tell you how hard we worked. Together, you know, in the laboratories. We were always together. In the evening we all three went out to supper together very friendly. We drank and laughed. We were all of us happy. My wife was as pleased at our discovery as we two were ourselves. Soon we should be famous, my brother and I."

He paused to take a few puffs at his cigarette. "Yes," he added with finality, screwing up his face, sucking deeply and exhaling the smoke across the room in a single jet. "Yes, we were very happy."

Rumanades was nodding forward in his chair, with his bearded chin cupped in the palm of one hand. He seemed to be asleep.

"One day," continued Fonvisin, "I found them." He nodded portentously round, and then stared painfully at his boot. "I found them and knew what it was that had been going on. I was very calm with my brother. He was younger than me, you understand? I was calm. But I hit my wife on the mouth until she bled and confessed everything to me. After that I did not know what to do. I was unhappy to see such a thing happen to me. And my brother was younger than me.

"At first I could have killed her, but then afterwards I knew that it would be wrong. It was difficult. I was not a savage, you understand, but a civilised man. Jealousy was a silly thing though I could not help it. I had known many women myself, of different kinds – all kinds: I was sorry for the women, too. I liked them very much and hated to see the men treat them like possessions, furniture – you understand what I mean? I wanted them to be open and free, to have life. But I myself was jealous when it happened to me. I was unhappy.

"It was not only that she had been untrue to me that was bad. It is important you understand that. It was unjust. But that alone did not make me sad. It was my brother. His love made me sad. Because the ties of friendship and companionship are greater than just love in the body. They are harder to break, and they are more unhappy. And my brother was younger than me."

He groped forward and slipped down into his chair, grunting with the effort.

"What did you do?" said Marlowe, his voice sounding to him unnaturally loud in the silence.

"For a long time I did nothing. When I thought of my wife I was only sorry; when I thought of my brother I was a little mad. I did not go near him for a long time, thinking I would feel well after a time. But I didn't feel any better. I was still mad to think of him. So one day I went back quite naturally and told him I had forgiven him. We shook hands, and he cried a lot, saying that he would never forgive himself for what had happened. I could have killed him in my hands while he was crying but I was kind, saying friendly things to him. You understand, I had no idea, then. I knew I was going to do something, but I did not want to kill. I had seen so much death in young people that I did not want to add to it. I waited until the chance came. It was the discovery that gave me the idea. He was a very brave boy, and said he would make a test on himself for the disease. We were so confident in our cure. So one day we pumped him full of the germ and put him to bed. Only my wife and I knew, you see. No one else. We put him to bed and watched the development of the disease. He did not know then that I had destroyed every scrap of paper in the laboratory. He did not think that I would never wake him. He dozed off with a slight temperature, as comfy as if he had flu. Well! there it was.

"He went through the various stages: and I kept trying to console my wife that our invention didn't work. Once he woke up and was quite lucid, but it didn't last. He has slept for years now. He will be thirty-five tomorrow. They feed him with pipes.

"Shortly after that there came trouble with the Bolsheviks. We had to leave Russia. In Poland my wife died in childbirth. My mother was getting on in years. She is seventy now. In her youth she was a famous opera singer. All the world praised her. She was heartbroken over Grigori going to sleep like that, and me not being able to wake him. She is a little mad herself. She spends her life travelling on tours which she did in the height of her fame. All over the world, for she has still got a great fortune. Wherever she goes she takes Grigori with her, in a coffin lined with velvet and with a mattress for him to sleep on. There is a glass top so she can open it and talk to him when she wants to. She introduces him to all her friends."

He stopped short with his mouth open and, turning, saw that across Gordon's face stretched a huge grin. Laughter, soundless and painful, was tugging at his chest. On his side of the arm-chair, he drew his knees almost up to his chin in an attempt to silence the demon of mirth.

Walsh, too, of a sudden, began to laugh, and turning to the piano beat out the sharp rhythms of a foxtrot, dry as sherry, and as invigorating in that smoke-laden room.

"No, but really," said Marlowe, leaning forward with an owlish expression on his face, "really, Fonvisin, you know. Really, my dear fellow." The firelight jumped and flickered, lighting up the shiny face of the Russian, and Gordon's mouth, wide with silent laughter.

"Yes. Yes," affirmed Fonvisin, gazing round him with benign humour. "Yes, indeed it is so." He put one finger in his ear and shook it violently inside the cavity. Then he lay back and sucked his teeth and began to doze.

The laughter came from Gordon suddenly, in a succession of harsh barks: so harsh and unnatural that the sound seemed to make punctures, visible rents, in the space that separated them.

"Astounding," said Marlowe, with inebriate dignity. "Amazing, my dear chap."

At last Gordon rose, wiping his eyes in the hanging sleeves of his blue shirt, and, leaning down, drew Francis to her feet. They retreated arm in arm from the fire to the outer floor. Then, gently latched together, they began to dance. Walsh, preoccupied, hung his head down over the keys and watched his bouncing fingers at work: the right hand skipping, mad with the interlacing syncopations, the left rapping out the long tenths like clockwork. From time to time he whistled scraps of the tunes he was playing, effortlessly accomplishing his nimble variations. The music streamed out, dead but sensually compelling to the body. Marlowe began to tap out the time on the floor with his shoe, jauntily refilling his glass as he did so from the bottle beside him. Things were looking rosy now. He could have got up and danced himself if he had only known how. He wished Rumanades or Fonvisin would wake up. How good it was to see young people together. Yes, how good, how warming in the stomach. The milk of human kindness. He got a real warm vicarious thrill to see the tall boy and girl in each other's arms, with their breasts and loins latched, treading this Zuluesque measure.

He wondered why the girl should look so solemn, with her brown face turned sideways over Gordon's shoulder. Francis was a sulky little bitch. All women were bitches, one supposed. He winked gallantly at the sleeping Fonvisin and took another swig.

The music had dropped into the dragging, sinuous rhythm of the blues. Throwing his head back, Walsh gave a shout of pure joy and began to sing their latest and most popular song.

> "*Ter be* (pom pom)
> *Or not ter be* (pom pom)
> *Is still the question* (pom)
> *With you and me.* (pom pom pom)
> *I've got no one to care for,*
> *Honey, what you there for?*
> *What do you give me the air for?*
> *Gee!* (rest) *you* (rest) *hou* (rest) *ri*
> *Ter be* (pom pom)
> *Or not ter be* (pom pom)…"

…and so on, with infinite pathos and rhythmic emphasis, and a series of the most astounding treble breaks.

Marlowe was captivated. Standing up in that din he too began to laugh, and applaud the ghosts of the hundred Hamlets which cakewalked among the rhythms with their behinds stuck out.

TER BE (*pom pom*) OR NOT TER BE (*pom pom*). The music took him by the throat and brought the tears to his eyes. He loathed it, and the mephitic mind that could make it, but he laughed and tapped his little feet on the floor. He was talking away too, from between his wine-wet lips, pointing his finger at Fonvisin: "Get thee to a nunnery." Oblivious, the dancers carried on, seeing nothing, hearing nothing.

> "*For who would bear the whips and scorns of time…*
> *When he himself might his quietus make*
> *With a bare bodkin?*"[145]

From outside the window filtered the omens of storm – occasional deep beats of thunder, at which the windows shook in their frames. Rain hissed and squalled round the house.

"What's that you say?" Rumanades was awake and shouting across the din, blinking his eyes. He was quite serious. Putting his hands to his mouth, Marlowe bellowed waggishly: "It falleth as the gentle dew from heaven. Get thee to a nunnery."[146]

Someone was calling Fonvisin. He turned and shook the Russian by the shoulder. "Someone wants you. Wake up." Marlowe in this *enfant terrible* mood was revolting. "Come on," he said, "wake up. Booo Fonvisin."

"Who calls?"

"Wake up."

Walsh, leaning over as if caught by the tides of his own music, raised his face from the piano and shouted: "You remember the mummy you made? The Spaniard? Remember?"

"The mummy?" Fonvisin struggled awake and groped about for his long since empty glass. "Yes."

"What was her name?"

The Russian blew his nose and shouted: "Manuela." And then again, as if he had not been satisfied with the noise, "MANUELA."

As he shouted a peal of thunder shook the house, and the wind twitched the curtains apart, to show, stark and apocalyptic, the landscape burning under lightning. Walsh was cowed and the music stopped. The reverberation of the thunder diminished, like physical pain, in the hills: and left the jangle of piano-strings in the room, a still small noise. Fonvisin began to hiccough loudly. The curtains swung together again, and Walsh began to play like a madman, the dancers to rotate, Marlowe to stand unsteadily on his heels and repeat, over and over again, the dark words that remained in the flesh of his conscience like barbs:

> "No more; and by a sleep to say we end
> The heart-ache and the thousand natural shocks
> The flesh is heir to."[147]

Only Rumanades sat silent in his chair, with his fists propping his chin, staring sideways at the rotation of the dancers with an expression of utter malice on his face.

This state of affairs might have lasted all night, had not Fonvisin been reminded that his flesh, too, was heir to a thousand natural shocks. Cropsick of a sudden, he reeled to his feet, staggered, rotated, drove the thumb of his right hand into his eye, and began horribly to cat in the fender.

It was a consummation devoutly to be wished.

He stood at the front door and shook hands with each of them as they passed, with his head down upon his chest, as if fearing to look at them. One by one they ran through the doorway into the rain, muffled in coats and papers, like curious grotesques: and each turned in the rain-swept light of the doorway, cried out and raised a hand, and then was spirited away by his shadow. The old man stood, backed by the line of jumping candle-flames, gripping the shaking door and watching them as they were lost in the blankness, one by one. Their voices sounded from very far off, crying "Good-bye," and thanking him. The wind wrenched their garments out on their stooping bodies like wings. "Good-bye," they cried: the voices of Walsh, Marlowe and Francis.

He shut the door securely upon the weather, and, assuring himself that the servants were long since gone, walked from pillar to shadowy pillar, blowing out the candles, until the hall was dark except for the lightning, and silent but for his own slow footsteps on the stone.

He mounted the stairs slowly, one by one, breathing hard, as if the effort needed were a great one. Somewhere in his mind he was searching for the idea which would govern his actions. He did not know what it was. Something was needed. Something was there at the back of his mind, which he must wait for: an agency which would direct him. This body of his walked in a dark trance of weariness and confusion, without direction, up the flight of stairs to the music-room. The candles dripped and dripped until he puffed them out, with a gesture like a kiss: and left the acrid smoke from burnt wicks hanging in the darkness. They were burnt right down to the black wood sockets of the sconces. He felt, of a sudden, very ancient and whimsical, and a little weary. With a quaint little smile he stopped and put his hand to the left breast of his coat, reassuring himself that his heart was still beating. A minute bumping communicated itself to his fingers. He gave a sniff of approval and pushed open the door of the music-room. The room was just as they had left it, with the lights still burning. His footsteps made very little noise upon the smooth wood floor.

He seated himself in the arm-chair, facing the dying fire, and with his face in his hands, concentrating. What was it he was waiting for? From where would it come? The occasional thunder seemed a hint of the nature of the things with which he was trying to establish contact in his mind. He waited in painful respect. Would it be a voice? As he waited he heard the sharp strokes of a bell wafted up to the house through the noise of the wind and rain. Uncertain he went to a window, and drew the curtain across in the face of the lightning. The olives had gone mad, jumping and twisting, and flinging their bodies up, raving at the sky. Against the light from the window the rain fell in lemon showers. The dim straits were humped and twisted in dark torsion, and the waves in the blow hole below Phaon beat like tom toms. It was funny that all this energy should be let loose around him, and he, of all humanity it seemed, safe and dry from it, in his little ark of masonry and plaster. Noah must have felt like this, looking out from the ark as from a watchtower across the immense waters of the world, snug and dry, but ineffably alone, with the soul weary in his old body, crying out for the symbol of a dove. The cypress trees, with an air of dignified lunacy, bent now this way, now, like pendulums, that, touching their toes. He gave a chuckle, and his eyes turned from side to side in his head, as he watched the landscape start up at him, and disappear again, swallowed by the night.

Again the sound of the bell. Running his dry tongue round his teeth, he stared out, trying to establish its identity in that world of chaotic sound. Illusion? Perhaps there was a fishing boat caught in the storm, and the priest was invoking the aid of the saint. Perhaps it was the bell in the church-tower.

There was a sharp sound of footsteps on the path of the house, re-treating, soon lost; and then the bell sounded again, beating across the valley and up the slopes. He knew then that in the monastery on the top of Leucothea the old monk was dying, or already dead. He could imagine the dead man's familiar, distracted by the weather-symbols of judgment, dragging the long bell-rope which hung in the yard, his eyes closed against the stinging rain, his beard turned to the sky, crying out the warning of God to the valley, and to mankind. So the monk, after all, was dead. For some reason he felt cheered by the thought.

He drew the curtains together again, shutting out the view, and re-turned to the arm-chair, rubbing his hands together as he might have done after a successful business-deal. The fire shone boldly on the glass bottles, though itself dying, and on the black piano. The fire was dying, the priest dead. Seating himself, he poured out a glass of the red wine, his especial favourite, which was brewed for him in one of the southern villages from grapes specially grown. Raising it he drank, letting the tepid sweetness of the liquid cling on his tongue, curdle along his palate, and send its fumes to his brain.

Sitting there, in all simplicity of mind, he contemplated his own death as something new and delightful; a divorce from the present which was perplexing, always perplexing, with its trivialities. Death, once beyond that partition of physical pain and fear, seemed to him made in the shape of his own desire. It would be a place of infinite understanding, in which there would be no bars for the roving intuition; everything would be open, and explored. Death must be a very spacious place, he heard himself think, in which so many heroes can be accommodated, so many mysteries solved. And thinking like this, in the warm first flush of exultation, he recalled to his mind all those things which before had done him hurt, trying to prove that the new strength was proof against them. As a man will press a bad tooth to see that it still hurts, he filled his mind with the unhappy things, but was at peace. Somehow the death of the monk had assoiled him and annulled his fear.

Still smiling, he got to his feet, and blew out the candles. In the silent corridor he paused for a second, looking at the floor, and then went to Manuela's room.

The shutters were drawn, and the musty air lay warm in it, and dark. He groped his way across to the French window, with a sense of impish excitement, and unlatched the window, letting the rain beat in upon the expensive tiles, and the lightning flash down, lighting up the furniture – the great bed and its counterpane decorated with the phoenix, the polished wardrobe, the line of bottles on the dressing-table.

For a time he stood at the mirror, watching his own smiling face light up with every flash from the wide windows.

Presently he went to his own room, leaving the window wide and the lightning playing upon the silk phoenix.

That night Fonvisin could not sleep. Sick, wet and weary, he had got back to his room in the tavern to find that the roof was leaking on his bed; and that one wall had absorbed the water like sugar, until its surface was coated in large dark stains.

The frightened peasants refused to get up and do anything to help, so that he was obliged to move the bed to one side and sleep in it as it was.

Outside, he could hear the rain and the wind playing their duet, and lying there, in the damp sheets of the great bed, he ground his teeth in rage and annoyance. He too heard the bell and wondered what it was; he did not think of the monastery at Leucothea, or the monk. Putting one arm over his eyes, he tried to sleep, but the dinning of the rain on the tin roof pierced his consciousness like riddling machine-gun fire. The lightning shone even through his closed eyes. From time to time he was partially successful, sinking into a troubled state of semi-coma, but no sooner would he find himself slipping into clear sleep than he would start up again at some sound, magnified by imagination of the imperfect functioning of sense. A bough of a tree beat and beat against the loose panes of glass in the window.

It seemed to him as he lay there that, sleeping, his mind was full of a nervous expectation, which these sudden wakings dispelled. There was something, just beyond the reach of his mind, which was tantalising him with a message. What it was he could not tell.

Presently it seemed to him that he was being called, though from where and by whom or what he could not tell. Across his closed eyes flowed a stream of disconnected images which gave him no clue. Sleep. He must sleep. He was still feeling sick.

It seemed to him then that the face of the old monk rose up out of the darkness at his bedside, with an expression of demoniac concentration on it. The old lips were drawn back angrily talking, while no sound came from them.

He reached forward to take the old man by the arm (for he should have been lying down, resting, not walking about in the rain) and found his own fist clutching vacancy. Immediately a cock crowed and he heard Walsh playing the piano. He reached out for the matches which lay on the chair beside his bed and lit a candle, thinking that these impressions must be produced by overdrinking and weariness. For a little while he sat, propped up in bed, reading, and then dozed off again, to the accompaniment of rain and the rapping at the window. The bell rang again, once, twice, in his dream, and, when he had begun to think that he was too far gone in sleep to be worried any more by the quirks and inconsistencies of his mind, he saw a sudden picture of the lightning flashing along the white sides of the Villa Pothetos. A voice said: "What was that?"

"Nothing," he croaked with a dry throat.

"There's something wrong."

"Nothing," he said again.

"In the light there."

"Nothing, I tell you. Nothing."

A black panel seemed to slide away before his eyes to show Francis and Gordon dancing round and round, madly, while above him, truncated, the figure of Marlowe laughed loudly. He laughed himself and dipped his fingers in the wine-glass, tilting his head and letting the drops run on to his tongue. They burnt like an acid. As he did so there was a sudden confusion outside, a door was pushed open, and a voice said: "For Christ's sake, Fonvisin, for Christ's sake."

He had hardly realised he was awake before he found himself out of bed, in the centre of the floor, putting on his clothes in great haste. Taking the matches, he ran down the passage and out into the night.

Out in the rain, for a moment the impulse which had been directing him seemed suddenly lost. He ran twenty yards down the road, and then halted, panting, in the shade of a tree. Drawing his coat round him, he felt the water spinning round his boots in the roadside puddles; the rain drilling his coat with spots of wetness. It was a terrible night and he cursed it, looking up to the sky and shouting in the face of the wind. As he waited he knew that the impulse would return and govern his actions.

All of a sudden he was off again, running heavily in his big boots, this time in the direction of the Villa Pothetos, without hesitation, and certain in his own mind of the direction. He crashed up the path, stumbling among the loose stones, and swearing as his footsteps threw up splashes of moisture on to his calves.

At the edge of the plateau he stopped and listened, holding back his own gusty breath to enable him to hear more clearly. Nothing. Only the wind in the cypresses. He stumbled on, his hands stuck in his pockets, his hat pulled down over his eyes.

As he came out of the crowding shrubbery he happened to glance upward, and knew what his forebodings had tried to tell him in their imperfect way.

It was like this:

The French window was wide open, and the room behind it bright with electric light which cut a broad yellow swath on the darkness. On the terrace stood the old man, naked, holding the parapet with both hands. He was staring out to sea with a fixed and gentle concentration which nothing could shake. Even the ugly lightning could not make him flinch. He looked very nice and naïve standing there, his naked body pouring with rain, and the drops hanging in his sodden beard.

Fonvisin called, Fonvisin whooped, Fonvisin danced about on the path raging at him, but it made not the slightest difference. He stood, looking out at the tormented sea, moving his lips very silently as if repeating a prayer.

Seeing it was no good, the Russian ran round the side of the house to the front door, swearing. The door refused to open, so he drove his fist through the coloured glass panel, and, shoving his arm in, unbolted it. The hall was dark territory which he crossed in a couple of bounds. Up the staircase he went in the dark, not thinking to switch on the lights which must then have been working. He burst into Rumanades' room and ran to the old man's side, putting an arm on his shoulder, his mouth drawn up in anger. The skin was wet and cold, and unresisting.

"Come," he said imperiously, and the old man, turning, wavered, as a tree wavers before it falls, and put his arms across the Russian's shoulders. He was very happy in a gentlemanly way.

Once inside the room (the few steps took him an age to accomplish, even with the Russian's help), he leaned sideways with one hand on the dressing-table, looking mildly at his own reflection in the glass. He began to tremble slightly and his teeth to chatter in his mouth. He seemed vaguely reproachful, and his lips still moved very slowly.

Fonvisin forced him down on the bed and, seizing a rough towel, enveloped him in it and began to curry his pleasant old body, hissing between his teeth like a groom at work.

"What did…you do that…for?" he grunted at last, towelling the bony back. And the old man sitting there quietly, jogging his body about under the roughness of the Russian's fingers, only smiled sweetly, as one who does not properly understand, and scratched his neck.

"The rain," he said at last, like a child between ecstasy and wonder. "It was only the rain." And he drew a deep shuddering breath from the very bottom of his lungs and lay back softly with his mouth twitching among his beard.

Fonvisin left him there, on the bed, and ran down the corridor, switching on the lights as he went. In the music-room the bottles of wine and spirits lay in different places, where the party had left them, and running here and there, he found a bottle of brandy, lying on its side half empty, in Gordon's chair. He grabbed it and, taking a wine-glass in the other hand, went back to give the old man a stimulant.

He opened the door, only to find the bed empty, the covers laid back. The window he saw at a glance was still as he had left it, fastened shut, but the other door into the corridor was wide open. He dropped the glass and the bottle on the bed and ran back into the passage. Empty. Looking down from the head of the stairs he saw the old man below him, walking down with great slowness and caution, chuckling as he did so. It was a splendid joke.

Fonvisin skipped down the flight and caught him up, talking to him as one would to a child. He carried him back to his room and put him in the bed, soothing the hair of his brow with his own hard hand.

"Ha. Ha," said old Rumanades playfully, and began to cough inside himself.

"Now you stay where I tell you," said Fonvisin roughly, wondering whether his forehead was hot enough for him to have a temperature. "That's right."

He went into Manuela's room and with great difficulty managed to bring her precious bed in and place it beside that in which the old man lay. Then, slipping off his sodden clothes, and taking a sip of brandy, he crawled in between the delicious sheets, and prepared himself to doze beside his patient.

The night passed very slowly, and by the time the first faint inches of dawn had reached the sky behind the hills of the mainland, the rain had slackened off a bit, and the thunder had slowly begun to roll southward.

Once or twice the old man woke and, sitting up in bed, gave a short, discursive and intelligible lecture on the flora and fauna of the island. And once Fonvisin woke to hear him weeping away to himself, snuffing under the bedclothes, and talking in snatches to a woman. By four o'clock, however, he had sunk into deep insensibility. At six, to his own and (subsequently) everyone else's surprise, he was dead.

Very weary, and with a foul taste in his mouth, Fonvisin lurched over to the window and unfastened it, intruding his bleary and drink-smelling carcass on the morning. The air was sweet as spring water, and the scents which the storm had crushed out of the flowers and foliage came up to the balcony in great whiffs like incense. To the east was the omnipassionate morning, opening its rifts of blood upon the water. The air was bitterly cold. From the east the light opened in long chinks and filters of wounded red, as if the morning were a pomegranate, casually prized open by the childish world.

In the hills the water still flooded the banks of the springs, sucking at the stones, skipping the rock-torrents. The shepherds, still fearful of snow, drowsed in their sheepskin cloaks. The sun which must be shining on the domes and minarets of Constantinople would soon shine for them too.

Nearer, there was the rough sound of footsteps on the road below the house. A man in a coloured smock, yawning, passed on his way to the village, praising the light. Fonvisin called to him, telling him to take the news of Rumanades' death to Christ. As he talked he found himself smiling and stretching his arms, gulping in the icy air, purging his weary and dirty body. The man crossed himself and, dropping his spade, ran down the hill with tears on his cheeks to call the priest and deliver the message. Fonvisin turned back into the room, laughing with tenderness at the morning, and patted the dead cheeks of the old man, saying: "Now if you don't mind, I'll have a bath."

He bathed at leisure, and, when the priest came, made him wait in the room while he dressed. The poor man was snivelling with cold, and aching in every bone with rheumatism and the fear of death. They sat on the bed beside the dead man and drank what remained of the brandy, while Fonvisin neatly disposed the slack limbs and performed all the necessary duties.

The priest stood for a long time at the window, saying: "Death is a terrible thing. It comes so suddenly. Death is a terrible thing." But he drank his brandy to the last drop and enjoyed it as a creature should.

While the priest prayed loquaciously at the white bedside, Fonvisin stood on the balcony consumed with the freshness and tenderness of everything, humming to himself an old song which he had not sung since he was a child. In the village the dogs had begun to bark, and a man's voice shouted something, indistinct. From the bay came the tattering of an engine and in a few minutes Christ's boat came nosing out into the still choppy water, heading for Corfu. He had instructions to wire the news to Rumanades' lawyers in Athens, who would notify the dead man's relations, if, indeed, he had any.

The Russian folded his arms tight, gripping his fingers under the arm-pits with a kind of ecstasy to feel his own life so secure in his body;

from somewhere deep inside him the laughter poured gently up through his lungs and his mouth, as if from some fountainous source of warmth and mellowness. The stone was wet with dew and the rain which still hissed along the wide gutters of the house. He put his arms inside the sleeves of his faded corduroy jacket, running his fingers along the newly washed flesh of his arms, so smooth and warm and hairy. Presently he went to Manuela's dressing-table and dashed sweet-smelling talcum on his freshly shaven jowls: and pinched a drop of eau de Cologne in his fingers before applying it to his nose as if it were snuff. Then back to the terrace again, to draw the icy morning into his very bowels and sing for well-being.

The priest came and stood beside him with a long face, telling him that the old monk had died in the night. It had been too wet to go up, but a shepherd had brought the news in at early dawn. At this Fonvisin laughed outright.

"It is a terrible thing," said the man reprovingly, "a terrible thing."

"Yes?" said the Russian and turned to stare curiously at the grubby man, with his belly-to-earth mien, his tangled black hair, and his festering shoes. "Yes?"

The priest returned to the dim room. The morning was too much for him. He knelt again, as one who was himself unworthy to perform the office. His beautiful voice, in tones of meek entreaty, began to pray for the spirit of the defunct Rumanades; the old man who lay there with many smiles on his mouth, enjoying some ancient and whimsical joke of his own.

It is a pity, thought Fonvisin, as he stood and watched the sun come up, that a corpse cannot laugh.

Presently Agathie came down the road, treading as proud as a peacock, with the pride which only that woman knows who has wearied and buried many husbands. Her skirt was prussian blue, spinning at her bare and lovely ankles, her loose blouse coffee-brown, with parti-coloured frills, and round her black and arrogant features she wore a vermilion head-cloth. In her left hand she carried a vast bunch of black grapes, with the dew still fresh on them; she sucked them one by one, spitting the pips grandly among the dust.

"God praise you, woman," said Fonvisin in a deep voice, and intensely. "Be happy. Your clothes are as beautiful as your body."

She turned up her bold face and stood there for a while, speaking to him, with the whole richness of life and fertility moving in her strong body. Then she raised her hand in agreement, with a powerful gesture, and went down the road again, sumptuous in the sunlight.

The contract that they made, he standing on the balcony, and she below, with her face lifted to him, shall not be revealed. But he was satisfied, and later, walking down the road, he too flourished his body, turning its massiveness from side to side, feeling the power to move in his loins and the heavy muscles of his arm. He too stopped and broke himself a hanging bunch of black grapes, wet on the skins and cold, eating them, tramped onwards, ripe as nut for life, and content.

# Chapter XIII

# The Curtain

BY TEA-TIME THAT DAY, life for the five of them had resumed its normal rhythm; but it was soon to be altered. Vague and evanescent their plans had been, and this simple one-act death on the part of the old man would force them to reconsider the chances. They were all at once a dispossessed court, left without a succession to save them. To Francis it mattered least: she had been going away in any case. Death she could not try to understand. Being told of death so near, she had gone frozen and mute inside herself, avoiding everyone except Walsh. To Gordon death had not very much force. He spent the day at the Villa Pothetos with Fonvisin, interviewing the hordes of peasants who came from the distant villages to make a gift to the dead man and weep at his feet.

But Marlowe, curiously enough, spent the day working as he had never worked in his life. He had slept late into the morning, been waked with the news of Rumanades' death, and after breakfast, without giving it much more than a passing thought, had sat himself down to his work of self-expression. Occasionally, from outside the armour of his scurrying thoughts, the words came to him, "Rumanades is dead. Have you heard?" but they created hardly any impact.

In the village there was weeping among the young and the middle-aged. The old men, glad of the sun, sat themselves outside under the trees with great placidity in their rush bottomed chairs, lit their smokes, and fell into pleasurable drowses, occasionally waking to take their nip of *ouzo* or wine. These, the real darlings of death, had seen enough of life not to fear it.

In the sunset, a scarlet seaplane of all things blew up from the south like a dove with an olive branch, and skidded into the Bay of Nanos. The entire peasantry of the island lined the cliffs and terraces to watch it disgorge two passengers: one, a specialist from Athens, complete with gold teeth, a fountain pen, a black suit, and a small bag; the other, Rumanades' lawyer, sober and dour as a death-watch beetle.

Late into that night there were consultations with Fonvisin, and discussions with Gordon, and exhortations to the peasants. The two business men moved about the great house with the assured decorum of vultures or mourners, trailing their grave coat-tails behind them.

A coffin was made, and while the doctor busied himself over the corpse, attended by the jaunty Fonvisin, the lawyer went about with a hammer and chisel breaking open cupboards and cabinet-desks with an air of slightly insane geology on his face. In the end, after he had cut his thumb and taken the creases out of his trousers, he found what he had been searching for – Rumanades' will.

Sitting down at the desk, he read it through several times, absently dusting the lapels of his coat with one hand as he did so. Nearly everything was left to Manuela.

He sniffed and raised his hands in the air, as one who would say: "What can you do with such a man?"

For years he had been trying to trace the girl, by advertisement, police, and private detectives; and it had all been in vain. She could have come to no good. Ah well, these Spaniards! What could one expect of them? They would have to keep up the hunt for a while longer, and if no trace were found of the girl, he supposed the whole estate of Rumanades would be claimed by the Government. He deplored the waste of so much good money. He toyed for a moment with the idea of falsifying the will; of inserting, say, a clause which would benefit him to the extent of several hundred thousand drachmae. But then, he remembered, as the family lawyer he could hardly do that; he must content himself by presenting a really fat bill for his professional services. Looking up, he caught Fonvisin's eye. Enigma.

There was one other clause of significance in the will, recently added. It stated that Francis was to receive annually the sum of two hundred and fifty thousand drachmae, with the good wishes of the deceased; and that the body was to be taken to Ithaca for burial.[148]

"It will be obvious to you," he said to Gordon that evening, "that it would be difficult for you people to continue living here while the estate is being cleared up. You understand?" His English was as faultless as was his taste in clothes. "After the island reverts to the Government, of course, it will be different. Visitors will be welcome. But just at present."

"Yes. I understand," said Gordon impatiently. He was thinking of the legacy to Francis which the lawyer had just read out. He turned to Fonvisin, who was standing by the window picking his teeth with a match-stick.

"Where will you be going from here?" he asked curiously, and the Russian scratched his lip, replying: "Not sure yet. Perhaps to Italy."

That afternoon, as they walked down the hill together, Gordon was elated by the knowledge that once more all the roads of the world were open to him. He would go south this time, Constantinople way, where the sun came from. He felt very strong and happy about it. Onwards again, into the blue!

"When is the funeral?" he asked.

"To-morrow morning at dawn. He's going to lie in state in the church next to the saint all night. In the morning the boats are going to row him across. The seaplane with the madman in it is going on to Ithaca to make arrangements."

"Shall we be going across too? Etiquette and that kind of thing?"

"On the contrary. The lawyer was angry when I said I would go. You'd have to get permission."

"I see," said Gordon. "Well, I only wondered."

They walked down the hill to the corner of the road, and paused for a moment as their ways diverged.

"By God," said Fonvisin with something that was remotely panic, "I might not see you all again. I'll be away a few days in Ithaca. Fancy that."

Gordon's elation vanished of a sudden, and he began to feel the fear and wonder of new adventures and places crowd his heart. It was the penalty of wandering, he thought, that there should be many good-byes at every stage of the journey.

"True enough," he said shyly. "We might not meet again. Christ goes north to-morrow evening. I imagine we go with him. In case we don't," he held out his hand stiffly, with a frozen propriety, "good-bye and good luck."

Fonvisin gripped his hand in his fist, wrung it hard for a moment, and gave a crooked transfiguring grin.

"Good luck," he said, all in a breath, and turning, swung down the hill.

The following night there was an unintentional festival in the village – for so many people had arrived that there was no accommodating them, and they either slept in blankets under the olives, or spent the night sitting about in the arbours round the wine-shop, drinking. They had come from everywhere, from the villages to the north and south of Nanos, in boats and by road, in all the colours of funeral and festival. With them too had come the beggars, who wandered in and out of the groups of seated men, doing a brisk trade in witticism. The old wooden-faced piper, who plagued Francis twice a day whenever he came down to Nanos (because she had a godly face), walked about, a little drunk, but in fine form. Every now and then, for the sheer fun of the thing, he would unbutton his vest, produce his pipe, and give a few toots and twirls.

Under the olives, here and there, lay dark groups of sleepers, while from the wine-shop door, blazing in lamplight, came roars of male laughter and the greasy slicking of cards. A stream of men entered this door. Festival was in the air.

Donkeys wheeled wearily down the road from the hills, stumbling among the boulders, and setting up wings of dust at the heels of each cavalcade. More people, and still more. In the bay a whole fleet of fishing boats and oil driven coasters had dropped anchor. The stone-shifters were in again with a fresh load, and the still air was bright with their commerce. In their flower-yellow straws they staggered up the slope with the materials for the church, helped by the women, laughing and chattering among themselves – a polyglot crew.

Outside the inn door, along the dusty wall, was piled a long row of melons, waiting for the ripening sun. The lamplight fell smoothly over them as they lay there, like hundreds of bland faces, green and yellow, fat and round, long and tapering, with the uniform expression of a coroner's jury sitting in judgment. The women moved across and across the yellow doorway, motley as birds of paradise, stepping proudly and with the assurance of their own colours and their duty to the dead. Someone had a guitar out there among the olives, and the plangence of its strings, slowly twacked, was joined by the fine tones of a voice, singing as if the limping, rising, falling melody would go on for-ever world without end. There was a deep suppressed excitement in the voices of the girls and the men under the olives, as they took up the burden, raising their faces to the roof of leaves from which shone yellow-green reflections of the light. There was devilry in the laughter of the lovers who prowled along the top of the cliffs, above the blank sea, linked of body and spirit.[149]

The little barn-like church was full of the reek of candles and incense. It had been newly swept and garnished, and the tin-nimbused frescoes of saints had been polished so that they shone with dark malevolence. The women, red, blue, saffron, yellow, mustard, cinnamon, magenta, walked about under a forest of candles as thick as a man's arm, each going up to the right-hand nook by the altar to kiss the case in which the rib of the patron saint was locked, before moving across the line of frescoes to gaze upon the dead face of Rumanades, and leave their offering of fruit, flowers or vegetables with the remaining Leucothean monk. He stood, poor man, with his red-rimmed eyes half closed and his beard on his chest, half asleep with fatigue, but doing his duty, on the left of the altar, with a candle in his hand, and appropriate prayer forming in his mind. He had buried his comrade that morning, with the help of a peasant.

The little anteroom at the back of the church let out strong earthy whiffs of fruit and flowers, whenever the door was opened. The offerings were stored there; and in the gloom it resembled the dressing-room of an actress, full of the gauds of a great success.

The priest, hollow-eyed from sleeplessness and rheumatism, moved about among all this with the dignity and unction of his office, now stopping to speak to someone, now turning aside to arrange the flowers, or snuff a curving candle.

At about midnight Francis and Walsh walked down to the church together to look at Rumanades, arm in arm, for they were both a little nervous.

They paused at the door, staring wide-eyed at the congregation of men and women who had made the pilgrimage to the dead. The priest, seeing them, came across and complimented her on the unfinished fresco which covered the short back wall of the building. In that yellow light it looked very bold and strong, in ripe colours, and she herself was proud of it.

They walked up the aisle together, hand in hand, for she had never seen death, and he still feared that motionless passivity which visits the human body when it dies. Their noise on the wide stone flags of the floor, newly swept and sprinkled with sweet water, was nothing in the soft hush and fall of voices around the altar.

In the side wall (which was being demolished) there were gaps in the brickwork, and outside these they could catch glimpses of children playing in the light from the tavern door. In a clear space among the olives someone had lighted a small fire of sticks, and round it squatted a circle of old women, laughing and talking, happy of an event which excused the wearing of their best clothes. The town was a hive of chatter: and above it, from time to time, threads of melody from the pipes pierced their ears. The old piper was in excellent form by now.

In the doorway at the other end of the church Vassili stood in his uniform, blear-eyed from weeping; while Christ, in his ceremonial shoes, creaked up and down, talking with gravity to anyone who would listen to him.

"Dear sir," he said brokenly to Walsh, gripping the boy's arm with his little brown fingers; "dear sir," squeezing his eyelids down hard in an effort to bring the tears to his eyes, "what a tragic, my dear sir. What a *tragic*." The light flapped down on his brown face from the swinging candles. They breathed in the hot sweet stink of molten wax. The old monk leaned heavily against the doorpost, weary of death itself, with his eyes drowsy red zeroes in his matted hair. He nodded to them, bowing his head in a gentlemanly way, and folding his mud-grimed fingers over his chest.

They went slowly up the two steps, past the altar-rail, holding each others' arm, to join the little cluster of peasants who waited their turn outside the holy of holies.

The rib of the patron saint lay in a large ornamented casket of the size of a child's coffin. At each side of the church-altar was a tiny nook, about five square yards in size, whose wall-surface was covered by a fresco of saints. In the right-hand chapel lay the patron saint; in the left, Rumanades.

They waited while the peasants kissed the pictures outside, and then, muttering a prayer, ducked into the dim doorway to pay the same tribute to the casket in which the saint's bones were reputed to lie. In the restricted space the fumes from the candles made it almost impossible to breathe. The line of dim saintly faces, circled in bright tin, glowed with a kind of ascetic malice. They waited in there for a few moments, in a kind of stupor, watching the swirl of women in the doorway, entering and kissing the silvery plates which circled the casket, running their lips round the ornamental flutings and knobs with a passion of religious fear.

Christ came in while they stood there, and began to kiss the silverwork with ostentatious loudness, smacking his lips against the metal which had been worn smooth by generation of hands and mouths.

He came across to them again when he had finished, smiling and saying, with a certain pleasure: "The saint is kind to us, dear sir."

"Christ," said Francis quietly.

"Yes, missy?" He was all attention, his violet eyes wide with expectation, his hands ready to gesture.

"What time do you leave to-morrow?"

"Very early morning. At sunlight."

"Come," said Walsh, and hooked his arm again through hers. "Let's go out now."

They walked past the front of the altar and the row of framed pictures, almost completely rotted away by the damp and neglect. In the semi-chapel on the opposite side of it, they paused staring in on the coffin which held the body of the old man. In detail this second nook was like the first; an ordinary bed had been placed in it, under the crowding brown faces of paint, and covered with cloth of some dark velvety material. On this lay the smooth coffin.

They entered together and stood for a long time, Without nervousness, looking down on his white face, composed and yet not severe. There was a slight compression at the corners of his mouth, as though a smile were about to break out on his face at any moment. The only unhappy thing was the stare which made his eyes so expressionless. He lay there glaring up at the fresco of saints above his head, like an absolute stranger in a strange place.

Francis withdrew her arm, and stood loosely beside the boy, staring at the enigmatic old man's face, without fear or prejudice: quite alien and strong in herself again.

The interminable muttering continued in the body of the church at their backs. The monk snoozed against the door-post, waking occasionally to give a little shiver of fatigue. He was beyond sorrow by this time; and beyond showing even the polite forms of it. Very far away, in the infinity that was night outside, a voice took up a song of lovesickness, with a slow lift and drag about it that suggested physical pain. The guitar, almost inaudible, squeezed the melody out drop by drop, as one would clean a wound. Through the hole in the wall they were able to see the circle of old women round the fire stir with the warmth of approval, warming to the lure of the sweet words. The singer was dying for them: and the old flesh on their bones ached for lovers. Not for the dead and forgotten men, the shades which lurked in grimy corners of the memory, but for new ones, young men with the brightness in them, haggard for women and the bodies of women. The singer was giving himself to them as Juan is said to have given himself, from pity, to an old woman who importuned him; and they, like that old and lovesick woman, were become new again and fresh for lust. Their faces were turned to the singing so that the firelight shone on the folds and pouches of their flesh: and they caught their hands together and squeezed them between their knees in a delight that was painful.

Inside the church the candles still sparkled, while the smoke of incense went up to the ceiling like steam. The boy and girl stood for a long time, staring at the face of Rumanades, rapt.

Then Walsh said: "Why are we all so dead? Why do we live so exclusively in the past and the future?" He was thinking of the old man's face on the night of the party, of Manuela's photograph, of Fonvisin's mummy, of Marlowe, but above all of himself, and his own want. He was in a rage with the girl for not flinging down every obstacle to grasp the delight within reach. Couldn't she see that nothing but immediate necessity mattered, not the codes, the complexes, the revulsions? Why didn't she accept?

"We're all dead," he said again with contempt. "We're the last of the romantics, between two worlds. Our emotions aren't our own any longer. We're shirkers."[150]

The girl said nothing but continued to stare at the smooth dead face, fixed in some abstraction of her own. She wanted, at that moment, to lean down and kiss the dead mouth: not for sentiment or anything like that, but simply for physical comparison with the warm mouth of Walsh so close to her.

"But we suffer," she said. "We face things and we suffer?"

"In the wrong way. Our suffering isn't real any more. We are wise enough now to break through our environment and conditioning. We need something new from life – life in the body, not the mind. The senses, Franz."

She was thinking of the way those old women had pressed their rheumatism-disfigured hands between their knees. The hiss of their drawn breath.

"That's what Fonvisin was always saying. He said I was a cardboard silhouette of a stock emotion. And you, and everyone. Gordon was the only one, he said, who took things as they came."

"And so we are. He's right. Don't you see, Franz?"

"But how – " she began impatiently.

"How? Oh! for God's sake let's be true to our immediate necessities, to our wants. Why complicate them and make tragic-comedy out of them?"

"Words," she said in bewilderment. "Words, Walsh."[151]

"I know."

"What do they all mean?"

"Simply that we're fools to deny life. It's to be or not to be all over again."[152]

He was so happy now that she was afraid he would spoil their decorum by laughter. Taking her hand up in his fingers he shook it from side to side, saying: "Don't you believe me? You've seen dead traditions before, history is thick with them. Francis, we must start in another direction. Look." Suddenly turning on his heels, he waved a hand in the painted faces of the saints, and laughed. "Look at them! There's a tradition gone bad. Sterile. Dry. Like bad sardines in a tin. Come, for God's sake, let's get out of here."

Almost running they left the church, Walsh skipping ahead and dragging her by the arm out into the cool night. Once in darkness, their pace slowed until they were walking at a snail's pace across the turf at the terraced cliff-head.

When they reached the first terraces, where their voices could not be heard by the merrymakers, they paused to stare out at the sea. Faintly it rose and fell in the gloom at their feet. Presently the moon would edge up over Epirus and the hills.

With a little sigh, as if the tangle was at last resolving itself for her, she turned to him, and said: "All right, then; I don't understand, but I'll believe you."

As they walked down the white dust of the road together, towards her villa, their bodies pressed together at each slow stride in a delicious contact, they noticed that a light was burning in Marlowe's Phaon. He was working like the devil. His head looked absurdly dollish, sitting there on top of a desk littered with papers. His little hand scurried up and down, holding a pen.

It is possible that he heard their slow, intimate laughter as they passed.

They were none of them awake at dawn to see the final ceremony, except Fonvisin, who was taking an active part in it, and Gordon; Marlowe had worked so long and so hard that he slept on well into the afternoon. Francis, through the numb content of her body, and the dreams which passed in her mind, heard the noise and bustle of the preparations.

At three o'clock that morning Gordon had packed some food in a knapsack, taken his binoculars and climbed the long cliff-paths to the Jump, alone, and very happy.

Now, at early dawn, he sat on the edge of the dancing-floor, dangling his feet in space, smoking.

Eastward the light crawled up the flanks of the mountains, and brimmed over slowly until it flooded the deathstill sea. Inland it had penetrated the valley, shining on the chequers of olive and vine, corn and barley.

In the village noise was growing up dimly out of silence. A man sang a few bars of a song. A door banged. Three ants in scarlet set out on the road to the bay.

Nanos looked like a glass bowl of water in which fruits floated – grapes, cherries, figs. The coloured boats bobbed gently, while from under the awnings sleepy men appeared, stretching themselves and yawning, stiff with the chill of damp. From the tethering-grounds among the olives came the sniggering of donkeys. A woman shouted something.

Gordon watched keenly, and saw the confusion growing, until the town looked like an armed camp preparing for an attack. From the white gates of the Villa Pothetos three dark figures emerged and began to walk down to the village. He guessed that they must be the lawyer, the doctor, and Fonvisin. Half an hour later the procession started.

From the door of the church pressed a coloured multitude of people, clustering round the black figures which bore the coffin on their shoulders. The priest and the monk were in full ceremonial costume; over their black soutanes they wore beautifully fringed and embroidered stoles, reaching almost to their ankles. In the right hand of each was clutched a tall candle, while the priest held one of the sacred books. Behind them came the crowding peasants, holding aloft the sacred eikons of the village, laughing and talking among themselves.

The procession went on down the hill, centred round the coffin and its bearers; down through the olives and past the lemon groves, until at last it left the cliff-paths, and emerged safe and sound on the jetty. Alongside the line of bobbing coloured ships there was a halt and conference while Christ manoeuvred his boat into position to receive the privileged mourners with the coffin. The others began crowding into the boats, laughing, with a great swinging of skirts and twirl of scarves.

Then the long line of boats set out southward in the keen air of morning, to Ithaca.[153]

THE END

## Notes

1 Brindisi is an Italian port from which a ferry runs to Corfu. This is the same port through which Durrell traveled and was delayed in 1935.

2 This refers, with heavy irony, to difficulties Durrell experienced due to strife over the Greek monarchy while he was moving to Greece. As with Marlowe, he and his wife Nancy were delayed in Brindisi en route. The republican constitution was revoked in 1935 after a royalist military coup and manipulated plebiscite. In 1936, King George appointed General Ioannis Metaxas as Prime Minister, which led to a dictatorship (drawing on Fascist models) with significant censorship, to which Durrell later alludes. Since he wrote *Panic Spring* after his arrival in Greece, these political contexts were fully available to his anachronistic broadening of the disruption into a Revolution.

3 Durrell's Anglo-Indian childhood, in particular his ties to hill stations such as Kurseong, plays a significant role in his first novel, *Pied Piper of Lovers*.

4 Since Durrell was stranded in Brindisi under precisely these circumstances, the implication is that he is an author prone to wit and satire. Reading these descriptions of the British and the Greek Revolution through satire alters the novel somewhat and anticipates Durrell's often-overlooked colonial satire and irony in his later works.

5 The capital city of Greece.

6 Samuel Johnson is an eighteenth-century author and literary critic particularly known for his dry wit and aphorisms.

7 Durrell's comments on Jews in this novel are conflicted, as they are in general in his early works. He later refers to "jew-boys" (243, 297) but appears to be appropriating a character's voice, and his own later support for Zionism was equally complex. His second and third wives were strongly Zionist, and Durrell's film scripts for *Judith* demonstrate he unequivocally felt the same until 1967, after which his attitude appears to have changed significantly.

8 Thule is a mythical island North of Great Britain in Strabo's *Geography*. In a more general sense, it refers to a distant and uncharted land. Ultima Thule refers to the limits of the known world.

9 World War I, also known as the Great War.

10 Miguel de Molinos (1628–1697), author of *Guida Spirituale* and chief reviver of Quietism, who died in prison for his beliefs.

11 This moment anticipates the notion of the "English Death" that Durrell would develop in his 1938 novel, *The Black Book*. Durrell's composition and revisions of *Panic Spring* overlap significantly with this later more influential work.

12 Mount Athos is the "Holy Mountain," a peninsula in Northern Greece that houses twenty Eastern Orthodox Monasteries. It is now the Autonomous Monastic State of the Holy Mountain. Although linked to the mainland, it is only accessible by boat.

13 A direct quotation from Shakespeare's *Hamlet* 3.1. The lines spoken by Hamlet refer to Ophelia, suggesting closeness in Marlowe and Latimer's relationship.

14 Patras is a port city on the mainland South of the Ionian Island of Corfu, nearer to Lefkada, Kephalonia, and Ithaca. Patras' reputation for producing fine mavrodaphne wines appears later in the novel. Durrell lived on Corfu while writing *Panic Spring*.

15 D.H. Lawrence's *Lady Chatterley's Lover* was at the core of one of the most infamous obscenity trials in Britain in the twentieth century. Durrell had been asked if he would testify at the trial, and he agreed, but was not needed at the time. When *Panic Spring* was written, *Lady Chatterley's Lover* was still banned.

16  A traditional Cumberland song set to the tune of the Scottish song "Bonnie Annie."

17  *Madama Butterfly* is a famous opera by Giacomo Puccini. Bathos refers to the juxtaposition of "high" and "low" or the serious and the ridiculous. The implication here is that the profundity of emotion in the opera is subverted by a trivial or ridiculous rendering.

18  This shift to a first person narrator here suggests that Durrell was, in characteristic fashion, drawing from his notebooks, in which he would record diary-like entries mixed with phrases or scenes for poetry and fiction.

19  Italian, "very good."

20  Rather than Italian, Marlowe has lapsed into French.

21  Like Patras, Piraeus is another port city on the mainland.

22  Kephalonia is a large Ionian island South of Corfu near to Patras.

23  More typically known as Lefkada, this is another Ionian island attached to the mainland by a bridge. It is South of Corfu. Being near Corfu and within full sight of Lefkada is not possible.

24  Marlowe's attention to Christ's feet aligns him with the Greek god Pan.

25  Caliban is a character in Shakespeare's *The Tempest*. Durrell significantly draws on the same play for the title of his travel narrative of Corfu, *Prospero's Cell*.

26  Simon Eyre is a character in Thomas Dekker's comic play from 1599, *The Shoemaker's Holiday, or the Gentle Craft*. Cicely Bumtrinket is the maid who annoys her master by farting in her sleep. Durrell's younger brother Gerald also named his boat Bootle Bumtrinket in his later semi-autobiographical book *My Family and Other Animals*.

27  A literal translation of the wine Μαβροδαφνε, mavrodaphe, a sweet and dark wine somewhat akin to a port or rich sherry. It is strongly associated with the port city of Patras, and the black grapes used to make it are indigenous to the area.

28  Until 1974, Greek coffee was referred to domestically as Turkish coffee.

29  The Albanian coast would be visible before the Greek coast on a trip from Brindisi. Corfu, a Greek island, is located largely North of the latitude of the Greek border when it reaches the sea.

30  A French newspaper.

31  They are traveling South between Corfu and the Albanian mainland. These images of Pantokrator and the Albanian snows recur in Durrell's works repeatedly, even in *Clea* (1960), the final volume of *The Alexandria Quartet*. The closest resemblance is to the openings of *Prospero's Cell* and "Oil for the Saint," both of which narrate an arrival on Corfu by boat. Pantokrator is the largest mountain on Corfu, on the Northern portion of the island. Durrell lived beneath it in Kalami. Lefkimo, which follows, is the southernmost and second largest town on Corfu.

32  The Durrell family identified their residences on Corfu by the colour of the homes, such as the White House Durrell and his wife Nancy rented in Kalami or the Strawberry Pink Villa the rest of the family rented in Perama.

33  A satiric response to John Farmer's Elizabethan madrigal, "Fair Phyllis I saw sitting all alone." The madrigal, like many, contains implicit sexual materials masked in the language of the pastoral, overlapping word repetitions in the different singing voices, and the stereotypical "Fa la la" when they "fell a kissing…up and down."

34  An Orthodox icon.

35  This mixes three languages, the French "très," the Italian "bella," and the Greek "Nea" (meaning "yes").

36  This adjective likely derives from D.H. Lawrence and relates to the development

of the movement in British poetry that would subsequently be called the New Apocalypse. This ties Gordon to Lawrentian vitality and shifting aesthetic norms.

37   As with Francis' work in an advertising firm in the subsequent chapter that bears her name, this is the first likely allusion to George Orwell's 1936 novel *Keep the Aspidistra Flying*. Orwell's work bears some resemblances to Durrell's previous 1935 novel *Pied Piper of Lovers*, and Durrell later referred to Orwell's flying aspidistras during a disagreement between the two authors in *The New English Weekly*. Orwell's protagonist is a poor poet who works as a copy-writer in an advertising house and who is also named Gordon. Durrell's allusion seems satiric here.

38   Durrell is likely referring to Herbert Read, whose correspondence with Henry Miller he was reading in 1935 and 1936. Durrell wrote a long response to Read's second speech during the London International Surrealist Exhibition in 1935, which was published in September 1936 in the fourth *International Surrealist Bulletin*. Read, prior to his more well-known anarchist beliefs, overtly tied art and politics via communism. Perhaps Read's most overt statements, to which Durrell objected, were "the Surrealist is naturally a Marxian Socialist, and generally claims that he is a more consistent Communist than many" ("Speech" 9) and "let us, in short, as artists no less than as Socialists, work for the transformation of this imperfect world" (13). For a thorough discussion, see Gifford (7–52). The other likely subject is Auden and the Macspaunday poets, against whom the New Apocalypse developed, in large part via Durrell's and Henry Miller's influence.

39   Although Durrell is often accused by critics of being unaware of political circumstances, this and many other passages in his novels and poetry point to his highly keen awareness of the political world around him, even while he placed emphasis on the individual. This presages, to some degree, Durrell's later complex ties to Zionism, the Balkans, and his political discussions in *Tunc* and *Nunquam*.

40   The allusion is to Cleopatra, but it also anticipates his later keen interest in Antony and Cleopatra in *The Alexandria Quartet*.

41   The airport is a point of local pride, and the site is still in active use. Durrell's family lived very close to the aerodrome of this period when they were in Perama.

42   Pothetos is a Greek surname, but it is uncommon for the Ionian islands. It might also be read as "desirable."

43   Leukothea is the White Goddess and is a form of the ancient sea goddess. In the *Odyssey*, she appears as a sea-mew offering Odysseus a veil to save his life. In Laconia, far South of the Ionian, she has a sanctuary where she answers questions about dreams, much like Asclepius. It would be anachronistic to parallel Durrell's invocation of Leukothea to Robert Graves' in his famous 1948 work *The White Goddess*.

44   The Bolsheviks (or "The Majority") were a party founded and run by Vladimir Lenin. It seized control in the October Revolution in 1917 and led to the creation of the Soviet Union in 1922. Fonvisin's politics are, in this description, not communist and are perhaps Tsarist. Fonvisin's name may be adapted from Denis Fonvizin, an eighteenth-century Russian playwright. Fonvizin's pro-Imperialist political sentiments would certainly have run contrary to the Bolsheviks, as would his mockery of the peasantry.

45   In Greek mythology, Phaon was a boatman on Lesbos. Aphrodite gave him an ointment that brought him youth and beauty. The poetess Sappho then fell

in love with him, and when he rejected her, she threw herself into the sea. Rumanades appears to be the elderly Phaon, especially with the novel's later emphasis upon his attention to the ointments that rest on his wife Manuela's vanity. This also foreshadows the tension in the scene at the Jump.

46 Casuistry is a branch of applied ethics that involves matching a given case to a paradigm. In this instance, it would involve adapting religious morals to modern times and circumstances.

47 In Greek, apollyon means "destroyer" from απολλυειν, but the likely reference is to the *Book of Revelations* in the *New Testament*, in which Apollyon is a fallen angel who brings the plague of locusts (*Book of Revelation* 9.7–11). The proximity to Rumanades' comments on the island's patron saint is striking, and Marlowe ends the chapter by commenting that he will think twice about becoming sick with such a doctor on the island. Durrell is likely aligning Fonvisin with Apollo as well, who is capable of both healing and destruction.

48 Epirus is the area of the Greek mainland that sits opposite Corfu, running along the coast and the Albanian border. This again ties Mavrodaphne to Corfu, since the other islands closer to Patras (with which the fictional island is also associated) are not near enough to Epirus to warrant this description.

49 Literally, "especially," but μαλιστα also means "yes" idiomatically.

50 Epirus is the region on the Greek mainland immediately adjacent to Corfu and the Ionian Sea.

51 This is not Molinos' writings but Marlowe's response to them and Durrell's response to Quietism. For more discussion, see Morrison (179).

52 A medieval logical school led by Adam of Balsham, which was named for its meetings at the Petit Pont in Paris.

53 Molinos' main work on Quietism.

54 Durrell discusses caves on Corfu in his other works, setting major scenes within caves on the island in *Prospero's Cell* and "Oil for the Saint; Return to Corfu."

55 This paragraph and the previous draw heavily on images from T. S. Eliot's *The Waste Land*, but it is set in contrast to Keats' "To Autumn." The blossoms, the dead self, the "unreal" sense, the "dead earth" and dead leaves all point to images drawn from Eliot and set in contrast to a more positive view from Keats. This contrast, especially with its ties to Greece, is crucial in Durrell's next novel, *The Black Book*. These particular images from Eliot, and Durrell's resistance to them, also recur across his career.

56 These images recur in the first chapter of Durrell's later 1974 novel *Monsieur*.

57 In *Genesis* 2:7, God breaths life and a soul into man through his nostrils.

58 This list ranges widely: John Donne, the metaphysical poet; the Protestant Reformation that began with Martin Luther; the jazz pianist Duke Ellington; the Symbolist poet Remy de Gourmont, who was a major influence on Durrell through Ezra Pound's translations, *The Natural Philosophy of Love* in particular; and Henry Miller, who wrote the infamous *Tropic of Cancer*, with whom Durrell had corresponded since 1935.

59 Permanganate would be used to induce abortion or to bleach skin. John Milton is here used in a general sense to refer to Puritanism, and Sloane's is a mixture for hot chocolate by the Cadbury Brothers, based on Sir Hans Sloane's invention of milk chocolate – Sloane's collection formed the basis of the British Museum. The last work refers to Jonathan Swift's satiric 1732 poem "The Lady's Dressing Room," in which the gruesome details of a woman's beauty techniques are displayed.

60 Rabelais' 1533 work *Gargantua and Pantagruel*. Gargantua, when born, shouts in a loud voice "Drink, drink, drink!"

61   Tarquin is also a major character in Durrell's third novel, *The Black Book*.

62   This paragraph is a direct quotation from Jeremy Taylor's very popular 1651 book *The Rule and Exercises of Holy Dying*. Taylor (1613–67) was an Anglican Clergyman, Bishop of Down and Connor, and Vice-Chancellor of the University of Dublin.

63   Both poems are quite dissimilar from Durrell's idiomatic poetic style of this period, so it seems likely they are either meant to characterize Ruth or are taken from another source.

64   This is one among several allusions to Shakespeare's *Hamlet* in the novel. This is the moment of Hamlet's death from the poison on Laertes' blade while Denmark falls to Fortinbras.

65   Barbuni is Red Mullet, fish.

66   Durrell also describes such late night fishing expeditions in *Prospero's Cell*.

67   From Stephen Spender's 1932 poem "The Funeral." The preceding line is "Death is another milestone on their way." The poem was first published in *New Signatures*.

68   Selene is tied to the Moon, and is one of the oldest of the Greek gods, though she was largely supplanted by Artemis who became Diana for the Romans.

69   The deleted words are unclear, but given the following "yoni of Eve" and discussion of the embalmed prostitute, they are likely the "cunt of a whore."

70   Evisceration "per anum" is Latin for removing the organs via the anus.

71   As previously, this is Lefkada on the Ionian Sea, Greece's West Coast. These references to landscape keep the island's exact location vague yet plausible. It would be anachronistic to parallel the island to Aristotle Onassis' private island in the Ionian near to Lefkada, Skorpios. The most plausible location for Mavrodaphne is somewhere between Patras, Kephalonia, Lefkada, and Ithaca – later references in the novel securely locate the island South of Lefkada and within view of Kephalonia and Ithaca.

72   Durrell had a strong interest in Ancient Egyptian mummification and embalming, which later resurfaces in his novel series *The Revolt of Aphrodite* as a satire. The descriptions here loosely align with ancient mummification. The likely source is Herodotus' *The Histories*, but this could just as readily be an amalgamation from various sources.

73   From Stéphane Mallarmé's poem "Tristesse d'été." The last two lines are originally in quotation marks. Loosely, "O, my fearful kiss, 'we will never be a single mummy under the ancient desert and the happy palm trees.'"

74   An archaic form of "packed."

75   This is a particularly political list of locations for 1935–7, when Durrell was contemplating and writing the novel. All were involved in the Spanish Revolution, which Durrell would certainly have had in mind. Durrell was also very likely thinking of the broadcasts from Nazi Germany of the Summer Olympics in 1936.

76   This is the first novel in which Durrell began to incorporate such stories, the most notably of which are the "Vampire in Venice" scenes from *The Alexandria Quartet*. As a working method, this illustrates his developing notion of "quarry books," in which he would sketch scenes or brief tales, sometimes transcribing or adapting, which he would then use later, sometimes decades later.

77   Durrell told the same story by moonlight on the beach, with his wife Nancy and his friend Dr. Theodore Stephanides as an audience (MacNiven, *Lawrence* 118).

78   In some versions of the mythology, Anubis invented mummification and embalming in order to resurrect his father, Osiris, who was reassembled after his murder by his wife Isis. Durrell, significantly, used the titles "Book of the

Dead" and "Lover Anubis" as stand-ins for his subsequent novels *The Black Book* and *The Alexandria Quartet* during their composition. Their concerns with mortality and the body, in this context, show a long genealogy and conceptual development.

79  Durrell was later fond of discussing the death of the discrete ego.

80  From Sir Walter Raleigh's *The Historie of the World*.

81  From "The Lord's Prayer."

82  As with the earlier references to Egyptian mummification, the ceremony of the opening of the mouth (to feed the mummy) and the breath of life relate to the resurrection of the dead. These descriptions also provocatively overlap Christianity, Egyptian mythology, and Durrell's interest since childhood in yoga, in particular Pranayama.

83  From Shakespeare's *Measure for Measure* 3.1. In the scene, Claudio soliloquizes on the nature of death and his own mortality.

84  *Georgios Averoff* was the Hellenic Navy flagship during the Balkan Wars. She survived World War II by fleeing to Egypt with the Greek fleet, and Durrell would surely have seen her in the Alexandria harbour during his years in the city. She then led the Greek naval forces back to Athens after the Nazi occupation of Greece. The ship also played a further role in Durrell's life when she sailed to Rhodes to commemorate the accession of the Dodecanese Islands to Greece, a historical moment in which Durrell was involved as a British Public Information Officer during his two years residence on Rhodes.

85  Durrell had a longstanding interest in Elizabethan authors dating to his teenage years. He claimed to have read nearly every extant literary work (most during his youth), and he planned a major monograph on the subject but never brought it to fruition.

86  Durrell is referring to Shakespeare's *Hamlet* and its origins in Thomas Kyd's *The Spanish Tragedy*. This statement is also significant in Durrell's developing notebook method and his notorious quotation from other authors. As noted previously with the mummy story, Durrell was constructing "quarry books" from which he would later draw phrases, scenarios, or descriptions. These notebooks had their origins in Durrell's constant "scribbling," his diary-like entries, and his paraphrasings or transcriptions of materials he read (sometimes even cutting and pasting in newspaper clippings, as in a commonplace book). This led to constant revisions and recreations of some particularly striking materials as well as his multiple perspectives on the same scenes in *The Alexandria Quartet*. This is also the stylistic origin of his "stolen" materials in later works, such as Nessim's cycle of historical dreams in *Justine*, which derive from Rex Warner's translation of Xenophon's *The Anabasis* (identified by William L. Godshalk) or Semira's nose in *Clea*, which derives from pyschoanalytic case-studies in Groddeck's *The Unknown Self*, and his reconstructions of Sophie Atkinson's *An Artist in Corfu* in his *Prospero's Cell*.

87  As is noted later, the poem is John Keats' "To Autumn." Allusions to Keats appear throughout Durrell's works. In comparison to Keats' other works, this poem is particularly rich in sensual descriptions of ripeness and over-ripeness. The later disjunction is between Francis' recognition of the sensuality of the poem and her own sensual attraction to Hilda, which she cannot articulate.

88  The Greek goddess of marriage.

89  Responsions were the first of the three examinations for a degree at the University of Oxford, taken prior to or just after matriculation. It covered rudimentary Latin, Ancient Greek and mathematics.

90  British slang for intoxicated or drunk.

91   D.H. Lawrence's 1921 travel narrative *Sea and Sardinia*. Lawrence's works had a strong influence on Durrell.

92   A 1913 novel by D. H. Lawrence.

93   *Georgian Poetry* was a series of five anthologies from 1912 to 1922, which appeared every two years. This likely refers to the 1922 publication. They contain several authors tied to Modernism and are named from the reign of King George in the early part of the century. D. H. Lawrence was among those published in the *Georgian Anthology*.

94   William Butler Yeats, the Irish poet and Nobel Laureate; the poet and playwright John Drinkwater; and the war poet Edmund Blunden.

95   Durrell wrote to Richard Aldington at this time, and after his move to France in 1956, he and Aldington became close friends. Through their correspondence, Aldington passed Durrell's *The Alexandria Quartet* to H.D. and conveyed her comments on the novel to him. The Durrell-Aldington letters were published as *Literary Lifelines*, ed. Ian S. MacNiven and Harry T. Moore. Durrell very favourably described Aldington's 1930 *Dream in the Luxembourg* throughout his career.

96   D. H. Lawrence was frequently derided for the erotic and sexual elements of his novels, and his *Lady Chatterley's Lover* was at the centre of one of the most important censorship trials in Britain in the twentieth century. Durrell later wrote a significant introduction to *Lady Chatterley's Lover* for the first Bantam edition in 1968 after the American ban was lifted in 1959, and he regularly defended Lawrence's work.

97   Stylistically, this passage is closely related to Richard Aldington's *Dream in the Luxembourg* (a highly sensual poem), but it is not a quotation from the poem, as is implied. It appears to be Durrell's own creation or perhaps a false recollection.

98   *Matthew* 5.3.

99   Cleopatra, the last Pharaoh of Egypt.

100  From William Dunbar's "In Honour of the City of London." Dunbar (1460–c. 1520) was a Scottish poet of the Scottish Chaucerian school, and he was the first poet to use, in print, the words "fuck" and "cunt" in 1503, which may relate to Durrell's interest. Durrell echoes this poem's "per se" in his own "Carol on Corfu," first published in 1938.

101  When Durrell lived in London, he frequented the galleries and the British Museum. He also had indirect ties and much interest in the 1936 London International Surrealist Exhibition (Gifford 36–64). He also frequented foreign films (Ekberg 3–4; MacNiven, "A Matinee" 163–4).

102  A Jack-of-all-trades. The term was famously used by Robert Greene in the earliest published description of Shakespeare.

103  European folk music was a major movement in art music in the early twentieth century, perhaps most notably through Zoltan Kodàly and Béla Bartok, but also with British and North American composers and musicians as well.

104  Identifying Constantinople by this name and as a part of Greece is highly political at this point, since Kemal Ataturk had changed the city's name in 1930 to Istanbul, and in 1922 the *Megali Idea* had collapsed with the Catastrophe of Asia Minor.

105  Woodbine was a popular cigarette brand.

106  A projecting angle or corner in a wall, typically decorative in a stone building.

107  Slang for a prostitute.

108  This scenario may, to some degree, derive from George Orwell's novel *Keep the Aspidistra Flying*, on which Durrell commented in the *New English Journal* on 4 November 1937.

109 Likely an allusion to T.S. Eliot's "The Love Song of J. Alfred Prufrock," to which Durrell repeatedly alludes in his third novel, *The Black Book*, in 1938.

110 Remy de Gourmont was a French Symbolist poet and critic. The reference here is to Chapter 10 of his *The Natural Philosophy of Love*, which Durrell likely encountered through Ezra Pound's translation. Durrell ends his previous novel, *Pied Piper of Lovers*, with his protagonist describing himself as de Gourmont's faun. Gourmont's influence on Durrell's early works is significant and echoes de Gourmont's influence on literary Modernism in general. The particular parallel here is to entomological sexuality.

111 These terms are increasingly racist as the series continues, likely characterizing Noah Silverstein and his worldview.

112 Blüthner was a particularly popular pianomaker at this time.

113 J.B. Priestly and Louis Golding were both bestselling popular novelists of the time.

114 T.S. Eliot and Ezra Pound are perhaps the two most famous modernist poets. Since this scene is cast retrospectively, it seems likely it refers to their most famous works from the 1920s.

115 The Nonesuch Press is a famous private press known for its quality editions at affordable prices, taking the example of William Morris' Kelmscott Press but using mechanical printing to produce editions at less cost.

116 Taylor's *Holy Dying* has already been cited with an extensive quotation in the chapter "Walsh."

117 T.S. Eliot's famous long poem, which was set out at the beginning of the scene. This scene of seduction parallels, to some degree, the "A Game of Chess" scene in *The Waste Land*.

118 A Swedish toast, "Cheers!"

119 Frederick Delius was an English composer who died in 1934. Durrell was likely attracted to his works for their experimentation and for Delius' use of Nietzsche's texts. Delius also pioneered the use of gramophone records to distribute classical music to a wider audience.

120 Jonathan Swift was an Irish satirist most famous for *Gulliver's Travels*, and Odo of Cluny is a Catholic saint.

121 Latin meaning "There is a filthiness in copulation and only brief pleasure." It is typically attributed to Petronius (fragment 54) and the translation given immediately after by Marlowe is verbatim Ben Jonson's translation. Both Jonson and Petronius had a significant influence on Durrell's later works.

122 This is Beethoven's Fourth Piano Concerto, to which Durrell was exceptionally attached. In a 1935 letter to Alan G. Thomas, written on Corfu, Durrell notes "In this quiet room above the sea I've just played the Fourth again. I know it now – every stitch of it – more intimately than I know Nancy. I've got it in my bowels. Sort of empathy. I've *been* it. I act it, sleep it, shit it, sleep with it – everything. And I can tell you that compared to it, the Emperor is a collection of musical platitudes written for a lavatory-paper musical box by a deaf mute. So there!" (*Spirit of Place* 34–35).

123 "Ashamed of you" although "ςας" should be spelled "σας." Durrell went on to develop fluent Demotic Greek but had not mastered the language by this point, although he was second in his class in Ancient Greek at St Edmund's School, Canterbury.

124 Beethoven's Fourth Piano Concerto, premiered in the last concert in which Beethoven performed as a soloist with orchestra. This was one of Durrell's favourite works.

125 The concerto is unusual in that it begins with the piano soloist without accompaniment, followed by a restatement of the theme in the strings.

126 Cape Lefkada has thirty meter cliffs from which the Ancient Greek lyric poetess Sappho is believed to have jumped to her death. From the cliffs, one can see Kephalonia and Ithaca to the South.

127 This creates a sacred landscape. The pediment is the triangular section above the entablature of a Greek temple. The temples on Corfu, where Durrell wrote the novel, are located near to the sea in naturally secluded or hidden areas, such as the Temple of Artemis in Kanoni and the Kardaki Temple in Paliopolis, both of which are very near to where Durrell's family lived in Perama. The Kardaki Temple in Paliopolis, perhaps dedicated to Poseidon, overlooks a secluded natural area popular for swimming, and it is very likely the inspiration for this description. This seems particularly likely given the association of the Kardaki Temple with the Kardaki spring and a cave that opens onto the sea, descriptions that align with Durrell's here. The cave becomes increasingly important as Walsh imagines his dive later in this chapter.

128 This shift to first person again shows Durrell's emerging notebook methods.

129 An Italian musical term for "all," meaning all players.

130 Basket weaving.

131 From Shakespeare's *As You Like It* 2.7. Motley was the garb of the fool, and Walsh is responding to Francis' comment.

132 A slight variant of this poem, which appears to be Durrell's own, is published in his letters to Alan G. Thomas in *Spirit of Place* (33–34).

133 A Greek cigarette company. It is now owned by Phillip Morris & Co.

134 At the moment of death.

135 A street in London that is particularly well-known for its specialist and second hand bookshops.

136 Ouzo is a Greek anise-based liqueur.

137 This phrase, the title of Walsh's song, infiltrates the novel at several points.

138 Latin, "Farewell."

139 Hail and Farewell.

140 Taylor's works, *Holy Living and Holy Dying* in particular, are alluded to throughout the novel. Apart from the thanatological preoccupations of the novel, Durrell's interest appears to be in Taylor's famously rich prose style.

141 Greek, "Ready."

142 This is a peculiar cultural mixture, offering a Greek libation (pouring an offering) to a Norse god of thunder.

143 Johann Strauss, a famous Viennese composer of waltzes.

144 Very likely one of Hitler's speeches. Durrell's composition of the novel overlaps with the 1936 Olympics, and he would certainly have heard Hitler's speeches over the radio. While the novel seems adamantly unpolitical (perhaps even in Herbert Read's anarchist sense of "The Politics of the Unpolitical"), Durrell did write to Alan G. Thomas in 1936 that he had invited as houseguests "a few Huns who loathe Hitler but are scared shitless to say a word" (MacNiven 136).

145 From Shakespeare's *Hamlet* 3.1.

146 The first sentence in the quotation alludes to Shakespeare's *The Merchant of Venice* and the second again quotes *Hamlet*, as do several subsequent comments in this section. The allusion to *The Merchant of Venice* 4.1 suggests mercy, as Portia explains to Shylock: "The quality of mercy is not strained. / It droppeth as the gentle rain from heaven / Upon the place beneath."

147 Again, a quotation from *Hamlet* 3.1.

148 The burial on Ithaca gestures back to Homer.

149 Durrell is anticipating one of his later and most common tricks: a good work should show, not tell. Without conceptually unifying the book's themes for

the reader, this paragraph draws together previous scenes, such as the sailors sleeping with melons in the sun, the motley fool when Walsh kisses Francis, Fonvisin's perambulating mummy, Walsh's guitar, and the lovers of the Jump. The reader's interpretation retrospectively unifies the scenes in the novel.

150 This likely alludes to W. B. Yeats' poem "Coole and Ballylee 1931."

151 Another allusion to *Hamlet* 2.2, this time to Hamlet's response "Words, words, words" to Polonius' query "what do you read, my lord?"

152 The series of allusions here are, overtly, to Shakespeare's *Hamlet*. Durrell was keenly interested in the play at this time and was examining both the first Folio and the Quarto editions. For more, see his "Hamlet – Prince of China" (38–45) and "The Prince and Hamlet" (271–3). Similar allusions appear, in a more complex form, in Durrell's contemporary short story series "Asylum in the Snow" and "Zero."

153 The return to Ithaca parallels Homer's *Odyssey* and Odysseus' long return journey. An ending that culminates in the beginning of a journey to Ithaca is, then, hardly an ending at all, but points to a much longer narrative.

*Afterword*

# An Unacknowledged Trilogy

JAMES A. BRIGHAM

What's become of the early novels? *The Black Book* has been available in an American edition since 1960, and it was finally published in England in 1973. But *Pied Piper of Lovers* (1935) and *Panic Spring* (1937) have both been out-of-print for more than forty years, and nothing is being done to reissue them. Mention them casually to Durrell and he'll laugh and say, "Good God! The family doesn't talk about them any more!" They weren't particularly good novels: *Pied Piper* is the predictable *Bildungsroman* of a twenty-three-year-old, and *Panic Spring* presents a set of character studies loosely linked by the presence of all the characters on the same island in the Adriatic. But Professors Wickes and Weigel were incorrect when they described *Pied Piper* as "an account of bohemian life in Bloomsbury" (Wickes 3) and *Panic Spring* as merely "a put-together job by a young writer who is impressed by and borrows from the best talents and minds of his time" (Weigel 43). Both novels contain some fine bits of writing, as Durrell himself was aware,[1] and they should be reissued as the early work of a major novelist, for they will repay the reader interested in Durrell with glimpses of themes and character types that would be prominent features of *The Dark Labyrinth* (1947) and *The Alexandria Quartet* (1957–1960).

And they will pay another, greater dividend: the attentive reader who is not deterred as G. S. Fraser was (*Lawrence* 10) and who reads right the way through *Pied Piper, Panic Spring,* and *The Black Book* will suddenly realise that he has been reading a trilogy. Taken separately, the three are so different in setting, structure, and characters that a reader might be forgiven for thinking that they have little in common; taken together, the three appear as complementary novels, panels of a triptych in which the setting changes but which are linked by small structural parallels and the reappearance of characters, and, more importantly, by textual echoes so clear that they cause one narrator to comment, "This is a piece out of another book" (*Black Book* 236).

*Pied Piper of Lovers* is itself a work in three parts, with a "Prologue," and an "Epilogue" which points to *Panic Spring.* The "Prologue" neatly births the eponymous hero, Walsh Clifton, who is the half-caste son of an English father and a Burmese mother, and almost immediately disposes of the mother. Thus we are left with the Cliftons, *père et fils,* whom we meet at the beginning of Book One when Walsh is six (*Pied* 25). In an early letter to Henry Miller, Durrell gave a biographical sketch which might have been a summary of the plot of *Pied Piper*: "My birth and upbringing?" he asks. "I was born in India. Went to school there – under the Himalayas. The most wonderful memories, a brief dream of Tibet until I was eleven. Then that mean, shabby little island up there wrung my guts out of me and tried to destroy anything singular and unique in me" (Wickes 60). In Book One, Walsh goes to school – both the formal one run by the Jesuits and the informal one presided over by a little native boy who becomes his friend – and, at the end, has a nightmare which brings all of the events of that book together with the realisation that he is going to England and leaving India forever (103–106). Book Two opens aboard the liner which is taking Walsh and his Aunt Brenda "home," and the boy is very quickly installed in a public school which, for the most part, he doesn't leave until the death of his father at the end of this section of the novel. Book Two is important to our discussion because it introduces Ruth and her brother, Gordon, who tells Clifton, "You're not a damned Englander yet.... They haven't got you yet.... [I'm English.] At least that's my nationality, but I don't stand for any of the things that your Englishman stands for. And you don't yet. They haven't spoiled you yet" (150), and thus introduces the idea of a spiritual sickness from which some of the characters in *Panic Spring* will suffer and which Durrell will identify as "the English death" in *The Black Book*. Book Three is really a rejection of "bohemian life in [a] Bloomsbury" which echoes hauntingly Wyndham Lewis' *The Apes of God* (1930). By the end of Book Three, Walsh has rediscovered Ruth and has begun to see England as a perverted nineteenth-century "heaven" rather than the "land of hope and glory" to which his father had once thought he was sending him. The "Epilogue" finds Walsh and Ruth earning a meagre living writing jazz tunes, and preparing to "move across the billow" (251) to a Greek island from which Gordon has been writing to them.

*Panic Spring* opens with the voyage to Gordon's island, a voyage undertaken, not by Walsh Clifton but by Christian Marlowe, a schoolmaster who has taken a leave-of-absence to write a book on Quietism. Like the rest of the characters, Marlowe is taken to a small island in the Adriatic by Christ, a boatman with curiously Pan-like feet (*Panic* 16). With such an obviously Lawrentian figure as a guide, we are prepared for the self-revelations and self-realisations that comprise the bulk of the novel. Upon his arrival on Mavrodaphne, Marlowe meets Francis and Fonvisin, Walsh and Gordon, and Rumanades, the owner of the island. The plot, such as it is, is sparse after this point: the various characters interact; Rumanades becomes ill and dies; and the rest all prepare to go their ways. But, where *Pied Piper* takes its linear progression from the biography of Walsh Clifton, *Panic Spring* is more like a collage in which several characters are juxtaposed. Each of the major figures has a chapter, and each character study makes clear the ways in which the character is suffering from a disease not unlike "the English death." Durrell originally called this novel "Music in Limbo," and a limbo is precisely what the major characters inhabit: Mavrodaphne is a point of rest from which they can analyse their own predicaments before moving on.

The structure of *Panic Spring* is not unlike the structure which Durrell would use in *The Black Book*: "I've tried," he wrote to Alan Thomas, "just for an exercise in writing to create characters on two continuous planes of life – the present – meaning the island and their various pasts. It does not progress as an ordinary novel progresses. The tentacles push out sideways while the main body is almost static."[2] *The Black Book* is composed of three quite distinct units: the present on Corfu; memories of the England which Lawrence Lucifer, the narrator, has left before the novel begins; and passages from the diary of Herbert "Death" Gregory. The whole novel is a chronicle of "the English death," which makes its point by juxtaposing characters and events from the three units to show that the disease is absolutely fatal unless one recognizes the symptoms and effects a cure by leaving England forever. "Dear Alan," Lawrence Lucifer writes in Book Two: "this is a very necessary valediction, not only to England, but, if you like to the world.... It was the temptation of the devil, the vision of the cities offered to me from an immense mountaintop. The devil! What should be more plausible than that you should be the Black Saint himself – panurgic, long-nosed, calculating bastard that you are! You were offering me, in your oblique way, the whole of England – the masques, the viols, the swans, the mists, the doom, the fogs: you were offering me a medieval death in which I could live forever, stifled in the pollen of breviaries, noctuaries, bestiaries: split silk and tumbrils, aesthetic horses and ruined Abbeys.... That is an England I am going to kill...."[3] While it recapitulates the themes of the earlier novels, *The Black Book* is also and more importantly an act of ritual murder, and the third novel ends with a narrator who has passed from the death-in-life which "Death" Gregory seems to have accepted through the limbo of indecision to a new state of being in which, for the first time, he feels truly alive (*Black* 213).

As we have seen, *Panic Spring* is structurally different from *Pied Piper*: the elements of its plot are grouped spatially around an "almost static" core instead of being arranged in a linear fashion. There is a passage near the end of *Pied Piper* that provides a key of sorts to the structural shift in volume two of the trilogy. In the letter to his room-mate, Turnbull, which comprises the "Epilogue" to the novel, Walsh Clifton speaks of "the eternal quibble with words. Failing to express to others what you have expressed to yourself. I think sculpture is the medium in which to express. Space against Time curves and stresses, structures and dimensions. How in hell can I express the volume of things by daubing ink on paper?" (250). The structure of *Panic Spring* is a response to Clifton's question, and so is the structure of *The Black Book*. There is a narrative progression in the third novel which parallels that of one and two taken together, but the structural mode is spatial rather than linear, and is the product of a logical progression from the biography of *Pied Piper* through the annihilation of linear time with the use of "memory" chapters in *Panic Spring*.

Just as Walsh Clifton's remarks on "the eternal quibble with words" foreshadow the techniques of the second novel, so, too, *Panic Spring* is tied to *Pied Piper* through the presence of Clifton on Mavrodaphne. Chapter VII of *Panic Spring* is devoted to "Walsh," and it may well be a chapter of *Pied Piper* which was cut out and replaced by the "Epilogue" as a more satisfactory way of ending that novel. There are more details about the life of Ruth and Walsh as described in the "Epilogue," some of which tie directly to the earlier novel. For example, Walsh's reference to the jazz tunes which he and Ruth had been writing is paralleled in detail. In *Pied Piper*, Clifton tells Turnbull, "The two which we've done while we've been here are called, respectively, 'Hold Your Woman'...and 'Never Come Back'" (272; italics mine). In the comparable passage in *Panic Spring* there is "a cheque for thirty pounds on the mantelpiece and a letter from Garland saying: 'Do you mind selling your soul? You do it well. This last tune of yours is good. As I see it you'll be rich before long. *Ecstasy to be in Love* is still selling mildly. *But I anticipate bigger things from this one, 'Never Come Back'*" (66; italics mine). Garland is also an echo from *Pied Piper*, and the Christmas card from "Gordon, Ruth's brother, with a beautiful Greek stamp" and the suggestion that Ruth bring Walsh down to "this Island" (*Panic* 77), is a retrospective link between the two books. These links are certainly not fortuitous, and this same section of *Panic Spring* contains references to characters who will appear in *The Black Book*. For example, Tarquin, the village schoolmaster near whom Walsh and Ruth lived in England, is a "memory" character in the second novel. He is not really presented as a character *per se* until he appears as a major figure in *The Black Book*. In this way, through the presence of characters in two of the three novels, Durrell provides clear links between the volumes of his trilogy.

It might be argued at this point that, rather than being involved with a trilogy as such, we are faced with one novel which Durrell clearly felt was his first true book ("Preface" 8), and that those passages in *The Black Book* which echo the previous novels simply appear because he wanted to condense his statement on "the English death" into one novel. In other words, the echoes are not intended to form any kind of summary tying the three novels together. This would be quite defensible if it were not for the details from *Pied Piper* and *Panic Spring* that appear in the third novel. Toward the end of *The Black Book*, this lengthy passage appears:

> Let us walk quietly in the declension of the season, smoke a pipe over the gate, take note of how the asphodels are doing. in the little house run over the accounts, select a book, doze over the fire, or at bedtime light the candles and start the piano hymning. It is all the same, for this is a piece out of another book. It is significant merely because Tarquin is mentioned. Over the fire and the crusader's hearth, in the smoke of pipes, Tarquin is mentioned. It is a strange immortality to be consummated here, in this cottage, drowned in flowers, under the glimmering bottoms of the books. I record it now merely to reassure myself that we are never forgotten. (236)

This passage echoes directly that portion of the "Walsh" chapter of *Panic Spring* in which Clifton's later relationship with Ruth is discussed and Tarquin is, indeed, mentioned:

> Walsh…would go instead for a walk, dropping in on his way home at Tarquin's cottage. Tarquin was the schoolmaster.
> Sitting in the threadbare armchair, puffing his pipe…, he would be again amazed at the huge, bald, gentle cranium of his host; the twists of silver at his ears. The mild eyes, almost olive-purple, with their fine lashes…. Tarquin was interesting because he was a splendid medium: through him one could reach history. No, it was more than that, for Tarquin was history. The perfect refugee to whom any age was more immediately accessible than his own, he lived between the fireside and the long shelves of dusty books which fed his insatiable taste for the living death. (73)

The parallels between these two passages are too exact to be accidental, and the excerpt from *The Black Book* actually stipulates that "this is a piece out of another book."

The correspondences between *Pied Piper* and *The Black Book* are not as direct – or at least not as directly stated. The clearest parallels are with Book One of the first novel: there are many references to Tibet or to India in the final volume of the trilogy. While most have symbolic significance, three specific references echo *Pied Piper* quite unmistakably.

The earliest reference is interesting because of the precise details from the first novel which it contains. "Letters with Indian stamps on them, Halma, Ludo, Baedeker, Old Moore, dripping, sequel, the green house lit with a green rain from heaven, the haggard fingers stitching a winding cloth for the morning..." (*Black* 56). The "green house lit with a green rain from heaven" is clearly "the house...called 'Emerald Hall'" to which the Cliftons move from Burma in *Pied Piper* (32). The "haggard fingers stitching a winding cloth for the morning" are the fingers of the old doctor who, with an Indian servant, "crossed the room to the bedside and started to sew a blanket about the body" of Clifton's mother the morning after his birth (*Pied* 17).

The next reference to the first novel, a passage much too long to quote here, contains numerous correspondences which would have to be picked out of *Pied Piper* page by page, and the catalogue would become tedious (*Black* 147–148). It is a reminiscence, virtually a resume of the sights and sounds of the Indian hill country described in the first novel. The opening sentence is significant: "When the drums begin, and the opaque lightning trembles in the night sky, I become a child again, in revisited history" (147). With this sentence, Durrell throws the reader back into the first novel and at the same time brings forward from that book the very presence of the Tibet which he employs as a symbol in book three.

The final clear reference to *Pied Piper of Lovers* in *The Black Book* is to some extent a continuation of the previous example as well as an amplification of the "brief dream of Tibet" to which Durrell referred in his letter to Miller.

> Tibet hangs like a sphinx over the revisited childhood which
> my dreams offer me: the craters crammed with jewelry; the hills
> curving up into their vertiginous flowers of snow; the dawn
> opening like a coral umbrella on Lhasa; the yak and the black bear
> the only visitors of that immense vista in time; the monasteries
> as remote as stars upon the hills; everything has fallen upon
> me in this stuffy English room with a pathos that is beyond ink.
> (237–238)

The heroes of the trilogy – Walsh Clifton, Christian Marlowe, and Lawrence Lucifer – all experience the same sort of despair that Durrell felt before he left England in 1935, but only Lawrence Lucifer identifies their common malaise as "the English death" and prescribes a rejection of England as the cure. In *The Black Book*, Tibet becomes Ultima Thule (230), the place to which the blessed are taken and a symbol of the breaking free of England. Walsh Clifton learns by the end of *Pied Piper* that England offers "a medieval death in which [he] could live forever" (271). In *Panic Spring*, Christian Marlowe discovers the truth about England, but – having found his own form of quietism – he returns, like the troglodyte to the Platonic cave, to tell anyone who will listen what he has found. And Lawrence Lucifer narrates *The Black Book* from Corfu, the island that was clearly the model for Mavrodaphne in *Panic Spring*.

W. Y. Evans-Wentz, in his preface to *The Tibetan Book of the Dead*, states that

> *The Egyptian Book of the Dead*, correctly entitled, is *The Coming Forth from Day*, with reference to the sacred Egyptian art of the coming forth from this life into another life.... Similarly, [the title of] *The Tibetan Book of the Dead* [implies] a yogic method of coming forth into *Nirvanic* Liberation, beyond the Cycle of Birth and Death. Each of these two books concerning death thus inculcates, by its own peculiar method, an Art of Dying and Coming Forth into a New Life. (xvi)

In a "Contributors" note to the September, 1937 issue of *The Booster*, Lawrence Durrell is said to be "now at work on *The Book of the Dead*" (*Booster* 49). At that point, *Pied Piper* and *Panic Spring* were in print, and – although *The Black Book* would not be published until June of the following year – the same note lists the third novel, and an excerpt from it actually appeared in the next issue. On what, then, was Durrell working? Future commentators may well discover that the whole of his prose fiction forms a multi-volumed "book of the dead." Certainly the first three novels constitute a trilogy that presents a guide to the thoughtful English reader who, having recognised that his culture is terminal, wishes to learn the "Art of Dying and Coming Forth into a New Life."

*Notes*

1 See his comment on *Panic Spring* in *Spirit of Place* (38).
2 See Durrell's letter to Thomas re: *Panic Spring* cited above.
3 Durrell's letter to Thomas re: *Panic Spring* cited above.

# Works Cited & Selected Bibliography

Barrie, J. M. *Peter Pan*. [novel] London: Penguin Books, 1995.

Bolton, Jonathan. *Personal Landscapes: British Poets in Egypt During the Second World War*. New York: St. Martin's Press, 1997.

*The Booster* 11.7 (September 1937).

Bowker, Gordon. *Through the Dark Labyrinth: A Biography of Lawrence Durrell*. New York: St. Martin's Press, 1997.

Brigham, James A. and Alan G. Thomas. *Lawrence Durrell: An Illustrated Checklist*. Carbondale: Southern Illinois UP, 1983.

Christensen, Peter G. "The Achievement and Failure: Durrell's Three Early Novels." *Lawrence Durrell: Comprehending the Whole*. Eds. Julius Rowan Raper, Melody L. Enscore, and Paige Matthey Bynum. Columbia: U of Missouri P, 1995. 22–32.

Clogg, Richard. *A Concise History of Greece*. 2nd ed. Cambridge: Cambridge University Press, 2002.

Durrell, Lawrence. "Asylum in the Snow." *Seven* 3 (1938): 43–54.

_____. *The Black Book*. Paris: The Obelisk Press, 1938. London: Faber & Faber, 1973.

_____. "The Booster." *The New English Weekly* 12.4 (4 Nov 1937): 78–79.

_____. "The Black Book (Coda to Nancy)." *The Booster* 2.8 (1937): 19–23.

_____. "The Cherries." *Masterpiece of Thrills*. London: Daily Express, 1936. 239–243.

_____. "Corfu: Isle of Legend." *The Geographical Magazine* 8.5 (1939): 325–334.

_____. "Down the Styx in an Air-Conditioned Canoe." *The Booster* 4.10–11 (1937–1938): 14–17.

_____. "From the Elephant's Back." *Fiction Magazine* 2/3 (Winter 1983): 59–64.

_____. "Gracie From The Black Book." *New Directions in Prose and Poetry* 4 (1939): 292–33

_____. *The Greek Islands*. London: Faber & Faber, 1978.

_____. "Hamlet, Prince of China." *Delta* 2.3 (1938): 38–45.

_____. "Heraldic Universe." *Personal Landscape: An Anthology of Exile*. Ed. Robin Fedden. London: Editions Poetry, 1945.

_____. "*Je est un autre*." *Collected Poems*. Ed. James A. Brigham. London: Faber and Faber, 1980. 106–7.

_____. *A Key to Modern Poetry*. London: Peter Nevill, 1952.

_____. "Landscape and Character." *Spirit of Place: Letters and Essays on Travel*. Ed. Alan G. Thomas. London: Faber and Faber, 1969. 156–163.

_____. *Monsieur or the Prince of Darkness*. London: Faber and Faber, 1974.

_____. "Oil for the Saint; Return to Corfu." *Spirit of Place: Letters and Essays on Travel*. Ed. Alan G. Thomas. London: Faber & Faber, 1969. 286–303.

_____. *Panic Spring: A Romance*. London: Faber & Faber, 1937. Victoria, BC: ELS Editions, 2008.

_____. *Pied Piper of Lovers*. London: Faber & Faber, 1935. Victoria, BC: ELS Editions, 2008.

_____. Preface. *Aeolia*. Ilias Venezis. Trans. E.D. Scott-Kilvert. London: Campion, 1949. i-vi.

_____. "The Prince and Hamlet: A Diagnosis." *The New English Weekly* 10.14 (January 1937): 271–73.

_____. *Prospero's Cell: A Guide to the Landscape and Manners of the Island of Corcyra*. London: Faber & Faber, 1945.

_____. *Spirit of Place: Letters and Essays on Travel*. Ed. Alan G. Thomas. London: Faber & Faber, 1969.

_____. *Tunc*. London: Faber & Faber, 1968.

_____. "Zero." *Seven* 6 (1939): 8–18.

Durrell, Lawrence and Henry Miller. *The Durrell-Miller Letters, 1935–80*. Ed. Ian MacNiven. London: Faber & Faber, 1988.

Ekberg, Kent. "Studio 28: The Influence of the Surrealist Cinema on the Early Fiction of Anais Nin and Henry Miller." *Deus Loci: The Lawrence Durrell Quarterly* 4.3 (1981): 3–4.

Evans-Wentz, W. Y. "Preface to the Second Edition." *The Tibetan Book of the Dead*. London: Oxford University Press, 1960.

Forster, E. M. "The Story of a Panic." *The Celestial Omnibus*. London: Snowbooks, 2005. 7–44.

Fraser, G. S. "Apocalypse in Poetry." *The White Horseman*. Eds. J.F. Hendry and Henry Treece. London: Routledge, 1941. 3–31.

_____. *Lawrence Durrell: A Study*. London: Faber and Faber, 1968.

Friedman, Alan Warren. "Place and Durrell's Island Books." *Modern Fiction Studies* 13.3 (1967): 329–341.

Gifford, James. "Surrealism's Anglo-American Afterlife: The Herbert Read and Henry Miller Network." *Nexus: The International Henry Miller Journal* 5 (2008): 36–64.

"Grecian Isle." *Times Literary Supplement* 24 April 1937: 307.

Hastings, Selina. *Evelyn Waugh: A Biography*. Boston: Houghton Mifflin, 1994.

Kaczvinsky, Donald P. "Panic Spring and Durrell's 'Heraldic' Birds of Rebirth." *Lawrence Durrell: Comprehending the Whole*. Eds. Julius Rowan Raper, Melody L. Enscore, and Paige Matthey Bynum. Columbia: U of Missouri P, 1995. 33–44.

Kazin, Alfred. *Contemporaries*. Boston: Little Brown, 1970.

MacNiven, Ian. *Lawrence Durrell: A Biography*. London: Faber & Faber, 1998.

_____. "A Matinee Idyll?" *Deus Loci: The Lawrence Durrell Journal* NS 2 (1993): 163–4.

_____. "Pied Piper of Death: Method and Theme in the Early Novels." *On Miracle Ground: Essays on the Fiction of Lawrence Durrell*. Ed. Michael H. Begnal. Lewisberg: Bucknell UP, 1990. 24–40.

_____. "Ur-Durrell." *Lawrence Durrell: Comprehending the Whole*. Eds. Julius Rowan Raper, Melody Enscore, and Paige Bynum. Columbia: U of Missouri P, 1995. 11–21.

Mallinson, Jeremy. *Durrelliania: An Illustrated Checklist of Inscribed Books of Lawrence Durrell and Gerald Durrell and Associated Publications, Letters and Notes*. Jersey: Bigwoods, 1999.

Matiossian, Vartan. "Kostan Zarian and Lawrence Durrell: A Correspondence." *Journal of the Society for Armenian Studies* 8 (1995): 75–101.

Miller, Henry. *Tropic of Cancer*. London: Granada, 1965.

Miller, Tyrus. *Late Modernism: Politics, Fiction, and the Arts Between the World Wars*. Berkeley: University of California Press, 1999.

Mitchell, Julian and Gene Andrewski. "The Art of Fiction XXIII: Lawrence Durrell." *Paris Review* 22 (1960–61): 32–61.

Montalbetti, Jean. "Lawrence Durrell, en dix mouvements." *Magazine Littéraire* 210 (September 1984): 78–85.

Mörne, Håkan. *The Melting Pot*. London: William Hodge, 1937.

Morrison, Ray. *A Smile in His Mind's Eye: A Study of the Early Works of Lawrence Durrell*. Toronto: University of Toronto Press, 2005.

Nin, Anaïs. *Diaries of Anaïs Nin*. Vol 1. New York: Harcourt Brace Jovanovich, 1985.

_____. *The Journals of Anaïs Nin 1935–1939*. Ed. Gunther Stuhlmann. London: Quartet, 1974.

Norden, Charles. "Ionian Profile." *Time and Tide* 4 Sep 1937: 1169–1170.

_____. "Obituary Notice." *Night and Day* 1.11 (1937): 8–12.

_____. "Sportlight." *The Booster* 2.7 (1937): 6–11.

Pessoa, Fernando. *The Book of Disquiet*. London: Quartet, 1991.

Petronius. *Satyricon*. Trans. M. Heseltine. London: Heinemann, 1913.

Pine, Richard. *Lawrence Durrell: The Mindscape*. London: Palgrave Macmillan, 1994. 2nd ed. Corfu: Durrell School of Corfu, 2005.

_____. "War, *Agón* and the Greek Literary Imagination." *The Literatures of War*. Eds. Richard Pine and Eve Patten. Newcastle: Cambridge Scholars Publishing, 2008.

Politis, Linos. *A History of Modern Greek Literature*. Oxford: Clarendon Press, 1973.

Pritchett, V.S. "New Novels." *New Statesman and Nation* 13 (1 May 1937): 741.

Read, Herbert. "Speech by Herbert Read at the Conway Hall." *The Surrealist Bulletin* 4 (1936): 7–13.

Roessel, David. *In Byron's Shadow: Modern Greece in English & American Literature from 1770 to 1967*. New York: Oxford UP, 2002.

Shephard, Ben. *A War of Nerves: Soldiers and Psychiatrists in the Twentieth Century*. Cambridge, MA: Harvard University Press, 2001.

"Shorter Notices." *Nation* 146 (1938): 753.

*Spirit of Place: Lawrence Durrell's Greece*. Dir. Peter Adams. BBC, 1975.

Weigel, John A. *Lawrence Durrell*. New York: Twayne, 1965.

Wickes, George. Ed. *Lawrence Durrell and Henry Miller: A Private Correspondence*. London: Faber & Faber, 1962.

Wilde, Oscar. "The Truth of Masks." *Complete Works of Oscar Wilde*. London: Collins, 1946. 1156–1173.

Yeats, W. B. *The Poems*. Ed. Daniel Albright. London: Everyman/J. M. Dent, 1990. 293–4.

## Colophon

BOOK DESIGN BY JASON DEWINETZ

The text face is Minion Pro, designed by Robert Slimbach for
Adobe Systems, Mountain View, California. Minion Pro is inspired by
classical, old style typefaces of the late Renaissance, a period of elegant,
beautiful, and highly readable type designs.

12345abcdefghijklmnopqrstuwxyz67890
ABCDFGHIJKLMNOPQRSTVWXYZ
ABCDEFGHIJKLMNOPQRSTUVWXYZ
αβγδεζηθικλνξοπρστυφχψω
0†ffi¶{&}§ffi‡j

The display and supplementary text is set in Fedra Serif B Pro,
designed by Peter Bil'ak for his Typotheque foundry in The Hague,
Netherlands. During the development of ELSE's first publication the
designer was in correspondence with Bil'ak as a newly updated version
of Fedra was in preparation. With various typographic issues related to
the design of that book in mind, and in the spirit of the book's theme, a
rewarding exchange developed as Fedra was reshaped and refined.

12345abcdefghijklmnopqrstuwxyz67890
ABCDEFGHIJKLMNOPQRSTVWXYZ
ABCDEFGHIJKLMNOPQRSTUVWXYZ
αβγδεζηθικλνξοπρστυφχψω
∗†ffi¶{&}∫ffi‡∗